# ROBIN HOOD

### AND

## THE ARCHERS OF MERRIE SHERWOOD.

BY

*The Author of* "*FOR VALOUR*," "*MIDSHIPMAN TOM*," *&c., &c.*

## IN THREE VOLUMES.

## PROFUSELY ILLUSTRATED.

## VOL. I.

Publishing Office:

HOGARTH HOUSE, 32, BOUVERIE ST., FLEET ST.,

LONDON, E.C.

# ROBIN HOOD

## AND THE ARCHERS OF MERRIE SHERWOOD.

### BY GEORGE EMMETT,

*Author of "Tom Wildrake's Schooldays," "For Valour," and "Midshipman Tom,"*
*"Captain Jack," Etc., Etc.*

MUCH, THE MILLER'S SON, RELATES HIS STORY.

"Come, listen to me, ye gentlemen,
  That be of freeborn blood,
I shall tell you of a good yeoman,
  His name was Robin Hood."

OLD BALLAD.

No country in the world ever produced a hero whose memory has lived through so many ages as that of Sherwood's forester—bold Robin Hood.

Much has been written about his doings, but among the many versions there has been but a slight sprinkling of the true life of this remarkable outlaw.

Endeared to the youth of England by the old songs, quotations, games, and proverbs which a few centuries since were made to his remembrance, it is surprising that the modern versions of his life, except in one or two instances, should be so totally at variance with the truth.

The old ballads, it must be admitted, were rude in composition, and faulty in the sequence of sound, which falls so harmoniously upon the ears.

But they suited our sturdy ancestors, for they expressed in good Saxon language a love of all that is manly and brave, and a contempt for all that is cowardly and mean; thus they appealed to the hearts of the free-born, manly youth of England, taught them to aid the oppressed, yet at times soared into the regions of romance, and stamped on every line the most prominent traits of the gallant hero whose life they portrayed.

This story of the remarkable outlaw's life claims precedence above the recent versions, upon account of the immense research the writer has had among the ancient manu-scripts and pamphlets, some of the latter dating as early as the first introduction of printing in this country.

Among these may be mentioned Wynken de Worde's black letter pamphlets, Ritson's Critical Edition, and the "Lytell Geste," of Robin Hood.

Long and patient has been the study to separate the dross from the metal; but now the task is ended, and the bold yeoman, who has been erroneously termed a robber, will be shown in his true character of one who hated, with a thorough Saxon hate, the Norman oppressors of the English nation; for Robin, when all else bent the knee to a Norman king, betook himself to Sherwood Forest, and kept up an incessant and preda-tory warfare against the Norman tyrants and enslavers of the people.

With this preface we commend our work, not to the critic, but to the youthful lovers of manly worth and gallant deeds.

---

## CHAPTER I.

### ROBIN HOOD, EARL OF HUNTINGDON.

Forth went this gentle knight,
In very rueful case;
The tears out of his eyes did run,
And fell upon his face.

MAY-DAY in the reign of Henry III.—the year one thousand, two hundred, and sixty-five; scene: a massive castle, towering proudly above the scattered dwellings which lay among the trees.

Facing the drawbridge was a broad ex-panse of level ground, in the centre of which was the May-pole, adorned with alternate stripes of white and black, and festooned with Flora's early productions.

Around this joyous emblem of the coming summer were congregated the villagers, old and young, and among them could be seen

scores of men-at-arms, their helmets reflect-ing back the sun's rays in glittering discs.

The battlemented castle was the strong-hold of a Saxon earl, and this merry-making was in keeping with the good old English customs, for opposite the flower-bedecked archway of the castle were a dozen targets, and some fifty yards to the right the prizes which were that day to fall to the most skil-ful in the use of the goodly yew bow and the cloth-yard shaft.

The most noticeable of these was a snow-white cow with gilded horns and a wreath of flowers suspended around its neck; displayed upon an oaken table were prizes of a less value, bows, quivers, arrows, a leathern purse containing three gold pieces, and several good Saxon broadswords, the blades fashioned from the finest steel.

But the prize which excited the greatest attention was an arrow with a golden head, and a shaft of solid silver.

Many a sturdy hand was stretched out to touch the prize, and many an eye wandered from the piece of crimson velvet on which it lay to the butts beyond.

The winner of the silver arrow would, besides the intrinsic value of the prize, be entitled to the much-coveted honour of being crowned king of the May-day revels, and when in the possession of his sovereignty he was at liberty to choose from the maidens present a May Queen.

Thus the prize became an object of more than common interest to the fairer portion of the revellers, and their whispered words to their sturdy companions caused a spirit of emulation among them which bade fair to make the coming contest one of more than ordinary excitement.

The throng began to thicken before the drawbridge, and the musicians, taking their place at the head of the revellers, stood with their eyes fixed upon the archway.

The blast of a trumpet pealing out from one of the towers caused those who were still hovering about the prizes to run across the green and join the expectant throng.

A second flourish from the brazen instru-ment caused the piper to inflate the bag of his instrument, and the player on the viol to flourish his bow.

A third time the sound was repeated; then issuing from the grim grey arch was a sight which caused the revellers to doff their caps and shout—

" Long live the Earl of Huntingdon !"

The piper, the player on the viol, and the flutist began a warlike march, and turning about prepared to head the gallant cavalcade.

First came the young earl, a bold, hand-some youth of little more than twenty summers, fair almost to a fault, large blue eyes, and masses of long golden hair, which fell in rich profusion upon his shoulders.

He paused when his foot left the draw-bridge, and raising his jewelled cap said in English :*

"Welcome, my friends; God send there may be many such sights as this in store for merry England."

"Long live the Earl of Huntingdon!" again shouts the crowd; "long live the Saxon earl!"

A courteous bow, then the cap was re-placed, and the musicians, now having a chance to be heard, lost not the opportunity.

Following the young Earl was a score of richly clad-gentlemen, neighbours of the Earl, and, like himself, of Saxon blood.

Then came a troop of men-at-arms, and following close upon their heels were the domestics, trundling before them a runlet of choice Malvoisie.

The Earl halted before the butts, and the competitors in the coming match came for-ward, many testing the soundness of their bowstrigs, others examining the peacocks' feathers upon their arrows. As these exa-minations had been going forward since the company first came upon the ground it noted the anxiety felt by the bowmen that their chance of victory should not be lessened by any failure on the part of their weapons.

Near the earl stood his henchman, John Gammell, or Little John, as he was named upon account of his gigantic height and immense strength.

Behind the henchman a couple of domestics held the wassail bowl full to the rim with ambrosial wine.

Little John, with the freedom of a favoured follower, leant forward and wispered in his lord's ear—

"Goodly wine, my lord, is waiting; it were a sin when so many thirsty throats are dry, wishing you life may exceed that of——"

"Of what, knave?"

"The accursed Norman oppression, my lord," said the henchman, finding a simile; "by my lady that would be long enough."

The Earl smiled as he said—

"The simile, knave, is but a promise of short duration for my life, for Leicester's good earl, backed by the people, has stayed this of which thy tongue wags."

"Aye, for a time, my lord; even now dark tidings come from the——"

"Peace, knave! mar not the day with that croaking voice of thine. Come, my friends—let the wine be tasted, then to work!"

The stout yeomen, when the Earl's lips had

touched the edge of the bowl, passed it to each other, then returned it to Little John.

"Body o' me!" muttered the giant as he cast his eyes at the empty bowl; "but the carles' throats are as dry as——"

"Thine, John," said a burly yeoman; "to say sooth that is dry enough."

"Or as dry as the cakes made from thy flour, Much," said the henchman; "body-o'-me! but they are as like unto the mortar be-tween the stones in the abbey as aught I know."

"Good for thy jaws," retorted Much the miller, joining in the laughter caused by these sallies; "were it not for this they would rust."

"If that were to happen," said a man-at-arms, "thy pouch, miller, would be without many broad pieces. Give thanks, man, give thanks to Little John, for he——"

"He'd break that back of thine," said the henchman, turning suddenly upon the re-tainer, "so keep a civil tongue."

The soldier backed out of range, and a movement at that moment among the com-petitors told the sports were about to begin.

The laughter and merry jests ceased, and the yeomen and maidens crowded around the competitors to watch, as the old chronicler says :—

He that shooteth the best of all,
And fair as an archer should,
At a pair of goodly butts,
Under the merry greenwood;
A right good arrow he shall have,
The shaft of silver white,
The head and feathers of rich red gold—
In England there's not the like.

The twanging of the bow-strings and the whistling of the arrows were the only sounds that broke the silence.

One by one the prizes were carried off, and the victors, as a reward for their skill, were the only archers allowed to shoot for the silver arrow.

There was some judgment in thus selecting the best archers, for the conditions upon which the good people of Huntingdon gave the prize rendered the shooting of an inferior archer a waste of time.

The mark to be hit was a silver coin, placed in the centre of the butt, and unless it was struck by an arrow the precious prize would be returned to those who gave it to be shot for.

To render the shooting more difficult, each archer was allowed but one arrow; thus the contest caused an eager excitement among the friends of the archers, which broke forth in words of encouragement as the eight sturdy yeomen took their places in line with the butt.

One by one the cloth-yard shafts flew on ward and were embedded in the target; but, to the dismay of the spectators, the silver coin, clearly conspicuous beneath the sun, remained untouched.

"By the soul of St. Quintain," said Little John, "it were a sad sight to see the arrow leave this part. Come, master of mine, thou hast some skill with the bow; try thy hand."

The young Earl rose from the place where he had been lying during the contest, and taking a bow from one of the discomfited archers, laid the arrow on the string.

A steady look at the glittering mark, then the arrow-head was raised to his ear; the twang of the string was followed by a joyful shout, and Little John, tossing his cap in the air, yelled with delight.

It was a marvellous shot: the silver piece was perforated through its centre, and a third of the arrow had gone into the butt.

Amid the uproarious delight which followed this welcome sight the Earl was announced king of the Mayday sports, and a chorus of lusty throats called upon him to select a queen.

The handsome noble's eyes sought but one face among the bevy of fair maidens—that one the fairest of the fair—the loveliest of the lovely—gentle, blue-eyed Maid Marian, old Much the miller's niece.

A few words from the Earl told the blushing girl of her envied fortune, then he led her by the hand to a flower-covered seat near the Maypole.

A hundred hands bedecked the young pair with flowers, then the barrels of old October were broached, the wassail cup refilled, and the lads and maidens joined hands around the Maypole, and began the merry dance.

Much the miller's son, was alone, for although a comely youth, he had joined the revels with his fair cousin, and her election having piqued the remainder of the maidens, they, with wonderful unanimity, refused to become his partner in the dance.

The Earl saw poor Much's troubled face as he was refused, with a haughty toss of the head or a cutting sneer, by the maidens, and not wishing to mar the day's happiness by causing the one he loved so well to suffer, he called the lonely swain to his side, and bade him take Marian to the dance.

Much's face brightened, and, truth to tell, Marian was as pleased to join in the dance as Much was to take her.

So the sports went on, peals of laughter were mingled with the piercing notes of the pipe, and the monotonous drubbing of the tabor; and young hearts were glad, young feet kept time to the music, and they danced as joyously as though sin, suffering, and sorrow were unknown.

The dance was near its end when the Earl chanced to look beyond the tripping circle,

and a dark shade passed over his face as he saw two horsemen approach the revellers and pull up their steeds within a dozen yards of the lofty pole.

His inward displeasure was shared by Little John, who still kept close to his lord.

"A fat ecclesiastic," he muttered between his teeth, "and a Norman knight who has helped to give him the substance of our fair land to fatten upon."

The elder of the two horsemen was astride a white palfrey; and, by his dress, a high dignitary of the Norman church.

His face had but little of that humility which is becoming a man who professed to follow a brighter object than worldly ambition.

He was stern, proud, austere—more befitting a mailed knight than a prelate. Even now, as his eyes wandered over the Maytime revellers, an angry flush came to his cheeks, and a cynical, cruel smile played upon his thin lips.

His companion was many years younger—of slight but sinewy form. His features, like those of the prelate, were of the Norman type, and would have been handsome had it not been for the haughty, supercilious expression they bore.

He was armed after the fashion of the times—a coat of linked mail, and a closely-fitting steel cap, with a crest of black feathers, showed that he had won his spurs upon a battle-field.

A rich baldric supported on the right side an anelace, or long dagger; on the left, a heavy cross-hilted sword.

His black charger—a powerful and swift animal—was caparisoned as though his rider was about to enter the lists, or a field of strife

The prelate was the first to speak, as, tapping the pommel of his saddle with his right hand, he followed the graceful figure of Maid Marian with his eyes.

"Methinks," he said, "these carles flaunt it bravely—as bravely as though they were masters of the land."

"They deem themselves so, my lord," said the knight; "but, had I my will, every Saxon hind should be driven into the sea."

"The day is not far distant, Geoffrey," was the prophetic reply, "when the Norman sway will be able to do more than even this."

The knight looked at his companion, and, with something of malice in his tone, said:—

"Methinks, my lord, you would be one of the last to utter these sentiments."

"Why, Sir Geoffrey?"

"Was it not these Saxons who curtailed the fat revenues of the Church?"

The prelate bit his lips, and his swarthy face crimsoned; but, before he could reply the knight sprang from the saddle, exclaiming:—

"By my halidame, that is the fairest maiden I have yet seen!"

The trained steed remained perfectly still as the mail-clad Norman strode to the very centre of the laughing group—for they had paused in the dance to give their feet and the tired musicians a rest.

The advent of a Norman noble had much the same effect as the appearance of a fox among a flock of geese.

The fairer portion of the sex fled from the path he was pursuing, and clung to such of the sturdy Saxons as had not already ran for their staves and short swords.

There was good cause for this dismay, for the insolence of the Normans was only equalled by their licentiousness, and so much were they feared that the majority of the English maidens sought the seclusion of a nunnery rather than live in daily fear of being carried off by them.

Marian clins to sturdy Much, and the miller's son, divining the knight's purpose, placed himself before the girl, and said—

"Marry, fair sir; do you not see how you have disturbed our company? Get thee to thy horse's back, lest, perchance, a Saxon arrow may find its way through Norman mail."

The knight heard, and choking back the angry words which came to his lips answered—

"Fair words, peasant, fair words! I am no hawk that these doves should flee at my approach. Come, I want but the hand of that fair maid, that I may join the dance."

He advanced closer as he spoke, and Much's Saxon blood getting the better of his prudence, caused him to raise his hand and push the intruder back.

"We want none of thee," he said; "back, or it may be worse for thee——"

The suppressed wrath burst forth at this indignity, and the Norman striking Much a heavy blow upon the chest with his gauntleted hand, said—

"Take that, peasant; stand aside, or my dagger shall slit that wagging tongue."

Much reeled under the blow, and would have fallen had not his father run forward.

He caught his boy upon his left arm, and flourishing a long oaken staff in front of the knight's face, kept him back, then he placed the good old English weapon in Much's hand, saying—

"Liquor his hide, lad; liquor his hide."

Much grasped the weapon like one who knew its use, and before the Norman could use his sword, the long staff fell upon his shoulders and struck him to the ground.

The Earl of Huntingdon had by this time reached the spot, followed by his henchman, Little John, who quietly remarked—

"Would it had broken his crown, the arrogant knave!"

Marian clung to the young earl, and he drew her away from the angry Saxons who were now standing in a compact body behind the miller's son, who said, as his adversary regained his feet—

"We have enough of the accursed meddling of thy race in this fair land; let this teach thee there are English arms yet strong enough to punish Norman insolence."

The prelate had watched this scene with lowering brows, and as the knight regained his feet he dashed towards him, and bending low in the saddle, whispered—

"Mount, Geoffrey, the spearmen are close upon us!"

His companion understood the purport of his words, and jumped into his saddle, the haughty churchman at the same time shaking his clenched fist at the group, said—

"Hinds, you shall remember this day! by the cross you shall!"

He turned his horse as he spoke, and with his companion galloped across the green sward.

As quick as thought Little John fitted an arrow to his bow, and as the shaft whistled through the air, he sang out merrily—

"Keep that, Sir Priest; it will remind you of your promise."

The cloth-yard shaft penetrated the wooden pommel of the prelate's saddle, and despite the efforts of the churchman he could not withdraw it.

His face went pale when first the arrow became fixed in such close proximity to his body, but when he found he was safe he turned to his companion and asked:

"Marked you the knave who discharged this arrow?"

"Aye, my lord, a peasant, a head taller than his fellows."

"He shall be a head shorter," was the fierce rejoinder, "before another hour is passed—ha! here comes our fellows."

As he spoke the glitter of a score of spear-points could be seen advancing, and when the troop were within earshot, Geoffrey Lois angrily said:

"A murrain on ye for knaves; while you have been loitering I have been nigh murdered."

He extended his hands towards the villagers as he spoke, and the men-at-arms wheeling into line, lowered their spears and prepared to avenge the insults their master had received.

The coming of the troop had been seen by the merry-makers, and now the maidens, conjecturing a strife was at hand, fled in a body towards the castle.

There also the retainers had hurried, to arm themselves; and the Earl, drawing his sword rushed to the front of the archers and called out:

"Lay your arrows—ready, my men. Aim at their horses as they advance, then to work with sword and buckler. Hurrah for merrie England, and confusion to the Norman knaves!"

The cry was taken up, and as Geoffrey Lois at the head of the foreign mercenaries who formed his train, came charging upon the Saxons, a flight of arrows brought down a dozen horses.

These animals were in the front; thus those in rear were thrown into confusion, and before they could fill up their broken ranks the incensed villagers were upon them.

The strife was but short. The bowmen closed with their assailants, horses were ripped open by their short swords, and the goodly quarter-staves swept the mail-clad horsemen from their saddles.

Foremost in the fray was the young Earl and his henchman, Little John, the latter wielding a pole, one blow of which felled the war-steed bestrode by Geoffrey Lois.

"Yield thee, ransom or no ransom," said the giant, "or bone o' my body I'll crack thy skull like an eggshell."

He was answered by a fierce thrust from the Norman's sword; then like a flail the stout pole whirled round, driving back those who came to their lord's rescue, and finally settling upon the noble's casque, split the tough metal and rendered the wearer senseless.

The war-cry of the Saxon retainers told the mercenaries a further struggle would be useless, so those who were yet able to manage their steeds turned and galloped from the fight.

The prelate's harsh voice rang out the church's direst curses upon their heads as they dashed past him; but they fell unheard, for the Normans thought more of their lives at that moment than any promised punishments hereafter.

The arrival of the Earl's retainers upon the battle-ground was the signal for the haughty churchman to follow De Lois's spearmen, for the Englishmen would have ducked the ecclesiastic in the horsepond without the least compunction.

Six of the spearmen were slain, and twice that number wounded. The Saxons had escaped without the loss of a life, but many bore ugly marks of the horsemen's long spears.

The Earl, seated upon the floral throne which had been erected for their May King, passed judgment upon the knight.

"For insulting a peaceful gathering," he said, "and drawing a sword upon an unarmed man—and further, for ordering the armed foreigner to shed English blood, you are sentenced to be stripped of your arms and your steed—these being the lawful trophies of my stout henchman, Little John, who subdued you in fair and open fight; your back to be bared, and for a good English mile you will be flogged with stinging nettles."

The punishment was in accordance with the rough justice of our sturdy forefathers, and when the nettles were found, the sullen captive's face was turned towards the road by which his followers had fled.

Once only he turned when the yeomen were driving him from the green, then he asked in malignant tones—

"I would know the name of him who sat in judgment over me."

"Robin Hood, Earl of Huntingdon," said the Earl; "forget it not, we may meet again."

"We shall."

The words were spoken in vengeful tones; then he started at a swift pace, followed by the noisy crowd.

## CHAPTER II.

### THE GATHERING OF THE SAXON BOWMEN.

Therefore they called a council of state
To know what was best to be done
For to quell their pride; or else they replied,
The land would be overrun.

SIMON DE MOUNTFORT, Earl of Leicester, the husband of Eleanor, the king's sister, had, at the head of the rebellious barons, held supreme power over England for nearly three years.

Then came a battle fought near Lewes, in which the weak and irresolute king was taken prisoner, and his army utterly routed by the popular party.

This victory made Leicester sole master of the kingdom; he confiscated the estates of eighteen barons who had fought on the Norman side.

It was when in this position of neither sovereign nor subject that Simon de Mountfort laid the foundation of the House of Commons, for he introduced a second order of men to those councils which had hitherto been held by the nobles, who cared but little for the common weal.

Two knights from each shire, and deputies from the boroughs, were ordered to attend and have a share in the Government of the State.

A wise and judicious measure, which made him popular with the people, and, as a natural consequence, hated by the most powerful of the barons, and the result was that many of them deserted the confederacy and joined the royalists.

This brief explanation will enable the reader to understand the event which was of such import to the hero of this story—the gallant Saxon Earl of Huntingdon.

It was now the month of July, and upon the drawbridge of Huntingdon Castle the retainers were lounging about enjoying the cool evening breeze.

Although the drawbridge was lowered, the appearance of the men was not as peaceful as upon the opening of the May-day, when the Earl was proclaimed king of the revels.

The men were armed at all points, and upon the battlements could be seen steel-capped sentinels, pausing ever and anon in their walk and looking towards the wood which skirted the roadway.

Besides the host of men-at-arms, there was mingled a goodly number of English yeomen garbed in buff jerkins; these were armed with the stout yew long-bow, and a sheaf of those shafts which had made the archers of England a terror to their mail-clad foes.

Others wore casques and gorgets of iron, and their arms were a short sword and buckler or a long lance.

In those days every man, according to his degree, was equipped for war, for by an edict issued some time before, every man having a knight's fee was compelled to have a coat of mail, a helmet, a shield, and a lance.

And the same description of accoutrements were provided by all, whether noble or commoner, for whatever number of knights' fees he possessed.

Every free man who had property to the amount of sixteen marks * was compelled to be armed in like manner, and every one that had ten marks, an iron gorget, a cap of iron and a lance; lastly, all citizens were compelled to have an iron cap, a lance, and a coat quilted with wool.

Thus it will be seen it was an easy matter to raise an effective army in an inconceivably short space of time; and in a few days the Castle of Huntingdon had within its walls all who had sworn allegiance to the Earl's banner.

The demeanour of the men marked this gathering as one far different from that of the May-day.

True all the sturdy yeomen who were present upon the latter occasion were now seen either upon the battlements or upon the level sward before the castle.

The summons had gone forth for the Saxon bowmen to gather under the Earl's banners, for dark tidings came to that peaceful village of the growing power of the Royalists, the Norman oppressors of the people.

* A coin worth about 13s. 4d

Amongst one of the groups who were canvassing the coming events was Little John, and near him Much and his sturdy father the miller.

The henchman had his hands crossed upon one end of a long bow, and his loud laugh could be heard as he jested with the yeoman.

"Lewes," said a stout farmer, driving the butt of his lance upon the ground, "should have taught the foreign minions a lesson, and made them fear the Great Earl and the people at his back."

"It should," said Little John; "but the same might be said with the crows you trap when they alight upon your fields; you catch and kill them, but I'd warrant there's plenty to eat the next crop."

"Aye, John, but I am there to prevent them, just as we shall prevent these Normans from devouring our liberties."

"May it be so!" responded little John, in a graver tone than he had hitherto used, "may it be so! I will give my good right hand to see Leicester's Earl master of the country and the Royalists beaten."

"But he is master. Shoulder of St. Hubert, thy speech smellest of more than the tongue utters."

"You are right, Randall—right."

"Come, man," said the franklin, "let us hear thy budget, for thou hast one, I'll be sworn."

"Marry but I have. Listen! a messenger came here but yester e'en; he had ridden far; he brought a message to our lord from the Great Earl to this import."

The bowmen gathered closer round the speaker as he continued,

"Prince Edward has escaped, many of the barons have left the league, the Royalists are meeting—that is the substance of his message."

"Substance sufficient," said Much, "to gather the Saxon bowmen—a gathering that will cost the Normans as much as it cost them at Lewes."

"With the saints' blessing, yes," said Little John; "and the sooner we are planting our shafts in the joints of their armour the better for England."

"What delays our lord?" Much asked. "Why does he not lead us to join Leicester?"

"For two reasons, Much," said the henchman; "two goodly reasons—one, he does not know where the Earl is collecting his forces; the second, many of the roads are even now in possession of the Royalists."

"The better for us," said the old miller; "I warrant the Huntingdon spearmen and the bows would make a passage to the Great Earl, even were the whole of the foreign minions who overrun our land to stand in our way."

"See," Little John exclaimed, suddenly, "here comes the messenger!"

A horseman emerged from the wood as he spoke, and when the foam-covered charger came close enough, the crowd on the drawbridge saw on the rider a tabard bearing the arms of Simon de Mountfort, Earl of Leicester.

The tired steed was led to the castle stables, and the messenger shown to the banqueting hall.

Here the knights of the shire were assembled, and, like their leader, the young Earl, they were cased in glittering mail.

Steel casques, ornamented with drooping plumes, were upon the table beside the link gloves, so cunningly fashioned by the armourer as to admit of the free play of every finger.

Against the wall were the long lances and shields, and behind each knight stood an esquire, in close attendance upon his master.

The board was strewed with brimming goblets of mellow wine, and, indifferent to the coming troubles, the gallant fellows laughed and jested as though the party were one of pleasure, in place of being a warlike gathering.

Those were times when feathered soldiers were unknown—days when kings and emperors led their armies in person, and by their prowess inspired their men to emulate the deeds of those who were ever foremost in the strife.

Bowing low to the earl, the messenger took a folded piece of parchment from beneath his gabardine, and said—

"From the Earl of Leicester, my lord."

The Saxon noble read the few lines the missive contained, then jumping to his feet, said—

"We must to horse, gentlemen;" then turning to his esquire, "Bid the trumpeters sound the call."

As the plumed helmets and mail gloves were being adjusted, the earl said—

"Prince Edward's forces are gaining strength, and many of the roads are in his power; there is bad tidings from Oxford, but of that anon   England needs her right arm to teach her oppressors that our liberties are not to be trampled under foot by Henry of Winchester's foreign favourites."

He spoke hurriedly, and paced to and fro the great hall, his armed heel ringing angrily upon the stones.

He said England needed her right arm, and by those words he meant the sturdy Saxon bowmen, and well they merited that name; it had been earned on more than one battle-field, where the cloth-yard shaft had done more to decide the fortunes of the day than the mail-clad knights and their army of spearmen.

---

## CHAPTER III.

### THE BATTLE OF EVESHAM.

Then Robin he took his noble bow,
And let fly his arrows all amain,
And Robin Hood he began for to smile,
As he went over the plain.

A FORTNIGHT after the day upon which this gallant array left Huntingdon Castle, the earl joined the forces of Simon de Mountfort.

The anxiety upon the great earl's face did not escape the Saxon leader's eyes as the former came forward and said—

"Welcome, Robin; thrice welcome, in this our hour of need."

"You are troubled, my lord. Is it the issue of the coming struggle which causes the gloom upon your brow?"

"Aye, Robin; the scurvy knaves who deserted my banner have ere this joined the Prince, and my gallant army is fearfully outnumbered"

"Did I hear aright?" the young noble asked, "that Gloucester commanded a wing of the Royalist force?"

"Too true, Robin. Ha! hither comes one of the advanced guard."

A man-at-arms galloped towards the great leader, and pulling up when within a few feet of him, exclaimed—

"My lord, from yonder hill I saw the banners of the Prince."

"Art sure, knave?—art sure it is not the banners of the barons I expected ere this?"

"Quite sure, my lord. As for the barons, report sayeth they have been met by the prince yesterday e'en and defeated."

Simon de Mountfort's lips twitched as he heard this news.

"I had expected this," he said, "but let it pass. We have still men enough left to do our devoir as brave men. Let the trumpets sound—to horse, gentlemen, to horse!"

The Earl of Huntingdon sprang upon his black charger's back, and closing his helmet, galloped to the spot where his banner formed a rallying point for the Saxon bowmen.

The confederate host was soon in motion—the Huntingdon archers in the front, headed by the earl and his gigantic henchman.

So close was the army of Prince Edward that the earl had but little time to form his men in battle array.

The Royalists, as they emerged upon the plain, likewise formed in battle array, and when the great leader beheld the overwhelming numbers which were advancing against him, he made use of these memorable words—

"THE LORD HAVE MERCY ON OUR SOULS,

FOR I SEE OUR BODIES ARE PRINCE EDWARD'S—HE HAS LEARNED FROM ME THE ART OF WAR."*

There was a pause as the rival hosts stood face to face, then Leicester placed the old king, who was his prisoner, in front of the confederate lines.

The weak and treacherous old monarch was encased in complete armour, and bestrode a war-horse of magnificent proportions; and much as he wished to escape from the earl's power, he dared not make the attempt, in consequence of twenty of the Huntingdon archers being placed near him, with orders to use their fatal shafts should it be necessary.

The Earl of Leicester, when these preparations were completed, beckoned for Robin Hood to come to his side.

A few bounds of his splendid charger, and the young noble was beside his leader.

"They outnumber us, Robin," Simon de Mountfort said, "three to one, but the English bowmen may yet give us the day—you understand me?"

"Well, my lord."

"See where the traitors are crowding around Edward's banner; bid your bowmen try their skill upon that point."

The Earl of Huntingdon bowed to his saddle, then turning his horse's head, galloped back to his men.

In spite of the superior force the confederate army had to face, the men were eager to begin the fray.

The knights brought their lances to the rest, and drew in the bridle reins; the cross-bowmen placed the bolts in their weapons, and the Saxon archers waited with their feathered shafts placed upon their bowstrings.

The latter had not long to wait, for their leader, after quitting Simon de Mountfort, dashed to the head of his men, and, pointing to the steel-clad host, said—

"Loose your shafts, men; find the joints in their armour!"

The twang of three hundred bowstrings was followed by a flight of arrows, and the cluster of knights and nobles who were near the Prince was seen to disperse, leaving one-third of their number dead or dying.

"Bravely done!" said Leicester, closing his helmet, and sitting himself firmly in the saddle; "may those shafts have found those who turned traitor's to their country's cause!"

The battle thus began, and in answer to the discharge of arrows there came a flight of quarrels from the Prince's crossbowmen.

For an hour the air was darkened by the missiles from slings, yew-bows, and crossbows, then a second line of steel-clad knights advanced with levelled spears upon the Saxon archers.

The latter plied their weapons still faster, and the glittering line was broken as men and horses fell before the deadly shafts.

But the gaps were soon closed, and the very earth trembled under the weight of the charging columns.

At a signal from the Saxon earl, the archers opened their ranks to allow Simon de Mountfort's knights to advance.

The Earl of Huntingdon joined the gallant body; then, spurring their horses, they rode full tilt at the advancing foe.

There was a mighty crash as the two lines met. Men and horses went down as though struck by lightning, then the struggling mass separated, and each seeking an opponent, a general hand-to-hand combat ensued.

The Earl of Huntingdon had selected a Norman knight, whose bearing he remembered as that of the disturber of the May-day revels.

The recognition was mutual, for Geoffrey de Lois called out, savagely—

"The Virgin has heard my prayer—we have met again."

The young earl made no reply, but as his vindictive enemy strove to drive his lance through the bars of his helmet, he caught the blow upon his shield; his own weapon at the same moment striking the Norman's neck, carried him out of his saddle.

He fell with a crash to the earth, and the victor would have driven his lance point even through the steel panoply, had not a fresh body of horsemen from either side carried him away.

The contest was fiercely sustained, although one half of De Mountfort's army had fallen.

Still the little band fought to conquer or die, upon that fatal plain.

The Earl of Huntingdon's spear was shivered as he rode at the powerful form of Prince Edward, and he would have been slain before he could have loosened his battle-axe, had not a weak voice near him said—

"Spare my life, I am Henry of Winchester, your king."

One of the Prince's army not recognising the old monarch in his armour, had already wounded him, and would have struck the fatal blow had not the Prince left the young earl, and dashed to his sire's assistance.

The Prince led the old king to a place of safety, then rode to join his troops who were now slowly forcing the confederate army from their position.

The young earl soon detached his battle-axe from the saddle, and his raven plumes were seen where the fight was thickest.

Twice he met the Norman knight, Geoffrey de Lois, but each time they were separated by the charging of fresh bodies of horsemen from the Royalist host.

A quarrel from a cross-bow slew the Earl's

* Vide "Bloomfield's History of the British Empire."

charger, and before he could disengage himself from under his horse he was surrounded by a score of Gloucester's men-at-arms.

They tore the battle-axe from his grasp, and would have slain him had not Little John seen his lord's peril.

With a two-handed sword, the henchman cut a path to the Earl's side; thus mowing down all who came near, he wispered—

"Rise, my lord, the day is lost, the remnant of De Mountfort's army is falling back—our archers alone stand firm—they await your coming—resolved if you are slain not to leave Evesham's red plain while a hand can fit a shaft to a bow."

"The Earl de Mountfort, where is he?"

"Slain, my good lord—with others as noble as himself. Come, we have not a minute to lose. See the victors! The foreign minione are revelling in England's best blood."

Little John's words were too true. The foreign mercenaries, enraged at the stubborn defence of the Saxon band, had been slaying the wounded and dying.

The Earl and his henchman fought their way to where the Saxon bowmen still held their ground; then the former, casting away his battle-axe, called for a bow and a quiver of arrows.

Thus armed, he slowly fell back with his unyielding men; and in answer to the repeated summonses to surrender, he sent a cloth-yard shaft through the hearts of those who made the demand.

Foot by foot the remnants of the gallant band he had led from Huntingdon left the field of slaughter, terrible even in their retreat, keeping at bay the mail-clad knights and their mercenaries, by slaying all who came within range of their terrible arrows.

Defeated but not subdued—his hatred burning still furious against the Norman conquerors—the Earl and his little band of not more than a hundred archers retired from the field of slaughter.

An exultant smile was upon his handsome lips as he brought down the leaders of the host who sought to capture the remnants of Saxon bowmen.

Until the darkness set in did this little band of heroes elude the advance of the mailed hordes, and when the next day's sun shone upon the plain, all traces of the stubborn Saxons who had survived that fatal day had departed.

## CHAPTER IV.

### ROBIN HOOD THE OUTLAW.

Some lost legs and some lost arms,
And some did lose their blood;
But Robin he took up his noble bow,
And is gone to the merry greenwood.

EVESHAM'S fatal plain spread sorrow and consternation throughout the length and breadth of the land.

Not alone for those who fell upon that fatal day was this sorrow felt—they had died nobly in their country's defence; but alas! their fall caused the bulwarks of the people's liberty to be trampled down, and left them at the mercy of the foreign minions whom Henry III. openly encouraged in their exultation at the downfall of the people's cause.

The minstrels sang the praises of those who fell on Evesham's plain, but their songs could not restore the dead, or give back to the hapless country the Saxon birthright—liberty.

True, there were many of the Saxon nobility who refused to bend the knee to the Norman court; and leaving their vast possessions to be bestowed upon the mercenary hirelings, they sought a home beyond the seas.

One among the nobles who claimed an English descent laughed the Norman power to scorn; and when all had fled from Henry's vengeance, he drew together the remnants of the bands of Saxon bowmen, and in the fastnesses of the northern forests struck many a blow for the land he loved so well.

This one was Robin Hood, so recently a belted earl, but now an outlaw; his estates confiscated, a price upon his head, houseless, his bed the green sward, his covering heaven's canopy, and nothing to defend him save the good yew bow and the cloth-yard shaft.

A few weeks after the overthrow of the confederate army, and while the Normans were yet rejoicing at their victory, Henry of Winchester caused a grand assembly of the nobles and barons to be held at his Court in London.

It was the last day of the term allowed for the Saxon nobles to make their submission to the king.

Many, to save their estates from being given to the foreign favourites, had already taken the oath of fealty, but a larger number still kept away from the Court, despite the mandate which had gone forth, the substance of which was that all who did not make submission to the party in power were to be outlawed by the king, excommunicated by the clergy, and their lands given to the knights of Normandy who had fought under Prince Edward's banner at Evesham.

It was a goodly sight; the weak and false King seated upon the throne, and wearing a robe of velvet and ermine over his armour, and surrounded by his mail-clad nobles, knights, and barons.

The proceedings were opened by the King asking his son whether the whole of the Saxon nobility had made humble submission to their King.

"All, sire," answered the Prince, "save these."

As he spoke he handed a packet to the King.

The face of Henry became reddened with anger, as he read the list, and when he had finished, he exclaimed angrily—

"So the rebellious varlets would seek an exile in a foreign land sooner than bend the knee to their lawful sovereign."

"It would seem so, sire."

"Well, let it be so; the day of grace has passed, let sentence of outlaw be proclaimed against all who do not attend the Court before the dial marks the hour of noon."

"Your mandate, sire, shall be obeyed."

"Tell me," the King said, "what is the meaning of this mark placed opposite the Earl of Huntingdon's name?"

Prince Edward glanced at the parchment as he replied—

"I know not, sire; unless it is that the Earl has died since the battle."

The packet was about to be given to the scriveners that they might copy the names of the outlawed nobles, when Geoffrey de Lois stepped forward,

"Your pardon, my liege," he said; "but I can tell you the cause of that mark being placed against Huntingdon's name, if I have permission to speak."

The King smiled upon his favourite, whose head was yet swathed in bandages from the effect of a blow he received from the Earl of Huntingdon, and said—

"Speak, De Lois, and freely, for Henry has not a more devoted follower than yourself. How goes the wound? Does it show promise of mending?"

"But slowly, my lord; but for the good steel of which my cap was made, I must have been brained by the blow."

"Well, well; we must see if we cannot find something out of the fat lands of these rebellious knaves to quicken the healing of the wound."

Geoffrey bent low, and his face flushed with joy at hearing this promise, for beyond the suit of mail and his sword, he had but little in the way of wealth.

"May I crave a boon, my liege?" he said, "a boon to elect my choice of the many posts now vacant by the death or flight of the rebellious carles who dared to raise their hands against the Lord's anointed."

"In good time, De Lois, thou mayest, but first tell me the meaning of this mark."

"Its meaning, my liege, my tongue trembles to explain; but under your favour, I will speak."

"Do so, good De Lois, for my curiosity is excited nearly to womanly feeling; so speak, and fear not."

"Robin Hood, Earl of Huntingdon, my liege, in open contempt for thy gracious proclamation, has publicly made avowal of his defiance to thy power, and now, with the remains of the archers he led to Evesham, has betaken himself to the forest of Barnesdale, from whence he sallies forth at times to rob or slay all who have any connection with thy Court or army."

The King heard Geoffrey's emphasised speech, with but ill-concealed anger, and when he had concluded, he sprang from his seat, and exclaimed passionately—

"Is it thus, my lords, you would see my power severed? You have troops of stout men-at-arms under your banner—how is it that I have true swords, and so many weeks have passed since this knave dared to openly defy me?"

Forth from the glittering crowd of mail-clad men stepped William de Valence, Earl of Pembroke.

"My liege," he said, "your barons have not forgot their duty to their sovereign, for twice has an armed party been sent to crush this nest of traitors."

"Well, well, my lord, and the result?"

"Each time, my liege, they have returned with broken crests, their men-at-arms slain, and all that was valuable taken by the outlaws."

"I make here a vow to the Virgin," the King said, fiercely, "that I will crush this gathering. Where is Mortimer?"

"Here, my liege," said the Earl, coming forward, "and ready to do my devoirs as a knight and a noble."

"It is well, Mortimer. Heard you all that has been said?"

"Every word, my liege."

"Know you aught of the matter?"

"I know this, my liege, that Huntingdon's rebellious earl has some seven or eight hundred bowmen with him in the fastnesses of Barnsdale, and their cloth-yard shafts have beaten all who have been sent against them."

"See to it, Mortimer! Take a thousand of your best men and crush this nest of vipers. Hark'ee, my lord; every success gained by them will but swell the dissatisfaction now so rife in the northern counties, and we may have another Evesham, and perchance not the same result."

"I will to horse, my liege," said Mortimer, "and by the hour of sunset the power of this rebellious earl will be nearer its end."

"May the saints grant a favourable result to your journey! Farewell, my lord, when next we meet I trust Huntingdon will be a prisoner."

"A dead one, my liege, for I swear to

hang him upon the bough of one of the trees which has afforded him shelter."

The Earl left the audience-chamber, and all who knew his great military skill doubted not the fulfilment of his words.

The King was about to break up the assembly, when his eyes fell upon Geoffrey de Lois, who, stood a few paces from the throne.

"Your pardon, De Lois," he said; "I was nigh forgetting you, for this matter troubled me sorely. Come forward, sir knight, and let me know the boon thou would'st crave."

De Lois bent his knee to the monarch and said:

"My liege, the shrievalty of Nottingham is vacant. May I crave to fulfil the office?"

"It is but a poor one, De Lois," said the King, "after the great work thy strong right arm has done for the State."

"I shall be content, my liege, if you grant it me."

"Be it so, De Lois; your boon is granted. But tell me why you should have chosen this post among the many that are now vacant?"

"My uncle, the abbot of St. Mary's, will be near the town. It is to receive his goodly counsels I crave the favour you have granted."

"A fitting reason. Thou art a good son of the Church and a brave knight, De Lois. Stay—thou wilt require money to keep up a fitting state. To do this I give thee the rents of the lands hitherto held by Robin Hood, of Huntingdon."

The gleam of malignant triumph which came to De Lois's eyes passed away before he took the monarch's hand and humbly kissed it.

"You are too generous, my liege," he said, "and my devotion to you, I hope, will repay such goodness."

"It will, De Lois, it will. Now, my lords, I will retire, for this matter of Barnesdale has moved me much; and in the privacy of my own chamber I may regain somewhat more composure."

Henry left the great council, and his nobles soon after dispersed and went to their homes.

The last to quit the great hall was the newly made sheriff of Nottingham, and a haughty looking man garbed in priestly robes.

The latter was de Lois's uncle, his companion on the day of the May-time sports, John of Langley, now abbot of the rich monastery of St. Mary's—a magnificent structure situate within a mile of Nottingham town.

"Thy success," the prelate said, as they mounted their steeds, "has been beyond even my anticipations."

A dark smile came to the knight's lips as he answered:

"And mine; but if Roger Mortimer slays this knave, it will be of but little avail."

"Save the fat Huntingdon land," said the Abbot, "methinks that ought to repay the flogging with nettles."

"But in part, good uncle; even were it to balance this matter, there is the broken head he gave me at Evesham."

"This you hope to settle by being Nottingham's sheriff. By the saints I cannot read this, Geoffrey. What hope is there for your vengeance to fall upon a man who tarries in Barnesdale."

"Every hope, good uncle of mine, unless Mortimer's meddling hand baulks me of my vengeance."

"Be plain in thy speech, Geoffrey, or perhaps I shall be tempted to give thee some of that goodly counsel which caused thee to crave thy boon from the king."

The pair laughed heartily at these words; then De Lois said:

"Listen, good uncle of mine, and thou shalt know the weighty reason for my wish to be at Nottingham; from the hour that I received that scourging from the Saxon's hands, I have had a watch kept over the Earl, and when he sought the security of Barnesdale, I bade one of my knaves join his band."

"A good thought, Geoffrey."

"So it has turned out, for the varlet has sent me knowledge of all that passes; and but yesterday he gave me word of the intent of the Outlaw to seek a better protection than that he now has, in the forest of Sherwood."

"It was for this," said the prelate, "you wished the shrievalty of Nottingham."

"For this only; should they escape Mortimer, I can do the King a service and obtain my vengeance."

"That head of thine," said the Abbot, "is better fitted for a statesman than a soldier."

Geoffrey De Lois smiled at the compliment; then they spurred their horses, and London was soon left far behind.

## CHAPTER V.
### THE BEGGAR'S BUDGET.

Robin stood in Barnesdale,
And leaned him to a tree,
And by him stood Little John,
A good yeoman was he;
And also did good Scathlock
And Much the miller's son—
There was no inch of his body
But it was worth a whole man.

THE wonderful increase of the human species since the time of which we write, has caused a complete change in the aspect of the earth.

ROBIN HOOD CHALLENGES THE EARL OF MORTIMER.

The mighty forests then so thickly studded with noble trees, the pleasant dingles and dells where the wild stag, the boar, and the wolf were wont to resort, have passed away before the giant strides ol civilisation.

Sweet shady glens, where our sturdy fore-fathers were wont to gather and exhibit their skill in the use of the yew-bow and other free and manly sports are now occupied by popu-lous villages; aye, in some instances, even cities, the sites of which cover the verdure-clad dells where the foresters roamed as free and as happy as the sunny air they breathed.

In the densest part of Barnesdale forest the sturdy Saxon bowmen and their gallant leader, Robin Hood, had sought refuge from the tyranny of the victors of Evesham.

The band numbered about a hundred strong-limbed foresters, whose deeds were in high repute among the ill-used people who were compelled to bear the Norman yoke.

The peasant, the artisan, and their wives and daughters already began to venerate the name of Robin Hood and his merry men, for all who lived within the vicinity of the forest had a story to tell of the outlaws' gallant deeds and open hands.

In some instances young girls would relate how they were beset under the greenwood by a Norman knight or baron, and when fleeing from their impertinent attentions, several men clad in Lincoln green suddenly appeared, and gave the Norman and his followers such a drubbing with their quarter-staves, that taught them there were strong and willing hands yet left in England.

In others, the peasant when about to be driven from his cottage, in consequence of not being able to pay the tithes and dues, had been saved by the generous outlaws' ready purses.

True, the rich ecclesiastics, the harsh land-owners, and the Normans who came to reside in the confiscated castles, told a different story when they fell into the hands of the brave foresters, and many a rueful face and empty pouch were evidences of the truth of their words.

In some instances the outlaws were not content with lightening these gentry's purses, but these were particular cases : for example, a rich landlord, who had been one of the first to swear fealty to the tyrants, and sought to ingratiate himself into favour with the Court by his cruelty to the poor upon his estate.

He ventured too far under the green bough, and, being caught, was not only lightened of the rents he had collected, but a stout deer-hide thong was laid upon his back, to teach him to be more merciful in future.

There is no doubt this popularity with the people enabled Robin Hood to forestall all the attempts made to dislodge him from his haunts, for, no matter how secretly the expeditions were planned against him, he was certain to have timely warning to prepare a warm reception for his foes.

It was near the close of a lovely September day that Robin and his followers first heard of the advance of Earl Mortimer, and the confiscation of Huntingdon castle.

The outlawed Earl's face did not lose its habitual smile when Little John gave him an outline of the scenes we have described at the Court of Henry of Winchester.

The appearance of the Saxon archers had undergone a great change since the fatal fight on Evesham plain.

The quilted coats, iron gorgets and helmets, had been thrown aside, and each burly form was clad in a jerkin of Lincoln green, tight-fitting hose, and russet boots with wide tops, so that the wearer, when on foot, could turn the tops down ; when mounted, draw them up to the knee.

Their heads were covered by caps of red and blue cloth, ornamented by a drooping feather fastened on the right side.

Their arms were the short Saxon sword, a buckler, a Spanish yew bow, and a baldrick, studded according to the taste of the wearer, was worn across the body, to which was fastened a sheaf of arrows, each a good cloth-yard in length. Drayton, the poet, thus makes mention of this famous band in his Poly-olbion :—

" Their arrows finely paired for timber and for feather,
With birch and hazel pierced to fly in any weather ;
＊　　＊　　＊　　＊　　＊　　＊

And of these archers brave there was not any one
But could kill a deer his swiftest speed upon."*

Thus armed and well versed in forest war-fare, they were more than a match for four times their number of England's choicest troops.

The group under the giant oak consisted of Robin, Little John, and Much, the miller's son, and as the former henchman watched his leader's face, he smote his huge palm upon his thigh and said—

" Body-o-me, master, but the news does not cause thee much concern."

" Why should it, John ?" said Robin ; " we have but thy bare word for it, and that, may-hap, may be influenced by the barrel of Mal-voisie you helped to empty yestere'en."

" Helped to empty !" Little John repeated, " there is some truth in that. I helped, but it was but little assistance the thirsty varlets required when they gathered round the goodly barrel."

" Yet," said Much, with a smile, " they tell how one Little John was seen swaying from side to side as the sun went down, and but for two of the foresters he would have ——"

" It's a foul invention, Much," said the giant ; " think you I would take more down my throat than my legs could carry ? Body-o-me, man, could not the sun have taken effect upon me when we were at the butts yesterday ?"

" It could," said Robin, laughingly ; " never heed them, John ; it was the sun, not the Malvoisie, which made my legs crook like two bent bows ; but come, man, thou hast not told me where they news was gathered."

" That is soon told, master o'-mine," said Little John ; " We have spoken of the sun, and body-o'-me, it made me wondrous athirst to-day."

" The monks," interrupted Much, " will tell thee it was a punishment, John ——"

" The monks' words are not worth a groat," said the giant ; " thou knowest that right well, or the monk thy fingers lightened of his gold, would have spoken truly, when he said a goodly bough would bear thy body before the week had passed."

" Peace with thy idle prating," said Robin, " Come, thou wast athirst."

" I was, master-o'-mine—I did proceed ; when I felt so wondrously athirst, and though

* Another writer, speaking of bold Robin, says:— " In these forests, and with this company, he for many years reigned like an independent sovereign at perpetual war with the King of England and all his subjects, with the exception, however, of the poor and needy, and such as were desolate and oppressed, or stood in need of his protection. When molested by a superior force in one place, he went to another, still defying the power of the law ; and making his enemies pay dearly, as well for their open attacks as for their clandestine treachery "

I looked well into every runlet, there was not enough of liquor in any one of them to wet the tip of a finger; body-o'-me, the thirsty knaves must have drained them last night."

"Mayhap they did, John, but thy story, man."

"Not mine, master, for when I walked to the edge of the forest to find the brook—for my thirst had grown prodigious—mayhap he sight of the empty runlets did this—be that as it may, master, when I had drunk and drunk again, I heard a laugh behind me. No knave shall laugh at Little John, I thought, and getting to my feet, I saw a sturdy beggar leaning upon his staff."

"Thy news, man," said Robin; "thou art as long in answering me as a maiden telling her love story."

"Patience, master, patience, as I told the fat friar I caught in the forest; patience, and thou shalt have the story word for word."

Robin stooped to caress one of the large hounds which lay at his feet, and Little John continued:

"Body o' me, when I asked the knave what he had to laugh about, he made an answer that brought the quarterstaff I carried on his pate, and the lusty varlet gave me as good a blow in return. We had a long bout, master, and my hide is sore yet; but the end was we became friends, and he told me all that I have told you—much more, mayhap, for his staff so rang about my ears that it's a wonder I remembered a word."

"Where is the knave?"

"Where I left him, master, sitting by the brook, bathing his pate."

"At the brook through the forest?"

"At the brook through the forest, master. I would he had come with me, but as that was not to be done without having a second bout, I left him."

Robin placed his horn to his lips, and blew three clear ringing notes.

"I will see this sturdy beggar," he said, "not only for the news he brings, but to get one so stout to join our merry men."

## CHAPTER VI.

### ROBIN HOOD AND THE BEGGAR.

He met a beggar on the way.
Who sturdily could gang;
He had a pike-staff in his hand
That was both stiff and strong.

THE mellow notes from Robin's bugle were answered by George-a-Green, who came towards the Outlaw, leading a white horse, and the chief, as he mounted the beautiful steed, turned to Little John and said:

"Go to the cellarer, John; he will give thee a posset to cure thy bruised hide."

Nothing loth, the thirsty forester, taking

Much with him, went towards that part of the forest where the provisions and wine were kept, and Robin galloped through the intricate paths, and soon reached the brook.

He found the beggar as Little John had described him—a sturdy, well-built knave; but in place of bathing his head, he was seated upon a fallen tree, coolly examining divers rents in his cloak.

He affected not to notice the horseman who drew rein within a few feet of the fallen oak, but as he turned over the ragged cloak he soliloquised loud enough for Robin to hear:—

"Ten holes has the scurvy rascal made in my cloak, and I did not break his thick skull for it—out upon the cankerly hind! Would I had him here now."

"What would'st thou do?" Robin asked, amused at the stout-built fellow's words; what would'st thou do, knave?"

The beggar rose from the trunk of the tree, and, leaning upon his staff, answered:

"Break his thick skull, as I will thine if you do not leave me in peace."

"A murrain on ye for a saucy varlet," said Robin, dismounting, and passing one arm over his steed's neck; "know ye who I am?"

"I neither know nor care," said the beggar, "but judging from thy green jerkin, thou art one of those fellows who deserve a thrashed hide—by our lady, one of ye had one to-day."

"You are a pert knave," said the Outlaw, "and were it not that other matters require my time I would give thee such a drilling as would make as many holes in thy hide as Little John has left in that clouted cloak of thine."

"Little John!" said the beggar, "callest thou yonder water-guzzling carle Little John?"

"In sooth I do; mayhap thy back can tell more of his quarterstaff than thy tongue his name."

"Ask him, green jacket, ask him whether his back felt Allan-a-dale's staff. Out upon ye, there is not a man among ye save one that I would give a pinch of meal for."

"Who is that one, then, pert carle?"

"Robin," answered the beggar, "good Robin Hood, an honest and true man—know you him, young free of speech?"

"Passing well. I am Robin Hood."

"The name acted like a spell upon Allan-a-dale; he dropped his pikestaff, and kneeling before the Outlaw, said:

"Strike off my head, Robin, with thy good sword, that the tongue which has wagged against thee may speak no more."

"Not so," said the Outlaw; "I would hear it wag of things thou hast heard at the court of him men call England's king—Henry of Winchester."

"Hast not thy fellow told thee, good Robin?"

"But in part, but in part. Come, man, let me hear all thou knowest."

"All I know, Robin, brings sorrow upon thee. Thy lands are gone, thy name is outlawed, and by the light of to-morrow's sun you will behold Earl Mortimer and nigh a thousand spears entering Barnesdale."

"We will do our devoirs, Allan, let them come."

"Well spoken, bold Robin, wilt thou have Allan's pikestaff to help thee; mayhap it will not be the first Norman crown it has cracked?"

"Right gladly, Allan, but I would not part with thee after we have shown Roger Mortimer the use of the yew bow."

"Thou shalt not. I will stay with thee if there is meat and drink to be found in the merry greenwood."

"There is meat and drink, Allan—aye, more, there is a Lincoln green jacket to replace thy clouted cloak, a good yew bow, a sheaf of cloth yard shafts, a sword, and a buckler for thy arms, and, more, a hundred marks a year as long as you stay with my merry men."

"That will be as long as England has a Robin Hood, and a forest to hold him. I will stay, and thou shalt never regret the bargain."

"I know it—thy hand. There, the bargain is made, and foul fall him who breaks it."

"Amen."

"Now, Allan, jump behind me; my steed will carry us to the greenwood."

Robin mounted as he spoke, and Allan, throwing his cloak and the leather bags that hung around his neck into the brook, jumped lightly upon the horse's croup.

"So my lands are gone," said the Outlaw, as they went through the forest: "dost thou know to whom the false king has given them?"

"Right well I know; Geoffrey de Lois, a Norman beggar, has thy lands."

"Ah! the disturber of the May-day sports; there is more in this than mere chance."

"It would seem so, good Robin, for he bears thee no good will."

"Thou knowest much for one of thy calling, Allan."

"My ears are open when men speak. Behind the hawthorn I lurked and heard the tramp of horses' hoofs, and when I looked I saw Geoffrey de Lois and a priest riding from the court."

"A priest, Allan, one dark of countenance and sharp of speech."

"The same, Robin, the Abbot of St. Mary's, and uncle to Geoffrey de Lois."

"Did the wind bring their words to thine ear?"

"Marry, but it did, and my ears were sharpened when I heard thy name spoken."

"It was well thou wert near—come, what said the proud Abbot?"

"But little, save in joy that his nephew had been made Sheriff of Nottingham."

"Sheriff of Nottingham!" exclaimed Robin, pulling up his steed sharply, "by him who died on tree, this smellest of priestcraft more than court favour."

"So thought I," said Allan-a-dale, "and my thoughts were not wrong, as I knew when Geoffrey de Lois said thou wert going to Sherewood, if molested at Barnesdale."

"By my knighthode the priestly brain is subtle. Well, Allan, didst thou hear how they knew I was going to Sherwood?"

"I did, good Robin; there's one of Geoffrey de Lois's knaves among your merry men."

"Ah, is it so? That tells how the foreign minion knew so much of our haunts. By our Lady he shall dangle from a good green bough, but go on, good Allan—didst thou hear more?"

"But little, good master, for my breath was nigh gone, running so long by the hedgerow, but this I heard——"

Robin pressed his steed forward as Allan continued.

"They prayed that Earl Mortimer would fail of his object."

"How so? I can scarcely understand the workings of the priest's crafty brain."

"They prayed he would fail, good Robin, that you might go to Sherwood; then Geoffrey de Lois and the priest would pay off some score they hold against thee."

"A goodly plot! By my knighthode these priests learn some craft in their cloisters. Dost thou know more, Allan?"

"Not one word, good Robin, for I was spent, and when I got strength I came across the country to tell thee all."

"Thou art a good fellow, Allan, and twenty marks shall be thy portion. Where is Mortimer's band now?"

"On the high road which leads to Barnesdale. I have been quick, master, for they rode hard to take thine and thy merry men."

"Thou hast, indeed, been quick, and nearly got thy head broken for thy pains."

"Not so, master," Allan answered, laughing. "Ask thy long-limbed man whose head was nearly broken."

"I know, I know; and have given Little John a posset to cure the wounds made by thy pikestaff."

"Hadst thou not given him so many or

he day before he would not have so nigh dried the brook. Bladebone of St. Peter, how the man sucked the waters down that throat of his, and how my fingers itched to lay my staff across his back as he buried his nose in the water!"

"Peace, Allan; here's the greenwood and Robin's men. Have a care over that tongue of thine, or there will be some skulls broken before thou hast worn the Lincoln green many days."

"I will, master, I will. Bone of my body, but this is a goodly sight—five score and more stout archers; there is work here for the Earl Mortimer and his foreign knaves."

"There is, Allan, work enough for him to remember Barnesdale and Robin Hood."

## CHAPTER VII.

### FOREST WARFARE.

. . . . ! It was a gallant sight
To see them all in a row,
With every man a good broad sword,
And eke a good yew bow.

THE Anglo-Norman troops, led by the Earl of Mortimer, presented a splendid and warlike appearance as they wound in and out of the quiet roads which led to Barnesdale.

The great Earl's banner was in the van; the rich colours with which the arms of his house were embroidered upon the fluttering silk and its mail-clad bearer was a beautiful sight in itself.

The emblazonry upon the shields of the knights who owed allegiance to his house, the glowing colours worked upon the housings of their chargers, and the pourpoints which each knight wore above his mail, and the rainbow-like tints of the scarves which crossed their bodies, the long ends of which, fluttering in the autumn air, gave them the appearance of men about to enter a tournament rather than the rude field of battle.

But this illusion, if any of those who saw the Earl and his knights as the little army went on its way through the many towns and villages, entertained such, was dispelled when the curvetting war steeds passed onward; and the plainly-clad spearmen passed in close order—their steel caps and the points of their weapons glittering in the sun.

These and the crossbowmen told that other matters than a tournay caused this martial array, for the knights seldom brought their numerous bands of retainers to these meetings, the most ostentatious being generally content with the attendance of a couple of squires, and at the most a half-dozen attendants.

Around the stern Earl fluttered the gay pennons on the knights' lances, and ever and anon came the blast of a trumpet, calling the men who had fallen out of the line of march to rejoin the ranks.

There was much laughter among the young knights at the object of their long journey, and many wagers were made that the Saxon bowmen would not stay to meet their steel-clad foes.

"A cloth jerkin," said one who rode close behind Earl Mortimer, "will be but a poor check against our lances and spearmen."

"A cloth jerkin," said the Earl, who knew the stubborn Saxon character too well to undervalue the men he had vowed to destroy, "has before this been a match for linkmail."

"Say their arrows, my lord," said the knight: "but in this instance I am afraid that we shall have had our long ride for nothing."

"We shall see, Sir Raymond. I hope it may be so; it will save us from slaughtering these misguided men. Ha! here is Barnesdale Forest. Sound the halt, trumpeter."

A youth, mounted upon a white horse and wearing a surtout richly embroidered with the Earl's bearings, placed his trumpet to his lips and sounded one long, shrill blast upon his brazen instrument.

The small army became motionless, then the Earl, turning to the knight he had addressed as Sir Raymond, said:—

"Come, sir knight, push forward with the trumpeter and sound a parley; tell the rebels if they will surrender their leader to our keeping, then quietly disperse, Roger Mortimer will return back whence he came."

The young noble would sooner have had the order given to dash into the forest and charge the rebels than do the Earl's bidding; but he dared not disobey.

Fastening a white scarf to the point of his lance, he rode forward with the trumpeter and was absent full twenty minutes.

When they returned, an angry shout came from the soldiers, for both the knight and his companion were shorn of their arms and fastened in the saddle, their face towards the horses' tails.

Earl Mortimer bits his lips when he saw the manner in which the foresters had answered his messengers, and giving the word for the troops to advance, he entered the forest.

Robin Hood, with Little John, Much, and Allan-a-Dale had met the knight and the trumpeter in one of the fairy-like glades in the great forest.

They seemed to be alone, for not one of the five score archers were visible to the knight as he drew rein and gave Robin the Earl's message.

"Answer him, Much, and you, John; and Allan, help Much to tell this sweet knight how the Saxon archers fear the Earl's threat."

The three sturdy fellows sprang forward, and before the knight or his companion could turn their horses they were both jerked out of the saddle.

The Outlaw's lieutenant wrenched the half-drawn sword from the knight's hand, then taking him by the waist as though he were a child, placed him in his saddle with his face towards the horse's tail.

Much and Allan-a-dale did the same office for the trumpeter, then Robin Hood, laughing aloud at the sight, said :—

" Hie thee back, sweet herald, to him who sent thee, and tell how little Robin Hood and his merry men care for big words, although the Earl may have twice five hundred spears and crossbows to back them."

A few stripes from Little John's yew-bow goaded the steeds forward, and the riders, clutching at the hinder part of the saddle, were soon born through the forest.

" Body o' me !" said Little John, " How the Earl will rave when he sees yon messengers back."

" Were he only to rave, said the bold Outlaw, " we need care but little, but peradventure we shall hear more of the whistle of a bolt from a crossbow than Mortimer's gentle words."

" We need care but little for the sound," said Allan, " did not an iron bolt come with it. Ah ! look yonder, my masters, and tell me if there is not a morion shining through the green leaves."

" Wondrously like it," said Robin, as he carelessly fitted an arrow to his bow, " but it's a fair mark, Allan, for a feathered shaft to teach the knave to wear a less bright covering for his thick skull."

The arrow whistled through the air as the forester ceased speaking, and the cry which came from the thicket told how well the mark had been hit.

" One knave the less," said Little John, " thou hast slain him, master."

" Not so," said the Outlaw ; " see, John, for thyself."

A slight opening between the trees showed one of Mortimer's spearmen running at full speed, his head was bare, the steel casque having been taken off by Robin's arrow.

" One of the foreign thieves in the pay of the Norman," said Little John, " he can take back word that cloth-yard shafts are plentiful in Barnesdale. Body-o'-me, heard ye that ?"

The loud fanfare of the Norman trumpets and the rattle of a species of kettle-drum were heard as Little John spoke.

Robin's lip curled with scorn, when he heard this signal, and looking towards the opening in the forest, said :—

" The varlet has told his story, I will answer the Earl's summons to horse."

He placed his bugle to his lips, and wound a shrill defiant call which echoed the length and breadth of the forest."

" There," laughed Robin ; " if the knaves follow that sound, we may lead them to the open glen. Ha ! by our Lady, hither they come. To your shelter, John, away ! Much and Allan, bid our merry men find the rivets of the Norman armour with their cloth-yard shafts."

They disappeared among the trees. Then Robin, sounding another defiant call upon his bugle, followed.

The force which now began to enter the forest was three times as great as that of the outlaws.

Their equipment was also better calculated for defence than the foresters' green jerkins, for not only were the men-at-arms and knights cased in armour, but even those who carried arblasts* wore iron gorgets, caps, and defensive armour for their arms and thighs ; but there was one weapon they lacked— that, the tough yew bow and the English shaft.

Riding at the head of his men, Earl Mortimer spurred his war-steed to the little glade, where Robin and his companions had so lately stood.

Not a glimpse of a green jacket was to be seen, and the Earl, turning to the knights who crowded around him, said :—

" Marry, but 'tis as I said, fair sirs, the sound of the knave's bugle was but the call for his rascals to flee."

" Thou liest ! Earl Mortimer," said a voice. " Draw to the ear, my merry men. Saint George for England, and confusion to the Normans."

Upon every side came a flight of arrows, which rattled upon the knights' impenetrable armour, and others finding an undefended part on the less skilfully-made covering worn by the men-at-arms, struck nigh three score of them to the earth.

The attack was so sudden, the shafts so well aimed, that men and horses had fallen dead or dying before a lance could be lowered, or eye had time to mark from from whence the arrows came.

The Earl saw he had been led into am ambuscade by the foresters, so spurring his black charger over the bodies of his fallen men, he called out fiercely :—

" God and Saint Denis, follow me, all true knights, follow me."

" God and St. Denis !" they repeated. " come forth, Saxon swine, come forth !"

The attempt to penetrate the surrounding thicket was a failure, so the Earl and his

*Arblast, a cross-bow : the missile, an iron quarrell, so called from its shape.

lances, after essaying to break through the thick brushwood, drew up their steeds.

The most profound silence had been preserved by the foresters during the time the mail-clad horsemen were endeavouring to force a passage through the bushes, and were it not for the heap of dead and dying who lay in the centre of the glade, with the Saxon shaft driven into their bodies, there would have been nothing to show the forest was tenanted by the Norman troops.

That every movement was closely watched Earl Mortimer soon found, for when he drew up his snorting steed in the midst of angry knights, a clear voice trolled out merrily from the brushwoood :—

> Robin blithely blew his silver call,
> And here the echoes slept,
> One hundred archers stout, and tall,
> Appeared at right and left.

The Earl struck his gauntletted hand upon his saddle, when the full, rich voice sounded so mockingly upon his ear, and with an oath called upon the arblast men to discharge their missiles into the surrounding bushes.

At the butts of the crossbows came to the men's shoulders, the voice of the Outlaw Chief could be heard shouting :

"St. George and Merry England, draw to the ear, my lusty bowmen, draw to the ear !"

The twang of a hundred bowstrings heralded the coming of a flight of arrows, and the foremost of the arblast men fell to the ground.

Earl Mortimer chafed like an angry lion as he plunged forward to within a yard of the bushes which held the outlaws commanded by Robin Hood.

"The foul fiend take them for lurking dogs !" he cried. "Come out from thy shelter, or——"

A cloth-yard shaft, impelled by no ordinary hand, struck the earl's corselet, and checked the completion of his speech.

"Have a care, Lord Mortimer," said the voice that had before spoken, "or the next shaft may find an entrance between the points of thy Spanish harness."

The earl gnashed his teeth, and backed the sable steed he bestrode from the dangerous points.

"Come, sir knights, have none of you heart of grace in this hour, no plan to advise your Earl ?"

Raymond, the knight of Bayonne, rode to his leader.

"My lord," he said, "he who would crush a nest of hornets must not fear their stings."

"By him who bled for us, I conjure thee to speak more fully, or three score more of our men will follow those who have already fallen."

"It is not meet that I should have spoken before having thy permission, my lord, and yours, sir knights. Our men have swords: let them cut a passage to these hinds; also, let the arblast-bolts be sent into the depths of the thicket."

"By my halidome, thou hast spoken well! Fall to, my men—fall to."

The sound of the troopers' swords and axes were accompanied by the hissing quarrells from the crossbows.

A space was soon cleared, and the Earl, flourishing his battle-axe, shouted:

"A Mortimer ! a Mortimer !"

The cry was taken up by the knights as they couched their lances, and followed the Earl to the glen, which spread to the right and left as clear of timber, and as soft as the richest carpet ever placed by Dame Nature upon the earth.

Then came a sudden check to the advance of the Earl and his knights; the foremost fell to the ground, and those in the rear were struck with confusion by a sudden flight of arrows.

The Earl was the first to disengage himself from his fallen steed; and as he sprang to his feet, he called out:

"Back—back ! The hinds have placed stakes for our horses."

The warning cry checked the dense crowd of horsemen, and as they pulled up there issued from the opposite belt of trees Robin Hood and his merry bowmen.

The Earl's angry shout when he saw the bold outlaws advancing so fearlessly towards the steel-capped host was aroused by a peal of laughter from their gallant leader.

———

## CHAPTER VIII.

### THE COMBAT BETWEEN ROBIN HOOD AND EARL MORTIMER.

> Their bows they bent, and forth they went,
> Shooting in company,
> Towards the town of Nottingham,
> Outlaws though they be.

THE indomitable leader of the Saxon archers did not permit his lightly-clad men to remain long enough in the open glade to face the line of spears which were levelled when the band issued from their covert.

A single note from his bugle caused them to disappear as suddenly as they appeared before Mortimer's angry host.

The Earl quickly marshalled his followers in line, intending to charge the foresters, and thus at one blow destroy them; but ere the heavy horsemen could strike their rowels into their horses' flanks, the archers had sought the shelter of the trees.

All save their fearless leader had gone, and he, as though loving the danger he had placed himself in, stood leaning upon his drawn sword, regarding the movements of his foes.

"A cloth jerkin," he muttered, "is but a bad shield against a lance head; my merry men are safer behind yon trees than out here. Marry but the Norman mercenaries like not the fact that a hundred grey-goose shafts are drawn to the ear behind this thicket."

The earl, checking the advance of his mailed cavalry, seemed uncertain how to act; as Robin had said the knowledge of a hundred unerring shafts being pointed at his followers caused him to act with prudence.

He felt no fear of the issue of a combat in the open ground; here his lances would have scattered the foresters like dust; but as they had gone to the thick cover, he knew as long as a quiver contained an arrow his men would be mere targets for the English bowmen.

While holding a brief consultation with the knights nearest to him, the Earl's attention was called to Robin Hood by Raymond of Bayonne.

"See, my good lord," the knight said, "yonder stands the leader of the outlaws, peradventure it may be to treat with thee for clemency toward his band."

The Earl looked towards Robin, who was now leaning against a tree.

"By our Lady," said the Earl, "thou art right, Raymond; yon outlaw has done wisely to yield to our clemency, and we'll have speech with the knave; although I may spare his men, he must hang upon the nearest tree."

He went forward as he spoke, then the two leaders were placed about half way between their bands.

The Outlaw smiled quietly when he saw the earl come towards him, and in reply to a whispered caution which came from the covert behind him, said—

"A malison on thee, John. Keep thine eyes upon the arblast men; leave the Earl to my care."

"But, master," answered the invisible lieutenant, "I pray thee forego this wish to have speech with yonder Earl. Seek the covert, master, and we will give these Norman such a flight of grey-goose shafts as——"

"Peace, knave. Do as I bid thee, or by St. Herman of the Wold thou shalt drink nought but water for the next seven days."

"Body-o'-me!" grumbled the giant, as he drew further into the covert, "body-o'-me! but I shall have but little strength left to bend the bow. Water! for seven long days! Body-o'-me! ugh!"

When the Earl came within speaking distance of the bold forester, the latter to show he trusted to Mortimer's honour, sheathed his sword, and, with the hand thus set at liberty, toyed with the rich tassel which hung from the bugle he wore at his hip.

Mortimer, not to be outdone in courtesy, also returned his ponderous sword to its scabbard; then resting the point of his triangular shield upon the ground, he placed his hands lightly upon the upper part, and began the conversation by saying—

"Have I mistaken thy meaning, my man, when I come forward to ha with thee?"

"Thou dost not err, Earl Mortimer," answered the Outlaw. "I sought speech of thee, thinking it were a shame this greensward should be red with the blood of my merry men; and for the matter of that, of thy followers, mercenaries though they be, and enemies to this fair land."

"Thou art right," said the Earl, not doubting but Robin was about to surrender; "it were a shame that blood should be spilt when by a timely yielding of thy body thou mayest pre——"

The ringing laugh which came from the forester's lips checked the Earl's speech, and placing his hand upon the hilt of his sword, was about to draw the weapon.

"Take thy hand from thy sword," said the Outlaw, "for as surely as an inch of the bright blade becomes visible above the scabbard's mouth will a grey-goose shaft pierce thine eye until it reaches the brain; so have a care my Lord of Mortimer, have a care."

The fame of the wondrous skill possessed by these bowmen had been spread the length and breadth of the land; thus Mortimer's earl knew the threat was no idle boast, and, though a brave man, he did not hesitate to remove his hand from the embossed hilt of his weapon.

"The fashion of the Norman Court," Robin said, "is to look upon the Saxon as but a slave to his conquerors—thy brain, Mortimer, has taken up this, or thy words would not have been so wide of the truth."

"In Heaven's name, then, disgrace to the spurs thou once wore," said the earl, angrily; "what caused thee to seek this parley, if it were not to yield?"

"A wish to save the shedding of blood, the blood of those who have nought to do with thy mission here. Mistake not my words as those of fear, for at a wave of hand five-score feathered shafts would be planted among thy followers, who look even now greedily upon the free land which holds England's merry bowmen."

The Earl was growing angrier every moment, and it is probable he would not have patiently heard Robin Hood's words to the end, had he not known that his slightest movement towards his men would have been the signal for a flight of arrows from the copse.

Well skilled in the then rude art of war, he did not wish to bring matters to a crisis while the outlaws had so much the advantage of position.

A position he saw, while conversing with the Outlaw Chief, had been rendered still more impassable for his mailed cavalry, by the row of sharp stakes, which were just visible abov the ground, behind which the bold woodsmen stood.

True, he numbered some three-score arblast men in his train, but the weapon being a foreign one, and but lately introduced into England, the men were not so well skilled in its use as he would have wished.

Knowing all this, and hoping yet to draw the foresters from their covert, he repressed his rising passion, also the strong inclination to draw his sword upon the Outlaw.

"My mission here," said the Earl, in reply to the forester's words, "is in obedience to the wish of my lawful—aye, thy lawful—sovereign, Henry of Wincester, King of England."

"Thou liest, Mortimer," said the Outlaw; "thy coming was prompted by the hate thou hast ever borne to me since my good lance rolled both thee and thy steed in the dust before the whole court assembled to witness the tournay."

The Earl's brow became as black as night at these words; he too well remembered his tournay of which Robin spoke, and his heart told him it was more in revenge for that defeat, which up to the present hour galled his proud spirit, than a wish to serve the King. that he had undertaken to subdue or slay the captain of the outlaws.

"The lie back to thy teeth!" he said angrily; "if I went down before thy lance, it was when thou wert a belted earl, not a leader of thieves and cutpurses; wert thou still a noble, and worthy of my lance, I would even now wipe out the trampling of my crest in that day's tournay."

"Gramercy,"* said the bold forester, "for thy courteous words, most puissant Earl, although my lands are given to the hungry Norman crew, I am yet as good a man as thou art. Aye, better, for my knee has not yet bent to the foreign yoke, neither has my tongue, with lip-loyalty, saved the possessions of my fathers."

The forester drew the buff gauntlet he wore from his right hand as he spoke, and holding it by the fingers, continued:

"Listen, Earl Mortimer, I will prove I am the better man of the two. Here we stand, in the merry greenwood, my coat but of Lincoln-green cloth, my cap but of felt, and my arms an English sword and buckler; yet, withal this, and despite the Spanish mail which covers thee from crown to heel, I challenge thee to single combat!—here, foot

to foot and hand to hand, let the issue be with the best man; if thou conquer, my men will yield thee true and lawful——"

"Body-o'-me!" growled a voice in the thicket; "surely, this mad master f mine will not fight that tower of steel. b nes of St. Hubert! but we will not yield while a shaft is left, or a hand to wield a sword."

"Prisoners," he continued, not heeding the interjectional growl of the sturdy lieutenant, "in proof of this, behold my gage."

He flung the leathern glove at the Earl's feet as he spoke, and the latter, trembling with suppressed wrath, stooped and picked it up.

"I accept the combat," he said; "but that men may not say I slew thee in unfair fight thou shalt have the loan of one of yonder knights' armour. Come hither, Raymond of Bayonne," he added, raising his voice, "I would borrow thy——"

"Stay," said Robin Hood, "I will not have even a helmet that has adorned a Norman head. I offer thee combat, and, as the challenger, have a right to my choice of arms— a choice thou wilt accept, unless thy heart has grown weak through mixing with the silken gallants at the court of him thou stylest king."

"Be it so," said the Earl; "I will leave thee for a few moments, that thy peace can be made with heaven; for, as sure as the sun gilds the leaves of yonder tree, thou hast seen thy last day upon earth."

Robin's rejoinder was a light laugh of defiance, and as the Earl walked swiftly to his followers, the Outlaw drew his sword and tried the temper of the blade by bending it until the point touched the hilt.

Satisfied that his weapon was to be relied upon, he loosened the straps of his shield and threw it behind him.

There was a dull thud as though the buckler had come in contact with a hard substance.

"Body-o'-me! ten thousand curses upon the buckler," rapped out Little John from his place of concealment; "thou hast well nigh broken my head with that target of thine."

"Keep thy head covered, John."

"Blessed St. Hubert," rejoined the gigantic forester, "would that I had done so. But hearken, master of mine, I was praying to the saints to give thee victory, praying, master, with head all bare, when thy shield came rattling about my ears. But, master."

"What now, knave?"

"You must be mad to engage yon steelcased Earl. Body-o'-me! shall I draw a good shaft ready to aid thee should he get the upper hand?"

---

* Thanks.

"Peace, knave, le tthy shafts alone, except yonder host advance. Where are the men?"

"Here, good master, stuck in this copse as thick as flies around a honey pot."

"Listen, and keep thy peace till I have done: should the day go against me let no hand move in my cause; they are too strong for us. To save thy carcasses from their spears I will do my devoir with this Earl; should I fall, take my body with thee in thy retreat, and give it a free man's burial. To thee, Little John, rogue as thou art, I give the care of our merry men; see to it, knave, and be less fond of swilling all the wine, whether good or bad, which comes in thy way."

"Body-o'-me! but I always choose the best, good master; if I am more athirst than my fellows my patron saint is to blame; but here comes thy foe; a grip of thy hand, master; may St. Hubert bring thee safe out of this grievous strait."

Little John's huge hand was protruded through the thick foliage, and Robin gripped it with a force which even brought tears to the giant's eyes.

A rustling among the bushes told that more of the foresters were coming forward to enjoy the honour of a farewell clasp of their leader's hand. So Robin, to prevent this, moved forward to meet the Earl.

"Hast thou," Mortimer asked, "made thy peace with heaven? or does thine heart, even at this moment, fail to second the words" ——

"Peace! we lose time," said the Outlaw; "draw thy weapon, man, for the arm which overthrew thee once has lost none of its skill; but stay—ere we begin I must tell thee my mind is changed. My merry men will not yield to thee if I fall."

"The better for yonder knights, who hunger to dim their lance points with Saxon blood. Now have at thee for a false traitor. God and St. Denis!"

Shouting the later words (the Earl's warcry), he made a downward stroke at the Outlaw's head, which, had it taken effect, would have cleft him to the spine.

The forester's trusty sword caught the blow, as he answered Mortimer's cry by calling out:

"St. George and Merry England, and confusion to the tyrant's minions!"

The combat lasted for some minutes without either party gaining an advantage, and those who watched the play of the trenchant blades, saw that Robin, despite the absence of defensive armour from his body, was by his superior skill and quick eye, quite a match for the Earl.

For some time the Outlaw fought purely on the defensive, and the Earl, being armed at all points, and covered by his shield, rained blow after blow upon his adversary.

Every stroke was met with a rapidity and coolness, which caused the fiery Earl to redouble his efforts to slay his antagonist.

Robin smiled when he beheld this; it was all he aimed at. Knowing the heavy armour the Earl wore would soon tire him, the Outlaw kept him at bay until the strong arm began to tire.

Now the forester in turn pressed upon his foe, his blade rang upon the steel armour and the large shield, until the Earl, tired and worn by the weight of his mail, began to retreat.

The hidden foresters could scarce restrain their joy at the sight, and Little John now understood his leader's motive for refusing a suit of mail.

The cumbersome armour, though very useful to a mounted combatant, was a decided disadvantage to the wearer when on foot.

Back, step by step, Mortimer went, the Bold outlaw seeking with his sword point every joint of his adversary's mail.

Back, back, until they were within three feet of the copse where the outlaws were concealed, and then the Earl's sword flew from his hand.

He raised his arm to ward off a blow which threatened his head, and quick as thought the forester changed the direction of the weapon, and the point entered the only vulnerable part of the Earl's body.

This was under the arm where the joints of the mail met.

"Yield thee, rescue or no rescue!" said Robin, as the sword point pierced the leathern doublet and began to cut the flesh; "yield thee, or by St. Herman of the Wold, I will drive this good blade through thy body until the point touches the mail on the opposite side."

"I yield," was the sullen answer; "withdraw thy weapon."

The Outlaw did so; and at the same time made a sign to Little John, who, with Allan-a-Dale, dashed from the copse, and seizing the Earl by the arms hurried him out of sight.

The knights and horsemen had dismounted at the beginning of the combat and so swift had been their leader's defeat that ere they could mount their chargers, he had disappeared from view.

Raymond of Bayonne was the first in the saddle, and waving his lance, he dashed the rowels into his charger's flanks, and shouted:

"A rescue! a rescue!"

His companions were not long in following him, and taking up the cry, and the weight of the heavy steeds, as they thundered across the glen, fairly shook the earth.

The spearman and those armed with the arblast followed as quickly as they could, and the horsemen, when within fifty paces of the copse, heard a voice call out:

"St. George and Merry England. Now, my men, now!"

The hiss of a hundred arrows through the air was followed by the rattle of the steel heads upon the knights' armour, the fall of horses, and such of the riders as were not armed in proof.

Checked, but not subdued, the knight of Bayonne sprang from his horse, and, drawing his sword, called upon the spearmen to follow him, but when they reached the copse it was untenanted.

---

## CHAPTER IX.

### THE EARL'S RANSOM.

In summer time, when leaves and flowers
  On every bough do spring,
It is merry in the gay greenwood,
  And the little birds do sing.
Listen to me, ye yeomen all,
  So comely, so courteous, so good:
One of the best that ever bare bow—
  His name was Robin Hood.*

THE mellow tints of the autumn sun flooded Sherwood's fair forest, and the timid deer were leaving their coverts to seek a crystal pond which lay in the depths of this romantic sylvan retreat.

At the base of a giant oak the ground was strewed with rushes and soft grass, and reclining upon this couch was the handsome and fearless Outlaw, Robin Hood.

His yew-bow and a quiver filled with grey-goose shafts lay near, and his right hand, although his senses were buried in a deep sleep, rested upon the hilt of his sword.

In spite of the price which had been put upon his head, the Outlaw's repose was as little troubled with a thought of danger as though he slept in the stone chamber of the castle which had once been his.

The Forest of Sherwood was, at the time of which we write, little frequented, save by those who were compelled to skirt its margin when travelling; even then, so great was the solitude of its avenues of giant trees and coverts of brushwood, that many an ave or pater-noster were said before venturing upon a journey fraught with so many real and unreal dangers.

Superstition had much to do in preventing even the peasants of the neighbouring hamlets from exploring the forest, for they held

---

* The ballad from which these verses are taken was given by Ritson to the public at the close of the last century. The original manuscript is preserved in the public library of Cambridge, and it is supposed to have been written during the reign of Henry VI. The above words are modernised.

---

a firm belief that nature's solitude was tenanted by woodland fays and nymphs.

The former, they believed, were gifted with the power of cudgelling any daring mortal who should attempt to penetrate the haunts of the deer; and the latter, by their wondrous beauty, were supposed to lure men to destruction.

If these causes were not sufficient to keep the forest from being invaded, the knowledge that a band of desperate outlaws had sought refuge in the mystic depths added to the ill-repute of the place.

Thus the peasant and swineherd, the farmer and trader shrank from Sherwood as a place of evil; and those who were compelled to traverse the more open parts did so with sinking heart and trembling limbs, starting at the rustle of a leaf, and expecting to behold either a spirit, a nymph, or a forester dart from among the trees.

It will be readily understood that a better place for the outlaw's home could not have been found in the whole length and breadth of the land; add to its repute the nature of its coverts which were impassable for horses, there is little wonder that bold Robin slept so peacefully and soundly in that sylvan glade.

True, no precautions were neglected to prevent a surprise, for the band had many powerful foes around them.

Upon every point of the forest which could be entered from the high road, there lurked among the brushwood and behind trees lusty green-clad outlaws, who gave timely notice of a foe's approach.

Their signal was certain notes upon the bugle-horn, and so well acquainted were they with the sound of each other's horns that the band could tell exactly where to expect an intruder.

Suddenly the profound silence was broken by a long-winding blast from one of the sentinels, and the Outlaw, springing to his feet, hastily donned his quiver, then as he leant upon his long bow, he passed one hand across his eyes as though to banish the hazy sensation which is felt when one is aroused from a deep sleep.

"That's Allan's blast," he muttered, after listening to the ringing echoes. "He is posted on the high road."

As though the matter was of no more import than the fact of ascertaining from whence the sound came, the Outlaw began to saunter leisurely to and fro beneath the wide-spreading trysting tree.

He paused when Little John made his appearance at the farther end of the glen, and judging by the lieutenant's face that nothing serious had arisen, he greeted the giant's advance in his usual good-humoured manner.

What knave," he said, "has dared to make the welkin ring with this rude blast, and disturb the slumbers of Sherwood's King? Is it a fat bishop, who has come this way in all humility to leave us his gold and silver? Speak, John."

"It is both gold and silver, muster-o'-mine," said John, "and a goodly bag, but not brought by a churchman. No, body-o'-me! they do not, these pious knaves, discard the goodly things of this world so easily, although they let the more sinful portion do so."

"Shorten thy preamble, John," said the outlaw chief, "which has been as long as a new-made monk's first prayer, tell thy story man, and a' done with it."

"Body-o'-me!" said the giant, for the first time displaying two well-filled bags; "this will tell the story, and in a pleasant way."

He shook the bags until the chink of the metal could be heard—certainly a pleasant sound.

"Mortimer's ransom!" said Robin, laughing. "It is welcome, John, for our royal coffers have been empty of late."

"Bones of St. Hubert!" said John, "but thou sayest true; for nothing but water has passed down my throat this week past. Body-o'-me! I have scarce strength to bend a bow in consequence."

"Shame on thee, John! dost thou forget the good monk they found with a bottle of sack under his gown?"

"I reckon that as nought, good master; it was but a good action."

"How, knave?"

"A good action I did, master. I both drank his sack, and cudgelled his hide, for letting me; but think, good master, the scandal I saved the Church by preventing the holy man getting in a state not seemly for one of his calling."

"Get thee out for a hypocrite," said Robin; "thou carest little for the sins of others when that throat of thine is dry."

"I will not gainsay aught thou sayest, good master; so we'll let the matter stand over until a more fitting time; but concerning these pieces of gold and silver, shall I take them to Much, our steward?"

"Do so, John; tell him to have the feast spread at once, that we may give this Earl an insight into our free and merry life; let him spread it in the glen where stands the hollow oak."

Little John's face expressed the delight he felt at the prospect of the banquet, and humming the refrain of an old ditty, he went towards the covert, but, ere he could pass through the foliage, Robin Hood's voice arrested his steps.

"Stay, Little John," he said: "when the feast is prepared, sound three notes on thy horn, to call in such of our merry men as be out in the forest, for this eve we will trust to the safe keeping of our patron, St. Herman of the Wold; and hark'ee, knave, keep thy itching fingers out of those bags."

Little John cast his eyes upwards, and looked the personification of injured innocence.

"Body-o'-me!" he said, as he went towards the glen, "had I but helped myself to one good piece, I had deserved it for the trouble of carrying."

During the foregoing colloquy between Robin Hood and his lieutenant, the sun had sunk so low that its dusky light was only visible through a slight opening between the trunks of the trees.

The Outlaw Chief, who had resumed his walk after Little John disappeared, paused when he saw the blood-red glow of the setting sun, and folding his arms, attentively regarded the small disc visible from where he stood.

"So," he said, half aloud, "the setting of this day's sun was to be my last hour upon this fair earth, unless I yielded the Lord of Mortimer without ransom. Such was the answer my messenger brought me. But yon blessed orb has seen a different result from the Norman's threats."

"Thanks to thy promise, good master, of wetting the feathers of a goose shaft with his proud Earl's blood."

Robin turned at the interruption, and beheld his stalwart follower, his big face brimming over with good humour as though some recent event had mightily amused him.

"What now, knave?" said Robin," "is it thus you keep my orders?"

"I have kept them, good master, and even now there is a feast being spread that would cuase the Norman King to die with envy were he to see it; and body-o'-me! it has all been done without Much looking at even a roast haunch."

"The pursing of thy lips," Robin said, "tells me that something has befallen Much. What is it thou'rt grinning at?"

"But what I expected," said Little John, laughing. "Thou remember'st I spoke of a Curtall friar I saw yester-e'en hunting a goodly buck?"

"I do, by Saint Herman. I'll teach the shavelings to hunt deer in our preserves. Well, about Much?"

"Body-o'-me!" said the forester, laughing until his sides shook; "little Much went to teach this holy friar not to hunt our venison; and—ho, ho, ho!—ha, ha, ha!—

"A malison on thy jaws. Tell thy story without such unseemly mirth."

ROBIN HOOD AND MAID MARIAN.

Little John drew the back of his hand across his eyes to efface the moisture which gathered there during his outburst of laughter.

"Patience, good master," he said, "and thou wilt laugh too, or thou art not merry Robin, the king of good fellows. Well, body-o'-me, when Much bid the friar leave the deer at peace, the holy man laid about him with a stout staff; and though Much fought like a very devil, he has come back so bruised from head to heel that he can neither sit nor stand. Body-o'-me—ho, ho, ho, ho! The shaveling has trounced the miller's hide —ha, ha, ha!"

The giant went off in another fit of boisterous laughter, and Robin, in spite of himself was compelled to join in the merriment.

"By Saint Herman of the Wold!" said Robin, when he regained sufficient breath to use his favourite oath, "thou shalt learn better than to laugh at the misfortunes of thy fellows. Here, knave, take thy good oak stave and seek out this lusty saint, and if thou dost not liquor his hide, not one drop of sack or malvoisie touches that thirsty throat of thine for twice seven days.

Little John's face lengthened at this command, and, well it might, for the expected feasting he had looked forward to was placed out of his reach.

"Body-o'-me! good master," he ruefully said; "would not to-morrow do as well as to-night? Think thou of the fast I have had so long. I am weak, good Robin, and the holy man's staff would ring upon my carcase like as though it were an empty——

3

"To-morrow, be it. Crack the rascal's shaven crown, if thou canst, and remember, if he beats thee, thy master must e'en try a bout with him."

"Beat me! Shoulder of Saint Hubert! I'll make jelly of the varlet."

Rising clear and ringing above the trees sounded the signal that the feast was ready. Arm-in-arm the outlaws went in the direction of the sound, Little John thinking more of the goodly viands than the trouble which awaited him on the morrow.

Robin left his trusty lieutenant near the glen where the feast was spread.

He went towards a small hut, or rather a cottage, for it was built with blocks of stone, and cemented rudely, but securely together.

Here Robin had kept the proud Earl; it was but a small prison for so great a prisoner.

---

## CHAPTER X.

### THE OUTLAWS' FEAST.

They washed themselves and wiped themselves,
  And down to their dinner sat,
Bread and wine they had enough,
  And venison plump and fat;
Hares and pheasants they had full good,
  And river fowl was there,
And there wanted never so little a bird,
  As ever was bred on a briar.

IT was a scene of rare picturesque beauty this feast of the green-clad outlaws; the chief, conspicuous from his men by the cap of green velvet, and jerkin of the same costly material, which he now wore in place of the ordinary Lincoln cloth.

There could not be conceived a more beautiful sylvan spot than the place where the long oaken tables were placed—a row of gigantic oaks, in so good a line that it seemed the hand of man had planned the acorns which bore such prodigious fruit.

Under the wide-spreading branches of these forest monarchs the feast was held, and so perfect was the covering which nature thus afforded the bold yeomen, that neither sun nor rain could pierce the leafy canopy.

Upwards of a hundred stout foresters were seated at the board, which was covered with the choicest viands the forest, the lake, or the adjoining swamp could furnish.

Upon a huge wooden trencher in the centre of the table were two smoking haunches of venison, and at each end there was a counterpart of this famous dish.

Upon smaller trenchers were to be seen roasted swans, pheasants, boiled capons, swimming in toothsome sauce, bowls of fresh fish, huge piles of barley cakes.

Nearer the sides of the table were huge flagons of nut brown ale, and beakers of sack, malvoisie, and other choice wines.

Beside each wooden plate was a horn drinking cup; and upon the grass near the lower end of the table and supported by large blocks of wood, were several huge barrels, containing a further supply of both good October ale, and the rich juice of the grape; and towards these goodly emblems of joy to a thirsty throat, Little John, from time to time, cast looks of the tenderest regard.

Earl Mortimer was seated upon Robin's right hand, and by the sullen, gloomy expression upon his face it was evident he did know how soon his captivity would end.

The Outlaw had treated the Earl with knightly courtesy, for although a prisoner held to ransom he wore his sword, and the sable crest upon his helmet floated in the breeze as freely as though he were an invited guest instead of a foe and a captive.

In these warlike days it was the custom to deprive a prisoner of his armour and arms; neither of these had the courteous forester demanded, although the Earl had more than once attempted to escape the vigilance of his guards.

When all were seated, the chief of the sturdy band doffed his cap, an example which was followed by all present; then grace was said, and the business of eating began in earnest.

It was not unfashionable in those days to have an appetite; so the Earl, however much he despised and hated his captors, did as much execution among the viands as the most lusty of the band.

Venison, fowl, and fish were carved by his dagger, for there were no knives and forks at that period, the dagger which every man wore serving the purpose of a knife with as much readiness as it would find a sheath in an adversary's body.

The feasting was carried on in silence save for a low-voiced remark or jest being spoken by a yeoman to his neighbour.

The fourth part of an hour sufficed to make sad havoc among the edibles; then, at a signal from Robin, a dozen stout fellows jumped to their feet, and carried away the wreck of the feast.

The horn cups were soon passing round, and tongues began to wag under the influence of the nut-brown ale.

"What think you, my lord," Robin asked, "of our forest life? Does not its freedom sit more easily upon our shoulders than being at the caprice of a false king?"

The Earl's temper had been a little improved by the good cheer, and divers horns of wine he had partaken of.

"I will not gainsay your words, Robin," he said, "yet I would not that I were compelled to lead a life fraught with such danger as threatens thee and thy companions, if taken in open outlawry."

"If taken—that was well said, my lord," said the handsome forester; "if taken—that day is far off yet."

"It would seem so," replied the Earl, a touch of anger in his tone, "or I had not been left in captivity so many weeks."

"How now, my lord, has thy captivity been a dungeon or a chain, that thou speakest in such covert bitterness. Saint Herman! thou hast had the forest to roam in, and the best cheer our poverty could afford!"

"Thy cheer," replied the Earl, "has been meet for a king—the forest a bridal chamber; but when the mind is far beyond these, then they are but like a dungeon wall."

"There may be some truth in this, my lord," said Robin. "I did not think thy captivity sat so heavily upon thee as this. I give thee joy, Earl Mortimer; thou art free to depart at any hour."

The Earl's face flushed with joy, and he seemed about to grasp the Outlaw's hand, but he checked the impulse before his companion noticed the half-extended arm.

"Has the good knight Raymond," he asked, "surrounded the forest with his spears, that thy tongue offers me instant freedom?"

"The knight may be among the silken nobles of Henry's court, or at the bottom of the sea for aught I wot," replied Robin; "no, my lord, when my messenger brought word that I should hang when this day's sun set, unless I released thee, I sent them back such answer to their message that soon brought the means of thy liberation."

The Earl's face expressed more than ordinary surprise as he listened to the Outlaw Chief's words. At first an incredulous smile played upon his lips, then, as this faded, he turned his eyes upon the bold forester with an expression in them that told he felt some admiration for the man whose hand had twice conquered him in fair and open fight.

"The means of my liberation!" he repeated; "unless it were a body of good spears; it must be the ransom thy boldness prompted thee to ask; but unless all who owe allegiance to my banner are turned traitors, they would clear this forest of thy band before paying a single mark for my liberty."

"You mistake, my good lord," replied the forester, smiling; "for I sent word to all who hold the name of Mortimer as their war-cry, that the sight of a steel helmet or a glittering spear-head being seen by my merry men would be the signal for a grey-goose shaft to pass through thy body."

The Earl started as these words were spoken, and gnawing the ends of his long moustache, he looked as though he would

have given much to have plunged the dagger into the Outlaw Chief's heart.

"And would'st thou," he asked savagely, "have kept thy word had the glitter of my spearmen been seen from thy coverts?"

"Would'st thou," said Robin, evading a direct answer, "have hanged me in the forest of Barnesdale, according to thy word plighted to Henry of Winchester, had the chance been thine?"

"By the Blessed Virgin," the Earl angrily answered, "I would, had'st thou ten lives!"

"By St. Herman of the Wold!" said Robin, "so would I have kept my word, hadst thou been Henry of Winchester, in place of Roger Mortimer. But come, my lord, a truce to this; you are my guest, and it smacks of scant courtesy to grumble with one who is under our hospitality."

"Thou art right, Robin," said the Earl, his passion giving place to a better feeling; "give me thine hand; there, Mortimer is thy friend, for a right good yeoman and true man is Robin Hood."

"Thanks, my lord, there is my hand, one that is always ready to strike a blow for England, and as a true knight thou canst not gainsay me when I say it is the better for that."

"Men think differently upon these matters, Robin," answered the Earl. "Perhaps ambition guides thy thoughts and deeds, but be that as it may, no matter upon which side we strike, we are friends henceforth, unless we meet in the field of battle; then each must do his devoir for the banner he fights under."

"Be it so, my lord, the day may yet come when this pledge of friendship may serve us both."

The forester's words were prophetic; for those unsettled times soon brought a change in the mind of the false King, and caused him to banish the very men who placed him upon the throne. But of that, as far as our hero is concerned, anon.

"Come, my merry men," the bold forester continued, "to your feet, fill your cups to the brim and pledge our guest."

The outlaws obeyed, and Little John to show his good-will to the Earl took up a large beaker of wine.

"Drain off thy goblets, knaves," said Robin when all were ready. "Drink to Earl Mortimer, and wish he may never meet worse friends than the merry men of Sherwood forest."

The pledge was drunk, and so heartily by Little John that he was well-nigh choked by the volume of liquor which ran from the beaker down his capacious throat.

Harm might have befallen the lieutenant, had not Allan-a-Dale snatched up a heavy mallet and began to belabour the giant's back with blows that would have felled an ordinary man.

"Thanks, good Allen," gasped John, "I am better; a murrain on thy cursed mallet, dost want to break my back?"

Allan-a-Dale desisted, and there was a roar of laughter from the foresters at the little scene.

"Silence, all of ye," said Robin. "Marry, but thy tongues have quickened full early. Silence, listen to Mortimer's Earl, he would pledge thee in return."

"Body-o'-me!" muttered Little John; "I fear my throat is twisted out of shape too much for me to do honour to my Lord of Mortimer; but I'll try. Let the mallet lie where it is, good Allan," he added, as he saw Allan about to raise the heavy wooden instrument from the ground; "let it lie. It was but my throat had become smaller in consequence of the long fast I've had from good wine——"

"Peace!" cried Robin; "pray heaven, John, to shorten that tongue of thine, for it wags from dawn to sunset without a rest."

Earl Mortimer was by this time upon his feet, and, holding a brimming goblet of rich wine above his head. The outlaws had also replenished their cups, and Little John possessed himself of a full beaker."

"To ye all, my merry men!" said the Earl; "may ye live here at peace until Roger Mortimer leads a foe to your retreat; for I swear by my knightly word and my oath of chivalry to do no harm to thee by word or mouth or by arms."

He raised the goblet to his lips as he concluded; then, at a signal from Robin, the outlaws again pledged the Earl; this time without Little John requiring the aid of Allan-a-Dale to rescue him from suffocation.

"Have a care, John," said Much, who sat near the giant, his hand bandaged and one arm in a sling; "have a care, thou swill-tub, or the fat friar will knock the fumes of that goodly liquor out of thy pate before thy tongue can repeat an ave."

"I care not a groat for the fat friar," replied Little John, "nor thee on his back. Give me but room to wield my staff, body-o'-me! were he the devil in a curtall gown I would break his pate. A murrain on thee! Have a care, thou thing of a miller's son."

"A malison on thee for a wine-swilling hog," retorted Much; "were not my body sore from the effects of that cursed friar's staff, I would have a bout with thee now. Listen, thou guzzling ox—here, before this fair company, I wager a runlet of wine against thy best arrow, that yon curtall monk —or devil, for I wot not which—tans thine hide for thee to-morrow."

"A wager—a fair wager!" shouted the foresters; "thou'lt lose thy runlet, Much,

for no forester can bout with John at quarter-staff, much less a shaven monk."

"Peace, my men," Robin said, and in an undertone to Earl Mortimer he added, "these knaves require watching, my lord, for when the wine begins to tell they would as soon fall to and break each other's heads as they would capture and rob a rich churchman."

The Earl smiled, and his face now showed that he enjoyed the scene quite as much as the foresters themselves.

"They are sturdy knaves," he said, in reply to Robin's words, "and little wonder we had such stubborn work to win Evesham —now, good Robin, the song thou hast promised."

"The rascals are quiet now," Robin said. "Ho, there, Little John," he added, "if that last sack has not twisted thy gullet out of place, give us thy famous song."

"Thy song, John," chorused the merry foresters, "the song of the Norfolk Turnip."

"Body-o'-me!" said John, clearing his throat, "that song has been trolled so oft that I expect to hear the very trees singing it at dead of night."

A rattling of the horn drinking cups told of the little patience possessed by the foresters, so the giant in a full rich voice trolled out the following humorous ditty:—

### *LITTLE JOHN'S STORIE OF YE NORFOLKE TURNIPPE.

> Some counties vaunt themselves in pies,
> And some in meat excel;
> For turnips of enormous size,
> Fair Norfolk bears the bell.
>
> This tale an old nurse told to me,
> Which I relate to you,
> And well I wot what nurses say,
> Is sacred all and true.
>
> At midnight how a hardy knight
> Was riding for the lea;
> The stars and moon had lost their light,
> And he had lost his way.
>
> The wind full loud and sharp did blow,
> The clouds amain did pour:
> And such a night, as stories show,
> Was never seen before.
>
> In vain he sought full half the night,
> No shelter could he spy,
> Pity it were so bold a knight,
> Starved with cold should die.
>
> Now voices strange assail his ear,
> And yet no house was nigh;
> Thought he, the devil himself is here;
> Preserve me, God on high.
>
> Then summoned he his courage high,
> And thus aloud did call:
> "Fairies, giants, demons, come not nigh,
> For I defy you all!"
>
> When from a hollow turnip near
> Out jumped a living wight;
> With friendly voice, and accents clear,
> He thus addressed the knight:

---

*Much of the quaint humour of this song is lost in rendering the obsolete spelling (as we found it in the Heronshaw manuscript) into a form better suited to the general reader.

"Sir Knight, no demon dwelleth here,
　　No giant keeps this house;
But two poor drovers—good man Veere
　　And honest Robin Rouse.

"We two have taken shelter here,
　　With oxen, ninety-two;
And if you'll enter, never fear,
　　There's room enough for you."

## CHAPTER XI.

### FRIAR TUCK'S CHALLENGE.

THE Earl of Mortimer joined in the uproarious laughter which greeted the close of Little John's story of the wonderful turnip, and the narrator as grave as an owl took no part in the mirth, but looked from one to the other as though angry they should doubt the truth of his statement.

"Body-o-me!" he said, "hand that stoup over, Allan, for my throat is as dry as though I had swallowed the Norfolk turnip."

"A just punishment," replied Allan, giving the giant the stoup, "for wishing us to swallow it. Holy Saint Dunstan! what's that!"

Allan's exclamation was caused by the stoup, which Little John was in the act of lifting to his mouth, being struck from his hand, and to the astonishment of all present an arrow was seen quivering in the oaken table opposite where Little John sat.

The giant's surprise was so great that he kept his seat while all the others sprang to their feet and seized their weapons.

He was so staggered at the stoup being knocked from his fingers that he could not credit his senses, until he heard the voice of his captain calling upon him to pluck the arrow from the table.

He did so, and passed it to Robin Hood, who uttered an angry exclamation as he took from just below the feathers a small slip of parchment.

"Stay," he said to the men, who were about to go forth, and discover the daring fellow who had shot an arrow into the very midst of the band; "stay, my merry men, here is a clerkly scrawl upon this parchment. I will read it ere you go.

He did so, aloud, and the writing at once allayed their fears of the forest being filled with King Henry's archers.

"*The curse of St. Dunstan upon you for brawling knaves;*" so ran the billet, "*is it not enough you have come to my land, and robbed me of the deer which otherwise would be mine, but you must scare the few that remain from their coverts? A murrain on that bellowing ox, and his song; by the saints, if I catch him away from the nest of thieves, I'll make him bellow to the tune of a good quarterstaff upon his hide.*

"*The devil fly away with the lot. I would not give a pinch of salt for the whole pack.*

"THE CURTALL FRIAR."

"The Curtall Friar!" repeated Robin. "By Saint Herman, he is a bold knave, and he can use a bow as well as the best of us. Heard you the name he gave thee, John?"

"Body-o'-me!" growled the offended giant, tightening his belt; "Blade bone of Saint Hubert! but I did—bellowing ox—a malison upon the shaveling!—my quarterstaff, Allan! —Bone-o'-my-body! but I'll make a jelly of his holy carcass, or my name's not Little John!"

The speaker had, while delivering these words, tested the strength of the stout oaken staff Allan-a-dale had given him. Then, to the amusement of the goodly company, he stalked off towards the thicket from whence the arrow had come.

"Bellowing ox!" he was heard to mutter, as he crossed the glade; "Ashes of Saint Dunstan! make me bellow, will he, the accursed priest! Body-o'-me! I'll break every bone in his skin!"

This incident caused much laughter, and the men again seated themselves at the board, and renewed their application to the good liquor before them.

"What of the runlet, Much?" Allan asked; "I would not give a groat for thy chance."

"John has not returned yet," replied Much, and when he does, it will not be with so many whole bones as he has taken with him."

"A song, a song," shouted the outlaws at the upper end of the table; silence for our Captain's song."

The Chief, in obedience to this call, tossed off a cup of wine, and, in a remarkably sweet and well-tuned voice, began

### ROBIN HOOD'S SONG.

As blithe as the linnet sings in the greenwood,
　　So blithe we'll wake the morn;
And through the wide forest of Merry Sherwood
　　We'll wind the bugle horn.

Our hearts they are stout, and our bows they are good,
　　As well their masters know;
They're culled in the forest of Merry Sherwood,
　　And never will spare a foe.

Our arrows shall drink of the fallow deer's blood,
　　We'll hunt them all over the plain;
And through the wide forest of Merry Sherwood
　　No shaft shall fly in vain.

Brave Allan and John, who ne'er were subdued,
　　Give each his hand so bold:
We'll range through the forest of Merry Sherwood;
　　What say ye, my hearts of gold?

"Bravely sung," cried Earl Mortimer, when the clattering of the horn cups and the shouts of the yeomen had subsided; "beshrew me, Robin, but if I stay with thee and thy gallant company longer, I shall doff the Spanish mail, and take a green jacket and bow."

"You would find good men and true here," said the Outlaw. "That's not the name those bear with whom you are about to mix. But come, my lord, it's growing dark, and I must break up the revel, or there'll be but few sleepless eyes keeping watch to-night."

He arose as he spoke, and taking the arms which had been laid aside at the beginning of the feast, carefully replaced them upon his body.

"To your stations, my merry men," he continued, "and keep good watch, for the Norman Sheriff of Nottingham meditates us harm. Come, my lord, don your helmet and sword, and I will see thee safely through the forest."

The Earl complied with the air of one who would as soon have stayed with such good company; but, when he had armed himself, he followed Robin through one of those unknown paths only trod by the outlaws.

— -

## CHAPTER XII.

### LITTLE JOHN'S RETURN AFTER HIS ENCOUNTER WITH THE FAT FRIAR.

This caused Much loud to laugh —
  He laughed full heartily;
There lives a Curtall friar in fountain's dell,
  Will beat both him and thee.

\* \* \* \* \* \* \* \*

"Take up thy staff," said Little John,
"Friar, at my bidding be."
"Whose man art thou?" said the Curtall Friar,
Come here to prate with me?"
"I am Little John, Robin Hood's man;
Friar, I will not lie."

BRIGHT Sol's rays had scarcely begun to gild the tree tops when the clear ringing notes of the bugle horn called the foresters from their couches.

The morning gathering took place near the oak where Robin was in the habit of enjoying his afternoon siesta.

Here the band were drawn up in military array, and their arms examined by their leader.

This important duty over, the Chief seated himself under the foliage of the giant tree and heard the reports of those who had kept, watch during the night.

"Thou wert at the north side of the forest, Allan," he said, "did ought occur during thy watch worthy of note?

"An old woman, please you," good Robin," replied the forester, "was all that passed my way."

"An old woman, Allan; had she no gossip about the doings of the town, or was it she was old instead of young that thy tongue spoke not to her?"

"She had lost her way, good master," said Allan, "and while I showed her the broad path her tongue wagged quicker than a dozen magpies could chatter."

"Said she ought of the matter I have spoken about?"

She did, good Robin, although may be it was but an old woman's gossip—but I will tell thee word for word."

"Thy master," she said, "is a trusty and a good man; he fed my children when they hungered, and the Blessed Virgin be good to him."

"I cried amen to this, master."

"Tell good Robin," she said, "that many meetings have of late taken place between the proud Abbot of Saint Mary's and Nottingham's Sheriff."

"Ha!" exclaimed the Outlaw, "proceed, good Allan."

"These meetings," she said, "have borne fruit, for even now the smith is busy casting bolts for crossbows, and the armourers work day and night fashioning steel hauberks too strong for thy arrows to pierce.

The captain laughed at this, and the men joined in the merriment.

"By Saint Herman of the Wold," Robin said, "they will have to fashion such steel as ne'er yet left the hands of an English smith —but go on, good Allan."

"I have told all," replied the forester. "I saw her on the high road and gave her a silver mark for her news, but whether true or false we shall see."

"Thou must find this out, Allan," said the Chief; "don thy clouted cloak and go to Nottingham this day; crave alms at the castle gate, and use thine eyes well."

Allan stepped back to the foremost rank of the stalwart foresters, to give place to George-a-Green, who came forward.

"Thou wert on the south side," said Robin. What is thy budget, good George?"

"Not of such import as Allan's," said the forester; "save for this goodly bag of silver which may make up for my scant news."

He gave the Chief a leather bag filled to the mouth with broad pieces, as he spoke.

"Thy watch and ward has borne goodly fruit," Robin said. "What is the name of this good man, who makes us this present?"

"His name I know not," George-a-Green answered; but he has left his mark upon two of my fellows, who were with me."

"His mark, good George?"

"Aye, master; the pen he used was as good a cudgel as ever grew on tree."

"Thy fellows," the Outlaw said, taking a handful of pieces from the bag, "will want a balsam to heal the marks. Give these to them, good George."

"Grammercy," said the forester; "they will not grumble at this. Shall I speak, master, of the doings of this lusty varlet?"

"Do, good George; it is our custom to hear all that passes in our kingdom, whilst the night birds are abroad,"

"It was past the midnight," said the forester, "when we heard the strokes of a horse's hoof coming from the road. I bid the rider stand, or have a cloth-yard shaft through his jerkin. He pulled up, and I saw by the hood he wore over his head he was of a quality to pay the toll which is due from all Normans. Had he been poor, master, and civil of speech, thine orders would have been obeyed, for we touch not the needy and oppressed."

"Such is our rule, good George, and those of my merry men, who break it, I will hang

the butts, to keep up the skill of Sherwood's merry men."

"I bid the carle stand, good master," answered the man; "and as he threw aside his hood, I saw the face of the Norman villain who holds the lands of good Saxon franklin, Hedwold, who fell on Evesham's plain."

"I know the varlet," Robin said; "and

THE MONK TUMBLES ROBIN INTO THE BROOK.

upon the bough of as good a tree as Sherwood boasts."

"A meet punishment," said George-a-Green, "for such as disobey thy lawful will. By the saints! I would be the first to string such a knave to the fair bough above us."

"Spoken like a good yeoman, good George; but thy story, man, thy story, for the sun nigh touches the point when we should be at

Nottingham county does not hold one w. has a harder hand upon the poor."

"My heart is glad, master, to hear this; for, by the broad pieces, I thought the knave had been collecting the rents of the lands he has stolen from young Hedwold."

"No doubt of it, George—no doubt of it."

"Well, master, this Norman robber drew a good oak sapling from under his cloak, and, instead of yielding his ill-gotten gains, he laid one of my men at full length upon the earth. Beshrew me, but the knave fought well for his money-bag."

"Quick, good George; see, yonder sun will find us laggards at our post."

"I will hasten, good master, but the story is worth the hearing; for when I saw our poor knave with his crown cracked I threw the Norman from his saddle."

"The Saints look down upon us, the knave was on his feet, and his cudgel felled another of our men, and he would have escaped had I not given him a tap with my staff to teach him not to do these things."

"That was well done," said the Captain, who took delight in hearing of the recitals of his men, and knowing the emulation this mode of publicly hearing their doings gave his band, he neglected no opportunity of holding meetings like the present; "I hope thou brokest his pate for him."

"I should, master," George-a-Green answered, "had it not been for the steel cap he wore; but, our patron Saint be blessed, the blow laid him beside our fellows."

There was a murmur of approbation at this, for the foresters liked not that any of their band should be punished without the punisher being served the same.

"My hand," continued the forester, "soon found this bag he carried at his belt, and our knaves getting to their feet we hoisted the Norman to his saddle, then, tying his legs, placed a bunch of nettles under the gelding's tail, and away he went—the Norman yelling for help, and his steed kicking as lustily as though he had been possessed by a legion of fiends."

There was a laugh, as the foresters conjured the sight before them; then George-a-Green fell into the ranks, and the leaders of the men, who were out on the other sides of the forest, came forward.

They had no story to tell; therefore, kind reader, we cannot break faith with thee by putting untruths into their mouths and destroying the confidence thou feelest in this veracious narrative.

The first part of the day's duty being over, the signal was given to march, and as the stalwart forms hurried towards the butts the Outlaw Chief, for the first time, missed his faithful follower, Little John.

"Saint Herman keep us from harm!" he said; "where is Little John? Speak, my merry men, hast one of ye seen our lieutenant?"

"Mayhap," Allan-a-Dale said, "he has been paying too close attendance upon the good barrels which were broached last night to do honour to Mortimer's Earl."

"Nay, Allan," said the leader walking beside his men; "John never yet slumbered after the first blast of the morning bugle, no matter how deep his potations had been the night before."

The men could not give any reason to account for the giant's absence, although Robin went from the rear to the leading files in quest of his stout yeoman.

"Saint Herman," he exclaimed, when this questioning ended, "now I bethink me, the knave went forth to trounce the curtall friar. Mayhap, being tired after the bout, he has gone to rest in some covert where the sound of our call has not reached his ears."

"Allan," whispered Much, "dost thou think I will lose my runlet of wine now?"

"Aye, that I do, Much, for as good Robin truly says, John has but gone to rest after the bout, and the deep draughts of sack. Thou knowest, Much, if men sleep oversoundly after one of these causes, what must they do after the two?"

"We shall see," Much answered, "we shall see."

They reached an open space, at the end of which the butts (square mounds of earth) were placed.

Here Robin, as was the custom, drew the first bow, and the arrow, although the aim had been a careless one, went true to the mark.

The foresters followed the example thus set them, and with more or less skill hit the small white disc placed in the centre of the mound.

It was good archery, for even those arrows which did not strike the mark, went but a few inches beyond; not one shaft went beyond the butt.

Not more than fifty of the foresters had gone through this pleasant pastime, when those who were lying upon the ground awaiting their turn, gave vent to a roar of laughter.

"What now, my merry men," Robin asked as he turned from the butts. "What now?"

"Look, Master, look," answered Much; "where the ash grove ends, and thou wilt see a sight that it were a pity to see."

It was in truth a pitiful sight to see, for from the ash grove there came a huge forester, his head swathed in bandages, one leg held from the ground as though in pain; under the arm above the wounded leg a portion of a broken quarterstaff was planted, and did goodly service as a crutch, and to finish this mournful sight the forester had his left hand held to his side.

"Little John by Saint Herman, and every saint in the calendar."

"Little John," repeated Much, the miller's son, and several of his companions. "Little

John, and as soundly trounced as ever man was."

These words were too true; it was the battered form of Little John, and when he came within hearing it was found he had neither lost his voice nor the thirst which habitually beset him.

"Body-o-me!" he roared, and his tones were as sweet as that of an angry bull. "Body-o-me, fetch a stoup of wine, or I die of thirst."

"I've won the arrow," said Much, as he rose and went for a stoup of wine, "and Little John has got a worse trouncing than the friar gave to me."

The angry flush which came to Robin's face passed away when he heard his trusty follower was no worse hurt than by the receipt of a good drubbing.

He had feared that matters were more serious, until he heard John's voice; then with the remainder of the foresters, he set up a hearty laugh at the giant's woful plight.

"This friar must be the devil himself under a grey frock," he said, "to thus thrash two of my best men. Saint Herman keep us from such holy men."

"Amen!" said Much, passing at that moment with a huge tankard of wine; "amen, good master; but, if I mistake not, the friar will thrash both thee and thy men before he's done."

"By the saints it will be proved full soon whether Robin can be beaten by a shaveling," the Outlaw said. "Go thy way, Much, and tend John, for he is in a sore plight."

The giant—who, by-the-way, was over six feet four in height, and had a pair of shoulders as broad as two of the lustiest of the land— stood and leant against a tree, when he saw Much coming with the stoup of wine.

## CHAPTER XIII.

### ROBIN HOOD AND THE CURTALL FRIAR.

> Robin Hood, he took a solemn oath,
> It was by Mary, free,
> That he would neither eat nor drink
> Till the friar he did see.
>
> *       *       *       *       *       *
>
> And coming into Fountain Dell
> No further could he ride—
> There he was aware of the Curtall Friar
> Sitting by the water side.

THE trial of skill was put an end to by the appearance of Little John, and the Outlaw Chief and his merry men crowded around the bruised hero to hear how a sham friar had overcome one so stout.

"Thanks, Much, thanks for that goodly draught," Little John said, after he had received the stoup; "I stand sorely in need of the free juice, sorely in need. Shoulder-blade of Saint Hubert! Much, thy friar has done all he promised."

"And lost thee a good arrow, John."

"Aye, it is so. Seek my quiver, and take the best, Much; and thou mayest as well fill the stoup as thou passest: it will not be out of thy way."

The Outlaw Chief and the band came up at this moment, and it could be seen by their faces how great was the difficulty they had to keep from laughing outright at poor John's plight.

"Thou hast met the friar, I see," said Robin; "and the saints be blessed! he has taught thee a little sound religion, John."

"Sound!" said the woful forester. "Body-o'-me! there isn't a bone left whole in my skin."

"He has a strong arm, this friar, John."

"Friar!" said the giant. "Call him a devil, master—a lusty, roystering, stout, and fat-paunched devil—and thou wilt be nearer the truth than calling him a friar. May the evil one roast him with pieces of his own staff say I."

"Thou hast fared ill, John," said Robin; "if thou hast strength left to speak, tell thy merry companions and thy master how all this came about."

"Strength, good Robin, I have no more strength of voice than a linnet. Nay, not so much."

"Yet," Robin said, smiling, "there was something of thy old voice left when thou call'dst out to Much for a stoup of wine."

"It was my throat that spoke, master, for I was wondrously dry, wondrously dry."

"Never mind thy thirst, tell thy story, John. By the blessed Saint Herman, it must be wondrous strange to hear how so stout a forester had his hide tanned by a friar."

"It is a wondrous story, good master," answered Little John, looking over the Outlaw's shoulder to ascertain whether Much was coming with a second supply of wine; a wondrous story, therefore, I will sit me on the green grass, and tell you how it came about."

Suiting the action to the word, the forester seated himself at the foot of a tree, and, by the grimace he made, it was plain the posture was not an easy one.

"You must know, my masters," he said, "when the devil's limb, the red-nosed, wine-swilling monk sent his challenge yester-e'en, I took my staff and went through the forest until I came to Fountain Dell.

"There, my masters, I saw a fat monk, who looked more like a barrel with arms, head, and legs, than aught I can compare the knave to.

"He sat near the waterside, my masters, a good oak staff laid across his knees, and when I saw him, I brought my staff end upon the ground to startle him.

"Body-o'-me! he cared no more for the noise than though it had been a butterfly resting on the grass, but looking up began to laugh and roll his ungodly paunch about, as though the sight of a forester was a show to be made sport of.

"Body-'o-me!" I said, "who art thou, Sir Saint, that thy sides wag at the sight of a good and true man?"

"'True man,' he said, 'and he laughed the more. Who art thou that comes to Fountain Dell so glib of speech?'

"Robin's man I said; dost thou know brave Robin Hood, a good and brave man?"

"'Know him," laughed the ungodly friar; 'know him, who does not know the arrant thief from Sherwood to Barnesdale?'

"'Thou liest,' I said; 'he is no thief, but a good yeoman, so take up thy staff and stand a bout, or by Saint Hubert I'll crack thy bones, even for the lies thou hast told in calling my master an arrant thief;' would I had cracked his crown then, for I should have escaped my hide being tanned. Body-'o-me, where's Much, the thief, has he not come back with the stoup?"

"All in good time, John," Robin said, "the wine will be here before thy voice gets weaker."

"Saint Hubert be thanked for that. Well, my master, the godly man—the devil's limb, I mean—up and told me he cared not a groat for Robin Hood, and his pack of thieves, and if any came to Fountain Dell, he would baste their hides, as—as——"

"He basted thine," said Allan; "that will do, John; it is a goodly simile."

"Well, my master, and merry men all," said the very much bruised Little John; "I kept from breaking the villain's pate—a malison on my fingers for not doing it when the churl came before me—and the shaven limb of devildom laughed to my face as he balanced his staff on one fat finger, and said—

"'I care not to break thy bones yet awhile, for I want to learn of thee ——'

"'Break my bones,' I shouted, for I was getting wroth. Body-o'-me! would I had broken his bare pate before he got to his feet; but it would have been un-yeomanly to have taken advantage—a shame even, would it not, my merry companions? Yet I wish now I——"

"Thy story, keep to it closer," said Robin, "or by the patron saint of all true foresters, and that is St. Herman of the Wold, not a drop of the red juice which I see Much bringing this way shall touch thy lips."

"'Break my bones!' I said, "break my bones!—get to thy feet, man, or by Saint Hubert, I'll rattle this good staff upon thy skull to such a tune as will make thine ears tingle again.'

"Well, my master, the knave did but laugh the louder; and when this was over, he looked up, and asked:—

"'Art thou the knave with the voice like an ox—the knave who plucked my shaft from the oaken table?'"

"'I am Little John,'" I said, for I liked not the name he had given me; "'and if thou art not on thy feet in the twinkling of this staff there will be no more fat monks in Fountain Dell in less than——'

"Body-o'-me! when I said this he came to his feet, and, holding his staff in as yeomanlike a manner as any of us merry men, he called out——is Much come with the stoup, master?"

There was a roar of laughter at this, and John, in spite of his bruises, joined most heartily in it.

"I meant not that," he said; for the fat friar called out—

"'Have at thee for a bellowing knave; have at thee—by my patron Saint I'll trounce all the singing out of thy body.'

"Well, my masters, we fell to and fought for three good hours or more, and although my skull was cracked and my bones sore, not a rap at the devil's pate did I get!

"Body-'o-me! even then I did not give in, but for nigh another full hour our strokes rang out, and my head had more knocks than the friar had knots in his girdle, and every bone in my body seemed broken.

"So we went on, masters, until my staff broke in keeping off part of his blows; Shoulder of St. Hubert! but his arm was like a smith's, and his staff like a sledge-hammer!

"When my staff broke I got another knock on the pate, and down I went; and, would you believe me, my masters, the knave trounced me the more when I was down, and at every blow called out—

"'Crave a boon, thou thief, or I'll make jelly of thy carcass.'

"Body-'o-me! I had no breath left to crave a boon, for no matter which way I turned, the accursed staff came down as hard as ever.

"Well good master-o'-mine, and you, my merry men, the shaven devil trounced me until he could no longer use his arm. Then he gave over and said——bring the stoup, good Much, I am sadly athirst again."

A long pull at the vessel Much handed to him enabled John to finish his story.

"'Send thy master,' he said, 'send thy best men, and I will serve them as I have served thee, and they shall see what it is to interfere with the deer on my domain.'"

"He left me, then, my master, and my body was so sore I could not move, but lay there until ye saw me come from the ash grove."

"By the Blessed Mary," said Robin, "I will neither go to the east nor the west, neither eat of deer flesh nor taste wine until I meet this friar. My oaken staff, George-a-Green; to your care, Allan, I leave our merry men, keep watch upon the Nottingham side. St. Herman of the Wold! trounce Robin Hood, will he?"

And with sword and buckler, and carrying his long oaken staff upon his shoulder, the bold Outlaw went to Fountain Dell; and no sooner had he passed through the trees, than he saw the object of his journey sitting quietly at the side of the rippling brook from which the dell took its name, looking as innocent and unconcerned as possible.

## CHAPTER XIV.

### THE CURTALL FRIAR DROPS ROBIN INTO THE BROOK.

Lightly leaped the friar off Robin Hood's back;
  Robin Hood said to him again;
"Carry me over the water, thou Curtall Friar,
  Or it shall breed thee pain."
The friar took Robin on his back again,
  And stepped in to the knee;
Till he came to the middle stream,
  Neither good nor bad spake he.*

ROBIN HOOD stood for some moments regarding the friar, and the latter without once raising his eyes, continued telling his beads, an occupation he was engaged in when the Outlaw first appeared.

There was but little of the ascetic about the monk's appearance, for his face, instead of being pale and marked with rugged lines, showing penitence, and a total absence of the good things of this life, was as round and as rosy as an apple.

His body was in keeping with the face above it, for although fat, and as Little John said, like unto a barrel, it was evident that there was a wonderful amount of strength in the brawny arms which were but partially concealed by the grey gown he wore.

Had not Robin Hood known so much of the godly man's character, it is possible he would have been deceived by the pious manner in which he told his beads, and by the motion of his lips seemed to be repeating his *Aves*, *Paters*, and *Credos*.

Even had the friar been a stranger, a nd look at his eyes and the pursed-up s, would have told Robin this outward sanctity was but assumed.

Another look would have told him the round face and dark eyes bespoke a fund of good humour and devil-may-care recklessness when there was no distortion, as in this instance, of features that were better suited to a jolly cellarman than to an austere monk.

After these thoughts which expressed his feelings, had passed through Robin's mind, he bent closer to the holy friar, and touching his buckler lightly with the end of the quarter staff, attempted to arouse the godly friar from his meditations.

The priest took no notice of this intimation, but continued with increased fervour to whisper his prayers and count his beads.

"Holy man," said Robin at last, "is thy sin so great that thou art compelled to tell thy beads at this time of the day?"

The friar looked up with the well-assumed air of one who had been disturbed in an act of the deepest devotion.

"Sir woodsman," he said, "for so I judge thee by thy jerkin, in heaven's name I pray thee pass on and leave me to my devotion; life is but short, and were I to tell my beads from sunrise to matin song, and from moonrise to sunrise again, there would be but scant time to keep the vow I have made."

The religious zeal with which these words were spoken, the upturned eyes and meekly folded hands for a moment staggered the Outlaw, and he could not believe the godly man before and the lusty player at quarterstaff were one and the same person.

It is not at all unlikely this belief would have gained ground with the forester had he not observed a smile flit across the monk's face, and seen his eyes furtively regarding the noble form of the Saxon leader.

"Holy father!" said Robin, "far be it from me to interrupt a good man at his devotions, but having by mischance left my steed in his stable, I would cross the brook, but a vow I have made prevents me from wetting my feet."

"I will absolve thee from the vow," said the friar, "if thou wilt but pass on and leave me in peace. Go, my son; *absolutionem pro——*"

"Stay, good father, my vow is not yet told," said Robin, with difficulty keeping from laughing at the part he was playing, for I swore to St. Herman that I would not receive absolution, and further, that any man or animal I found near a brook I would compel to carry me over, or——"

"Thou compel!—at least, I mean, my good son, my patron saint is of more weight than thine; therefore by him I can absolve thee."

"An absolution I cannot take, holy father; therefore, prepare thyself in all humility to carry me across the stream; or by the blessed St. Herman, I shall be compelled, according to my vow, to use this carnal weapon upon thy shaven pate."

He held the oaken staff towards the friar

---

* From an old black-letter pamphlet, in the collection of Anthony-a-Wood, printed about the year 1610. There is also an earlier copy in the Pepysian Library.

as he spoke; and the holy man, losing all sanctity at the moment, rose to his feet.

"A murrain upon thee," he said, "and thy saint. Use thy staff! Blessed Saint Wilfred! had I not foresworn the carnal weapon men call a quarter-staff, I would make thee eat thy words."

"Softly, good father, and prepare to do my bidding, or by all the saints, canonised and uncanonised, I will make thy fleshy carcass as sore that the softest couch will seem a bed of stones."

"Thou do this? thou do this?" roared the friar. "A malison on thy hang-dog face! knowest thou who I am?"

"By report," Robin answered. "A sturdy, roystering knave, who can play a bout with a quarter-staff, empty a flagon, and kill the king's deer with the best woodsman of the forest."

"Repute is a foul calumniator," said the friar. "I am but a poor brother of the Grey-friars order; but nevertheless, should'st thou try to use thy staff upon me, this goodly fist shall deal thee a buffet which will stop thy prating tongue, as my——"

The friar paused, as though he had said too much; and Robin gave vent to a merry peal of laughter.

"As thy staff stopped the moving of my man's limbs," Robin said, finishing the friar's speech; "well, thy confession gladdens me, for I came to make thee do my bidding or pound thy fat carcass to a jelly."

"Ho, ho!" said the friar, putting his rosary out of sight again; "thy man? then thou art the chief of the cut-purses who royster in this forest; art thou? Blessed be St. Wilfred for sending thee here. Ho, ho! thou art the arrant thief, Robin Hood! Art thou?"

"I am, and thou art Friar Tuck, as great a rogue as ever let fly a shaft among a herd of fallow deer. Bless the Saint Herman for sending me to this spot, for now I am more resolved than ever to make thee carry me across, so prepare thy back either for my body, or a taste of this good staff."

"To the devil with thee and thy staff! Hark'ee, thief, cut-purse that thou art! behind yonder tree there stands as good a cudgel as ever grew; thou shalt feel it!"

He made a sudden rush towards the tree as he spoke, and would have got possession of the staff had not Robin stepped nimbly towards him, and tripped him up by the heels.

Placing his foot upon the Curtall* Friar's chest, the Outlaw flourished his staff so close above the fallen man's head, that he closed his eyes, as though expecting to feel the weight of the stout stick upon his skull.

---

* So called from their short smock, or rather because this monastery belonged to the order of "Cordeliers."

"Now," laughed Robin, "my lusty monk which shall it be, a good trouncing with this cudgel before thou takest me across, or wilt thou take me without the trouncing."

"Without the trouncing," said the friar, with wonderful subservience for his character "Let me rise, good Robin, and no mule ever carried pack-saddle with better grace than I will carry thee to the opposite side."

The Outlaw allowed the friar to regain his feet, then, setting his face towards the water, Robin leaped lightly on his back.

The Friar bent not beneath the Outlaw's weight, but without a word walked into the stream, and Robin, delighted at his victory over one who had beaten two of his best men, began to troll out the burden of a famous hunting-song.

His music came to an abrupt stop when they reached the middle of the stream, for the Friar suddenly parting Robin's hands which had been clasped under his saintly chin, gave a sudden spin round and dropped his burden in the deepest part of the water, and, raising his voice, blithely sang—

"Choose thee, choose thee, fine fellow,
Whether thou wilt sink or swim."

Taken so completely by surprise, Robin floundered about on his back for a second or two, his face only visible above the water.

But when he regained his feet, he dashed through the water after the friar, his trusty blade naked in his hand.

The saintly man stayed not to encounter the Outlaw's wrath, for before Robin's foot touched the bank, the fat friar had broken through the bushes and disappeared from sight.

## CHAPTER XV.

### ROBIN HOOD AND THE NORMAN SPY.

"He shall not go free," the other replied,
    So straight they were seizing him there
To kill him; but Robin Hood cries:
    "I pray thee, my men, to forbear."

When the indomitable friar had gone beyond all hope of being overtaken, the Outlaw Chief shook the glittering drops from his body, and gave vent to a peal of laughter.

"St. Herman," he cried, good-humouredly, "yon monk has behaved more like a lusty yeoman than a shaven crown. He has the chance this day, but I swear, by the Blessed Mary, I'll not rest until I have met the lusty varlet foot to foot, oaken staff to oaken staff. Hear my vow, good St. Herman of the Wold, and foul fall me if it is not kept."

Having made this vow the Outlaw took his way through the nearest path to the trysting tree where he knew his merry men would be anxiously awaiting his return.

ROBIN HOOD AND THE PIOUS MONKS OF ST. MARY'S.

"Marry," he muttered, "the knaves will laugh when they behold their master in this forlorn plight. A malison upon the cursed friar; he has spoilt my best and newest jacket, for which favour I'll yet thank him with as good a staff as ever yeoman handled."

Muttering thus to himself, he came to within half an arrow's flight of a dense copse, and from the dark foliage he beheld the glitter of a bright disc, which to his practised eye was no mystery.

"A hauberk, or helm," he said, "and in the very heart of Sherwood. Dolt that I have been, to leave my good bow under the greenwood tree, but for that, I would put a mark upon yon object that would spoil its brightness."

The sheltering trunks of the young trees

afforded a covert, from which he could, without being seen, watch the movements of him who wore the shining panoply.

"Valour," Robin said, in self-communion, "would bid me go forward and lay about yon knave with my good sword; but discretion, which is a goodly part of valour, bids me remain where I now stand, and watch for a sign by which I may know how yon varlet came to the heart of merry Sherwood without being seen by my yeomen."

While the Outlaw's thoughts ran thus the wearer of the steel cap was seen to change his position, and, evidently unsuspicious that he was watched, he left the covert as though with the intention of crossing that part of the forest where Robin Hood stood.

"By Saint Herman," the Outlaw said

4

'this knave must have more lives than ordinary men, that he flaunts it thus bravely in the greenwood. Ha! blessed Mary, he wears the badge of one I have but litttle cause to love."

The wearer of the glittering morion was habited in a garb not so rich as that worn by the knights of the period—yet it was richer than the esquires were wont to dress in.

The steel helm has already been mentioned. Except this, he wore no defensive armour. A gaberdine of thick brown cloth was gathered in at the neck, and depended from thence to below the knees.

The cuffs, shirt, and collar were trimmed with rich fur; and embroidered upon the breast was the figure of an eagle, with outstretched pinions and extended claws.

His hose was of the same material as his gaberdine, and his feet were encased in leather boots, the toes without the absurd points then worn by the Norman nobles.

The stranger's arms were a long cross-hilted sword, a dagger, and a spear, such as was used in the chase.

The fellow held an office new to England: he was in the employ of the Sheriff of Nottingham; his duties, to apprehend all who disregarded the law as represented by Geoffrey de Lois.

"So, master," Robin muttered, "thou hast trusted to thy valour too much, if it has brought thee here to take bold Robin or any of his merry men. Ah, whom have we here?"

As this exclamation left his lips a man entered the glade at the opposite side—a man garbed in Lincoln green, and armed, as all Robin's followers were armed, with a bow, a quiver of arrows, and a good sword.

The Sheriff's man evidently expected the arrival of him clad in Lincoln green, for he went forward and greeted him, as one friend would greet another.

"By St. Herman," muttered the Outlaw, his hand wandering to his sword-hilt, "but this smelleth of treason. Ha! by the holy and true Saint, this is the knave who came to my band after Evesham had been fought. Aye, Allan-a-Dale was right—there is a traitor and a spy among my men."

The two, after they had greeted each other, walked to and fro in open conversation. Thus the Outlaw Chief heard every word that passed between them.

"How fares it with thy goodly schemes?' the Sheriff's man asked. "Yet I need scarcely ask, for had that arrant thief, thy master, but the faintest suspicion of thy purpose thou would'st not be here."

"True," answered he of the Lincoln green, "I would not; but I have good cause to know he does not suspect I am aught else than a good yeoman of his band."

"Thou hast played thy part well," the Sheriff's man said, "and our good master, the noble Geoffrey, will reward thee according to thy due."

"Unless," thought Robin, "I am first to give thee the reward thy cunning has so well merited."

"I know it," said he of Lincoln-green; "for our master, though somewhat harsh in matters touching his dignity, is good to those who serve him well."

"Which thou hast done, good Bayston, and well art thou in the favour of our good lord and the holy prior of St. Mary's Abbey."

"'Tis something to be in such——hark! heard'st thou a noise at——hark! there it is again."

"'Tis but a hare," said the Sheriff's man; "see there—it seeks refuge in yon thicket."

The noise which at first attracted the men's attention was caused by the Outlaw Chief drawing his sword.

"Thy cheek palest," the Sheriff's man continued, "even at the sight of——"

"Not that, De Morley," answered the forester, "not that, it was the thought that mayhap one of Robin's men had passed this way—yet no, that could not be, for I so well arranged that this part of the forest has been left to my charge."

"Then the bird can be taken to-night?" De Morley said, interrogatively; "if the charge of the forest or this part is in thy hands it will be easy for thee to guide us to where the arrant thieves sleep. We can then take the leader and—holy St. Hildebrand defend us——"

De Morley's exclamation was caused by seeing the Outlaw Chief break through the thicket.

The sudden appearance of Robin Hood caused the Sheriff's man to turn from his companion, and flee across the greenwood towards the trees from which the Outlaw had seen him emerge.

"Had I but a good shaft," said Robin, "I would stop thy legs; but it matters not, I shall know the knave again."

The spy seemed at first inclined to follow the example of his companion, but seeing the gallant forester was without his bow and arrows, he merely retreated out of reach of the angry chief's arm.

"So," the Outlaw said, "this is thy gratitude, thou who hast eaten at our beard and drunk our wine, to league thyself with the minions of Geoffrey de Lois. Answer me, knave, what hast thou to plead for this foul work?"

The man retreated still further; a he had gone between fifty and si from the Outlaw Chief he fitted an arrow to his bow.

"This," he said, "is my answer. Take it, thou arrant thief!"

Robin's good steel buckler was upon his arm, and as the cloth-yard shaft cleft the air he raised the bright disc before his body.

The arrow-head passed through the steel plate, and before the shaft had ceased to vibrate, the spy again drew his bow-string to his ear.

Warned by the inefficiency of the steel buckler to ward off the arrows, Robin did not raise it in this instance, but with a swift blow with his keen blade he cut the arrow in two.

The shaft was well aimed, for when he cleft the touch wood the point was within a foot of his throat.

"A curse upon thee," said the Spy, "thou art in league with the Evil One, for no woodsman could possess such skill as thou hast this day shown, nevertheless I will try another shaft upon thy carcase."

"If thou dost" said Robin, advancing upon his enemy, "the lowest branch of our trysting-tree shall bear thy body."

"What clemency" the spy asked, as he drew the third arrow to his ear, "will be given if I yield without sending this shaft at thy carcase."

"None," answered the Outlaw; "thou knowest the laws of our band—a fair trial—death if judged guilty of a deed like this."

"A murrain on thy laws; St. Ulrick send this shaft through thy body."

He discharged the third arrow as he spoke, and the Outlaw, without any apparent effort, cleft it as he had cleft the one before.

The spy's quiver was not empty, and he would have fitted another arrow to his bow, had not the Outlaw run swiftly upon him, and severed the bow-string.

"Yield thee, false knave," said Robin, "or, by St. Herman of the Wold! I will slay thee at my feet."

"I yield," was the sullen answer. "But spare my life, good master, for, had not the Sheriff tempted me with his red gold, I had not been so false to one so good and true as bold Robin Hood."

"Your repentance comes too late," answered the Outlaw; "red gold would not have tempted a good and true man."

"Thou sayest true, master," the spy said, sorrowfully, "yet many men have risked much for the bright, broad pieces."

"Aye, Bayston, and brought themselves to a plight similar to thine."

"Not all, master, not all; some have won: those who play so high a game must content to lose."

is of more value than gold," the forester said. "Life is the stake you place against a few broad pieces."

"I will not gainsay this, master. Thou art merciful and good; and, although I would have taken thy life but a few minutes since, there is no trace of anger upon thy face. By this sign I know thy voice will not be silent when the laws of the foresters doom me to death."

"Shall I crave thy life, that thy brain may hatch more mischief against my merry men by so vile a plot as mine ears were open to near Fountain Dale?"

"No, master; I was thy foe, then, a mean-souled traitor; and, although a Saxon, a spy in Norman pay."

"True, by St. Herman! I wonder why tongue likes the office of telling these things."

"It does not, good Robin, but I must speak the truth, Aye, although the words blister my mouth."

"Quick with thy speech, man, for I see the green jerkins of my merry men at the end of these trees,"

Bayston's face went pale when he looked towards the spot where the stalwart bowmen were gathered.

"I have but little to say," he responded; "but little to crave. A few minutes past I was thy foe, and would have driven a cloth-yard shaft through thy breast, until the features were dyed with thy noble blood——"

"I need not thy telling to know this."

"True, good master; but it is part of the speech I have craved to make."

"As thou wilt."

"Yes; I was thy foe," he continued, "and when thou hadst conquered me in fair and manly fight, no words of anger came from thy tongue, no expression of vengeance upon thy face; no, thou didst not even bind my hands, but walked beside me, and with fair and gentle speech told me of the great wickedness I had meditated against one so good."

"Hast thou turned priest? for by the saints thy tongue is wondrously glib."

"I have not turned priest, good master; although I may soon stand in sore need of one. Well, thou hast done all this when others would have cleft my skull with their swords."

"It will come to about the same, my poor knave; only in place of a cloven skull thy neck will be stretched."

"Even so, master, it is but what I deserve, although were you to let me live there is not one among thy merry men would serve thee so well, and not one could be of such value to thee and thy band."

"How, knave, how could thy services be above all others of my band?"

"I could tell thee, good master, of the designs of thy proud foe, Geoffrey de Lois."

"How? tell me; surely the arrogant Norman does not hold a knave like thee in his confidence."

"He does, master, as far as the devilry concocted by him and the dark Abbot of St. Mary's Abbey is concerned."

"I begin to umderstand thy meaning: should thy life be spared thou wilt betray thy Norman master as thou wouldst have betrayed me,"

"I will tell thee of all the evil they mean; tell in time for thy merry men to prepare for their coming; a knowledge thou couldst not gain unless one of the bowmen were in league with the Sheriff's man."

"Out upon thee for a double-faced traitor—hark ye, knave, Robin Hood and his Saxons would sooner meet their foes foot to foot upon the green turf than have aught of this double dealing."

"When thou goest to do battle with a man," Bayston said, "thou should'st bear the same arms as he bears that there may be no disadvantage on either side; listen, master, in the battle thou wilt have to fight with the subtle Churchman and his kinsmen thou must use craft against their craft, or else they must conquer."

"Ha, there is some truth in this knave's words. Well, if I consent to ask thy life, what surety have I that thou wilt not play me false?"

"None other than my word and vow to the Blessed Mary."

"The oath thou tookest when you joined our band?"

"Yes, master, and I would have kept it, but for the Abbot's absolution."

"He gave thee absolution! Saint Herman, but the day will come when I will teach his priestcraft to find others than my men to practise his knavery upon."

"The good Saint Wilfred send the day, master, for I owe neither the Abbot nor his kinsmen much good will."

"Yet, thou wert in their pay?"

"Yes, master; but not a single piece of their money have I fingered, and when I spoke npon the matter I received but a haughty answer; one not calculated to make me love the masters I served. Thy speech has done more to set my heart against them than a hundred of their golden crowns would have made me hate thee."

"Peace; I will think this matter over, there may be much truth in thy professions, but there is as much cause to doubt."

They walked side by side until they came within sight of the foresters, and when the latter saw Robin's saturated garments, a shout of laughter greeted his approach.

"Body-o'-me," roared Little John. "Body-o'-me, master-o'-mine, has the fat monk rolled thee in the brook?"

"He has, John," replied Robin, good-humouredly; "but he did not trounce my hide."

"That pleasure is to come, Master," "the giant said. "Ho! ho! no! but this monk is a lusty knave to punish all who come nigh him, as he has punished Little John, Much, and bold Robin—

> "Oh, what shall I do, said Robin,
>   If the friar he doth see me ?
> No mercy he'd show unto me, I know,
>   And my hide well-tanned will be."

"Peace, thou roystering knave," said the Chief; "thy bawling is like the roaring of an ox, 'twould be better wert thou to tell thy beads oftener, and spend less time in singing lying songs."

"Body-o'-me! master," replied the giant, stopping short in his song, "I have but little mind to patter an ave for many weeks to come, for the good friar who baptised thee in the brook absolved me with his saintly staff, and——"

"The fiend take thee and the friar on thy back. Sound a call upon thy bugle to assemble our men; that is, if thou hast recovered as much of thy strength as thou hast the use of thy tongue."

"Good sleep and a draught of malvoisie, master, have done much to heal me, since thou went to take thy baptism in——"

"Peace, knave; sound thy bugle, for we have a matter of some import to bring before Sherwood's merry men."

The duration and pitch of the notes Little John sounded upon his bugle gave unmistakable evidence that his lungs had not received any injury from the trouncing the Curtall Friar had given him.

Long before the echo had died away among the trees, the yeomen came running towards the trysting place.

Under the spreading branches of the giant oak Robin stood, and, as the men came towards him, a wave of the hand directed them to their stations.

They formed a circle before him, leaving a clear space of nearly thirty feet.

It was a goodly sight, this gallant band; their Lincoln-green suits, studded baldrics, the shining hilts of their broad swords, their drooping feathers, and ruddy, honest faces beaming with good humour.

It was a fair and goodly sight; so thought the gallant Outlaw, as he looked at his band.

Close behind Robin stood Allan and Little John, and in the open space before them, Bayston was placed.

An empty quiver hung at his shoulder, a swordless scabbard at his hip, and at his feet an unstrung bow.

His limbs were free, for the Saxons practised not the disgraceful fashion of binding a man's limbs.

The most profound silence reigned during the time the Outlaw Chief related his encounter near Fountain Dale, and the yeomen as they lent upon their long bows, cast many an angry glance towards the culprit.

Bayston stood with folded arms and drooping head anxiously listening to Robin's words, and when the Chief had concluded, he cast a furtive look at the faces of the band.

He saw but little to give him hope; all traces of the habitual good humour expressed upon their countenances had passed away, and given place to sternness.

"You are his judges," Robin said in conclusion; "deal with him as thou wilt."

Little John stepped forward.

"Body-o'-me!" he said; "our master's journey to Fountain Dale has well-nigh bred him harm. What think you, my merry companions, should be done to a knave who would thus draw an arrow upon the king of good fellows—bold Robin Hood?"

"He deserves death!"

"Well said, good yeomen; but there must be more voices pronounce the knave's doom than made me answer."

"Raise your right hands," said Allan-a-Dale, "all who wish to see yon carle's neck stretched."

A forest of sturdy green-clad limbs were held aloft.

"Thou seest, good master," Little John said, "the wish of thy bold yeomen. Now it wants but thy consent and our trysting-tree will soon bear bad fruit."

Robin did not answer for some minutes; he was well calculating the effect such a spectacle would have upon his men.

They were enraged now; and when calm reason returned there would not be one among them but would be sorry to behold a fellow-creature suspended by the neck to a branch of that tree, under which their merry meetings were held every eve at sundown.

Another reason for Robin's silence was the aversion his generous nature felt to take away life.

True, the man had most grievously offended, but as it was the first time since the Outlaw's band had been formed, Robin thought he could with safety to himself and his merry men spare the poor wretch's life.

"I must withhold this consent," he replied. "We must be merciful, my merry men, as we hope to meet with mercy ourselves."

There arose a murmur of approbation at these words, and the reprieved culprit came forward and threw himself at the magnanimous Outlaw's feet.

"Rise," Robin said; "it is not meet a free-born Englishman should bend the knee, except to the Blessed Shrine."

Hugh Bayston arose, and pressed the hem of the Outlaw's jerkin to his lips; then faced the yeomen, who began to crowd around their leader.

"Hear me, bold hearts," he said: "hear my oath; for I swear by Him who died on tree, to devote the life ye have this day spared to the good of ye and our noble master. If I fail in my oath may perdition seize my soul!"

## CHAPTER XVI.

### ROBIN HOOD AND THE CELLARER OF ST MARY'S.

They made the monk himself wash and wipe,
  And at his dinner sit.
Robin Hood and Little John
  Served him with honour fit.
"Gladly eat," said Robin,
"Gramercy answer me,
  Where's your Abbey when you're at home,
  And your patron saint, who is he?"
"Saint Mary's Abbey," said the monk,
  "Though I be simple here,"
"In what office?" said Robin,
  "Sir, the High Cellarer."

THE man was received again into the fellowship of the stalwart band, a new bow was given to him, also a quiver of arrows.

"Go," the Outlaw said, "take thy post on the Nottingham side of the forest, and keep good watch upon all who leave the town, and you good George-a-Green, go with him, for it is not meet to trust one who has once played us false until we have proved his faith."

"That shall be proved ere long, good master," Hugh answered, "for at matin song I expect the cellarer of Saint Mary's here with a hundred marks in good silver."

"Are the marks payment for the treachery thou didst meditate."

"No, good Robin; the proud abbot has a needy relative to whom this cellarer takes a part of the proceeds of the abbey revenues."

"Is this relative a Norman?"

"He is, master, one of the hawks whom the favour of Henry of Winchester has spread over the fair face of merry England, to fatten upon the labour of her people."

"Saint Herman, but I am right glad I saved thy life, were it only to rob this fat monk of the silver he bears to the lean and hungry Norman. Proceed, man, let our merry men hear how much thou art mixed up in the matter."

"I will, master," Bayston answered; "the Abbot knowing my treachery to thee, sent word by his minion De Morley, the knave thou sawest in the forest glade—"

" I know the carle."

" He brought me word to pass the cellarer in safety through the forest, in order, as he said, good master, those arrant thieves should not despoil the good monk."

" Body-o'-me," said Little John, " but I will make this cellarer say a string of prayers which are not to be found in the missals of Benedictines, Bernardines, or the Grey Monks of Vallambrosa, nay not even among the Cistercians or——"

" Thou wilt keep that prating tongue o' thine quiet," said Robin ; " or I will give the monk over to thy keeping ; and only those big ears of thine shall hear the good man's benisons, and——"

" I am quiet, good master," said John, hastily—" as quiet as a chauntry* of monks when the Superior is away. Body-o'-me, I would sooner be cooped up with forty devils than one sleek monk. Quiet, by Saint Hubert ! I'll not speak for seven long days."

" Touching the affair in which thou promised to aid," the Outlaw said ; " thinkest thou there will be a opportunity of proving thy faith by leading the Sheriff's men to the heart of the forest after nightfall."

" I will, master ; although I fear the Sheriff's man has ere this run with mouth agape to his master, and told of thy appearance ; yet he may return ; if so, my master, I will lead them to the covert."

" Do this," said Robin, " and by my valour, our oaken staffs shall ring a Saxon tune upon the Frenchmen's skulls that will take them long to forget."

The Outlaws were delighted at the prospect of trouncing their foes, and many were the injunctions given Bayston and George-a-Green as they went to met the high cellarer of St. Mary's Abbey.

Then the foresters went to their various occupations ; not the least important, by-the-way, were the preparations made for dinner, and the savoury odour which came from a fat buck which was being roasted whole, caused Little John's mouth to water.

There remained now but Much, the miller's son, John, Allan-a Dale, and bold Robin ; and when the giant had regaled himself with several sniffs of the roasting venison, a broad grin came over his features.

" Master," he said, " what name did the saintly man give thee to-day ?"

" One akin to that he gave thee, John."

" Body-o'me ! then there's but little chance of either of us forgetting the good priest's services ?"

" True, John," laughed Robin ; " he has

* Chauntries were chapels used for the singing of masses for the souls of the departed. The jocose forester's simile no doubt inferred that when the Superior was away but few masses were sung by the lazy, overfed priests.

baptized thee and Much with good English oak, I, more lucky, received water for my allowance. There is one here yet who has not seen the meek friar of Fountain Dale. What sayest thou, Allan, to an interview with the shaven devil ?"

Allan stroked his long beard, and eyed Little John and Much mischievously.

" I care not," he said, " for any yeoman in England, and would stand a bout with the best among them ; but, like Little John and Much, if I were foot to foot with a saintly priest, I fear me I should not let him cudgel me soundly, and not return a blow !"

" Body-'o-me !" said John, " the shaven devil would keep thine arm too much at work to let thee get a fair blow at his shining pate."

" Aye, that he would," said Much ; " that he would—take thy staff and try him, Allan."

" Gramercy," said Allan, " for the offer ; but I would not cast a doubt upon the statements of three such good foresters, by going for proof of thy words ; no, I believe thee as devoutly as though thy words had been sworn upon the book."

" Thy belief," Robin said, laughingly, " is most convenient, Allan."

" How so, good master ?"

" It saves thy hide, man—it saves thy hide ! Ha ! that's from the Nottingham side !"

" Aye, master, and George-a-Green's bugle."

When Hugh Bayston and his companion reached the thicket which skirted the high road, they plunged into the deepest part, and there remained until the jingle of bells proclaimed the coming of an ecclesiastic, for the pious ascetics loved to bedeck their mules with housings fringed with silver bells.

The ungodly foresters, who cared no more for a mitred bishop than they did for a poor monk of the Greyfriars order, were wont to accuse the Churchmen with a love of display. But the good fathers, in that meekness of spirit so characteristic of the sons of the Church, scorned the accusation, and averred the silver bells were placed upon the saddle-cloth to remind them of the monastery chimes, so that no matter how deep their meditations were when they travelled, they could not forget the hours of prayer.

" The priest !" said George-a-Green, " and upon a sleek mule, I'll warrant."

" Aye," responded Hugh, " the office of high cellarer and treasurer to such a wealthy abbey as St. Mary's gives to him who holds it much of the ostentatious display of his superior."

" He will be in a state, as far as worldly goods are concerned, more befitting a monk when he leaves Sherwood than when he entered it."

"By St. Ulrick he will," Hugh said. Here he comes; now I think me, George, it will be better for thee to meet him, for were I to do so it would get to the prior's ears, and the good I would do our noble master will be out of the question."

"True," said George-a-Green, "should'st thou lead him to our master all will be known: take my bow, and I will get before the goodly

His rosy cheeks and small eyes, which twinkled good-humouredly, told he loved the good things of this life more than the rules of his order, which enforced strict prayer, fasting, and scourging for five out of the seven days.

The mule was as well fed as its rider, and in spite of the thumps which were administered every now and then by the monk's heels

CUTTING THE ARROW IN TWO.

man, so that the meeting may seem one of chance."

The forester passed through the thicket with that silence which proclaimed him a good woodsman, then running towards a line of noble trees he emerged upon the high road.

The cellarer was a portly jovial monk, just past the prime of manhood.

upon the animal's plump sides, he did not move a bit the faster.

No doubt the animal considered a solemn, reverent pace befitting the service into which he had fallen; and to do him justice, he did not depart from it, no matter how much his rider drubbed away with his heels.

"Unconcerned brute!" muttered the cellarer, out of breath with his exertions, "had

I my will thou shouldst fast full and often. A plague take the beast! were it not for my saintly vows, I would cut a goodly switch, and so belabour thy stubborn hide! Get on, thou over-fed dev—beast!

The mule was proof against this exhortation, and to the friar's disgust, walked into the centre of the road.

"A murrain on the beast! he has taken me where the sun will take several pounds of good flesh from my poor body. Ah, thou evil one, didst thou find it too hot that thy carcass seeks the shelter of the good trees—trees—that recall to my mind the knave I am to meet, and, the saints be praised, here he comes."

The priest caught a glimpse of George-a-Green's cassock as the forester turned the angle of the road.

"He seems a good youth, for he comes towards me with slow and reverent gait and bowed head. Now let me try and remember the little Latin I once learnt; it will sound well upon this arrant rogue—for rogue he is, although the proud abbot does receive him in the Locutorium."*

The good monk failed to recall a single sentence of Latin to his memory. So trusting to the forester's ignorance upon the subject, he determined to use a language which should serve to impress the outlaw with profound respect for one so learned.

The cellarer's mule now condescended to desist from cropping the herbage which grew by the road side. This habit by-the-way was a source of much discomfort to the good man, for the reins being very short caused the friar to lean over the brute's neck in a way that was not suggestive of ease or grace.

"A fair day, worthy father," said the forester as he came within hearing, the weather is somewhat hot."

"*Benedictine*, my son, *Notus sumus O dryalus meltabus.*"

"No doubt, holy father, but being English born I know not the meaning of thy learned words."

"Neither do I," thought the friar; "then aloud, the meaning my son is soon told, I returned thy greeting and said the day was indeed warm."

"It is, holy father, and a day that makes one's throat feel a dryness——"

"True," said the friar, smacking his lips, "true my son; the throat does feel somewhat dry about this hour of the day. Knowest thou of the whereabouts of a clear stream wherein I could slake my thirst?"

"I know of none such about this part of the forest," said George-a-Green, "but my master, who dwells not far from this, has a goodly cask or two of soothing liquor, which,

* An apartment in which visitors were received.

by the brand on the oaken butts, must have come from the Rhine."

The friar turned his eyes piously upward, and played with the bridle of his mule before he made any reply to the forester's words.

"The juice of the wine, my son," he said at length, "is denied to my order; yet, if there is no stream within reasonable distance —for I have but little time to spare—I do not think the saints would be angry if I took a cup of thy master's wine to prevent my dying with thirst; although, understand, my son, I would much prefer a draught from the rippling streamlet."

"I know it, good father, but in this instance thou must be content to drink what comes in thy way. Thou saidst something about having but little time to spare, good father; mayhap, after all——"

"I can find time, my son, to go to the door of thy master's house, for the knave I have to meet will not be here until the noonday sun is at its zenith."

"There is plenty of time, then, good father, for it wants a full half-hour of the sun reaching its meridian."

"I am glad thou sayest so; but before we go towards this good master of thine I would know what and who he is."

"The head forest-keeper, holy father."

"And thou?"

"I am a simple woodsman."

"Enough, my son, lead the way; no, it were better for thee to get behind this beast of mine, and, with the good staff I see in thy hand, to belabour him until he moves at a pace that will save his rider from dying with thirst."

George-a-Green complied with this request; and, much to the sleek mule's astonishment, he used the quarter-staff until the brute struck into a sulky trot, which caused the bag of silver under the monk's frock to chink most musically.

The unusual pace shook the portly friar so much that he called out for George-a-Green to cease belabouring the mule.

The forester did so, but the offended beast disregarded the frantic tugs at the rein and the voice of the holy man exhorting him to stop.

He had been driven to move at an unaccustomed pace, and, whether from spite, or because he liked it, he would not stop until he carried the friar right into the midst of Robin Hood's merry foresters.

## CHAPTER XVIII.

FRIAR CUTHBERT BESTOWS A BENISON UPON THE OUTLAWS.

If thou hast any silver bright,
 I pray thee, let me see.
The monk he swore a full great oath,
 That no silver had he.

Who is your master? said the monk.
  Little John, answered Robin Hood,
He is a strong thief, said the monk,
  Of him I never heard good.

THE shout of laughter which greeted the monk upon his arrival among the merry foresters caused the mule to lower his head and raise his hind quarters, and, at the same time, his hind legs were shot out with such velocity, that they acted like a lever, and the astonished cellarer flew out of his saddle, and lay sprawling within a foot of Little John.

The giant assisted the good man to regain his feet, and with much affected concern smoothed his gown, at the same time bidding him welcome.

"My master greets thee," he said, "and bids thee welcome to a poor foresters' dinner, which is now being served."

The friar looked around at the stalwart foresters, then at his traitorous mule, who had made such a show of him before the band. He seemed to form a pretty shrewd guess respecting the company among which he had fallen, for he hugged the bag of silver closer under his arm, and mentally thanked his forethought for having prompted him to fasten it around his body with a stout leathern thong.

"Thy master," he said, "bids me welcome! Pray, who is thy master, Sir Green-Cassock?"

"Robin Hood," said the giant; "Robin of Sherwood."

"A cutpurse and a robber," said the friar. "Oh, woe is me I came amongst ye!"

"Gramercy, Sir Priest," said Robin, coming forward; "is it thus thou givest thanks to an offer of a slice of as fat a buck as ever fed?—is it thus thou repayest the wish we have for thee to drink a cup of good wine with us? Out upon thy courtesy!"

This sounded well—a slice of venison and a cup of wine; and as yet the bag of money was safe.

These thoughts caused the cellarer to feel more at his ease, and, being hungry and thirsty, he adopted a more civil mode of speech.

"I crave thy pardon, good Robin," he said; "and would not have spoken so uncourteously had not my mind been filled with sorrow at the unholy behaviour of yonder mule. I give thanks for thy offer, and will gladly taste of thy viands, the smell of which comes sweetly to my nostrils."

"Sound a blast, John," said the Outlaw Chief, "and call my men to dinner; for it is not meet that we should keep the good father waiting."

A long and well-sustained note from Little John's bugle called the foresters together, and Robin, leading the friar to where the table was laid, gave him a seat on his right hand.

One of the yeomen handed the monk a long dagger, and the good man was about to attack the smoking joint before him when Robin arrested his hand.

"I crave your pardon," he said, "but it is our custom here in the greenwood to have a blessing said before we eat."

"A goodly practice, my son. Shall I utter the words of grace?"

"Do, good father."

The outlaws uncovered their heads while the friar mumbled out a few words, then the signal was given, and one and all began an attack upon the smoking viands.

The monk was not the worst trencherman present, as he soon proved by the manner he sliced off collop after collop of the rich venison, and when the wine was served he emptied a tankard at a draught.

"I have feasted right royally," he said, folding his arms complacently over his capacious stomach; "and I give ye all thanks for this courtesy, and although the buck may belong to the king, it nevertheless has the true flavour we poor monks so seldom taste."

"The buck, good father," Robin said, "belongs to none save him who slew it. God sent the beast for men's food, not for one man, although he may call himself king, to have the control of the——"

"Stay, my son, my order will not allow me to listen to thy dangerous doctrine respecting the forest laws, so let us have that tankard, and we will pledge each other like good and true men."

"The holy father," struck in George-a-Green, "much prefers water to good red wine. Shall I go to the brook and——"

"Nay, my son, nay, do not disturb thyself upon my account; I will, for this once, drink the same drink as thou drinkest, and if I sin by so doing I will do penance in my cell."

The foresters laughed at the haste in which these words were spoken, and the eager clutch the friar made at the stoup of wine.

Robin watched the monk as the good liquour gurgled down the saintly throat.

"Drink thy fill," he said, "mayhap the time will come when thou can'st ask me to drink with thee."

"Ask thee, Robin!" said the Cellarer, whose head was not quite proof against his libations, "ask thee! By the relics of St. Usurla, if thou will come to St. Mary's any time after evensong and ask for Father Cuthbert, thou shalt taste of the finest brand in the cellars—what sayest thou?"

"It's a bargain," said Robin; "I will come to-night and join thee and thy brethren after the day's prayers are——"

"Hush! what knowest thou of our jovial meetings in the refectory, surely; but no, thou can'st not know aught, for the poor brothers of our order are compelled to scourge themselves every night, that their bodies may be——"

"I will join in the scourging," said Robin, "so be at the gate after nightfall good father."

"I will, here's my hand on't, don't then fail to come."

"I shall not fail. Now good father, that the remains of the feast have been taken away I will ask thee a few questions."

"A thousand; if I can answer them I will."

"What brought thee through the forest to-day, good father."

This question partly sobered the monk, and he closed his arm tighter upon the bag.

"Ah! my son," he said; "'tis a sad and painful story, and I would not bring grief to the hearts of this merry company by talking of my errand,"

"We would well like to hear it, good father, for although we dwell in the happy greenwood we have not forgotten there is suffering beyond our kingdom."

"Since it must be," answered Father Cuthbert, "I will speak. Knowest thou a town some three or four arrows flight beyond the forest?"

"I know a small hamlet of that name."

"Well, town or hamlet, city or village—call it by any name thou likest best. I must tell thee there dwells there a poor man, grievously afflicted in mind and body; 'tis to him I am going, for he seeks the advice and aid of the only true church."

"Poor knave! Art thou going with empty hands upon so sad a journey? Does not the afflicted man need other things beside ghostly comfort?"

"He does, good Robin. A box of salve and a bag of herbs, I have for him under my ——, that is hanging to my saddle, unless that ungodly beast has broken the strap and lost it on the way."

"Is that all thou hast for him?"

"All, my son, all."

"No silver. No money to relieve him in his sore strait?"

"Silver! Blessed be him who died on a tree! What would a poor monk do with silver?"

"Yet, when thou alighted'st from thy mule, I could have sworn I heard the chink of good broad pieces. Mayhap, I was mistaken."

"Thou wert, my son (a malison on the accursed mule), thou wert, mistaken."

"It gives me pain to hear it," Robin said gravely; "for it is a law among our merry men to make all who have dinner with us to pay for it in bright broad pieces."

Father Cuthbert's face fell when he heard this, but the wine he had drank having given him an artificial courage, he determined to stick to the story he had told.

"Thy custom is a good one," he said, "and no doubt when a rich knight or merchant accepts thy hospitality, it is far better for this good company than a dozen poor churchmen."

"Not so," said Robin: "we have found the fat priests pay better than their lay brothers."

"The saints defend us! Robin, wherever can they get money?

"Generally from a leather bag, holy father."

"And if, good Robin they have no bag—how then?"

"If they say they have no bag of silver, holy father, we strip them of their garments and flog their hides with nettles."

> To bid a man to dinner,
> And then him beat and bind,
> It is our old custom, said Robin,
> To leave but little behind.

"Saint Uurula! Saint Dunstan! defend us, growled the monk; then I must suffer, for no silver have I."

"Thou liest, monk," said Robin; and for thy lies, thou wilt lose the hundred marks thou art carrying to heal the lame and hungry Norman who awaits thy coming at Blythe."

"*Misere ōōomine pater*——"

"Cease thy bewailings, and listen; and, for doing this before this merry company, thou art sentenced to pay me over and above the hundred marks thou hast about thee, twenty gold pieces——"

"*Misere oh*——"

"Peace; for these twenty pieces I will call upon thee to-night after evensong; and beware, if they ate not ready when I have joined the holy brethren in the refrectory—for I will keep that promise also——"

"Twenty devils, thou thief! a murrain on thy hang-dog face!" roared the monk. "Where dost thou think I can get gold pieces?"

"From under the stone in the buttery; the stone——"

The Friar gave a howl.

"Ten thousand curses!" he cried; "how in the fiend's name know you where I kept the little savings of——"

"How know I where you kept the pilferings of thy stewardship? I will tell thee, Monk. I saw thee hiding thy gains when I looked through a win——"

"Peace; thou shalt now have the twenty

crowns; but not a word to anyone of that stone in the buttery floor."

"I am dumb," Robin said. "Now, good father, the hundred marks, then depart in in peace."

"Hundred marks! thou art mad, Robin, mad! Where did'st thou ever find a poor monk possessed of so large a sum?"

"This very day," answered the Outlaw, "as Little John shall prove."

> "Come forth, Little John
> And hearken to what I tell,
> I do not know a yeoman that
> Can search a monk so well."

Little John did search the monk well, and found the bag under his arm.

"Body-o'-me," he said, "but it were a sin for a hungry Norman to finger these good pieces."

"The sin is saved," said Robin. "Now, Sir Monk, mount thy mule and return to the Abbey, and forget not to-night after even-song, or by Saint Herman, I will remember the stone in the butt——"

"I shall not forget," said the monk, angrily, as he mounted his mule; then as he gathered up the bridle he added to himself, "nor wilt thou if once I have thee inside the Abbey."

> "The monk then beat his mule,
> No longer could he chide,
> Have a parting cup, said Robin,
> Before you farther ride.
> Greet well your Abbot," said Robin,
> And your Prior I you pray,
> And bid him send me such a monk
> To dinner every day."

So sang Little John, but long ere he had finished, the good father was out of hearing. He had had enough of Robin and his merry men for one day; and as he rode through the forest he swore by all the saints he would sooner starve than pay so high for a dinner.

## CHAPTER XIX.

### ROBIN HOOD VISITS SAINT MARY'S ABBEY.

> The Abbot he rode to the Sheriff,
> With all the haste he could;
> And to him he told everything,
> Exactly as it stood.

In a sequestered valley about midway between the confines of the forest and the town of Nottingham, stood the monastery of Saint Mary's.

It was a spacious and noble structure; on one side was the church which differed but little from the beautiful cathedrals which still exist.

At the southern side of the nave was the great cloister, which had a door at the eastern and western ends of the aisle, so that the great processions could enter and leave the place with that dignity so befitting the splendid rites which took place in the time of which we write.

Over one side of the cloister was the dormitory of the monks, a spacious chamber divided into small cells, each furnished with a bed of rushes, a mat, a rug, and a blanket.

A desk and a stool completed the internal arrangements of these solitary dwellings.

From this apartment a door led into the church, in order that the monks should at all times be near the altar, and ready to attend the summons of the sonorous bell.

At the side of the cloister, and facing the church, was the refectory, where the holy brethren took their meals, and near this was the locutorium, an apartment where visitors were received, also where the monks, between the intervals of prayer, sat and conversed.

Beyond this room were the kitchens; adjoining was the buttery.

On the eastern side of the cloister were the chapter-house, the library, and the scriptorium, where the monks employed their leisure in copying and illuminating manuscripts.

On this side also was the treasury, where the coffers, the plate, and church ornaments were kept.

The abbot and the chief officers of the abbey had each a separate house: these dwellings stood on the eastern side of the cloister, where also were situate the nurses' chamber, the infirmary, and the almonry.

Surrounding these buildings was a high wall, which included within its precincts not only the places referred to, but large gardens, abounding with choice fruits and the rarest plants.

In one place only in the wall was there a means of access to the abbey: this was an embattled gate-house, and within the massive gates a monk was in attendance both day and night.

True, all who knocked at the grim portals did not gain admittance, for, by the means of a sliding panel, defended by a strong iron grating, the monk in attendance was enabled to scrutinise all who stood without.

The soft light from a thousand tapers streamed through the mullioned windows of the cloister, and the clanging of the great bell floating upon the evening breeze told the pious wayfarer who chanced to pass within view of the abbey, that the holy brethren had gone to evening prayer.

Standing upon a knoll which commanded a good view of the abbey and its grounds were three forms, draped from head to heel in long cloaks, which seemed more for concealment than warmth, for the evening was as balmy as the evenings are wont to be in this fair land.

As the cloaked figures turned from time to time in speaking to each other, the hem of their long garments became displaced, and a glittering object became visible just eneath, which, by its size, and the way in which it hung against the leg, could be no other than the steel tip of the long, straight, double-edged sword, then worn by all who could afford to purchase so good a weapon.

The monks' voices rose in full, rich tones as the bell ceased ringing, and before they had reached more than halfway through the chant, the door of the gatehouse opened, and allowed the egress of a man, who, as soon as he saw the portal closed and the light from the monk's taper fade away, ran nimbly towards the knoll where stood the trio.

"Body-o'-me!" said the tallest of the three, as the man from the abbey came within hearing; "hast thou been joining yonder shavelings in their chant?

"Nay, John," replied the man; "I have but a sorry voice at the best, and one hour with yon full-throated carles would——"

"Leave this jesting," said another of the cloaked forms, "to another time. Speak, Bayston, of all thou hast heard?"

"But little more than thou suspected'st, good master," said Bayston; "the Abbot is very wroth at the loss of his hundred marks, and he swears by St. Dunstan and the devil to hang thee before long."

"Ho, ho!" laughed Little John. "Body-o'-me! but I would——"

"Hold thy tongue, I pray thee," said Robin, "and let us hear more of this Abbot's prating. Go on, good Bayston?"

"I told him, good master, of the Sheriff's intent to bring his men to Sherwood to-night."

"Ah, what said the proud priest?"

"He called for his palfrey to be saddled," Bayston answered; "and told me he would tell the Sheriff of a better plan than taking his men to Sherwood."

"Did he not tell thee so much that thou might'st judge of this new plan?"

"He did not, good master; but I shall know more of it to-morrow at matin-song, for he bade me come to the——"

"And so far," Robin said, "there is nothing to be done save to wait the coming of the Abbot. Dost thou think he will be attended, Bayston?"

"Only by his shaven esquire, Friar Elmo—a stout knave he brought from Normandy."

"Gramercy for this," laughed Robin. "Now, John, thou had'st better follow this priest, and take thy opportunity to pull the squire from his mule, then thou canst take his cassock and girdle, and follow the Abbot?"

"Body-o'-me," said John, "I like the office well, but, good master of mine, I fear me I shall be sorely tempted to hit the Abbot on the pate before we reach Nottingham town."

"At thy peril, knave, do that! St. Hubert, have I not made a vow to catch this proud Abbot, and bind him to a tree, there to make him sing mass to our merry men? At thy peril crack his crown. By the saints, wert thou to do this I would send thee to meet the Curtall Friar of Fountain Dale for thy pains."

"Enough, good master; the Abbot's pate is as safe from my staff as though he were my own brother."

"Ah! yonder he rides. Follow him, John."

The Abbot and his esquire emerged from the gate-house as Robin spoke, and Little John, gathering up the skirts of his long mantle, ran swiftly from the knoll.

"Now, Allan," Robin said, "we will crave admittance to yon place. Hie thee to the greenwood, Bayston; and, should we not return by midnight hour, bring our merry men hither to give us freedom; for, unless you hear my horn, thou mayest make sure we have been caught in a trap."

"The shavelings may catch thee, good master," answered Bayston, "but we will pull their abbey down, stone by stone, before they shall hold good Allan and thee for long."

"Well spoken, Bayston," Robin said. And as the men went towards the forest he added: "there may be some good in this fellow, Allan, after all."

"Aye, master, there may be," Allan answered, "for he seems as ready to serve thee as he was to serve the Norman. I like the man well enough, but I like not the sorry manner in which he changes from side to side."

"He is a Saxon, Allan. Peradventure he will be as faithful to us as any of our merry men."

"If our Good Lady wills it so; but, thanks to little Much, this knave will have but scant chance of doing us harm."

"What has Much to do with him, Allan?"

"Only this, master: he has set himself to watch every act of this change-coat, and will do so until he can avouch the knave's fidelity.

"A good scheme; but, Allan, what is best to be done to gain admittance to yon building?"

"The plan I have advised, master; for it would be but folly to show thyself at the gate in such guise as would make thee known to the wrathful cellarer.

"Perhaps it is best to follow thy advice, so we will ask admission as two poor-brothers of the Franciscan order."

"The long cloaks they wore were soon arranged as monkish gowns; the hoods were drawn over their faces; and, bending their stalwart bodies, they leant upon their staves, and went slowly towards the gate.

ROBIN HOOD AND THE BEGGAR.

ROBIN HOOD AND THE FIGHTING FRIAR.

Neither the first nor second summons was answered by the surly porter; therefore Allan beat such a tattoo upon the carved door, that it was heard at the farthest end of the building.

The faint gleam of a taper was soon visible under the door, and, when it became stationary, the panel was drawn back violently, and a very red and wrathful face was seen the other side of the grating.

"Saint Mark! St. Ursula! bring a murrain upon thee," said the owner of the angry face.

"Dost thou think the house of God is an ale-house? Pass on, whoever thou art, and, for fear of Our Lady's wrath, disturb not the holy men of this abbey with thine unseemly noise."

Having delivered himself of this speech with more acrimony than it is possible to describe, the monk closed the wicket.

"The devil have his shaven crown!" said Allan, "and, were he within reach of the good staff I hold, I would trounce his hide until he needed no more absolution for his sins. Bones of St. Herman! master, what shall we do now?"

"Assail the door, Allan, until the surly churl give us admission. Raise thy staff, and I will help thee."

The din created by the united efforts of the foresters was for some time disregarded; but, as the two warmed with their work, it was evident the porter's wrath could not much longer keep him from resenting the attack upon the sacred edifice.

Robin's arm began to tire, and he was about to rest for a few moments, when the door was flung violently open, and, before either of the foresters could step back, the monk rushed through the open portal.

He was too angry to speak, and, without the least warning, Robin and Allan were felled to the ground by the thick, oaken cudgel the monk had armed himself with.

Full upon their pates they received the knocks, and, as they sat, too much astonished to speak, or attempt to rise, the monk danced around them, flourishing his cudgel.

"The devil palsy thine arms!" vociferated the monk. "Did I not warn thee of the just punishment thou would'st receive for disturbing the abbey at this unseemly hour? Get to thy feet, thou pair of roystering carles, or, by Our Lady! I'll pound thee to a jelly. Get up, I say!"

Both Robin and Allan felt a little dizzy from the knock down, yet the love for a good bout at quarter-staff was so strong a part of their nature, that, had they not a very powerful motive for wishing to gain admittance to the abbey, they would have repaid the monk with large interest and in similar fashion.

But, ruled by the desire before mentioned, they sat perfectly still, save that their right hands were tenderly rubbing their crowns, and assuming as meek a demeanour as was qualified to soothe the monk's just wrath, they waited patiently until the holy man had exhausted his energy by the joint occupations of cursing them, dancing, and twirling his heavy cudgel.

"Holy brother," Robin said meekly, when the monk paused, "hold thy hand, I pray thee, for we meant not to disturb the pious brethren, at this——"

"Meant not! meant not to disturb them?" retorted the monk wrathfully; dost thou think it possible that the devout brothers could say as much as an *ave* with the infernal din thou madest at the door?"

"We crave their pardon," said Robin in great humility; "and thy pardon, good and holy brother; and had not the night been of such blackness we would have wended our way to the shrine of Our Good Lady, and——"

"Our Good Lady!" repeated the monk, lowering his cudgel and stooping to look at the pair; "what art thou, then, that thy tongue pratest so glibly of the blessed patron,

whose goodness has raised this humble edifice for her devout sons?"

"We are two poor brothers of the Franciscan order, worshipful sir. We are lately from Palestine, and, being both hungered and athirst and footsore, we came but to crave a few hours' shelter from the storm which is gathering apace."

"Franciscans? I have heard of thy poor order, but I think it would better have become thee to have asked admission in a manner more beseeming thy poverty than like a pair of roystering knaves."

"We would have done so, please you, holy father," said Allan; "but had not time before the wicket was closed in our faces——"

"Get thee to thy feet," said the monk, "I will risk our lord Abbot's wrath for admitting thee; so follow on."

With due respect for their guide, the pair of poor friars kept some distance behind him, and by the shaking of their limbs it seemed they were wondrously agitated at beholding the interior of the sacred edifice.

So thought the monk when he turned and looked at the forms of the Franciscans; but could he have seen beneath their cowls he would have beheld a pair of jovial, laughing faces, and the trembling of their limbs he would have found was caused by the difficulty they had in suppressing their laughter. He saw none of this, but inflated by the humble manner in which he had been addressed, he became more communicative as they neared the Locutorium.

"The brethren," he said, "are at supper, and, if thou wilt wait my return, I will bring a sufficient portion for thy wants."

"Holy father," Robin said, "it is long since we had the ghostly comfort of sitting in a refectory; and, if the good brethren would not deem it too much for such humble sons of the church as we are, we would most humbly crave admission to their company."

The monk considered for a few moments before he replied to this humble request.

"I will ask the brethren," he said at length. "Meanwhile thou canst sit here until I return."

The Franciscans bowed low, and the lusty monk took his departure.

"Allan," whispered Robin, "how feelest thy pate?"

"There is a knob on top, master, as big as an apple. How feels thine?"

"Much the same, Allan. By St. Herman, if I do not raise two on the shaven knave's pate, make a show of me before our merry men."

"I'll break his back," said Allan, spitefully, "or may I be choked with the string of my good bow."

"We must wait, Allan, until we get him

near the greenwood. Huah! here comes the usty-armed thief."

"The holy brethren," said the friar, "have been pleased to listen to the humble request ye have made; therefore, arise, and follow me."

The Franciscans hobbled after their guide, and were by him ushered into the refectory.

"Welcome, my brothers," said a fat, jovial monk, who sat at the head of one of the tables: "welcome, in Our Lady's name, to our poor fare."

Robin mumbled out a few words, which he intended for Latin, and room was made at the centre table for the poor brothers.

"We are English monks," said the fat friar who had welcomed the Franciscans, "therefore, my good brothers, spare your Latin, for we much prefer to hear our mother tongue spoken."

"The saints be praised for that," thought Robin; "for I feared for this test."

"I'll give a silver piece to the shrine of my patron saint," thought Allan; "for the Latin I feared would betray us ere long."

Considerably at their ease upon this point, the Franciscans accepted a platter of dried peas and roots, which were placed before them, and neither could repress a grimace at the meagre fare.

A goblet of clean water garnished the platter, and added much to their discomfort, for they knew that for appearance's sake they must suffer martyrdom by partaking of it.

----

## CHAPTER XX.

### THE MONKS' CAROUSAL.

FRIAR JOHN: What is the name of yonder friar,
　　　　　With an eye that glows like a coal of
　　　　　fire,
　　　　　And such a black mass of tangled hair?
FRIAR PAUL: He who is sitting there,
　　　　　With a rollicking,
　　　　　Devil-may-care,
　　　　　Free-and-easy look and air,
　　　　　As if he were used to such feasting and
　　　　　frolicking?
FRIAR JOHN: The same.
FRIAR PAUL: He's a stranger. You had better ask his
　　　　　name,
　　　　　Where he is going, and whence he came.
FRIAR JOHN: Hallo! Sir Friar.
　　　　　　　　　　　　　　　　*Longfellow.*

THE slow movements of the hungry Franciscans' jaws somewhat belied the story they had told respecting their starving condition.

Allan's grimaces as he masticated the tough supper were equalled by the wry face Robin made when he took a draught of the cold water.

The jovial-looking monk keenly watched the proceedings of the Franciscans; and by the merry twinkle in his eyes it was evident he secretly enjoyed the martyrdom the poor brothers were suffering.

"Holy brethren," said the jolly monk, demurely, "your long fasting has rusted your jaws, for the best supper we have had for many long nights stands almost as it did when first it was placed before you."

"Brother," replied Robin, ruefully, "we have fasted long—we have plucked the unripe fruit from the trees in the Holy Land—we have held a pebble between our teeth for many days to exorcise the pangs of hunger; yet," he added, savagely, "by our dear Lady's shrine, such a supper as this is worse than anything we have yet had."

"Forget not thy vow of humility," responded the monk; "forget not these roots were the food of our blessed patron saint—this water her drink. Pray, my brethren, for Him who died on tree to bless this food and drink; and ye will be nourished as we are by the simple and wholesome means the Lord has sent us."

"Brethren," said Allan, "your prayers must have some wonderful powers of nourishment in them; for, by the saints, your bodies are sleeker than those who daily partake of rich wines and fat venison."

"There is much of truth in thy words," the monk answered, complacently folding his hands across his stomach. "We have faith, brother, strong faith. By us the dried roots and green herbs are thankfully eaten, and we praise Him who——"

"Two stoups only of the old oaken butt. A malison on the abbot for draining the barrel of the rich juice!"

These words were spoken by one of the brotherhood as he entered the refectory; and their effect was to disturb the solemn gravity which the monks had hitherto kept, both in word and look.

The monk placed two tankards of wine upon the table; then, for the first time, became aware of the presence of the two brothers of the Franciscan Order.

"Greet thee well," he said, casting one eye upon the platter of roots and the pitcher of water; "greet thee well, holy brethren."

One of the stoups of wine was placed within reach of Allan's hand, and before the confused friar could take it way again the forester's fingers had closed round the handle.

"Greet thee well, good brother," he said, "and gramercy for thy kindness in bringing us this draught of good water. I drink to ye all."

The forester, after he had taken a goodly draught, handed the stoup to Robin.

"Our Lady's blessing," said the chief, "upon the well from whence such water as this comes."

The monks looked from one to the other; then at the two Franciscans, who had by this time nearly drained the wine stoup.

It was evident the jovial brotherhood wished to partake of the good juice; but first they mutely asked each other whether the strangers were to be trusted.

"Good and holy brethren," said the stout monk, who had first given the friars welcome, "in the haste, prompted by your thirst, ye have drunk a cordial intended for such of our order as fall sick."

"I crave pardon," said Robin, "but in the monastery of St. Julian, blessed be the saints, we poor brothers were always sick, and drank but of exactly such a medicine."

"St. Julian," repeated the monk, grinning, "where is the shrine of that good saint?"

"At Walsingham, good brother."

"Walsingham! Thou hast travelled much at home as well as abroad, good brother."

"I have," said Robin, "so has my brother. Tell them, good Allan; thy tongue is given to sweet rhyme; tell the holy brethren of our travels."

The forester looked around at the faces of the monks, as he crossed his hands meekly, and began ;—

> "We are strangers well ye wot,
>   And much have travelled and have viewed
> The Lord's sepulchre and the grot,
>   Where he was born of maiden true.
>
> The Shells of Cales, in sign of grace,
>   Adorn our heads; and ye may see
> A vernicle, * with his dear face
>   Impressed, who died on Calvary.
>
> Upon my cloak Saint Peter's keys
>   Were drawn at Rome, with crosses wide,
> And relics from beyond the seas
>   We bear, or woe may us betide.
>
> The snow-topped hills of Armeny,
>   Where Noah's Ark may now be found,
> We've seen—in sooth we do not lie—
>   Told o'er our beads and kissed the ground.
>
> At Walsingham our voice we've raised;
>   At Waltham eke and at Coleraine,
> And to Saint Thomas we have prayed,
>   Who near the Holy Rood was slain." †

"By Our Lady!" Friar Cuthbert said, "ye have seen much, my poor brothers; but have ye ever seen a fairer abbey than this of our Lady's?"

"Few fairer," Allan said; "many not as fair. But," he added, with a sly look at the Outlaw Chief, "I never yet saw so fat a body of monks thrive so well upon these dried roots and green herbs, together with the cold water ye gave to us!"

"Ah, brother!" Friar Cuthbert said;

---

* A vernicle—a miniature copy of the picture of Christ, which is supposed to have been miraculously imprinted upon a handkerchief preserved in the Church of St. Peter, at Rome; and those wandering friars who visited the Eternal City usually brought back as a proof of their pilgrimage certain tokens of the places they visited.

† Joseph Strutt is the author of these lines, and the chronicle is headed, "May-day Pageant in the 15th century."

---

"there are many godless men whose evil tongues say we do not thrive upon the simple food the Lord sends us."

"If ye do," Robin said, "ye are the first goodly brotherhood we have met who has done this. Come, holy brother, does not your cupboard hold better comforts than roots and water?"

The friar's jovial face became over with a smile as he looked at Robin, a. meeting the frank, handsome features of the Outlaw Chief, he saw therein that which told him the poor Franciscans loved a good carouse, and would not betray those with whom they joined in this flagrant breach of monastic discipline.

"Brother," he said, "to such as ye who have travelled so far, I will not gainsay but what we poor monks do at times —that is, when our surly abbot is away—enjoy the carnal pleasures of the wine-cup and the table, and if ye will promise, by the vernicle upon your hoods, not to betray us, ye shall join us in such a carouse as ye have never before seen in monastery, or any place where the grey-robed brethren are wont to assemble What say ye?"

"Betray ye!" Robin said, "by the splendour of Our Lady's brow I would scorn so mean an act. Bring forth the contents of thy cupboard, and if ye do not find us as quick with the cup, the song, and the jest, may Our Lady doom us to walk barefoot from here to Mount Ararat, our food the dry roots here, and our sandals filled with grey peas."

Further parley was not required, for the fat monks had longed to begin their carouse during the abbot's absence, and many an unsaintly wish had passed through their minds when they saw the Franciscans enter the refectory.

"Brother Denis," said Friar Cuthbert, addressing a monk who sat at the end of the table, "I pray thee bring forth the black bottle from yon cupboard, and you brother John, go to the buttery and bring the pasty, and what is left of the noble haunch of the fat buck the saints sent us yester-even."

The two monks obeyed and while one went to the cupboard and the other to the buttery, a third spread over the table a cloth of the finest linen.

"By Our Lady's beauty," said Robin, when he, in common with the rest of the company, attacked a huge pasty, "the saints selected one of the finest bucks for the good brethren of their order.

"Ours is a good and kind saint," said Friar Cuthbert, who had already partaken of several goblets of wine, "she always tells brother John where to find—I mean she—that——"

"Holy brother," laughed Robin, "seek not

to fasten the sin of killing the king's deer upon thy saint; speak like a true man, and acknowledge that brother John has more to do in this than the whole calendar of saints."

"Well, brother Franciscan," said the Friar, "I cannot gainsay thy words; this unholy brother of ours has a fashion of *falling over the wall* at night; and, mind ye, he is fast asleep when he does so."

"I have heard of such things," said Robin; "In Palestine it is common for men to walk about when their eyes are sealed in sleep."

"Such is the case with brother John," the friar gravely said, "and when in this condition he takes a good yew bow and a sheaf of arrows, and as he wanders through the forest he shoots right and left, and sometimes his arrow will by accident, or by Our Lady's will, find a lodgment in the carcass of the fattest buck. Mark ye this," continued the friar, "our good brother, although mind ye, he is asleep, takes the buck across his shoulder and falls over the wall again.

"Does this occur often?"

"It does, brother Franciscan, I may say it occurs whenever we stand in need of venison pasty, or a good haunch—not oftener than this, good brother."

"Give thanks then to our Lady," said Robin, "for her mercies in thus giving brother John such wondrous dreams that he goes forth when in full sleep to shoot his arrows right and left. Pass the stoup, Allan, and we'll pledge all good monks who can let fly an arrow so bravely."

They pledged the monks and the monks pledged the Franciscans in return, and soon the good wine began to loosen the tongues of the saintly men.

Many a lively ballad was trolled out by the friars, and the refrain was taken up by Robin and Allan, who had both good voices.

It was during the uproarious laughter that was caused by one of the monks' songs, the Outlaw Chief's grey robe became unfastened at the throat, and revealed his green cassock and sword-belt beneath.

Friar Cuthbert was the first to notice the Franciscan's under garments, and, stopping short in the middle of a chorus, he sat with mouth agape, gazing at the unexpected sight.

"Our Lady preserve us!" he exclaimed at last. "Tell me, brother, do the Franciscans wear green jerkins and long swords under their robes?"

"The order to which we belong," Robin cried readily. "Come, brother, heed not the jerkin; keep up thy song."

The friar, in spite of his heated brain, remembered the admissions he had made respecting the manner in which the monks became possessed of the deer, and thinking Robin was one of the king's forest-keepers,

he began to repent most heartily for admitting the pretended Franciscan to the revels.

The majority of the brethren were too far gone to notice the cause of Friar Cuthbert's discomfort; so those who had not fallen from their seats kept up the chorus of the song in thick voices.

"The saints help us!" muttered the friar, "for our grey gowns will not save us since this keeper has learnt——"

Robin leant over to the astounded monk and whispered a few words in his ear.

The effect was magical, for Friar Cuthbert's face changed, and gripping the Outlaw's hand he handed a flagon to him.

"So thou art bold Robin!" he said. "Gramercy for this! But I thought we had a keeper amongst us—a malison upon them! But drink, Robin, drink, king of good fellows, for I wot thou would'st sooner send a grey-goose shaft through a ranger's heart, than tell how the monks of St. Mary's come by their venison."

"Aye," that I would!" said Robin, throwing off his grey robe. "Pledge me all of ye, pledge Robin of Sherwood!"

Many of the monks arose, and as they swayed from side to side, they pledged the bold Outlaw.

"Robin—hic—Hood—hic—bo—hic—ld—Ro—bin—hic!"

And, having stammered this out, three of the number quietly settled down under the table, and from time to time there could be heard a faint sound of Robin's name, mingled with the chorus of the last song.

More bottles were brought, and soon emptied, more songs were sung; and, as Robin trolled out the following ditty, Friar Cuthbert took the forester's horn, and, blowing upon it, added to the din:—

## ROBIN'S SONG.

There lived a vile miser so greedy of pelf,
  That he first robbed his neighbour and then robbed himself;
He starved in the midst of his glittering ore,
  For, though he was rich, yet he made himself poor.

At length, with old age and with sorrow opprest,
  Grim death, with a frown, the vile miser addressed—
    Derry down—derry down, &c.

"I've come to demolish thee this very day,
And to bear thee to my warm regions away."
    But the miser replied—
      "Derry down derry down!

"Before I set out, I'm desirous of knowing,
  If gold can be got in the place that I'm going?
Because if there's none, here I'm willing to tarry,
  Or, at least, a few bags along with me I'd carry.
    Derry down, derry down!"

To this old grim Death answered—
  "Here no longer, thou covetous fool, shalt thou stay,
And not one of thy bags shalt thou carry away;
  In the land where thou goest no good shalt thou gain,
And the devil shall plague thee with horrible pain.
    Derry down—derry down!"

To this the miser howled—

"The devil, I'm certain, will do me no ill,
For he helped me with money my coffers to fill;
Yet, since where I'm going, no gold I can find,
It taxes me sorely to leave it behind.
                    Derry down—derry down!"\*

Friar Cuthbert wound up the chorus by an extra flourish upon the horn, and deluging the monk who sat next to him with the contents of the bottle he held, he roared out:—

"Well sung, Heart of Oak; well sung, Green Jacket. Take thy horn, and I will give thee a roystering stave that will——Oh, holy saints defend us!"

The refectory door was flung open as this exclamation left the monk's lips, and to his horror he beheld the stern abbot and the high cellarer standing in the portal.

Robin's hand went to the hilt of his sword, and he looked around for Allan, but that sturdy forester had disappeared. He had left the refectory some time before Robin began his song.

## CHAPTER XXI.

### ROBIN HOOD AND THE ABBOT.

Said the Abbot, by God and Saint Richard!
Thou art ever bearding me.
With that, came in a fat-headed monk—
The High Cellarer was he.
The Abbot and the High Cellarer
Were standing out full bold,
And the High Justice of England,
The Abbot then did hold.

THE Abbot's eyes blazed with fury as he looked from the daring Outlaw to the forms of the monks, who were too far gone to be aware of his presence.

Many of these continued to repeat the chorus of Robin's song, and, from time to time suck the empty black bottle they so affectionately grasped.

At last the Abbot spoke, and, so great was his rage that the veins on his forehead stood out like black cords.

"What means this, ye heathen devils?" he said; "is this an ale-houses, that ye drink and bawl like so many peasants returned from their day's labour? Curse ye for a crew of drunken villains. Is it thus the house of God is defiled, if I but leave the abbey? To your cells, all of ye, and scourge yourselves, or, by God's dear Son, I'll have ye flayed alive."

The abbot and the high cellarer advanced to the centre of the refectory, and such of the monks as were able to stagger out of the abbot's sight slunk away.

"Pour water over these swine," the angry Superior continued, pointing to those who lay about the refectory, "and harkee, Sir Cellarer, let their names be inscribed in the

black book; for by Him who made us I will have as much blood drawn from their shoulders as they have drunk of this subtle liquor."

The high cellarer went upon his errand; then the abbot turned to the gallant Outlaw, who kept his seat, and laughed heartily at the sorry appearance the monks made.

"So," he said, sternly, "thou above all others art here, and, like Satan, tempting these good men from the path of sobriety and virtue. Answer me, thou arrant thief, and tell me what thou hast to say that I should not have thee hung over the gate-house as a warning to others of thy gang."

Robin laughed aloud at the abbot's words; and much to the latter's wrath, he helped himself to a stoup of wine before making a reply.

"What have I been doing here, Sir Priest," Robin said, "thou hast evidence before thee. What I have to say against being strung up over the gate-house of this abbey is, thou wilt find the task one of more difficulty than thou thinkest."

A malicious smile played about the abbot's lips when he heard these words, and stepping back until his hand came within reach of a bell-pull he grasped the silken cord.

"No bird," he said, "ever had less chance of escaping from the fowler's net than thou hast of leaving the Abbey alive; day and night have I waited to have thee in my power, the hour has now come."

"Has it, Sir Shaveling?"

The Outlaw again laughed, and quaffed the red wine from one of the goblets before him.

"Rise, dog," said the abbot, savagely, "darest thou sit before me—darest thou beard me to my face—rise—go upon thy knees and crave thy life, or by the saints thou wilt never behold another sunrise!"

"Rise, and pay thee respect!" said Robin; to the devil with thee and thy drunken crew! I care not a groat for ye, although I am, as thou sayest, like a bird in the fowler's net—but have a care, Sir Snarer, I do not cut the fowler's hands with this good blade if he attempt to draw the net closer upon me."

"Knave! caitiff! dog! darest thou threaten the Lord's anointed!—harkee, one pull of this cord and twenty lusty novices who have not yet taken their vows, will be upon thee, so have a care, or I will forestall the Sheriff in his work, by hanging thee from the highest point on the abbey walls."

"Sacrilege!" laughed Robin, "sacrilege! To rid this fair land of one of the lazy Norman priests who swarm like locusts in merry England. Harkee, Sir Shaveling, I would pin thee to yonder wall as I would a noxious reptile; therefore depart and leave

\* The chorus of "Derry down," dates back as far as the days of the Druids.

LITTLE JOHN OVERHEARS THE PLOT AGAINST ROBIN.

me to finish this stoup of good liquor before my patron saint tells me to pollute my sword with thy foul Norman blood."

"Depart! leave thee in peace!" roared the abbot, beside himself with rage; "a murrain upon thy tongue! may the direst curses of the Church——"

"Peace, noisy priest! disturb not a good man over his liquor. Away—leave me! Already my fingers tingle to grip thy throat and beat thy thick skull against yonder wall!"

These words, and the cool, defiant attitude of the speaker maddened the abbot.

Used as he was to the slavish obedience of the monks, the Outlaw's bold speech and open defiance caused him to forget his saintly character, and use language more befitting a man-at-arms than a follower of the Cross.

The Outlaw laughed the louder at this.

"By St. Herman!" he said; "the master of this goodly crew pollutes his lips with words that the most ungodly of my merry men would not use. Out upon thy living hypocrisy, thou Norman thief; doff thy robes —don a buff jerkin, and meet me upon the green sward—blade to blade, foot to foot, for I like not the killing of even such a false reptile as thou art unless thy hand held a good blade——"

The entrance of the high cellarer caused Robin to pause and throw himself back in his seat, and laugh until the tears came from his eyes.

"Ha, ha, ha! Sir Monk," he laughed; "when wilt thou have dinner with the merry men of Sherwood again? Ha, ha, ha! or dost thou think the charge too high?"

"Aye, laugh," said the cellarer spitefully; mayhap thy jaws will not wag so much between this and sunrise."

"Marry, but they will!" Robin said; "and my pouch will be the heavier for the twenty crowns thou owest me. Remember, if they are not paid, I must e'en help myself from the place thou knowest of."

The high cellarer's face paled; he feared these words would cause the abbot to question him respecting the Outlaw's meaning, and he knew if the proud Norman learned the little secret respecting the stone in the buttery floor there would be a vacancy in the abbey—that is the office of high cellarer and treasurer.

Perhaps the most unpleasant part of his thoughts was the knowledge that the late high cellarer had been an inmate of a certain dungeon beneath the abbey, where all who entered abandoned all hope of seeing the outer world again.

"Heed not this arrant thief's prating," he said; "heed it not, noble abbot, but summon the novices and have him taken to the black dungeon beneath the aisle there; he can tell the rats of the sinful sights he has seen in the abbey—sights, noble abbot, that will not give to Saint Mary's the odour of sanctity were they told among those who even now malign us with their false tongues."

The cellarer's suggestion was most acceptable: yes the dungeon was the best place for one who had seen so much of the godly brotherhood, and to the dungeon he should go.

"Drench these senseless swine," the abbot said, "and get them to their feet, for I would not for the best golden candlestick we have that the novices should see so shameful a sight; get them to their cells," he added in a whisper, "then this thief and scoffer at our order and my authority shall be removed."

The cellarer had brought with him two large vessels containing water, and in a few moments after the abbot had thus spoken the former aroused the drunken monks by raising the collars of their gowns and pouring the cold stream down their backs.

They scrambled to their feet, a most uncanonical oath in most cases falling from their lips.

When their blear eyes encountered the abbot's stern face, they gathered up their wet skirts and reeled from the refectory.

"Ha, ha!" laughed Robin, "what think ye . . . . Sir Norman . . . . By Saint Hubert

the devil must laugh aloud when he sees such saintly men."

The abbot made no reply, save by a malignant scowl, and before Robin could cut the bell-pull he gave it a sharp jerk, and the clang of the alarm bell rang out loud and clear in the still night.

The bold Outlaw took no notice of this, but continued to sting the abbot with his biting sarcasms, making the ecclesiastic bite his lips until the blood came.

He would not reply, although the ill-kept retort caused his frame to shake with anger, until the door which led from the body of the church was thrown open, and a dozen of the novices entered the refectory.

"Seize and bind yon thief," he then said, exultingly, "and convey him to the dungeon beneath the aisle."

The novices were about a dozen in number, and as the foremost of them advanced upon the Outlaw Chief, he sprang to his feet.

A lioness suddenly disturbed by the hunter could not have changed her mien quicker than our gallant hero did his.

The handsome face and lithe form, which had been all repose and good humour, became rigid with anger, and his right hand plucked his sword from its sheath, and his left drew the long dagger which hung at his belt.

The flash of the weapons cowed the boldest of the embryo monks, and they slank back as the long straight sword was levelled in a line with their breasts.

"Back, shavelings!" the Outlaw said; "remember, the first who comes within reach of this weapon dies. This I swear by St. Herman!"

The abbot foamed at the mouth with rage, and he threatened the novices with the direst punishment if they did not advance and seize the gallant forester.

"Show thy dupes the example," said Robin. "Come, sir, first; let yours be the task to take Sherwood's king."

The abbot looked fiercely at the bright blade, and, clenching his hands until the nails cut deeply in the flesh, seemed, for a moment, as though he would have sprung upon the leader of the Saxon archers.

The high cellarer, who had mighty reasons for wishing the capture of Robin Hood, sidled up close to the abbot.

"Sir Abbot," he whispered, "when there was a rising expected among the peasants, and they vowed to sack the abbey, thy good friend, the Sheriff, sent thee a score of weapons to be used in case of need. They are now in the buttery, and, as these men have not yet taken the oath to refrain from using carnal weapons, they may serve to aid in overpowering this lusty thief."

"Go thou, with *two* of the novices," replied the abbot, in the same low voice, "and bring sufficient of those weapons to serve our purpose."

The cellarer left the refectory, making a sign to two of the neophytes to follow him.

They did so, and Robin who gave a shrewd guess at the purpose of this movement, forced his foes farther back, and, before they could prevent him, he sprang upon the table.

Above where the table stood was an oriel window, and through this the Outlaw turned the bell of his bugle-horn, and sounded three long blasts.

Scarcely had he done this when there came a clatter of arms as the cellarer and his companions threw the swords and spears they had brought outside the refectory door.

The three men entered, each armed with a sword, and the remainder of the novices soon possessed themselves of like weapons.

Robin smiled defiantly at the formidable array, and placing his back against the wall awaited their onset.

It would have gone hard with the Outlaw Chief had not his bugle been heard, for the Normans, confident in their numbers, advanced boldly to the attack.

There was a clash of steel as the boldest of the assailants' swords were met by Robin's weapon.

The two foremost of the novices fell back, one with his cheek laid open, the other stabbed through his arm by the anelace.

The abbot snatched a sword from one of the wounded men, and cursing the neophytes for cowards, rushed upon the forester.

Their swords met, and although the abbot, in common with all of Norman blood, had learnt the use of arms in his youth, he soon had his weapon torn from his hand, and with a howl of rage and pain he staggered back, the blood flowing from a wound in his neck.

In a body the neophytes advanced, and were about to make an attempt to beat down the Outlaw's sword, when a monk, pale and breathless, rushed into the refectory.

"My lord abbot," he gasped, "the abbey is besieged by more than four-score archers, and their arrows find an entrance through every window and loophole in the abbey."

"Upon him!" shouted the abbot; "once in the dungeon, I care not if every leaf upon the trees in Sherwood were an outlaw, and every outlaw at our gates."

"My lord," said the monk; "in heaven's name give up this man, before the gate is battered in and the abbey despoiled."

"Battered in! the gate battered in!"

"Aye, my lord; when I fled for the gate-house, the outlaws were endeavouring, with the trunk of a tree, to break down the gate."

As the last word left his lips there was heard a terrific crash, then a shout, as the band, led by sturdy Much, dashed through the gate-house.

Robin took advantage of the confusion this caused, and, striking down all who stood in his path, rushed from the refectory.

"Bar the doors!" said the abbot; "bar the doors! or the church will be sacked!"

Too late!

The heavy door was hurled back, scattering all who had thrown themselves against it, and Robin, at the head of his men, entered the refectory.

"Seize yon abbot," he said; "and ye whose hands are idle trounce well the backs of those accursed monks, who would smite with the sword. Lay on, my men! lay on!"

They wanted no second bidding; and as the abbot was seized and made prisoner, the tough yew-bows were applied to the neophytes' backs until they yelled with pain.

"It will save ye from scourging your carcasses," the Outlaw grimly said; "now, my merry men, open yon door, and as ye drive these vermin out spare not your blows!"

When the door was opened the novices made a rush, and, as a natural consequence, there was a crush and the whole body were, for a moment, tightly wedged in the doorway.

It was not pleasant for those in the rear, as their howling testified; and the foresters, warming with this congenial occupation, laid about them with no gentle hand. The refectory was soon cleared.

Among those who received more than their share of the punishment was the high cellarer, and for many days after his head and body most unpleasantly reminded him of the Outlaw's visit to St. Mary's Abbey.

The foresters would have sacked the church, had not one of the band who had made a circuit of the place returned with the intelligence that all the silver cups had been taken from the altar.

There would have been a search for the costly ornaments, had not their leader taken the archers from the abbey—the abbot in their midst, his face pale with the probable fate in store for him.

Like most evil minds he judged others by his own standard, for had his and the outlaws' position been changed, he would not have scrupled to have hung their captain upon the first tree they came to when they returned to the forest.

## CHAPTER XXII.

ROBIN HOOD'S ENCOUNTER WITH THE CURTALL FRIAR OF FOUNTAIN DELL.

If thou wilt forsake fair Fountain Dell,
Every Sunday throughout the year,
A noble shall be thy fee;
And every holiday through the year

Changed shall thy garments be,
If thou wilt go to fair Sherwood,
And there remain with me.
The Curtall Friar had kept Fountain Dell
Seven long years and more ;
There was neither knight, lord, nor earl,
Could make him yield before.

THE morning after the events recorded in the last chapter, Robin Hood, according to his usual custom, assembled his men under the trysting-tree.

He heard the reports of those who had been on watch during the night, but, as there was nothing in them to interest the reader, we will pass on to the butts where the men were practising their skill with the long bow.

Before this trial of skill was ended, Hugh Bayston came hurriedly towards the Outlaw Chief, his face expressive of matters of more then ordinary import.

"Well, Bayston," Robin said, "thy haste heralds news from Nottingham, or I am mistaken."

"Not mistaken, good Robin," said the man; "I do, indeed, bring strange news."

"Thy report, Bayston, for this morning's gathering has been somewhat scant in news."

"Mine will make up for the shortcomings of our merry men," Bayston answered; "for I have much that is strange to tell."

"Let us hear it, then, for I see by the faces of thy companions they are more than usually anxious to hear that which thou hast to tell."

"It is of Little John, master."

"Little John! has the giant met the Curtall Friar again?"

"Not so, noble Robin; he is now in the Castle of Nottingham."

"Ha! by my valour, a prisoner?"

"Not so, good Robin. He is there of his own free will."

"St. Herman defend us! What shall we hear next? John in Nottingham Castle, and of his own free will!"

"Aye, master, thou shalt hear his message to thee."

"Speak, man; I am as curious as a woman to hear of this. What says the knave?"

"Thou knowest when he left thee last night to follow the Sheriff?"

"Aye, right well I wot of that."

"Well, master, he met a ranger near the town, and wanting the ranger's clothes, he cracked his pate and took them from him."

"The knave! Well?"

"After that he met a serving man and did the same by him."

"What, stripped two men?"

"Not so, master, for he gave to the first his suit of Lincoln green, and to the second the ranger's clothes; thus he went to the castle in the garb of the serving man."

"By St. Herman, this sounds strangely; but go on."

"Well, master, the Sheriff stood in need of a stout serving man, and Little John took the post."

"The saints defend us, but this is madness."

"Nay, good master——"

"But I tell thee it is, for John's face is well known to the Sheriff as it is to me."

"That matters not; Little John has n seen the Sheriff, nor will he, for the serving man was wanted to assist the cook, and by the cook he has been engaged."

"I see the knave's purpose. Tell me his message."

"It was but this. Tell Robin, he said, I am for a few days the Sheriff's scullion, and when I return to the merry greenwood, I doubt not but I shall bring tidings of all the Sheriff's doings, and mayhap a present for our master."

"St. Hubert keep him from harm, for this is somewhat venturesome. Hast thou told me all?"

"All, good master."

"Get thy bow then, and practise at the butts."

Bayston moved away, and Robin again turned to watch the shooting.

He was not long left in peace, for Allan-a-Dale, carrying a large leather bag, came towards him.

"Greet thee well, Allan!" said the Chief; "I am right glad to see thee safe amongst us again."

"Glad I am, Robin, to be here, for I have done heavy penance for leaving the monks' banquet."

"How so? I thought thou hadst left the abbey before the abbot entered."

"Would to the saints I had! No matte When I left thee and the monks it was to visit the buttery and the treasure-room of the abbey."

"And this bag is the result?"

"It is, master; but I'd like to have made the acquaintance of a certain dungeon beneath the aisle of yonder monastery."

"So had I, Allan; but, thanks to the saints, we are free!"

"Aye, master; the saints be praised, we are."

"Let us hear thy adventures, Allan, or the day will be spent before our good archers have shot their arrows."

"Thou shalt hear. Thou remember'st the time I left thee carousing with the monks?"

"I do."

"Well, master, I found my way to the buttery, and I also found the stone where the cellarer keeps his hoard, and, thinking he mayhap would forget to pay the broad pieces due to thee, I helped myself."

"To how many? the debt was twenty pieces, Allan. I hope thou acted honestly, and took no more than our due."

"I was in doubt, master, whether it was twenty or fifty pieces : so I made sure and took the fifty."

"Well," Robin said, smiling; "we owe the honest cellarer thirty pieces. Remind me, Much, I pay him when he passes this way again."

"I will," said Much; "that is, master, if thou dost not find out some poor peasant's family in sore distress, and empty our coffers to relieve them."

"If so," said Robin, "we can still owe the monk the money. Now, Allan, what happened after this?"

"Not content with the fifty pieces," Allan said, "I must needs go to the treasure-room, and being a good son of the Church, I did not touch the candlesticks of silver or the vessels of gold which belonged to the altar, but I found three cups of pure silver. Here they are, master. Thou seest they have the Norman abbot's bearings, and knowing they were made from the silver collected from the poor Saxon peasants for tithes, I brought them away."

"Thou didst quite right, Allan."

"Being athirst, after so much trouble in selecting these things, I found my way to the wine vault, and, while tasting of the different brands, in came a drunken friar, to fill the flagons he carried; and I, being too much engaged to notice him, did not know the wine-swilling knave had shut the door after him, until I wanted to come out."

The Outlaw Chief and Much laughed at the rueful face Allan made at the recollection of this mishap.

"Well, master," he continued, "I hammered at the door until I was tired, but no notice was taken, and I thought I must have gone mad when the alarm-bell rang, for I knew you were in danger."

"I was, indeed, sore pressed."

"Well, master, then came the shout of our merry men as they smashed in the door of the abbey, and rescued thee. After that, I had only to wait until one of the shaven knaves came, and that was not more than an hour since; then one whose throat was parched came and opened the door, and, for fear he should see me, and not let me pass, I waited until he entered the vault, and then I knocked him down with this bag. After being chased like a wolf by a dozen of the shavelings who were in the refectory, I ran through the gate, and came here."

"Thou art welcome," said Much, who, in his capacity as treasurer to the band, had al-

ready relieved Allan of the spoil he brought "May thy fingers ever fall upon such a goodly haul."

A stalwart forester, who had been appointed the abbot's guardian, now came towards the Outlaw Chief.

"Well, Clym," Robin said, "why is thy haste?"

"A message, good Robin," Clym answered; "a message from St. Mary's Abbot."

"Its import, Clym."

"He craves a boon, master."

"A boon, by St. Herman! the only boon he should crave ought to be——"

"A short rope!" said Much; "and——"

"Peace, Much," laughed the Outlaw Chief. "Although thou art pretty near the truth, I do not think the priest will crave either a short or long rope, for these Churchmen cling to life as strongly as the more sinful portion of the world."

"Aye, they do," said Much, "they do."

"Now, Clym," said Robin, "what is the boon this shaveling would ask?"

"This, good master," Clym responded. "He begs thou wilt, as a man, listen to his prayer. He craves thou wilt let him depart upon payment of such ransom as the poor coffers of the abbey will pay."

"Poor coffers," repeated Robin; "by St. Herman! were I to ask as a ransom his weight ten times over in gold, I doubt not but I should get it."

"This abbot is lean of limb, master," said Much; "would it not be better to have ten times the weight of the fat cellarman?"

"Hold thy tongue, thou greedy knave," Robin said; "and you, Clym, return to the abbot. Tell him we will attend to his ransom to-morrow."

Clym returned to his captive, and the Chief was about to leave the butts, when two bruised and battered foresters came towards him,

"By the saints!" he said, "this is not a comely sight upon so fair a morning. Speak, knaves, if either of ye have a tongue left, and tell how this came about."

One of the bruised archers, a man of powerful frame, and known to be one of the best wrestlers among Sherwood's merry men, tenderly rubbed his bruised pate, and slunk behind his companion.

"Answer me, Tom of Wakefield," said Robin; "and without trying to hide behind thy companion, who is of the two much the sorest."

Wakefield Tom shuffled to the front again.

"Well, master," he said, "Will Cloudesley and I were keeping watch in Fountain Dell for a fat buck we had long been chasing, when he passed us driven by a shaven friar, who sent a shaft through the deer's side with as sure a hand as the best among us."

"The Curtall knave again, by St. Herman! I'll stop his roaming among the fallow deer; but go on with thy story."

"You must know, master," Tom continued, "Will Cloudesley had sent a shaft from his bow at the same moment, and it struck the buck within a finger's length of the shaven devil's arrow."

"It were a pity it did not hit the knave's body," said Robin, "a murrain on the lusty thief."

"Would it had, master, for when we jumped from the bush to claim the deer, the monk turned upon us, and without a word began to liquor our hides with his quarter-staff."

"Aye," said Robin, "and ye had such respect for this son of the Church that your hands were idle while he thrashed ye."

"Nay, master," said Will Cloudesley, "shame fall upon us if we were as thou sayest."

"Yet your hides and skulls are beaten by this shaveling as though thou wert two beardless boys, in place of being two strong-limbed foresters."

"Master," said Wakefield Tom, "we laid about us like good and true men, but I take the blessed saints to witness the short-frocked friar gave twenty blows to one of ours."

"It is true, dear master," said young Will Cloudesley; "no matter how we fought, back hand or short staff, down came the friar's cudgel upon our pates, until he left us so well trounced that we were fain to lie upon the ground until a little of our strength returned."

"Friar, dost thou call him?" Tom of Wakefield said, "by the saints I believe he is one of the devil's lustiest imps, sent to the forest to trounce all who come within reach of his arm."

"Friar or devil," Robin exclaimed; "I swear by St. Herman I'll thrash his saintly carcass before the noonday sun reaches its zenith! Go thou, Will, and bid George-a-Green bring hither my horse."

Retaining only a short sword, such as was then used in the chase, the Chief handed his bow and buckler to one of the foresters, then, jumping upon his horse's back, would have gone thus armed to meet the lusty friar, had not a forester ran towards him with a stout oak staff.

"Tarry one moment, master," he called out, "here is something to absolve the Curtall Friar with."

Robin took the staff, and, bowing his handsome head courteously until his long fair curls were mingled with his charger's silvery mane

he wheeled round and dashed towards the ash grove.

The forester reined in his charger when he came to the Dell, then, placing his horn to his lips, he blew a long winding call.

"St. Herman!" he said, laughingly; "if that does not arouse the holy man I know nothing that will."

Robin was not mistaken—the rousing blast did arouse the fat friar; for he became visible at the end of a double row of trees

The saintly man bestrode a sleek mule, and as the tough animal came nearer to where Robin sat, the latter could scarcely forbear giving vent to a hearty peal of laughter.

The lusty friar as he rode forward, was looking keenly from side to side among the trees for the daring intruder; he had a stout quarter-staff tucked under his arm, his left hand held his rosary, and the fingers of his right were busy telling his beads.

"*Ave Maria*," he muttered; "blessed be the saints if I catch the knave who has dared to wind his horn in my domain! I'll make a jelly of his carcass! *Benedicite!* good Saint Wilfred! am I to be disturbed in my devotions by these deer-stealing thieves? The Lord forbid it! ha! it is the chief of the arrant rogues!"

The forester pressed his horse forward to meet the friar.

"Give thee good day, holy father," he said; "thou art early abroad."

"Early abroad!" repeated the friar; "it is the hour for morning song; but before I had half told my prayers the blast of a thief's bugle disturbed my devotions and called me forth to give the rogue a sermon, which will make him remember there is danger in disturbing the Lord's anointed. A malison on the knave! Would he had blown his two eyes out when he sounded that blast!"

"I crave thy pardon, good father," Robin said, "for disturbing thee."

"Oh! it was thou—wast it! By the saints, I should have thought the ducking I gave thee wouldst have taught thee to keep from Fountain Dell."

"Far from it, father," said Robin. "I have brought a staff which has been blessed by the patron saint of all good foresters—the blessed St. Herman of the Wold; and if it does not leather thy saintly hide, I shall place no more faith in our good patron."

The friar put away his rosary and tightened his girdle.

"Thy patron saint!" he said; "a plague upon both him and thee! Harkee, green jacket, I have a goodly branch here which grew upon the tree planted by St. Wilfred's own hand. Four of thy thieves has it smote to the earth; and by the blessing of Him whose saint I am it shall smite thee, or I will

ROBIN HOOD TO THE RESCUE.

leave fair Fountain Dell and become chaplain to thy gang of cut-purses."

"A bargain!" Robin cried, "a bargain! If my good staff fails, I swear by Saint Herman to pay thee every Sunday throughout the year five silver marks; so get off thy beast, thou thief of a friar."

The priest rolled off his mule, and, twirling the oak staff above his head as though it had been a willow wand, he roared:

"Get off thy beast, thou hang-dog-looking cut-purse, get off; or by St. Wilfred! I'll lay about thee where thou now sittest."

Robin leaped lightly to the ground; and the animals, as though they understood the danger of being too near the long staves,

trotted away to a green spot, and began to graze side by side.

"Have at thee, shaven devil!"

"Have at thee, hang-dog cut-purse!"

Exclaimed the combatants, as they stood foot to foot, and raised their weapons.

For a full hour there was nothing heard but the rattling of the oaken staves as the combatants alternately attacked and defended.

It was a rare exhibition of skill. Not in the whole history of the noble game of quarter-staff is there such an account as the old manuscript details of this long and obstinate battle.

Robin Hood's yeomen excelled in the manly exercises of the day, and their leader was the best and most skilful with bow, sword, or staff; in fact, it is said he could beat any three of his men with the last-named weapon: yet, for a full hour had he tried to crack the friar's pate, and could not touch him.

The priest tried his most skilful points with the forester, but failed to get an opening. Thus they fought, until both were utterly exhausted.

"A boon, friar," Robin said; "let us rest our arms."

"To the devil with thy boons!" he answered. "Fight on, or yield thee to the power of the good stick which grew upon Saint Wilfred's tree."

"A murrain upon thee and thy saint's tree! Take that for thy shining pate."

Robin's haste caused him to overreach himself, and the friar, catching the blow upon the centre of his staff, brought his hands together, as the forester prepared for another blow or for defence as the case required.

As quick as thought the priest took advantage of Robin's open guard, and making a feint as though to strike his opponent's fingers, he dropped one end of the staff under Robin's guard.

Although the blow was deprived of a considerable amount of force by being delivered so short, it caused the forester to reel backward.

"Yield! yield to St. Wilfred's blessed staff!" shouted the friar, "yield, and forget not the five marks thou hast to pay me every Sunday throughout the year."

Dazed a little by the blow, Robin continued falling back before the friar's vigorous assault, until the latter, feeling certain of his victory, paid less attention to his defence than he had hitherto done.

This was the Outlaw Chief's opportunity. He made a sudden spring forward—beat down his adversary's guard, and the next moment the lusty friar measured his length upon the green sward.

"Blessed be Saint Herman!" Robin said, as he stood over his foe. "Crave a boon, thou lusty thief, or by my valour I'll thrash thy fat carcase until thou art so sore that for forty days thou shalt neither move hand nor foot!"

"I crave thee, hold thine hand,'" said the friar, ruefully. "May the devil fly away with the saint who could not put more virtue in a tree of his own planting than he has in this."

"Saint Herman! before all thy calendar," the Outlaw said. "Dost thou yield to him?"

"Since it must be so I e'en must."

"Get thee to thy feet. We will return to my merry men, and they will make thee welcome, for we have long wanted such a chaplain as thou wilt make."

The jovial friar grinned at the Outlaw's words, and as they went towards the place where stood the animals, he gave a sly look every now and then at the red mark his staff had made across Robin's cheek.

Judging by the expression of the monk's face, his defeat did not greatly trouble him; possibly he was of opinion that it would be quite as well for him to join the band as to attempt to hold Fountain Dell against so many strong arms.

Whatever were his opinions about the matter, one thing is very certain, he seemed full of glee as he mounted his mule, and laughed and joked with his conqueror in the most genial manner.

---

## CHAPTER XXIII.

### HOW LITTLE JOHN GAINED ADMITTANCE TO NOTTINGHAM CASTLE.

Harken and listen, ye gentlemen,
　　All that now be here,
Of Little John, that was Robin's man,
　　And good mirth ye shall hear.

THE Abbot of Saint Mary's and his companion, the high cellarer, when they left the monastery were closely followed by Robin Hood's stout lieutenant.

The forester had hoped to have dragged the cellarer from his mule by disguising himself in the portly churchman's garments, and glean some intelligence of the movements of the Outlaw Chief's enemies.

He was prevented doing this in consequence of the pair riding so closely together, and before he could mature one of the many plans which come into his head, the embattled tower of Nottingham castle frowned above them.

"Gramercy for this long robe!" said the forester; "for by its aid I hope to pass yonder portals unquestioned."

The warder's hoarse challenge was answered by the abbot, and when the drawbridge was lowered, little John, with matchless effrontery, placed one hand upon the saddle-cloth of the abbot's palfrey, and boldly followed the pair inside the fortalice.

The armed mercenaries who served under De Lois, bowed their heads and crossed themselves when the Norman priest gave his benediction, and Little John who had by this time released his hold upon the palfrey's trappings, drew the cowl of his long-cloak over his head, and spreading out his hands right and left seemed to be showering blessings upon the steel-clad foreigners who lined the court-yard.

Here the abbot and the cellarer dismounted, and Little John placing himself before the groom, who advanced to take the priest's palfrey, he boldly caught the bridle and led the animal away.

The abbot and the cellarer were too much occupied with the matter which had brought them to the castle to notice the disguised forester; thus Little John was enabled to carry out successfully the bold plan he had determined upon following.

At the door of the great hall the churchmen were met by the major-domo of the vast establishment, who greeted his master's visitors; and giving the cellarer over to the care of the butler, he stalked before the abbot, flourishing his white wand, much after the fashion of a modern drum-major.

Little John watched this edifying sight from under his cowl, then beckoning the groom to approach, he placed the palfrey's bridle in his hands.

"Tend well this beast, my son," he said, "and our saintly abbot will well reward thee for it."

"I will, holy father."

"In which chamber is the Lord Abbot being shown?" Little John continued, "for my duty compels me to be at his side, wheresoever he may go."

"To the oaken chamber, holy father."

"Thanks, my son; canst thou do me a favour, by telling me of a nearer way to reach the oaken chamber, than the way by which the Lord Abbot has gone?"

"Aye, good father, I can, a much nearer way; if thou usest thy legs, thou wilt be there a good ten minutes before thy holy master."

"Gramercy for thy kindness. Remember, if thou should'st ever stand in need of the Church's prayers, forget not to come to St. Mary's and ask for Friar John."

"I shall not forget, holy friar, for truth to tell there are some matters I would fain consult one of thy order about——"

"Fear not; but come and open thy lips freely; thy mind shall have ease, and thy pocket be none the lighter. But be quick, my son, with thy directions, for I fear me, the lord abbot will reach the oaken chamber first, and his wrath will be great against poor Friar John."

"Follow me, holy father," said the groom, as he gave the steed to the keeping of one of his helpers; "follow me, and if I do not bring thee to the door of the oaken chamber before the pompous major-domo even begins to ascend the large staircase, may I be refused absolution for my many sins."

He led the pretended monk to the great hall, and passing through a door at the side, he reached the corridor by ascending a narrow staircase used only by the domestics.

The groom kept his word, for as Little John pushed open the heavy doors, he heard the major-domo and the abbot in close conversation as they ascended the grand staircase.

"Thanks, my son," said Little John, turning upon the threshold and spreading out his hands, "receive my blessing and depart."

The man crossed himself, and bowed his head, until the forester had finished mumbling a few words, which passed for Latin with the ignorant and superstitious servitor, who, like all his class, felt the greatest fear and reverence for the ruling powers of that dark age.

"Body-o'-me!" muttered the giant as he stood and surveyed the vaulted chamber; "so far has my impudence brought me safely. Will it as safely carry me out of these stone walls?"

While holding this mental debate, he looked about for a place to hide his huge form.

The few articles of furniture which stood in the chamber, although of the most massive make, were so placed that he could not secrete himself behind or at the side of any one piece.

There was no time to alter the arrangement of the winged cupboards or the carved seats, for the abbot's voice told he was near the top of the staircase.

"Saint Impudence defend me!" said John, as he ran towards the table which stood in the centre of the chamber; "last thought of, but not the least. Gramercy, Master Sheriff, for having such a long covering upon your table."

He had only time to draw his long limbs under him when the abbot entered the chamber.

"Thy master," he said, looking round, "is not here. Has he been apprised of my presence?"

"He has, most noble abbot; and he begged thou would'st be seated for a few moments, as he is engaged writing a report of the state of this part of the country to our brave Prince Edward."

The abbot threw himself into one of the chairs near the table, and Little John had the greatest difficulty in refraining from pinching the saintly leg.

"I hope my noble kinsman," said the abbot, "has not been angered by the obstinacy of the Saxon churls, who are as thick as weeds in this part of the land."

"Truth to tell, Sir Abbot," replied the garrulous chief servant, "the hinds took it somewhat sore the appointment of forest-keepers, and the issuing of other laws similar to those we have in beautiful Normandy, as thou mightest know, noble abbot; such laws and ordinances are too good for the government of these boors——"

"Yes, yes—much too good; yet thou sayest they resented their being put into force?"

"They did, my lord abbot; so much so that our good master of Lois was compelled to hang about a score of the peasants and burn the cottages of about as many more."

"Was their defiance so open, then?"

"It was, Sir Abbot; for the first of the new keepers who went forth upon their duty were found with a cloth-yard shaft driven through their bodies, and but for the example our good master, the Sheriff, made of those I have already spoken about, I do not doubt but the castle would have been attacked."

The abbot made no answer; and the servitor, well versed in the ways of his master's kinsman, took this silence as a hint for him to retire, which he did with the profoundest bows, and his face kept towards the mighty churchman.

"My brother's son," muttered the abbot, "has a strong head, yet not too strong, for these brats require harsh means to keep them in subjection."

"Do they?" thought the concealed listener. "Take care ye do not go too far, my gentle Norman, for it would be no miracle for a Saxon arrow to pierce thy priestly robe, even wert thou sitting in thine own chamber in the abbey."

The doors were then opened by a servitor, and Geoffrey de Lois entered the chamber.

"A fair greeting, my lord," he said, extending his hand to the abbot. "What urgent matter has brought thee to Nottingham?"

"Sit thee down, Geoffrey," replied the abbot. "Thou shalt hear of matters that will make thy blood tingle unless the air of this island has changed thee from what thou wert."

"Beshrew me, fair sir," said the Sheriff; "it would not do for a scion of the house of Lois to be changed. Although poor, I may say we have kept the pure blood untainted."

"Aye aye, I believe thou hast; for, enriching thyself in the land our swords have given us, does our race honour. But it was not of this I came to speak. Draw thy chair closer, and help me to a goblet of wine."

"I will help myself," thought Little John, "when ye have gone. Body-o'-me! it makes me sorely athirst to hear the good juice going down the throats of these Norman knaves."

The abbot placed the goblet upon the table, much refreshed in body, if not in mind, by imbibing the contents of the rich vessel.

"Knowest thou," the abbot asked, "of the sore strait our countryman D'Egremont has placed himself in?"

"I have heard some rumour of a Jew varlet having lent him money."

"Rumour has spoken truly for once," said the Abbot; "for D'Egremont was in hourly fear of falling into the unbeliever's clutches, when he sent a messenger praying I would advance for his present needs the sum of one hundred marks."

"Which thou didst, good uncle?"

"Assuredly, for our coffers, by chance, were pretty well filled; therefore I sent him the sum by a trusty bearer; but ere he could cross the path that skirts the forest he was waylaid by the cut-purse gang, and robbed. What thinkest thou of such open insults to our power?"

The Sheriff's dark face flushed angrily, and he bit his nether lip until the blood came.

"The curse of my race upon the dogs!" he said wrathfully. "Were this story to get abroad it would give the churlish peasantry heart of grace to again defy. There, this Robin Hood and his band must be destroyed, good uncle."

"I have heard thee use the self-same words many times."

"True! but my vow has lost nothing by keeping, or my hate become the less because every attempt I have made has failed."

"It is strange," the abbot said; "thou should'st be so openly defied by these knaves. Stranger still when thou hast a trusty spy in their very midst."

"Not the least strange, good uncle, when it is considered that for the one spy I have, this outlawed thief has fifty."

"Now, Geoffrey—beshrew me, this sounds strangely coming from thy lips who should'st be master of this part of the country."

"I hope to be so ere long, but first I must rid the forest of these knaves, and if all goes as well as I have planned, it will not be long before this happens."

"The saints prosper the undertaking, Geoffrey. Tell me what mean thy words when thou saidst the cut-purse knave had fifty spies to thy one."

"Had I said five hundred it would have been nearer to the truth," De Lois said with bitterness; "do you not know, good uncle, this varlet robs from all of Norman blood, and gives the gold and silver to the poor and sick among the Saxon boors? Thou seest now how it is he has so many eyes watching every movement among my men; by my halidome! I do not believe a steel cap glitters beyond the drawbridge but a messenger swift of foot bears him intelligence. Thus it is, good uncle, I have so often failed."

"This must be altered. St. Hildebrand! I will excommunicate from the altar all who touch money that has passed through this knave's hands, I——"

"Anger not thyself, Sir Abbot, neither raise thy voice from the altar steps; none of these will serve our purpose—draw closer, I would not the bare walls even heard the echo of my words."

---

## CHAPTER XXIV.

### LITTLE JOHN'S NEW SERVICE.

Now is Little John the Sheriff's man,
    And well with him does he thrive,
But Little John said, I will pay him out,
    As sure as I am alive.
Now so God me help, said Little John,
    And by my true loyalty,
I shall be the worst servant to him,
    That ever yet had he.

THE Sheriff's plot to entrap Robin was soon told.

It was his intention to hold an archery meeting under the Castle walls, and feeling sure the bold Outlaw would attend, he resolved to have him slain by a bolt from a crossbowman, who would be placed on the ramparts for that purpose.

"Of the success of my plot," the abbot said; "I have no doubt, but should the truth reach the ears of King Henry, I would not give much for thy post as Sheriff to this fair country."

"Yet," said Geoffrey, somewhat amazed at the abbot's words, "our King's favour is all for those who come from Normandy; I have thought he cared not a groat for the lives of the Saxons ·who yet encumber the land."

"Neither does he, Geoffrey, but to countenance a deed like this would arouse the discontent of the wealthy Saxon nobles who have bent the knee in homage to him; and thou must remember there is yet enough of the churls left, were they collected under a good leader, to work even Henry of Winchester and his Norman army mischief."

"There is much of truth and prudence in thy words; yet I would not give up this goodly scheme without I knew another which augured so much success."

"Has thy brain no other?"

"None; for it has been racked month after month with some scheme or other which has always failed the very moment I felt certain of success."

"Let me aid thee, Geoffrey," said the subtle priest; "although better versed in using bell, book, and candle, yet I have no doubt a little of the craft left such as is used by those outside the abbey walls."

"Marry, fair uncle, but thou hast; for the solitude of the cloisters seems to wondrously sharpen the inventive powers of those who dwell therein. Speak, fair sir, my soul yearns to hear thy counsel."

"It is this, Geoffrey," said the priest; "hast thou forgotten a certain blue-eyed maiden of surpassing loveliness thou sawest at a certain May-day gathering before the good King Henry triumphed over his foes?"

"Forgotten her!" exclaimed Geoffrey; "by my valour, I fear her face has been more often before me than that of the blessed Mary!"

"That were a sin, nephew," said the ecclesiastic; "nevertheless, I will absolve thee from it, for this maiden is wondrously fair."

"Wondrously! good uncle, she is; but I crave what can the maiden ever be to me?"

"Everything thou couldst wish."

"Ha! dwells she in these parts, that thou art so sure of speech?"

"In these parts; hast thou not seen her since she came to Nottingham?"

"Never once, I swear."

"Yet," said the abbot, with that slowness of speech which proved he felt a secret pleasure in adding to the feverish eagerness his listener displayed, "she has dwelt within an arrow's flight of the castle ever since thou camest here."

"Impossible, uncle; thou must be mistaken, for, by my knighthood, there is not a maiden's face within five miles of Nottingham but what I have seen."

"Yet," said the abbot, smiling, "thou hast overlooked the fairest of them all."

"I pray thee tantalise me no further, but tell me where dwells this pearl of loveliness, that I may see her, and, Saxon though she be, tell her of the quenchless fire that consumes my heart."

"Thou hadst better do this when alone with her, for she is guarded by one who would as soon crack thy skull as he would a serving man's."

"Nay, good uncle; keep me no longer in suspense——"

"Patience, foolish boy, thou shalt hear. Knowest thou a certain miller, the sails of whose mill thou canst see even from this window?"

"Aye; I know the varlet's right arm. It was his lusty arm that beat my men when they went to his mill to gather the tithes I had imposed upon all who dwelt upon the lands near the castle."

"He paid thy dues, then?"

"Aye, by breaking the heads of some of my best men, and beating the hides of as many more."

"Well, Geoffrey, here's a success to thy wooing! for yonder miller is the guardian of the pearl of loveliness—for so thou art pleased to term a woman of earthly mould."

"So much the better. I will have him brought to the castle, and this fair girl shall sue at my feet for his life—that is," Geoffrey added, "if she dwells beneath the carle's roof."

"She does; and by the manner in which she has been kept from thy sight, thou canst understand how well the miller tends his charge."

"It shall be my care to assist the miller," said Geoffrey; "but thou hast not told me in what manner this girl can aid me in capturing the forest thief."

"Thou wilt be the best judge," said the churchman, "when I tell thee that the pearl of loveliness, as thou namest her, meets the forest cut-purse every eve near St. Ann's Well."

"The Sheriff sprang from his seat as though he had been suddenly stung by an adder.

"By the mass!" he said, as he hurriedly paced to and fro the chamber, "thou could'st not have told me aught to goad me on to encompass the arrant rascal's death better than this. Rest content, my lord abbot, that the insult thou hast received will soon be avenged."

"I knew it would be," said the churchman, "or I would not have left the abbey after dark to visit even Nottingham's Sheriff."

He arose from his seat as he spoke, and was about to leave the room, when Geoffrey de Lois paused in his hurried walk.

"Forgive my scant courtesy," he said, taking his relative's arm; "do me the honour of tasting a cup of burnt sack, which is by this time ready in my chamber."

He drew the abbot from the oak-room as he spoke, and, before the churchman could reply, the hanging-doors closed behind them.

Peering out from beneath the tall cover, Little John made sure he was alone before he drew his long limbs from the cramped position they had been compelled to assume.

"Body-o'-me!" he said, as he seated himself at the table, "I am not much the wiser for the conversation I have heard. Ah! I see a good bottle of canary close to my elbow. I will empty it before I begin to think what is best to be done."

The giant's capacious throat not only swallowed the canary, but the contents of the whole of the remaining bottles.

"St. Hubert be thanked for that!" he said; "it was a goodly draught, and has set my brain in the proper place; and I think unless I find my way to the courtyard, my good master will be a knave the less." "Yet," he added, "I would fain have learnt more of this Sheriff's purpose; but I suppose I must e'en make the best of the little news I have gathered."

When he reached the courtyard the warder had just lowered the drawbridge; so Little John, not waiting to rejoin the abbot and the cellarer, walked slowly across, devoutly blessing such of the men-at-arms as were in his path.

"Safe out of the lion's mouth," he said, when he reached the open space before the castle. "Yet I am loth to go with such a small budget of news; but I—St. Hubert! what knave is this? I would fain know who comes so boldly towards the castle. Stand friend!"

A few minutes after the forester had crossed the drawbridge, the abbot and his companion descended to the courtyard, and, while the groomsmen were bringing the animals from the stable, one of the men-at-arms came towards the cellarer.

"Thy companion," he said, "has left the castle, holy father."

"My companion, my son! I came here with the lord abbot, none else."

"Was not that tall friar with thee? He came across the drawbridge with his hand upon the abbot's housings."

"Tall friar," exclaimed the cellarer, and the abbot, hearing his words, turned towards his puzzled attendant.

"What is this," the abbot asked, "that mystifies thee so?"

The cellarer repeated the statement made by the man-at-arms.

"Thou hast been drinking too freely over thy evening meal," said the abbot, sternly, "or thine eyes would not have conjured up——"

"Nay, my good lord," said the soldier, "I have been on the ramparts since sunset, and only came to the court-yard as the monk passed over—Ah! by the rood, here he comes to bear out my words."

As the soldier spoke, a tall figure was seen hurriedly coming towards the court-yard, and when he came within a dozen paces of the man-at-arms, the abbot said—

"Is this the knave?"

"It is, my lord, I would swear to his gown, which, as he passed me I thought was made too short for so tall a monk."

"Seize him," said the abbot, and when the soldiers held the monk firmly, he resumed, "Who art thou to dare, by hanging upon our skirts to gain admittance to this castle."

"Holy father! roared the man, in a voice which expressed both fear and surprise, "I have never set eyes upon thee——"

"Thou liest!" said the warder, coming forward. "I saw thee both enter and leave the castle."

"A murrain upon thy lying tongue!" roared the man, as he struggled with his captors. "I swear by the holy rood, I have never before placed foot inside this castle."

The groom came up at this moment, with the abbot's palfrey and the cellarer's mule, and, hearing from one of the men-at-arms the

A JOLLY TRIO

cause of the disturbance, came to the abbot, and added his testimony to that which had already been given.

"My lord abbot," he said, "I swear, by the cross to this knave. I knew him by the clouts upon his frock. He came in with thee and the high cellarer, and took thy palfrey when thou didst please to alight."

"Hearest thou this, knave?" the abbot said, sternly. "Surely thou canst not have heart to deny the words of these men,"

"My lord abbot," the man said, "I never until now, saw the——"

"It's a foul lie!" said the groom. "Didst thou not tell me thou wert of the abbey of Saint Mary's, and the favoured monk of the lord abbot's? Didst thou not tell me it was thy duty to reach the chamber set apart for his use before him? Deny this, thou false knave, if thou darest."

"I never saw thy hang-dog face before," said the man sullenly. As for this robe by which thou swearest to me, I have not yet worn long, for when I came towards the castle, I was met by a lusty varlet, who robbed me of my clo——"

"Stop his lying tongue," said the abbot, "if he will speak with such boldness against the words of these men; go on with thy questioning," he added, turning to the groom, "that I may hear more of the knave's doings."

"Thou must know my lord abbot," the groom said, "when the knave told me this, I took him by a side stair to the oaken chamber, and saw him enter; then, my lord abbot, I left him and saw not his face until now."

"By the mass!" said the churchman; "the knave has been hidden in the oak chamber during the time I spoke with thy master; run, varlets, run, and fetch the Sheriff!"

Geoffrey de Lois came in answer to the abbot's message, and when the story was told to him he sent a servitor to the oaken chamber to examine the wine-cups.

"For," he said to the abbot, "if this knave has been there, he could not for his life have passed the wine untouched."

The servitor returned with word that every bottle was drained, and further, by the marks upon the polished floor he could swear a man had been hidden beneath the table.

The Sheriff's brow became as black as a thunder-cloud, when he heard this.

"Gaudolin! he said to a grim-looking soldier, "take this knave, and place him where it will not matter how much his tongue wags of that which he has this day heard."

The unlucky wretch's eyes seemed as though they would burst from their sockets when he heard this order given.

"Mercy, my lord!" he shrieked; "cast me not into a dungeon. I swear by the Blessed Cross, and by Him who bled for us, I have been robbed——"

"Away with the lying knave! said the Sheriff; "take him hence. Varlets! have I to speak twice?"

Struggling and yelling for mercy, the man was dragged away to the dungeon; then the abbot and his companion left the castle.

They had not gone many paces from the drawbridge when they met a tall and stout man wending his way to the castle.

He was humbly garbed, and as humble in manners, for he crossed himself when he saw the holy men, and bowing his head said—

"The saints preserve thee, holy fathers; the saints preserve thee from harm!"

"Gramercy, my son, for thy wish," the abbot said; "here is a piece of money for thee; take it, and our blessing with it."

The man meekly accepted the coin, and bowed in the most abject manner. This so pleased the abbot that he reined in his palfrey.

"Thou art a good son of the church," he said, "or thou would'st not pay such respect to her followers; what is thy name, and where art thou going?"

"My name, reverend and worshipful sir," the lusty varlet answered, "is Roger Green-law, and I am going to the castle of his high mightiness, the lord Sheriff, to crave of the chief cook the post of scullion."

"Thou seemest better fit to wear a steel cap, and bestride a war-horse," the abbot said; but mayhap thy heart is not in keeping with thy body."

"Reverend father," was the meek answer, "I am but a scullion at heart, although my limbs are somewhat large, my valour is the smallest thou hast ever known; for the whizz of an arrow or the sight a naked sword causes my knees to totter and my heart to quake; thus thou seest I but fit to help the noble cook of the lord Sheriff—the saints be good to him!"

"Thou mayest be all thou hast said, yet thou art a good son of the church, and thy respect for her followers bids me do thee a kindness. Go to the cook, and tell him the Lord Abbot of St. Mary's sent thee, and thou wilt be appointed to the post thou seekest."

This kindness caused the man to bow so lowly that his face was hidden, and while he was in this position the abbot rode forward.

"Body-o'-me," laughed the servitor, as he watched the churchman ride away; "little does yon Norman priest know how my fingers longed to pull him from his horse and duck him in the ditch! Ho, ho! by St. Hubert! but this will be a mirthful tale to tell good Robin and his merry men! Ho, ho! twice in one night has Little John deceived this cunning knave!"

Laughing until his burly frame shook, the disguised forester reached the castle as the drawbridge was being raised.

After a short parley he was admitted, and conducted by a man-at-arms to the presence of the chief cook, and by that high functionary engaged to chop wood, draw water, and wash the platters.

How he acquitted himself we must leave another chapter to relate.

## CHAPTER XXV.

### LITTLE JOHN AND THE SHERIFF'S COOK.

The cook was most uncourteous—
There he stood on the floor,
He started to the buttery,
And shut fast the door.
Little John gave him such a rap,
His back was nigh bent in two;
And should he a hundred winters live,
He'd be the worse for that blow.

THE interior of the grim fortalice, built by William the Conqueror, was a sorry exchange for the sunny green-sward for Little John.

More than once during the first few days of his dwelling there, the Outlaw's trusty follower felt much inclined to lay a quarter-staff about the cook's back, and then make his escape; for the cook, like most Jacks in office, was fond of showing his authority over his helpmate.

"Bones of St. Hubert!" growled the forester, as he washed the platters in a dark corner of the kitchen, "would I had not taken the r ouble to come here. Body-o'-me! what with scant fare, bad beer, and the prating of this varlet's tongue, I shall be a dead man before I find anything out for my dear master."

"Quick with those platters, thou lazy knave," shouted the cook, " or I'll lay this rolling-pin about thy broad back. Dost thou hear? Is our most noble master to wait his dinner?"

His brawny arms bare to the elbow, the scullion for the nonce came humbly towards his master, a pile of platters held before him.

"A murrain upon thee!" continued the cook, "for a lazy carle. Move thy feet quicker, or by the—— To the devil with thee! Oh, oh! thou careless thief, thou hast broken my foot!"

Little John, boiling with the anger he did not deem it prudent to show, suddenly, and as though by accident, fell forward, and shot the heavy pile of platters upon the cook's feet.

No monk's face, when kneeling at the shrine he worshipped, could have equalled in penitential expression that of the lusty scullion when he saw the cook dancing about like a hen upon one leg, and yelling with pain.

"Thou awkward fool!" roared the cook; "thou art more fitted to lead swine to the forest than to be here. Out upon thee for a hang-dog thief. Wert thou not so great a coward, I would pound thy hide well."

At the conclusion of this speech the exasperated knight of the kitchen snatched the wet dish-cloth from whence it hung over Little John's arm, and began to strike the scullion over the face, neck, and arms with it.

The cook was a fat, stumpy little man, and John, who affected the most arrant cowardice, ran from the wet dish-cloth, holloaing at the top of his voice:

"Hold thy hand, good master! hold thy hand! Would I had broken my long neck ere I let fall the platters upon thy feet. Hold thy hand, for the love of Him who died for us!"

As nimble in his movements as a deer, the forester led the incensed cook round the kitchen, until the poor little man was thoroughly exhausted, and was fain to sit himself upon a stool, where he puffed and blustered wrathfully, until one of his assistants ran to him with the awful intelligence that the Sheriff was very wrath at his dinner being delayed beyond the usual time.

"A plague upon this thief," said the cook; "this all comes of my goodness in taking a varlet like this into my service. Get out from my sight with thy hang-dog face, or by the blessed Ursula, I'll drive this spit through thy carcase."

Little John retired to the scullery, and while enjoying a hearty but silent laugh the pompous butler entered the kitchen.

"Gaucher," he said, addressing the cook, "can'st thou lend me one of thy knaves to aid in moving some beer casks, one that is strong of limb, for I want not a dozen varlets to know the passage to the beer vault?"

"There's a lusty thief in yon corner,' Gaucher said, facing round and pointing to John; "take him, in the saints' name, for he is but little good here."

"Come with me, knave," the butler said; "thy master is willing, and I will reward thee with a tankard of beer; but," he mentally added, "it will be from the barrel whose contents went sour after the last thunderstorm, he! he! he! By Our Lady, thou wilt remember it,"

"Worshipful sir," John said, "cringing before the great man, "I am ready to do thy bidding."

The butler led the way to one of the vaults near the dungeons, and much to Little John's delight, when the door was unlocked, he beheld a row of oaken casks bearing the brand he so much loved.

"Good October," he thought. "By St. Hubert! a brave array. Body-o'-me! but it will be as well to have free entrance to this vault, therefore I will take this good key into my keeping."

While the butler was busy igniting a torch, the forester noiselessly drew the key from the lock, and concealed it in the breast of his jerkin.

"This way, knave," said the butler. "Art thou strong enough, thinkest thou, to bring yon barrel and place it upon this stand?"

"I will try, worshipful master."

The giant rolled the empty cask away then with as much ease as though he were handling a bag of meal, he clasped the full one in his arms, and placed it upon the place indicated.

"Bravely done," said the butler; "bravely done; thou hast not even disturbed the sediment, for this thou shalt have two tankards if thou likest them."

Little John, as the reader well knows, was always troubled with thirst.

"Gramercy, for thy goodness, worshipful sir,' he said, wiping his mouth with satisfaction; "would I had to do thy bidding every day."

"No doubt, knave," said the butler, "but I allow none to enter this vault but myself, for fear the wrong barrel should be drawn from."

"A wise rule, master," said John, smacking his lips, and wondering how much longer the butler would be before he filled the black-jack he held, "for it would be a sin for every knave to have access to these good casks."

"Thou art right, knave, and I warrant me there is such liquor in this vault as thou hast never yet seen, much less tasted."

"No doubt, master, for the beer we poor knaves get in the kitchen is but thin stuff."

"Thin stuff!" said the butler, facing round, "how now, knave, would'st thou have flagons of the nut-brown ale, brewed in October, and seasoned in wine casks, sent to thy table! Marry, for this insolence I will not give thee the draught I promised."

"I crave pardon, good master," said the forester, humbly, "if by my freedom of speech I have offended; but I swear by the saints I have not this opinion of the good liquor thou sendest to the lower board, it is but the words of the men-at-arms, who grumble the whole time they drink of thy bounty."

This polite speech restored John to the butler's favour, especially the last words, for the butler felt assured the scullion looked upon him as the master of the castle.

"The men-at-arms," he said, "are an idle pack; had I my will they should have nothing but water, for I cannot see of what use they are, except to flaunt with all the women-servants of the castle, and turn their heads with the lying stories they tell of their valour on the plain of Evesham."

"Aye," said Little John; "thou art right, good master; they are, indeed, of little use, and it would be as well their tongues were clipped, they cannot say a good word, even of thee."

"I thought this," the butler said; for, like most of his class, he liked his ears tickled with tales of the sayings and doings of those in his master's service; "a plague upon them, but they shall find it will not be the better for them to malign my name; harkee, good fellow, seest thou yonder cask?"

"I do, master."

"It is one of but a poor brewing, at best; but since the last thunderstorm, its contents were turned to as vile an acid as thou hast ever tasted. The cask, knave, shall be the portion of those varlets until every drop be gone. He, he, he! by my faith, if they are not sorely troubled with colic, I am no true man!"

"I shall remember that cask," John thought; then aloud, "a proper drink for the base knaves to speak ill of so good a master."

"Thou art right, knave; I am a good and bounteous master, and, as thy bearing so well pleases me, I will tell thee the virtues of each of these barrels."

He drew a foaming tankard as he spoke, and placing the vessel upon his knee, much to Little John's inward disgust, sipped the bright liquor while detailing the merits of each cask.

"Body-o'-me!" John thought, has the knave forgotten that I have a mouth, and a throat as dry as a new sponge? I would remind the carle, but he may beseem me too bold, and I shall lose the opportunity of learning which of these barrels hold the best liquor. Shoulder of St. Hubert! were I to do that, it would give me much trouble to have to taste them all before I found the best."

"Thou seest this one," the latter began. "Ah, by the saints! it holds a true and well-flavoured cordial. See," refilling the tankard, "how it sparkles and dances as it flows into this good vessel. Drink! by Our Lady, that were a draught to touch the soul. I love this cask, knave, and the one next, and none other lips than mine and the Sheriff's ever touch their contents."

"There will be another added to the list," thought the tantalised forester. "A curse upon the fellow! his head is of wood, for he has already drunk four flagons of the sparkling brew."

"See this cask, knave?" the latter continued, his voice becoming thick, "see how the good ale sparkles as it flows? By my faith, man, it is clearer than the finest wine, and, for my part, I would sooner have one goodly flagon of this to cheer my heart than all your sack, canary, or malvoisie. What say you, knave?"

"I am of your worship's opinion," Little John answered, "although, truth to tell, my mouth is so dry I can scarcely speak."

"Ah, I have promised thee a tankard; thou shalt have it."

"Gramercy, good master, would I had to serve thee every day."

The butler staggered from his seat, and Little John, with a rueful face, watched him reel towards the barrel he had set aside for the use of the men-at-arms.

"Ashes of Saint Hubert!" muttered John, "the villain has gone to the sour cask. The foul fiend fly away with him! Does he want to give me the colic?"

"Here, knave," said the butler, reeling forward, "drink this; it will quench thy thirst. I would give thee a better draught, but as thy head is not used to bear even as good a liquor as this, I should be doing wrong. Be quick, and empty the measure, for I must return, and see that my knaves have done their service properly towards the Sheriff?"

He handed the tankard to Little John, who, when the butler turned his back to extinguish the torch, poured the ale upon the ground.

"Hast thou drunk it?" asked the butler

as he stumbled through the door. "Ah, I see thou hast—and find it good, I'll warrant.

"It was good, worshipful sir."

"I told thee so. Come, lend me thine arm. No, stay, I must first lock the door. A plague take it! Where can the key have gone?"

"It is not among those at thy belt, master?"

"There is one there, but I have two, one not attached to the bunch, for they make such a noise when I have to unlock the door, that all who pass know I am at the vault."

"I can feel no key in the lock, master."

"It matters not; perhaps I did not bring it with me. Take the bunch, thou wilt find the longest of the three large keys will fit."

The forester locked the door, and, as the butler's steps were every moment becoming more unsteady, he was compelled to cling to the strong arm held out for his support.

"Harkee! knave," said the upper servant, "I like thee well, keep in mind all that is said by the varlets about me, and thou shalt guzzle as much of the prime ale thou hast not long since tasted as thou likest. This way, good fellow, this is the buttery."

There was a roguish smile upon the forester's face as he steered the butler to a seat, and when he was about to leave, his companion called him back.

"Harkee," he said; "I have but little love for that knave, thy master, the fat cook, so if thou canst contrive to give him a good trouncing, I shall not forget thee."

"But, good master," little John said, "I shall lose my place, if I do this."

"Fear not for that, fear not for that; I will stand thy friend, and none here, except our good lord, the Sheriff, has any power in the——The saints be good to us, here comes thy master, I know well his footstep; he comes to rate me for keeping thee so long; have at him if thou hast a chance; forget not, I will bear thee out."

The buttery door was flung violently open as he ceased speaking, and the cook, armed with a long rolling-pin, or, as it was then termed, a pastry-roller, entered the buttery.

He was very red and very angry, and his eyes glanced first at the butler, then at the scullion.

"How's this, knave," he roared, "that thou hast left thy duty? I did but lend thee to move a cask, and thou hast been gone twice the turning of the glass."

"I humbly crave——"

"Aye, that is is all thy cry! Get thee back to the scullery; get thee back, or I'll quicken thy lazy feet with——"

"Nay Gaucher," said the butler, adding fuel to the fire; "the poor knave is not to blame, it was I who——"

"Aye, thou; I should have known this when I lent him to thee; no doubt ere long thou wilt have made him as great a beer-swiller as thyself!"

The butler was a younger man than the cook, and had he been able to have kept his legs there would have been a set-to after he had received this insult.

But as it was, and while John was thinking the butler could not have made him a beer-swiller upon the contents of the sour cask, the cook flung the wooden roller at his head.

It missed, and terminated its flight against the butler's stomach, who rolled from his seat, and lay gasping to regain the breath which had been so rudely taken from him.

When he could speak he scrambled to his feet, and making a sudden rush upon the cook, caught him by the nose.

"Shut the door," he called out, and John obeyed. "Hold it fast, good fellow, while I baste this varlet's hide."

The cook, nothing loth to vent his long-cherished ill-feeling against the butler, clutched his opponent's hair; for, as in our more civilised days, there was about the same amount of jealousy and ill-feeling in those rude times among the servants of a large household.

Little John, with his back against the door watched the fight—if fight it could be termed—when one of the combatants held tightly to his opponent's nose, and the other clung by a handful of hair to him who held the most useful and ornamental feature of his face; their right hands being thus engaged, they did not long leave the others unemployed, and to Little John's amusement, the pair struggled and spluttered all over the buttery floor.

"I'll tweak thy nose off, thou greasy varlet," roared the butler; "beer swiller, and I'll teach thee manners."

"I've long waited to baste thee," roared the cook in return, "now thou shalt feel I am thy match."

"Body-o'-me!" thought Little John, "but this is a fair sight."

How long the encounter would have continued it is hard to say, as it came to an abrupt termination through the agency of the stalwart forester.

He had not forgotten the manner in which the cook had belaboured him with the greasy dish-cloth, so when the pair rolled against him he gave his master a blow on the back.

The cook gasped out an unsavoury oath, then fell to the ground doubled up with pain.

So skilfully had the forester put in this blow, that the cook felt assured the butler had taken an unfair advantage of him.

This belief was strengthened by the latter standing over him flourishing the rolling-pin he had picked up, and in the language of the knights, he said:—

"Yield thee, ransom or no ransom! or I will slay thee without mercy!"

The cook was unable to reply, so Little John came forward, and taking him in his arms carried him off to the kitchen.

## CHAPTER XXVI.

### WHAT LITTLE JOHN HEARD WHEN HE WENT TO THE VAULT.

When they had eaten and drunken well
Their troths together they plight,
That they would both with Robin be,
That very self-same night.
And then unto the treasure-house
Full quickly were they gone.
The locks, that were of very good steel,
They broke them every one;
Fine silver vessels they took away,
And all that they could get;
Pixes, and drinking-cups, and spoons—
Not one did they forget.

LEAVING the bruised knight of the spit to the care of his assistants, the forester, with glorious visions of the nut-brown ale floating before his eyes, went towards the vault.

"By Saint Hubert!" he thought, "that rap I gave the knave has served two purposes: it has pleased the butler, and carrying the cook away has pleased him well. Body-o'-me! were I to stay here long, I should have the two fighting who should have me."

When he reached the vault there was a gleam of light perceptible at the opposite end of the long, gloomy passage.

This sight quickened the forester's movements, yet, before he could unfasten the ponderous lock, the light began to grow larger, and, by the time Little John held the door open, he saw the glare of a torch dancing upon the shining mail shirt of Geoffrey de Lois and the steel caps of two men-at-arms who were in attendance upon him.

"Body-o'-me!" muttered the outlaw; "if yon rascally Norman comes to this vault I am lost, and Sherwood will count a knave the loss. Ah! they stop! The saints look down upon the poor wretches in these dungeons. I will have a draught of the cask set aside for the butler and his master, then I will try and find out the cause of these knaves' visit to this unsavoury part of the castle."

He had no difficulty in selecting the barrel the butler had pointed out, and by the sound that followed it was evident the October came pretty near the description set forth by the keeper of the cellar keys.

"Body-o'-me!" said John complacently, "but it is a fair and wholesome drink. I have not tasted better even in the merry greenwood. I shall keep this key, and

if there is any truth in that knave Bayston's words, about there being an outlet from beneath the castle to the woods, I will often do my devoirs to the good barrels."

Having made this resolve, the forester left the vault, and after carefully fastening the door, he stole softly towards the dungeon where he had seen the Sheriff enter.

The streak of light which came from the partly closed door told the outlaw that his foe was still inside the dungeon.

Creeping as close as prudence would safely warrant, Little John heard the Sheriff fiercely threatening the wretched captive.

"Darest thou," the Sheriff said, as John came within earshot, "repeat thy lies to my face?"

"Sir Sheriff," answered a voice the forester recognised as belonging to the unfortunate man he had stopped near the drawbridge, "I swear by Our Lady I never saw the inside of thy gates until thou gavest the order for me to be seized and brought to this accursed place."

"Dog!" said Geoffrey de Lois, "thinkest thou to escape thy doom by repeating such a sorry tale?"

"It is true, by Him who died for us, it is."

"I have told thee," rejoined the Sheriff, angrily, "if thy neck is of value to thee, thou hadst better tell who sent thee to spy upon my acts."

"I have spoken only the truth," the man answered, sullenly, "and I leave the issue to the saints who will bear me out of my trouble."

"Thy saints," the Sheriff said, grimly, "will have to be strong of arm to help thee now, for at sunrise to-morrow thy carcass will swing from the oaken beam across the castle gate."

"Saint Hubert," muttered Little John, "is a good and lusty saint, I will invoke his aid for this poor knave."

The Sheriff and his attendants left the vault as the forester drew back and concealed himself.

"Let the knave have the consolations of our confessor," the Sheriff said; "and harkee, Berthold, I may require the secret door. Have the tangled brushwood cut away from the exit to the wood."

"I will see to it, my lord."

"It is well. See it is done before to-morrow's noon."

The man-at-arms made a lowly bow.

"After thou hast seen to this matter," the Sheriff continued, "hie thee to a covert near the mill kept by old Much; thou knowest it, I suppose?"

"Right well, master, the man said, grimly; "for I was one of those the old thief tanned with his quarter-staff."

THE COMBAT IN SHERWOOD FOREST.

"Thou wilt be the more eager to aid me," the Sheriff said, "for I shall require thy aid to-morrow."

"To the end of my life, noble sir——"

"Aye, I knew thou would'st, Berthold; but peace, and pay heed to my words. The old miller goes to the hamlet of Radford to-morrow, at noon. At that hour bring with thee two steeds, and I will give to thy care the Miller's niece, the fair Maid Marian. I wish not to be seen in this matter; therefore, thou wilt bring her to the secret entrance, and lodge her in the chamber overlooking the courtyard. Thou understandest these directions.

"Right well, my lord, and they shall be carried out."

"If," thought Little John, "the good St. Hubert and my master do not interfere."

Geoffrey de Lois and his men left the gloomy passage, and the forester, after watching him ascend the steps, returned to the beer-vault.

"Body-o'-me!" he said; "but it's a great boon to have this good array of beer-casks to amuse me, while I await the coming of the good and pious confessor."

The black-jack was several times filled and emptied before the shuffling of a pair of sandalled feet caused the Outlaw to creep from the vault.

He saw the holy man apply the key to the dungeon door, and, stepping close beside him, John entered the dungeon at the same

moment. The confessor's stout form and
flowing robe concealed the forester's bent
form from the hapless captive.

"I give thee greeting, my son," the reverend
father said; thy hours are but few in this
world, therefore repent."

"Hold thy prating," said a voice, which
caused the prisoner and the friar to start;
"hold thy prating, Sir Priest, this good fellow
has more of life in him than either thee or
thy master can take away."

The prisoner stood with mouth agape,
staring blankly at the man who had robbed
him of his clothes; but the friar, recovering
from his surprise, turned upon Little John
wrathfully.

"Interfere not," he said, "with the office
of holy Church; quit this cell, thou rude of
speech and hard of heart.

"I will," John said; "and that full soon;
come," to the prisoner, "what is thy name?
Speak man, if thou hast a tongue."

"I am called Will Scarlet by my kith and
kin," answered the man; "but it can matter
little to an arrant thief like thou art what
my name and condition is."

"Tie up thy tongue, Will Scarlet," the Outlaw said; "I have done thee wrong, but I will
now repair it; come, I have a path open for
thee to sniff the fresh air again."

"Art thou serious?"

"As serious as the Sheriff is in his intent to
hang thee."

"I am with thee, then; lead the way."

"Not so fast," said the priest. "I cannot
suffer a prisoner to leave this place. What!
ho! without there! a rescue! a res——"

Little John's arm was passed round the
priest's throat and tightened until the godly
man was well-nigh choked.

When he fell to the ground, the forester and
his companion left the cell, carefully locking
the door after them.

"Come, Will," the forester said, "we will
refresh ourselves from a barrel I wot of, then
we can bid adieu to the Castle of Nottingham."

"A draught of October," said Will Scarlet,
"would be a boon, for I am but underfed
with the bread and water these knaves have
given me."

They went to the beer-cellar, and the
forester was much gratified when he beheld
the manner in which his new companion
emptied the tankard.

"Body-o'-me!" he said, "if thou canst
draw a bow and use a quarter-staff as well as
thou can'st empty a tankard thou art fit to be
one of our merry men."

"Thy merry men?"

"Aye—Robin Hood's."

"Who art thou to prate of such a good
man as bold Robin, the king of good fellows?"

Little John gave a hearty laugh.

"I am Little John," he said. "Hast thou
ever heard the name before?"

"That have I," answered Will Scarlet.
"Give me thy hand, good fellow. I forgive
thee the vile trick thou hast played me."

They shook hands, or, as the old ballad
has it, "plighted their troth."

"I make my vow to God," said Little John,
"And by my true loyalty,
Thou art one of the best drinkers
That ever yet I did see.

Could'st thou shoot as well with a bow,
To the greenwood thou should'st with me;
And twice in the year thy clothing
For new should changed be."

"What sayest thou?" John asked. "Wilt
to the greenwood?"

"Thinkest thou bold Robin would have me
in his company?"

"Thou art stout of limbs. Aye, marry,
that he will if thou hatest the Norman foe as
we do."

"A plague light upon the whole race,"
Will Scarlet answered. "Would they had
but one neck, and that neck in my grasp!"

"Say no more," exclaimed the forester,
"thou art one of our true hearts; come,
Will, let us to the greenwood."

"But how, surely the warders will not let
us pass?"

"We shall not trouble them," laughed
John; "come, let us haste, for I have news
for my master, and as we trip merrily to the
bonny greenwood I will tell thee why I bor-
rowed thy clothing.

"It mattereth not, thou hadst a goodly
reason, for it is not the fashion for bold
Robin's archers to rob a man who has
been beggared by the grasping Norman—
hark! what is that?"

"The priest," laughed John, "listen to his
holy words! I marvel, Will, if he learnt
such piety in the monastery wherein he was
reared."

Will Scarlet laughed, for the holy man's
words coming faintly upon their ears, savoured
but little of the odour of sanctity.

To speak the truth, he was cursing them
with all the vehemence of an ungodly trooper.

"It would be a sin," Will Scarlet remarked
as he passed the tankard to Little John, "for
us to leave this Norman stronghold without
taking a present for the master."

"By St. Hubert! thou art right, it is a
goodly thought, and goes far to show thou
art fit to be one of our merry men."

"Hast thou heard since thy stay here the
whereabouts of the strong room?"

"I have heard it spoken of by the kitchen
knaves as a place filled with cups of the
purest silver and pixes* of pure gold."

* In using this word the author adheres to the old
manuscript, although of opinion that by so doing is
open to criticism.

"A goodly place," said Will Scarlet, "and should we find it, bold Robin, will be well pleased with the presents we bring him."

"It must be hereabouts," said Little John. "Come, we will make search for it."

They drank to each other, then fastened the cellar door, and began their search for the treasure chamber.

All the doors were examined with care, until they came to one which had a lock of the finest steel.

"This must be it," said the forester; help me with yon key, Will."

The key was a huge stone, and the pair dashed it against the lock, which flew into fragments, and the Sheriff's treasure lay before them.

Little John made a bag with his jerkin, and it was soon filled; in addition to this they found two leathern bags filled with money equal to three hundred pounds of our coinage.

"Body-o'-me! John said with a grin; "the rascally Norman little thought, when he gathered his tithes, we should fall upon it."

"'Tis a fair punishment," answered Will Scarlet. "Come, John, let us breathe fresh air while we have the chance, for, peradventure, some of the men-at-arms may find their way down here, and we shall change places with yon priest, who clamours and swears more like a caged tapster than a holy man."

"Thou art right, Will; but it grieves me sorely to leave so many good vessels behind; can'st thou not make room for another?"

"Not one, John, not one; I am as well laden as a lazy monk's mule, when the shaven crown goes upon a journey."

Reluctantly Little John left the treasure-chamber, although he staggered under his load; he would have stripped the place, were it possible to have carried all the wealth away.

"If we must e'en leave this," he said, "let us at least have one more draught of humming October to give us strength to bear our load."

Against this Will Scarlet had nothing to say, for his throat was of a kindred nature with Little John's.

## CHAPTER XXVII.
### MAID MARIAN.

A bonny fine maid, of a noble degree,
With a hey down, down, a down,
Maid Marian called by name;
Did live in the North, of excellent worth,
For she was a gallant dame.
For form, and face, and beauty most rare,
Queen Helen, she did excel;
For Marian then was praised of all men
That did in the country dwell.

THE abbot's description of Maid Marian did not excel her wondrous loveliness. Formed in the most exquisite proportions, and somewhat above the middle height, the Saxon maiden looked as noble and queenly as the highest lady in the land.

It wanted an hour of noon the day following Little John and Will Scarlet's doings in the treasure-chamber of Nottingham Castle.

Maid Marian was seated near the open casement; the sun, lighting up her fine tresses, gave her head the appearance of being surrounded by a golden mist.

There was a marked sadness in her large blue eyes, as she looked out upon the green-clad heath, and more than once a deep sigh escaped her lips.

"I would," she mused, "that Robin gave up that strange, wild life. He is nobly born, handsome; so handsome, that when I look into his eyes I fear me he will see one of nobler blood than myself. Ah, me! should he do so, it will be a dark hour for poor Marian."

There was a suspicious moisture about her eyes as she gave lowly utterance to the fears which beset her heart, and but for the sudden entrance of her uncle, the burly miller, this would have swollen to tears.

"Well, girl," he said, "still pining like a caged linnet. Out upon it! I love not to one of thy years mope like a maiden whose knight-errant has gone to the Holy Land."

"I am not pining, good uncle," she said; "if my face speaks of a saddened heart, it is no truthful guide."

"Nevertheless," said the lusty miller, "it does speak to this effect—What is it, girl? tell thine uncle. A murrain upon all pining and sadness! Such a thing was never known when England was free. Peradventure it came with the hungry Normans, who fatten upon our substance."

"Not upon thine, uncle," Marian said, smiling, "for thy taxes were paid with thy quarter-staff."

"Aye, girl; thou art right; it was so far a payment that the knaves have not called for their tithes and dues. Tithes and dues—a plague upon the names! Such things were not known in my father's time, but then, girl, England was free!"

"I fear for thee, good uncle," the girl said; "for this proud Sheriff may work thee harm. Confide not too much in his forgetfulness of the manner in which thou visited the exactions of his men. Trust a woman's mind, uncle——"

"Saint Mary, preserve us! Trust a woman's mind! Well, I forgive thee, girl, I forgive thee, for thou art but a timid—— Well, well, I will not chide thee, thou meanest well, but as for this hang-dog-looking Sheriff, I care not this for him."

The miller snapped his fingers as he spoke,

then shook his huge fist in the direction of the castle.

"Now, girl," he resumed, "tell me what ailed thee when I came here; out with it. Come, hold up thy head, or I shall think thou art not speaking as a maiden should?"

"Well, good uncle," she said; "I was thinking of poor Much, thy son, for one thing——"

"Aye!" said the miller; "I will gage my good right hand, thou wert thinking of another green jerkin at the same time. Thou need'st not blush, girl, it is but natural, for bold Robin, the best and bravest of our Saxon race, is comely enough to win a maiden's heart. As for Much, my sturdy son, I would ten times rather see him with good Robin, outlaw though he be, than sheriff of this fair county, and he to bend the knee to the Norman tyrant who rules in this fair land. The saints preserve good Robin and his merry men, for of all our race, they alone bid defiance to the French robbers who despoil merry England."

"But the danger they are in, good uncle——"

"Danger, girl!" roared the miller, as though the word tickled his fancy; Robin and Much in danger, with six score good and true men to draw a bow in their defence? Go to, girl, thou knowest not of what thy tongue pratest!"

"True, uncle, I know but little; but my tongue is guided by my heart."

"As a maiden's speech should. May thy tongue always be thus guided. Now I must away, girl; I came but to say farewell, but thy speech has kept me waiting here; a fair good-day, child—remember thou keepest within doors, and should any of the silken gallants from the town pass this way, close the casement."

"I will follow thy advice, good uncle."

She kissed the lusty miller's cheek, and he, in return, caressed her golden locks.

"Thou art a comely wench," he said: "indeed thou art; the saints preserve thee until my return."

She watched the burly miller mount his horse and ride towards the road to Radford, then resting her head upon her hand, she became lost in a deep reverie.

Her mind wandered to the greenwood, and she saw in fancy the handsome form of her outlawed lover, as he stood beneath the trysting-tree, and, in her heart, she wished it were her lot to share his joys and sorrows.

Absorbed in these sweet fancies she heard not the door of her chamber open, nor was aware of the presence of a second person, until the ring of an armed heel caused her to look around.

She gave a low cry of affright, and started from her seat, then retreated slowly towards the furthest corner of the room.

The intruder was Geoffrey de Lois; he was cased from head to foot in link mail, and above his shining harness he wore a white gaberdine, emblazoned on the breast with a red cross, as a proof he had fought against the infidels in Palestine.

He stood for some moments dazed by the girl's wondrous beauty, and remained as silent as a statue until she reached the further end of the chamber.

Then he spoke, and his voice told how powerful his passion for the girl was influenced by being in her presence.

"Marian," he said, "fairest of all the maidens of thy race, why fearest thou me?"

"I fear you not, Sir Knight," she answered with a boldness her pale cheek belied, "yet I would be more at ease if thou wouldst leave this chamber where thou hast no right to enter."

"Thou speakest well, maiden," he said; "I have no right here, save the right of one who comes to tell thee how he has sighed and sought to obtain a glimpse of the sweet face which has haunted him from the hour when first we met."

"It is a pity, Sir Knight," she said, with a contemptuous curl of her lip, "thou didst not choose a time to tell me this, more befitting thy knightly vow and my fair name."

"Love waits not for the most fitting time; yet another reason I could urge, fair girl: I saw thy uncle, the good miller, leave this place, and I know the forest abounds with lawless men; therefore, I came to keep thee from their clutches—for, were they to know this place were without thy brave guardian, they would ransack his coffers, and peradventure carry thee off."

"Much, the miller, and his niece have nothing to fear from Sherwood's bold archers," she answered; "therefore, Sir Knight, thy protection is not necessary: and, as I would fain be rid of thy presence, depart as thou camest, or I shall have to summon my uncle's men to teach thee thy duty."

The knight smiled grimly.

"Thy sweet voice," he said, "would be raised in vain, for the miller's varlets are shut in the stone chamber of the mill, and a dozen of my crossbow men prevent them from leaving; therefore, thou seest thou must listen to my words, no matter how sorely it runs against thy wishes."

The girl's cheeks flushed with anger as she turned her bright eyes towards the speaker. The Saxon beauty was no coward, and had there been a weapon within reach, she would have boldly seized it, and bid defiance to the mail-clad intruder.

She would have done this, although there

was not the least doubt respecting the knight's instant victory over her feeble hand.

"Fitting words for one who has sworn to protect the weak and defenceless," she said, scornfully. "Go, Sir Knight, if this is thy Norman chivalry, give me the plain Saxon manners, at which thy class scoff; they, at least, know what is due to a helpless woman."

The girl's words, her defiant yet timid attitude sent a thrill of anger through the Norman's frame.

He had never before been thus spoken to, and it galled his haughty temper. Folding his arms and frowning angrily, he strode towards the maiden.

"Girl," he said, and his cheek alternately flushed and paled, "thy words bespeak thy race. Know that a Norman maiden of thy condition would hail with joy the wooing of a free-born knight."

"The manners of the French maidens are not ours," answered Marian, "the saints be praised for it! Take thy wooing to those complaisant dames, and learn that a Saxon maiden, however lowly, would sooner listen to the suit of a Saxon swineherd than mate with one of thy accursed race!"

"By the mass," the Sheriff said, stung to the quick by these words; "thou art as bold of speech as thou art fair of face; listen, girl, since it must be open war between us— I came here to woo thee as a knight, to utter my passion in the soft language with which heaven has favoured my race; but thou wilt have none of this: I must therefore tell thee I have determined to make these mine, and if fair speech will not serve the purpose, I am prepared to use harsher means."

"There speaks thy base nature!" the girl said boldly, although her heart faltered as she spoke; "but deem me not defenceless, false knight; were I but to raise a cry there would be many and strong hands come to my assistance."

"Let them come," exclaimed the Sheriff, clutching the maiden's wrists tightly; "let them come and save thee now."

She struggled wildly in his grasp, but his hand was like the grip of a vice, and the dove might as well have struggled to free itself from the talons of the hawk as Marian to escape from Geoffrey de Lois.

His passion getting the better of his manhood, he was deaf to her prayers and cries, as he ruthlessly dragged her towards the door.

"Help, help! she shrieked; "Arnulf, Arthur, Segwyrd! help, help! haste, knaves, haste and save thy mistress! they hear me not; God of my Fathers; is there none to help me? is there none to save me from this monster?"

There came a mighty voice, rising above the maiden's screams, as the clarion in the field of battle rises above the roar and shouts of the combatants.

"There is!" said the voice, and the chamber window was darkened. "Unhand the maiden, false knight! stain of thy race; false-souled caitiff! Unhand, I say, or by Saint Herman, I will cleave thee to the neck, were thy steel cap forged by the gods instead of mortal hands."

The speaker sprang lightly to the ground while giving utterance to these words, and the flash of a bright blade was seen as he raised his sword to strike down the Sheriff.

With a suppressed cry of fury Geoffrey de Lois hurled Marian from him, then drawing his ponderous sword, stood face to face with Robin Hood.

The Norman's dark features flushed with joy as he drew his sword.

"Hast thou made thy peace with heaven?" he said, fiercely lunging at the outlaw's heart; "if not, thou wilt pass from earth unshriven."

Robin parried the savage thrust with the ease and skill which proclaimed him master of the weapon he wore.

"Thou," he said, "standest in more need of a confessor than I—have at thee, false knight; were thy limbs ten times covered with armour of proof, thy false heart should feel my blade."

"Have at thee, thief! keep thy boasting, and learn how a true knight can rid the earth of such arrant knaves as thou art."

Their blades crossed as they thus hurled defiance at each other, and the maiden crouching low in the corner of the chamber, prayed that he whom she loved would be spared.

The mail worn by the Sheriff was forged by a cunning armourer of Milan, and although the gallant forester more than once got beneath the knight's guard, the blade failed to make any impression upon the glittering links.

"Foul fall the hand that forged thy steel jacket," thought Robin, as he parried the Sheriff's blows, "but for that my sword would long ago have reached the foul traitor's heart."

The Sheriff, confident in attaining an easy victory over the unprotected forester, became maddened with rage when he found every blow turned aside by the Outlaw's skill.

The Norman wielded one of those long-handled blades which could be used with both hands upon an emergency.

This course he adopted, and, had one of his heavy downward cuts taken effect, the bold chieftain would have been cleft in two.

The combat was too vengeful to continue much longer, for Robin's arm began to tire in meeting the Sheriff's blows.

There seemed no hope for him; the Sheriff's proof-mail defied his sword, and it seemed Robin must succumb to the odds against him.

His valiant heart knew no fear. He warded off blow after blow; drove the point of his sword against his foe's impenetrable breast.

In silence they fought, each with his teeth hard set.

Neither spoke as they stood thus, foot to foot and blade to blade, and the poor affrighted girl crouched yet lower—the fierce clatter of the blades ringing upon her ears, and telling that the combat which she dared not raise her eyes to look upon was not yet ended.

## CHAPTER XXVIII.

### LITTLE JOHN'S RETURN TO SHERWOOD.

God save thee my master dear,
    Said Little John,
    Then answered Robin,
Welcome may'st thou be,
    And also that fair yeoman,
Thou bringest there with thee.
    What tidings come from Nottingham
Little John tell thou me.

THE lieutenant of the foresters and his companion had not been long in the beer vault when the ring of an armed heel was heard on the stone passage outside.

"Hearest thou that, Will?" said Little John. "Body-o'-me, but if we are caught here there will be a pair of ornaments for the oaken beam across the gateway."

"It is but one man," Will Scarlet answered, after he had leisurely drained the black jack, "and may be a thirsty soul, who has come this way; if so we'll bid him welcome."

"If not, Will; if he does not turn out to be a man who likes the good dame Nature provides, what then, honest Will?"

"We must break his head, John, or choke him, whichever may be most fitting. Fill up the good measure again. Here's to merry Sherwood."

"If we get there," growled Little John. "Nevertheless, we will have another goodly draught—a malison upon the shaven priest, would I had choked him with his own rosary. Heard ye that, Will?"

"Marry, but I did, the holy man hears the knave's footsteps; and our sweet saint bless him, he calls out most lustily to be let out from his cage—pass the measure, John."

"For a Norman brew, Will, this is goodly ale; the saints be good to us, hear ye that, Will?"

"Mine ears would be but little use otherwise—aye, the knave has opened the door and the holy man is loose again."

"Bladebone of St. Hubert!" growled John, "I deserve to be held up for a show."

"What is the matter, John?"

"Aye, thou mayest well ask," Little John ruefully replied. "Strike my thick skull with the black jack, Will, but be careful thou empty it first."

"Strike thee for what, John?"

"For being a dolt, an ass, an idiot, a wittol, a fool, and everything else thou canst think of—ugh!—body-o'-me! I left the key in the door of yon dungeon."

"True, thou didst; well, it cannot now be helped—hush, by St. Gregory, John, they come this way—let us seek refuge behind yon barrels."

"Wittol, again, art thou, Little John," said the forester, as he filled the black jack preparatory to hiding, "for thou hast left the key in this door."

The red glare of a torch heralded the coming of the priest and his liberator, and when the forester and his companion had concealed themselves, the saintly man, and Berthold, the Sheriff's warder, entered the vault.

"No doubt, holy father," the warder said, as he entered, "thy throat is somewhat dry after shouting so lustily; and thou mayest well wish a benison upon the butler for leaving the key in the door of this cellar."

"Ugh!" growled Little John, mentally, "I hope the draught ye take will choke the pair."

"It is indeed, fortunate," said the priest, "for failing the clear water from a spring, good ale is not a bad substitute."

"Shaven-crowned hypocrite!" whispered Little John to Will. "Don't take too long a draught, for we may have to wait some time without getting another taste of the clear-running ale."

Berthold placed his torch in an iron socket which was placed in the wall, then he began to search for a vessel to hold sufficient of the good liquor to appease the churchman's thirst and his own.

"A malison upon the knave!" he said; "there is not even a horn left to taste the contents of this good barrel. Little wonder the rascal left the key here."

"My son," said the priest, "waste not thy words or time. Thou hast a steel cap, and, like unto the fainting soldier upon war's red plain, we will taste of the poor substitute for water. Fill it up, my son; the nearer the liquid is to the brim, the easier it will be for us to drink; we can throw away that which remains."

"Ugh!" whispered Little John, "I should be wondrously athirst before I drank from yon knave's greasy cap; what say you, Will?"

"It is not over-tempting, John," was the reply, "yet a dry thirst is a sore thing to bear."

The priest and the Sheriff's warder seated themselves upon an empty barrel, and, in the

THE WINGED MESSENGER.

most amicable manner, passed the steel cap to and fro, and interlarded their discourse with long draughts from the copious measure.

"I marvel much, Sir Priest," the warder said, "how this mischief befell thee."

"Of which dost thou speak, friend—the confinement in the dungeon, or having to drink of this bitter liquor in place of good, clear water."

"Touching the first, Sir Priest."

"But even as I in part told thee, a lusty knave entered the dungeon, and well-nigh strangled me; then went off with the rascal I was about to shrive."

"It will be unwelcome news to our master," the soldier said; "so for my part I would advise that we appear in ignorance of it, and let those who come to stretch the knave's neck find it out."

"I think thou art right, Berthold," said the holy man; "although falsehood is interdicted by the Church, I am of opinion that in this instance I had better bear the sin of appearing to be ignorant of this matter than deprive our good master of his sleep : for were he to know of it to-night, I feel sure his anger would be so great that he would not rest; therefore, thou seest, good Berthold, it is from a good motive we do this."

"Listen to the cunning priest," muttered Little John. "By the good Saint Hubert, the devil would have but few holidays were his priests to leave off lying."

"The veriest wittol," Berthold answered,

"could see your reverence's goodness in thus bearing the sin of falsehood."

"A sin, my son," interrupted the priest, taking the steel cap, and forgetting all about his resolve to throw that which remained away, "that I shall have to answer for by prayer and fasting, and the scourge well laid on my shoulders; for these things I must do when in the solitude of my own chamber."

"There is none more than myself," said the warder, "knows of your true and noble piety; yet, as thou sayest, a falsehood borne from a good motive, I should think, would be less wrong than the telling of lying words by the profane."

"Assuredly, my son," answered the holy man, "not the most learned divine could have placed the matter in a better light. So, good Berthold, as thy cup is now empty, and the close air of this place affects the linings of the throat, we will again taste of the liquor, which, although a poor substitute for water, is not so bad a draught as I had thought."

The warder slipped from the barrel, and while in the act of refilling his steel cap, the sound of coming footsteps was heard.

"Haste, good Berthold," said the alarmed priest; "I would not that we were seen here—at least that I were seen; it would be a lasting scandal upon my name."

The new-comer, as though the sight of the open door caused him more than ordinary surprise, quickened his pace, and before the warder could rise from his stooping position, the butler entered the vault.

He paused on the threshold, and, looking first at the priest, then at the soldier, tried to speak, but rage, choking his utterance, he was only able to articulate a confused sound.

When his speech became clearer his wrath burst forth in a torrent.

"A priest," he roared, "and a worthless man-at-arms, and in my cellar! May the foul fiend fly away with ye both for arrant thieves! Thou, Sir Monk, is this thy training, is this thy piety, to sneak like a rat into——"

"Peace, my son," said the priest, "peace I say. We should not have been here but for a——"

"Peace! dost thou preach to me, thou shaven thief? A pretty priest, forsooth—a dainty son of the Church. Out upon thee for a smooth-tongued, lying hypocrite——!"

"My son, forbear; invoke not the wrath of the Church upon thy head by abusing one of its chosen agents. Peace, I command ye!"

"Wrath—the Church—you command me!" spluttered the angry butler. "By Our Blessed Lady's favour, thou speakest too boldly for this once; but go, leave this place,

if thou canst walk, which I much doubt, by thy red face."

The priest sneaked out, and when safe the other side of the doorway, he turned.

"This profanation," he said, "will be punished by the——"

"To the devil with thee," roared the butler, advancing upon the holy man with clenched hands, "go, or by the mass I will pound thy carcase if thou wert ten times a priest."

The monk, seeing his sacred character would not protect him from the butler's anger, beat an ignominious retreat, and left Berthold to settle the matter

The latter, seeing there was no escape, seated himself upon the empty barrel, and during the time the butler and the priest were at high words, prepared for the share of abuse due to him, by refreshing himself from the contents of his steel cap.

"So," the enraged knight of the buttery said, as he faced the grinning warder, "thou hast turned thief, hast thou?"

"Hard words, good friend," said the other, coolly, "I found the door open, walked in, and saw a row of goodly barrels, and did as thou wouldst have done, tasted——"

"Tasted," roared the butler, his anger rising yet higher at the soldier's coolness, "tasted! beast that thou art; thou hast drunk of the barrel which is set apart for our good lord, the Sheriff; may the foul fiend take me if I do not tell our master of this."

"Do," said the warder, "and by all the saints, I will tell him how well thou keepest thy trust, then I will baste thy fat carcass——"

The butler's endurance was passed; to be insulted in this manner in his own dominion was beyond even the temper of a saint, much less that of the choleric servant.

With a roar like an angry bull he rushed forward to grapple with the soldier, but the latter, knowing the result should he be tumbled off the barrel, sent the contents of his steel cap fair in the butler's face.

The strong ale blinded the butler, and while he gave vent to a string of choice oaths, and struck madly right and left, the warder slid from his perch and left the vault.

Little John and his companion were well-nigh suffocated with suppressed mirth, and it was as much as they could do to refrain from giving vent to a hearty peal of laughter.

When the butler found his enemy had beaten a retreat he wiped his eyes, and thus poured forth his feelings upon the matter.

"A priest and a soldier; a lying, fat, hypocrite, the one; the other, a lazy, skulking, lusty thief—both robbers. Would I had twisted that Berthold's neck, for he, of the two, has been the—— Blessed Saint Ursula what is that? Oh, I know; it is the knave who is to die to-morrow. No wonder he groans. Yet—oh, there it is again. I could have sworn the sound came from behind yon barrels, but that cannot be. Fancy the ghost of an empty barrel groan—oh!"

The butler stopped abruptly, and his mouth resembled the letter O, for, to a certainty, there came a prodigious groan from the darkest corner of the vault.

The long silence somewhat recovered the servant, and, rising from his knees—for he had assumed the attitude of prayer—he advanced boldly to the door.

"It's that knave Berthold," he said. "He he—he—the thief, knows the story about the butler I replaced being found dead in this very vault. But, what matters? He has not come back—oh, blessed and holy Saint Ursula, be merciful, and drive away the evil spirit."

The hollow groan was repeated, and down went the butler upon his knees. Then came a crash, as Little John hurled the black-jack at the torch, and knocked it from the socket.

The flaming brand fell close to where the butler knelt, his hair bristling with fear, and his trembling lips vainly trying to give utterance to the half-forgotten prayers he once knew.

The noise made by the torch—for the flame had fallen in the pool of ale—increased the domestic's fright, and when it went out, he desisted from praying, and fairly howled with fear.

This was the opportunity of which Little John and his companion availed themselves to leave the vault; and the former, as he passed the howling domestic, placed his large cold hand over the poor wretch's face.

The butler could bear no more. He gave a prolonged yell, then tumbled face foremost on the ground.

Little John and Will Scarlet debated for a few seconds respecting the propriety of pouring a tankard of cold beer down the prostrate n's back.

They drew the vessel full to the brim for the purpose, but Little John could not find it in his heart to waste so much good liquor; therefore, the well-matched pair drank it between them.

"Now, Will," said the forester," "for the merry greenwood. Follow me, and be careful thou dost not lose any of the good cups of silver or the vessels of gold."

The forester must have had the organ of locality very strongly developed; for although he had only gleaned the position of the door which led to the secret passage from the gestures of the Sheriff when he was in conversation with Berthold, he went straight to it, and much to the surprise of both, they found it unlocked.

"Body-o'-me !" said Little John, "the Sheriff's warder has been kind to us."

"How so, John?"

"He is preparing the passage for to-morrow—ho, ho! Body of Saint Hubert! but that morrow will tell a different story."

When they neared the outlet the blows of an axe could be heard, and Little John going forward to reconnoitre, saw Berthold busy hewing down the tangled brushwood which grew before the door.

There was a few moments' consultation respecting the best mode of passing the warder. They could easily have done so by using force, but this did not suit the forester.

He wished, if possible, to pass unseen, then the man would have no story to carry to the Sheriff, consequently his suspicions would not be aroused respecting the character of the visitor who had worked so much mischief in the castle.

Chance favoured our adventurers; the soldier paused in his labour, and stood with his back towards the entrance

There was a torch stuck in the ground; and by its ruddy glare the warder had seen to do his master's bidding.

This torch must be extinguished—but how?

Little John soon found the means; picking up a stone he flung it at the light.

His aim was true, and the place was in darkness.

"A malison upon the light," growled the soldier, "and a double malison upon my careless fingers for placing the sticks where they could fall upon the torch—marry come up with a wennion."

With this hearty curse, he took up the smouldering torch and began blowing the glowing end to fan it into a flame again.

While he was thus engaged, the forester and Will Scarlet stole quietly past, and, despite the heavy loads they laboured under, they started at a quick pace and were soon tracing the high road which skirted the forest.

They had not passed many yards from where the trees began when two figures sprang out into the centre of the road.

"Stand!" said one of the men, "and pay toll to good Robin."

"I'll break thy back, Much," answered Little John, "If thou dost not stand out of my path; to the evil one with thy *Pawage\**."

"Is it thou, giant?" said Much; "we are right glad to hear thy voice again; there has been some talk among our merry men of one Little John, who had turned his sword and bow into a dishclout."

---

\* Pawage was the old Saxon expression for toll.

"Aye," answered John, "I'll warrant the tongues of our band have clacked like a flock of geese taking to the water, and their jaws have wagged when they thought of Little John washing the platters—see thee this, thou thief of a miller?"

"Aye, I do right well, and by its sheen should warrant it were made of silver."

"Right for once, wittol—how thinkest thou I came by them?"

"Found them, mayhap."

"Cudgel thy brains again, Much. No, I'll spare what little thou hast of that article—harkee, they are my wages for being scullion to the Sheriff."

"The saints be good," laughed Much, "but the Sheriff pays wondrously well; but tell me, John, who is this lusty yeoman? He has, I see, also got his wages."

"Yes," answered Little John, grimly, "he has been my helpmate."

"Pass on," said Much. "Thou king of liars! pass on."

"Body-o'-me!" said John; "had I not such presents for our master, I would stay and break thy back."

Much and his companion had by this time returned to the thicket, and, to Little John's amazement, the merry miller's son trolled out the following impromptu verse:—

"Some they will talk of bold Robin Hood,
And some of Little John,
But I know how he served the proud Sheriff
When he served him as scul-li-on."

"A plague upon thy bawling!" growled John. "This way, Will; but heed the trees, man, or thou wilt find thyself with a broken pate."

This caution was necessary, for they had entered a part of the forest where the lower boughs of the trees were not more than five feet from the ground.

They had not gone far through this almost impassable path, when a surly voice demanded—

"Thy name, friend; stand! or a clothyard shaft shall pierce thy body!"

"Hold thy prate," answered Little John, "and keep thy shafts for thy foes, most trusty Allan."

"Little John!" exclaimed Allan; "welcome to the greenwood, good scullion, the cooks have many platters for thee to wash."

"The fiend take thee!" said Little John, angrily. "At every turn I am met with like gibes. Come, Will, let us move; and may the saints send a wet night."

Will Scarlet was surprised at the vigilant watch kept by the outlaws, and his desire to become one of the band increased.

"Never mind their gibes, John," he said;

"thou hast more to show for thy service than all the scouts who are out to-night.

"Aye," answered the giant, "that is the only balm I have, for these knaves will not forget this scullion business until I crack their pates. Come this way, Will: stoop well thy head, for this path is but used by the deer when they lead their fawns to drink at the stream."

Will Scarlet had good reason to wish the path had been left only for the deer, for his head received many sore bruises before he went far through the tangled path.

"The foresters," he said, not pretending to heed the sore blows he received, "keep good watch, John."

"Ashes of Saint Hubert! yes. Harkee, Will, the forest is some twenty-one miles in length, and seven wide, yet I'll gage my manhood a ferret could not enter among the trees unseen."

"There must be many men in your good company?"

"Some seven score, Will, and every day some good fellow like thyself joins us."

They went on for nearly half a mile, the forest opened, and they crossed a glade tolerably shut in by the trees.

In the centre of this place stood a square-built stone hut, and Little John went to the door and imitated the cry of an owl.

The signal was understood, for the door was opened by a boy garbed in the finest green velvet trimmed with gold lace.

"Does our master sleep, Aylmer?" said Little John; "if so I will come in the morn, and tell him strange news."

"Enter, pigmy," cried a voice from within. "Welcome to the greenwood."

Little John and Will entered, and Robin, when he saw the stalwart form beside Little John, smiled.

"What news from Nottingham, John?" he said, "and who is thy lusty companion?"

"Great news, good Robin; my companion is one who would fain join our band."

"What are these vessels of silver and gold, John, which ye both carry?"

"Presents from the Sheriff, master—right royal presents."

"They are welcome. Be seated: I will hear thy news first. But stay, does thy companion know the rules of our band?"

"But in part, good master; but I will warrant he agrees to all if thou wilt take him."

"Upon thy word I will. What is thy name good fellow?"

"Will Scarlet, please you, bold Robin. Stout Will I am called by my kith and kin."

## CHAPTER XXIX.

### SHERIFF AND THE ABBOT MEET UNDER THE TRYSTING TREE.

Then Robin set his horn to his mouth,
And blew out blasts three,
Then quickly anon there came Little John
And all his companie.

"What is your will, master?" said Little John,
"Good master come tell unto me."
"I have conquered the Sheriff of Nottingham,
Therefore I bring him to dine with thee."

THE chamber in which the Chief of the Outlaws was seated was, for the period of which we write, fitted up in the most luxurious manner, and many of the ornaments, especially the lamps, which hung from the ceiling by silver chains, looked suspiciously like the filagree work lately imported into the country by the Normans.

The couch upon which the Outlaw reclined was covered with leopard skins, and surmounted at each end by lions' heads of solid silver.

Robin Hood's hunting dress was laid aside and in its stead he wore a loose robe of quilted silk trimmed with ermine and fastened by loops of gold thread.

This oriental magnificence contrasted strangely with the rough stone walls of the dwelling, the rush-covered floor and the chinks of the window frames through which the cold night air whistled.

At Robin's feet lay two large deer hounds, whose white fangs gleamed disagreeably when they turned towards Will Scarlet, for the sagacious brutes know every man in the band, although neither by look nor gesture did they show the slightest affection save to their master.

They were powerful, strong-limbed brutes, and well might Robin boast that with his good sword and buckler and his pair of hounds, he feared not twelve ordinary men.

"Now, pigmy," said the Outlaw good-humouredly, "for thy news."

Greatly to Robin Hood's amazement, Little John related his adventures in the castle; but, when he came to the recapitulation of the conversation between the Sheriff and Berthold, the Outlaw Chief's face reddened with anger, and he sprang from his seat, and the watchful dogs, as though they thought Little John was the cause of this display of temper, raised their massive heads, and snarled angrily at the giant.

"Down, Herod! down, Sylman!" Robin said; "have ye no better manners than to show your fangs to your friends?"

The dogs, rebuked, laid their heads upon their paws, and contented themselves by watching the visitors.

Little John continued his story, and, at its placed the spoil upon the table.

"These presents," Robin said, smiling—for his anger had passed away—"are welcome, John, for our treasury is but poorly supplied.

"Body-o'-me!" the forester said, "I never knew it other than empty. What, in the saint's name, hast thou done with the good coin thou hadst when I left."

"Given it away, John; for I could not hoard up riches and know so many of the poor were suffering through the rapacious locusts who infest our land."

"Thou art ever good," said Little John, "and, were harm to befall thee, the poor would lose a friend."

"And the rich an enemy," said the chief. "Seek thy rest, John, and take with thee this fair yeoman, who seems well able to use a staff or drive an arrow among the fallow deer, or, better still, through a Norman's coat of mail."

"Aye, that he is, master. Now, a fair good night! Come, Will, let us seek a cover for the night, for, to-morrow thou wilt have to prove thy skill in the use of bow, spear, sword, and staff."

The foresters left, and Robin's page, closing the door after them, retired to an inner chamber.

For some time the Outlaw Chief continued to pace to and fro, and by the red flush upon his face alone showing that his mind was disturbed.

"So," he said, as though in answer to his own thoughts, "this priest has set the bloodhound upon the abode of the dove. By my halidome, but he shall hang from the highest branch of our trysting tree if harm befall the gentle girl. What, ho, Aylmer!"

The richly-dressed page glided to his master's side.

"Hie thee to the place where the abbot is confined," the Outlaw said, "and bid his guards bring him hither; be quick, boy, for the matter will not brook delay—rather," he added, when the boy left, "my mind may not long keep in this mood."

The abbot, roused from his slumber by Robin's sudden message, was hurried to the stone building, and brought face to face with the angry Outlaw.

The proud Norman first met the forester's gaze with a contemptuous look of defiance—although a prisoner, he deemed himself too powerful to be confined by the chief of the Saxon archers.

"Harkee, Sir Priest," said Robin sternly, "thy brain hath hatched a plot for the destruction of one who is dear to me—but I swear should harm befall her, I will suspend thy carcass from a green bough—by the holy rood I will! Should ye," he added to the stalwart foresters, who guarded the abbot, "hear three mots from my bugle to-morrow at noonday, stay not for my coming, but hang this priest as ye would hang a rabid dog. Now, away with ye, and forget not three mots from my horn will be the abbot's death-warrant."

The abbot's face went pale, but he retained sufficient composure to walk steadily from the Outlaw's presence. Then again Robin threw himself upon the couch, and soon fell into a deep sleep.

When the morning came he inspected his men, heard their reports, and examined them at the butts, and Will Scarlet, who proved himself a good yeoman, was admitted into the band.

As the morning advanced the outlaw's calmness began to leave him, and when the dial showed it was now the hour Geoffrey de Lois had determined to visit the mill, Robin selected a dozen of his best men and left the forest.

When they reached the vicinity of the mill the foresters concealed themselves among the trees, and Robin went forward alone.

He had gone as far as the miller's dwelling when a scream caused him to pluck his sword from his scabbard, and recking not of the force which might be opposed to his single hand, he dashed through the window.

What followed has already been related.

The odds were all in favour of the mail-clad Sheriff, and as he was armed with a much heavier weapon, it was a wonder the lightly-armed Outlaw did not succumb to his foe.

The wondrous skill he possessed alone saved him from being slain, and this skill enabled him to take a sudden leap forward, as his sword blade snapped in two, and before the Sheriff could deal the fatal blow he was seized by the throat.

There was a brief struggle, then a crash of steel, as the Norman was borne to the earth.

Like a flash of light Robin's long hunting-knife leapt from its sheath, and his throat would have been pierced, had not Marian sprang forward, and catching the Outlaw's hand, said—

"Shed not his blood, Robin; let other hands than thine do this."

The blow was arrested, and the Outlaw arose, placing one foot upon his prostrate foe's neck.

"Yield!" he said, "or despite this maiden's prayers I will slay thee."

"I yield," was the sullen answer, "since there is none other to be done; but the day will arrive when I shall meet thee again, foot to foot."

"For that meeting," the Outlaw answered, "I shall be ready; but keep thy boasting until thou art clear of my hands."

The Sheriff regained his feet, his swarthy face black with passion, and in spite of his

knightly word which he had pledged when he surrendered to to the gallant forester, he made an effort to snatch his sword from the ground.

The forester's quick eye anticipated the treacherous movement, and before the Sheriff's hand could touch the hilt the weapon was kicked out of reach.

Geoffrey de Lois scowled savagely, and as though a sudden thought had come to his mind, he placed a silver whistle to his lips and blew a shrill note.

"False caitiff!" said Robin, "is this the way thou regardest thy plighted word? Out upon thee for a recreant! Listen to the answer to thy call."

Robin sounded a blast upon his bugle, then taking up the Norman's long sword he awaited the coming of his men.

"The devil," the Sheriff said triumphantly, for he believed that Robin had come to the mill unattended, "will not save thee; to-morrow shalt thy neck be stretched. Listen, here come those who will bear thee to a dungeon, and this maiden to a chamber, in Nottingham Castle."

As he spoke the door was thrown open, and Berthold, at the head of a dozen retainers armed with sword and buckler, entered the room.

"Seize yon thief!" said the Sheriff. "Ha, ha!—have I not spoken truly, thou cut-purse?"

"Thou hast told a foul lie," answered Robin Hood, as he whirled the two-handed double-edged sword around his head, and kept back the men-at-arms; "judge for thyself."

As the last words left his lips, the men-at-arms were hurled aside from the doorway, and Little John, followed by the foresters with bent bows, ran to their leader's assistance, the giant using his clenched fist to clear a path, and the steel-capped retainers going down before it as though a sledge-hammer had been used upon their skulls.

"Make way, knaves!" Little John said, seconding every word with a blow, "or mayhap my fists may batter the iron pots through your skulls. Now, master, what means thy lusty call?"

"Only this, John," the Outlaw said; "bind yon Sheriff's arms, then put a rope round——"

"Upon them knaves!" roared the Sheriff. "Use the swords ye hold, and cut these thieves to the earth."

"Ho, ho!" laughed Little John; "large words, master, large words. See thou these clothyard shafts. Open thy bawling mouth again, and thy men will be pinned to yon wall."

The men-at-arms drew back, for six of the

ROBIN HOOD A PRISONER.

foresters fitted arrows to their bows, and stood with the strings drawn to their ears.

"Draw to the ear, my merry men," continued Little John, "and if one of the knaves stir hand or foot, send a good yard of birch and hazel through their jerkins."

Three of the outlaws placed their bows against the wall after detaching the strings; these they knotted together, and, seizing the Sheriff, began to tie his arms behind him."

The Norman fought like a tiger, but his strength was as a child's against the stalwart fellows who held him in their grip.

There was not only the disgrace of being thus pinned before his men that galled him, but Robin's unfinished speech left him in doubt as to the use of the bowstring that was to be passed round his neck.

"Now," said Robin, when their prisoner was secured, "pass a loop round his neck, and lead him to our trysting tree ; and thou, Much, should he lag on his way, walk behind him and prick his hide with thy sword, if thou canst find a crevice in his armour for the point to enter."

"His mail," answered the delighted Much, "would have to be forged by the devil if I did not find space enough for the point of this good blade to enter."

"What about these knaves, master ?" Little John asked, baring his brawny right arm. "I think a good basting with our unstrung bows would be neat punishment for them."

"Thou art right," laughed Robin, "therefore set about it, John."

The hindmost of the retainers, seeing those of the foresters who had not their arrows fitted, busy loosing their bow-strings, fell slowly back through the door, and the example, spreading like an infectious disease among the remainder, the whole forty turned tail and left the miller's house.

But quick as they were they did not quite escape, for sturdy old Much riding towards the door and seeing the Sheriff's men upon his domain, struck spurs into his grey gelding's sides, and with the long whip he carried, laid about him right and left.

The old fellow came back chuckling with his victory, and to his astonishment he saw the Sheriff being led out like a convict, and his son, young Much, walking behind the prisoner with a naked sword held in an unpleasantly suggestive manner.

"What now?" demanded the old man, pulling up his steed, "art thou going to give the devil a day of merry-making by hanging his chosen friend?"

"Maybe so, father," answered Much, "but if he goes not on faster than this, I shall let out his black blood long ere we reach the merry greenwood."

"Good boy," said the miller, "by our ancestors this is a goodly sight—string him up, the knave—but where's good Robin, Much?"

"Ask Cousin Marian," answered Much, mischievously; "I saw him holding her by the waist lest she might fall."

"The knave," laughed the lusty old miller, "I'll teach him better manners."

"Do, father—and harkee."

"Well, knave."

"Didst thou grind up flint stones to fill the last flour sacks thou sent to the forest?"

"Out upon thee for a saucy varlet."

The old miller made a cut at his son with the whip, but the latter dodging aside, the thong came smartly across the Sheriff's face, and caused him to make an exclamation not generally used by so mighty a knight.

The foresters laughed, and led their prisoner away, and Robin soon overtook them.

When they reached the trysting tree, Robin Hood wispered a few words to Little John, who, when he heard them, began to grin, and finally bursting out into a hearty laugh, he left the spot, his person swinging to and fro with merriment.

When Little John disappeared, Robin placed his bugle to his mouth, and sounded a long mot for the foresters to assemble.

They came from every part of the forest, and the Sheriff's face, although he would have concealed it, expressed the greatest surprise at beholding the many stalwart green-clad forms gather around the handsome chief.

When the men were all assembled, the Sheriff's nerves received another shock, for Little John appeared leading the abbot towards the group.

"A friend of thine," said Robin to the Sheriff; "I have brought him here that thou shouldst not be the only one of thy race among the many of Saxon blood."

The abbot started when he saw his nephew, and would have spoken had not astonishment and rage kept him silent.

"Well, John," the chief said, "as we have such good company suppose we go to dinner."

"It would be a sin, master, to let the good roast meats be over-done. Disperse ye knaves, and spread the board——"

"But, master——"

"Well?"

"Dost thou not think that it would be as well to hang the Sheriff before dinner?"

"Nay that would be very unyeomanlike—he shall dine first, John, and pay for his dinner, then we can hang the knave."

Not pleasant for the Sheriff this—for he took the foresters' joking for earnest.

The lieutenant set about the arrangement of the board, amusing himself while doing so by singing a ballad of which the following was the refrain :—

> "The Sheriff is welcome here,
>  For I know he will honestly pay,
> And I know he has gold if it be but well told,
>  Will serve us to drink a whole day."

The verse was soon taken up by the outlaws, and the Sheriff bit his lip with passion at being made such an object of ridicule, among the men he had been wont to despise. Robin, with his back against a tree, listened to his lieutenant's voice, and by the smile upon his lips, it was evident he felt much amused.

## CHAPTER XXX.

FRIAR TUCK RETURNS FROM PRAYERS, AND THE ABBOT SINGS A MASS TO THE MERRY FORESTERS.

> "Now let him go," said Robin Hood;
>  Said Little John, "that must not be;
> For I vow and protest he shall sing us a mass
>  Before that he go from me."
> Then Robin Hood took the Abbot,
>  And bound him fast to a tree,
> And made him sing a mass, God wot,
>  To him and his yeomanry."

THE feast spread by the foresters resembled in many particulars the description of that given to do honour to the Earl of Mortimer.

When one of the servers announced everything ready, the chief desired the Sheriff's bonds to be cut, and then invited him to be seated.

However much the haughty Geoffrey and the prelate disliked having to accept the invitation, they had the good sense to hide their feelings, and heartily wishing the first mouthful of venison might choke their entertainers, they sullenly took the seats indicated.

Robin Hood was about to give the word for the ready daggers to fall upon the smoking viands, when looking first up one side then down the other, he missed the rubicund face of the fat friar.

"Hold thy hands," he said, "it is not right we should dine without asking a blessing. Where is our roystering chaplain?"

"I saw him," said the forester, "go towards the north side of the forest before you returned."

"Was it long ago?"

"Perhaps an hour, good master."

"To your feet, knaves," said the forester, "and search for our jolly clerk; for I swear not to eat until he's found."

The men were saved this trouble, for at the moment as a score or thereabouts rose to their feet, a lusty and somewhat thick voice could be heard singing—

"Ye gentlemen and yeomen bold,
    Or whatsoe'er you are,
To have a right good story told
    Attention now prepare;
It is about bold Robin,
    A man much talked upon,
And who was once a man of fame,
    And styled Earl of Huntingdon,
Bold Robin was his name."

The friar suddenly desisted from his song, then his voice was raised in expostulation to some one near him.

"The foul fiend!—that is, blessed be the saints!—for giving us good liquor. Keep thy feet, men, keep thy feet; for it would be a sinful sight for our master to see ye both in this unseemly state."

These words were uttered in a voice that left but little to be imagined respecting the state of the friar and his companions.

"Our fighting priest," laughed John, "and drunk, or I'm a false prophet."

"Out upon thee for a pair of knaves," the friar was heard to say. "Dost thou not know both feet ye have were given to ye to walk upon, not the hands. Keep upright, or, by all the saints! I will leave ye both without the support of my arm. Come, ye varlets, tune up, and bear me out in a right good stave."

There was a short pause, then the saintly man burst out with the following fragment—

"Ah! sweet are the flowers that bloom in May,
Like wing-gifts dressing the gaily-dressed day,
And smiling like beauty o'er heart-bending sway;
But sweeter to those than the thirsty soul's throat
Is the——"

"A plague take ye both! thou art drunk; tune up, or, by the saints! I'll split this——
A fair, good day, my merry men, and masters all."

It was a strange sight which burst upon the assembled company when the lusty friar uttered this greeting—a sight that caused Little John to roar with laughter.

Emerging from the trees, were seen the lusty friar, and two foresters behind, arm-in-arm, swaying two and fro, as they alternately flashed black bottles over their heads, and took up the last line of Friar Tuck's song, and, with drunken gravity, endeavoured to sing it as a chorus.

"What now, ye roystering knaves?" said Robin: "is it thus ye come before us? Out upon ye. What, drunk! and the sun scarcely beyond noon-time."

"Drunk!" hiccupped the friar, reclining on the arms of the foresters; "thou doest us great wrong, master, we have been to prayers, and feeling athirst after, we drank of Saint Ann's Well, and as thou well knowest the waters are by a miracle of a strength not befitting our poor weak heads."

"Go to, thou knave," Robin said, "here have we kept this company fasting a full hour through thee. Make thy obedience to the Lord Abbot here, then say a fitting grace for this goodly feast."

Friar Tuck's companions who had escaped by this time, were seated at the lower end of the board; when the monk found himself thus deserted by his allies, he screwed his face into a comical expression of repentance, and addressing the abbot said:

"I crave your reverence's pardon for not making my obeisance sooner to one of our cloth, but I wot the Lord Abbot knows full well what it is to drink of the waters of Saint Ann's Well, or may be waters of similar strength, and his reverence knowing this will pardon my——"

Here the jolly priest, who had been swaying to and fro, suddenly lurched forward, and losing his footing, fell into a huge dish of smoking venison, and sent the hot gravy all over the Sheriff's face.

The latter sprang up with an oath, which was repeated by the abbot, who chanced to be seated opposite to where the friar fell, and the latter in his efforts to regain his feet, rolled forward and overset the mighty churchman.

The laughter from the foresters was long and loud at this ludicrous scene, and the fat friar, scrambling to his feet, rubbed his shaven crown.

"The saints preserve us," he said, ruefully, "here have I scalded a good knight and upset a reverend head of the Church, and it all came about through Saint Ann. Out upon ye for blessing the waters of the well; is it thus ye would serve one who pays the shrine such homage."

"The Sheriff, who had by this time cleared

his eyes of the hot gravy, smarting under the scalds his face had received, made a rush upon the fat friar.

"Drunken carle," he said, "ungodly desecrator of a priest's robe, I will wring thy neck."

He made a clutch at the friar's robe as he spoke, but the stout priest suddenly ducked his head, and taking the astonished Norman by the waste, held him aloft.

"Now, my master," he cried, "shall I crack this knave's skull or fling him over yon tree?"

The Sheriff's position was not the most enviable in the world, for the strong-limbed friar held him with as much ease as though he were a child.

"Come, thou roystering devil," said Robin, "set our guest upon his feet, it will be time if he does not pay for his dinner to crack his skull or throw him over yon tree."

The priest placed the Sheriff upon his feet, and Robin, in the most courteous manner, begged him to be seated.

Geoffrey de Lois complied; he found he was no match for the Outlaw's chaplain, and knew it would best serve his purpose to ingratiate himself with the Outlaw.

With a forced smile he reseated himself.

"It would be more seeming," he said to the Outlaw Chief, "if this lusty friar of yours would seek the Well he worships less often, and much better for the comfort of thy guests."

"There is much truth in that," answered Robin, "but the knave is deaf to all good advice—come, sir friar, when thou hast done twisting thy face about we shall be glad to hear grace said, for our merry men and the guests here are somewhat tired of waiting so long for their dinner."

Friar Tuck was about to say grace, but ere he could begin the abbot jumped to his feet and sternly said:

"Peace, thou drunken varlet, thinkest thou I will sit here and listen to the Church being profaned by thy words."

The fat friar meekly crossed his hands, and a broad grin overspread his face.

"Far be it," he said, "reverend father, for one like myself to contradict the words of one who draws such fat revenues for wearing our cloth; I am dumb, Sir Abbot, and wait with due humility for thee to perform the office thou willest me unfit to perform.

The Abbot scowled at the fat monk.

"How is this," Robin said, what, two of a cloth at bariance? Come, Sir Abbot, the dinner's cold, and the mouths of my merry men water the more when they see good viands before them, and wait but for the proper words to begin the meal. Come, as

thou likest not the grace of the friar, say one thyself."

"Use my holy office," exclaimed the indignant churchman "for the benefit of such cutpurses as ye are! not a word wilt thou get from my lips; and as for yon grinning disgrace to priestcraft, would I had him in my abbey!"

"Ho, ho!" laughed Friar Tuck; would thou wert safe back there thyself, Sir Abbot; by Our Lady, were it in my power I would make thee use thine office or flay thee alive!"

"Accursed be such as ye——"

"Stop, Sir Abbot," Robin said; "thou hast used words which are but scant courtesy for all we have done for you. Arise, Allan, and thou, Much."

The foresters obeyed.

"Pass a looped rope over a strong bough of yonder tree."

This order was likewise obeyed, and the proud prelate's face paled.

"Take the abbot," Robin continued, "and put the loop around his neck, but strangle him not; I want him to have the power of speech."

The abbot's face grew paler, and his legs shook as he was led beneath the dangling noose, and his neck encircled with the cord.

The Sheriff sat aghast, but he moved not, for he saw Little John had unsheathed his heavy sword, and was keenly watching every movement of their foe — Nottingham's treacherous sheriff.

"Now, Sir Priest," said the Chief, " sing us a mass, or by the splendour of Our Lady't face, thou wilt be a dead man."

"Geoffrey," said the abbot, "thine arms are free, help me! By Our——"

"If he stirs but an inch," said Little John, "I will cleave him to the chine."

"Now, Sir Priest," said Robin, "sing us a mass, or thou hangest!"

The abbot made no reply, but his head fell forward as he reflected over the certainty of the fate with which he had been threatened.

Life was sweet to him—very sweet, but to have his pride humbled by the Outlaw was almost as bad as death; yet, he thought, "the time may come when I shall be able to avenge this insult."

"I yield to thy demand," he said, raising his head and looking fiercely at the Outlaw Chief; "but, rest content, the wrath of the Church will fall upon thy head!"

"When it does, Sir Abbot," said Robin, "I will obtain absolution from our confessor here; wilt thou grant it, fat friar?"

"Aye, right willingly," laughed Friar Tuck, "and as willingly as I grant it to sundry of thy merry men, who come to me in virtue of my holy office.

"Enough," said Robin; "thou hearest, Sir

Abbot; now sing us a mass, and in full voice too, or the stinging nettles I see being gathered shall make acquaintance with thy back; thy kinsman here, the Sheriff, once tasted them he will tell thee they are far from pleasant."

Geoffrey de Lois darted a look of hatred towards the forester for mentioning the degradation he had undergone when he disturbed the Saxon merry-making.

There was a deep silence during the time the abbot's voice was raised, and all paid deep attention to his words, save the ungodly Friar Tuck, who rolled his body from side to side, and once or twice disturbed the silence by laughing outright.

When the abbot had concluded his unwilling office, the noose was taken from his neck, and he was conducted by Allan-a-Dale and Much to his seat.

"Now, my merry men," said Robin, "fall to and show our guests the extent of a forester's appetite."

The men required no second bidding; they fell to with a will that soon made sad havoc with the huge joints.

When the servers brought in wine, Little John looked at his chief, a mischievous smile upon his good-humoured face.

"Master," he said, "have we not other vessels save those of horn to set before our guests? if not it were a sin to expect them to enjoy good wine."

"Now I bethink me," Robin answered, "the reserve cups of silver are more befitting the rank of our guests. Go thou, Much, and fetch them hither."

Secretly pleased at this mark of distinction were the Abbot and Sheriff; but when Much returned, laden with the cups Little John and Will Scarlet had brought from the castle, Geoffrey de Lois uttered a cry of rage.

He recognised his property, and ground his teeth in impotent rage, as he saw the grinning Friar Tuck weighing each cup in his hand, as though calculating its worth.

> "The Sheriff was to dinner set,
>   And served with silver white,
> But when his own silver vessels he saw,
>   He could have cried for spite.
> Make glad cheer, said Robin Hood,
>   Sheriff, for charity,
> For this is the way we order our life
>   Under the greenwood tree."

"Come, drink, Sir Sheriff," said Robin, "and do honour to our merry men."

The Sheriff could not answer.

He sat like one who had suddenly seen a ghost, and, although his lips moved nervously, no sound came from them.

"This is but scant courtesy, Sir Sheriff," continued Robin; "nevertheless, I will pledge thee in good red Rhenish wine; and thou, Sir Abbot, will I pledge, and pray ye are both well kept until our next merry meeting."

He drained the silver cup when he ceased speaking, then held it out to be refilled.

"Master," Little John said, "the cause of our guest's silence is soon told."

"Do thou tell it then, knave."

"That will I. The good Sheriff seems to have forgotten he sent thee these cups of silver as a fair greeting of friendship."

"I!" the Sheriff said in amazement, "I send these cups! Tell me, knave, how came they here, since it was but yesterday, at matin hour, I saw them safe in my treasure vault?"

"Sayest thou this?" said Little John. "It is most passing strange, for I brought them to our good master yestere'en."

"Thou, thou broughtest them, thief, cutpurse, robber. How camest thou near the castle?"

"The good abbot there sent me," said Little John, "and bid thy cook tend well so good a son of the Church."

The abbot started, and looked keenly at the forester.

"The knave's voice seems familiar," he thought, "yet I know not where I could have heard it."

"Reverend father," said Little John, using the same words as when he met the abbot and the cellarer outside the gates of Nottingham Castle, "I am but a scullion at heart. Although my limbs are somewhat large, my valour is the smallesr thou hast ever known, for the whizz of an arrow or the sight of a naked sword causes my knees to totter, and my heart to quake. Thus, thou seest, I am but fit to help the noble cook of the Lord Sheriff. The saints be good to him!"

"Ha!" exclaimed the amazed abbot, "the very words used by a serving man whom I met when leaving thy castle, Geoffrey."

"Yes, reverend sir," said Little John, "and the very lips which used them, and the very ears that listened to thee when thou wert pleased to call me a good son of the Church."

"Ho, ho!" laughed the fat friar; "I will burn six candles at the altar of my patron saint for this. Ho, ho! an abbot outwitted by Little John. Ho, ho, ho!"

The abbot was amazed at hearing this; and the Sheriff, seeing there was but little chance of regaining his lost treasure, concealed his vexation as well as he could, and, taking up the full cup which had been placed before him, drank in return to Robin Hood's pledge.

# CHAPTER XXXI.

### HOW THE ABBOT AND THE SHERIFF RODE FROM SHERWOOD FOREST.

Let me go then, said the Sheriff,
    For Saint Charity,
And the best friend ever you had,
    I will be to thee.
Thou shalt swear me an oath, said Robin,
    On my bright brand,
Thou shalt never waylay me for harm,
    By water or by land.
And if thou find any of my men,
    By night or by day,
Upon thine oath thou shalt swear,
    To help them that thou may.

THE wine was of the best, and both the Abbot and the Sheriff failed not to do honour to its goodness, and by the time a few flagons had been emptied, the foresters' tongues became loosened, and more than one heart-stirring song was sung.

The Normans began to thaw in their demeanour towards the foresters, and the abbot so far forgot the humiliation he had suffered, as to address a few civil words to the fat friar, who had by this time paid pretty good court to the juice of the grape, and was quite in a mood either to sing a song or fight a good bout at quarterstaff.

"It is sad," the Abbot said, leaning over towards Friar Tuck, to see thee, holy brother, so forgetful of thy cloth as to appear before thy flock in a state so unseeming for thine office."

"Unseeming," said the friar; "by Our Lady's favour, Sir Abbot, may I ask if the monks of Saint Mary's never get beyond the state thou seemest to think I have but little right to reach?"

The monks of Saint Mary's," said the abbot, "are a holy and zealous brotherhood, who would not taste of the juice of the vine, save in the most extreme case of bodily sickness."

"By the rood then," said the friar, "there must be much of sickness in the abbey, for when my master here——"

"Hush," said the abbot, "believe not the scandal—it is but a lie of thy master's, and one I know so good a priest as thyself wilt not believe."

"But I do," returned Friar Tuck, "and if there be any lies told it is from thy lips, not my master's."

"How now, knave," the abbot said, angrily, "is it thus thou accusest me?"

"Marry, why not?"

"Forgetest thou my rank in the Church?"

"Not I; neither do I care though thou wore all the silver mitres in the world."

The churchman's face flushed, and there would soon have been a quarrel between the pair, had not Robin interfered.

"Tune up thy voice," he said to the friar, "and give us a good stave: it will be better than quarrelling with the abbot."

"By the Rood, thou art right, Robin," said the lusty friar. What wouldst thou have me sing?"

"Give us the 'Maiden and the Knight.'"

"Aye," chorussed the foresters within hearing—"The 'Maiden and the Knight,' friar: it is the best of thy budget."

There was but little bashfulness about the friar: so, without more ado, and in a good mellow voice, he sang the following characteristic song of the age, when religion and chivalrous vows were so strangely blended.

### FRIAR TUCK'S SONG.

"A warrior knelt at the holy shrine,
And he thought of the home he had left behind,
He thought of his love, and he blamed the oath
That called him far from her gentle troth.
' Oh,' he sighed from his inmost heart,
' Light of my bosom, why did we part?'

"A maiden knelt at the sacred tomb,
Her dark hair shrouded her cheeks of bloom,
And she looked on the knight with a wild amaze,
But he turned aside from the stranger's gaze.
Her love lay calm on her breast of woe,
Like moonbeams on the driven snow,
And the wild tear shone in her eyes of light,
Like the first star of a summer's night.

"The warrior knelt at the shrine again,
His faith had dispelled his heart's keen pain,
And he prayed aloud that no Pagan hand
Should again defile the Holy Land.
But a thought of nature gently fell,
To mould a prayer for his Isabel;
' Oh, keep her from all but love's alarms!'
He rose—and his maid was in his arms."

"Well sung, fat priest," said Little John. "Body-o-me, but it would have served the knight according to his deserts had the maiden stayed at home, instead of following her recreant lover to the Holy Land."

"How so, thou mountain of flesh," asked Friar Tuck; "methinks it was but proper the maid should follow her knight. I wot thou wouldst think so were it thy case."

"Body-o-me," said John, "it would never be my case, for I should stay with the maiden I loved in merry England, and leave the Pagans to swallow the Holy Land if they liked."

"Out upon thee," laughed the friar, "for an unblushing knave; come, tune thy pipes and give this company a song."

Little John complied after a few moments reflection, and trolled out the following verse.

In Sherwood lived bold Robin Hood,
    An archer great, none greater,
His bows and shafts were sure and good,
    Yet Cupid's were much better.
Robin could shoot at many a hart and miss;
    Cupid at first could hit a heart of his.
      Then hey, Jolly Robin ho! Jolly Robin.
      Hey ho! hey ho! Jolly Robin.
Love finds out me as well as thee,
So follow, so follow, so follow me,
And sing hey, Jolly Robin, oh! Jolly Robin.

"WHAT HAST THOU DONE?" CRIED ROBIN HOOD.

"Peace, knave," said Robin Hood, "stun not this good company with thy bawling; come, my merry men, let us show our guests some skill in archery."

The foresters arose, and taking their bows went towards the butts, singing the chorus of Little John's song, the giant and Friar Tuck's voices leading the chorus.

"By my faith," said the abbot, as he followed the merry foresters, "thou leadest a happy life here, Robin."

"Aye," answered the Outlaw," we have but little to disturb us; the red deer supplies us with food, and such generous knights as the Sheriff keep us in vessels of gold and silver, and thy high cellarer and others fill our coffers with bright money."

The Sheriff smiled grimly at this allusion to his loss, but he made no remark; his prudence forbade that, and his brain was busy hatching a plan whereby he might recover his lost treasure.

The Normans were astonished at the yeomanry they beheld, for, in a trial of skill between Robin, Little John, and Friar Tuck, three white wands, not thicker than a man's little finger, were set up, and each of these doughty foresters split the mark at the first shot.

Then followed quarter-staff and wrestling; and the lusty Friar, tucking up his long gown, thrashed all who opposed him with the oak staff, and in the wrestling, he threw more than one stalwart forester over his head.

The evening was now coming upon the earth, and the Outlaw Chief led his guests beneath the greenwood tree, and, surrounded by his band, he named the conditions upon which he would release them.

"Thou," he said to the abbot, "must send, by one of thy fat, lazy monks, full two hundred marks in bright money."

"Two hundred marks!" repeated the abbot. "Surely, Robin, thou art joking. Thou oughtest to know full well the poverty of my order."

"Aye, I do, Sir Abbot," laughed the Outlaw. "Nevertheless, if thou dost not pay this sum, I warrant I can keep thee here, and make thee head priest to this worshipful company, and then thou wilt have but our jolly confessor to do battle with for the mastership of the office."

"I will have no other priest here," said Friar Tuck, "unless he can well trounce me with the stout oak staff. If he cannot do this, he will have to be my bondsman, and, if he fails to serve me well, he will be sorry the day ever came that brought him to the world."

"Thou hearest this," said the Outlaw, "and, from what thou hast seen of our curtal friar's arm, methinks it will be better for thee to even melt down the ornaments of the abbey to pay the ransom than abide with us."

"May the saints send a plague upon thee and thy band of cutpurses!" said the abbot angrily; "is it not enough that I have been kept in thy power so long, but thy thievish fingers must want to rob me?"

"Choose thee, Sir Abbot," said Robin; "choose thee between paying the ransom I have fixed and being the bondsman of our fighting confessor."

"Has the power of the Church fallen so low," the abbot said, "that I could be left among this pack of thieves without an arm being raised to effect my rescue?"

"Listen, Sir Abbot," said Robin; "the minions of a foreign court have more than once sought to crush Robin Hood and his merry men; but, while there are good English arms left to draw a bow and clothyard shafts to fit to the string, Robin will be King of Sherwood, and all who may be, like thyself, in his power, will be as far from a rescue as though locked in the deepest dungeons of a Norman castle."

The abbot knew the truth of these words, and with a determination to wring twice the amount of his ransom out of the poor Saxon peasantry, he sullenly agreed to send the money before sundown on the following day.

"I rely upon thy word," said Robin; "but if thou playest me false thou shalt repent of it until thy dying hour. Now, Sir Sheriff,"

he added, "I will liberate thee upon condition that thou wilt never do aught to molest or try and capture any of my merry men."

"I will not interfere with thee or thine," the Sheriff said, "if thou wilt let me free."

"I have had proof of thy knightly word," said Robin, drawing his sword; "swear me an oath by thy knightly vow upon the cross hilt of this good sword."

He held the hilt of the sword towards Geoffrey de Lois as he spoke, and the Sheriff kissed the sword, and swore by his vows never to waylay, or cause to be waylaid for good or for evil, any of Robin's band.

"Thou hast sworn," the Outlaw said; "remember thine oath, or by St. Herman-of-the-Wold! I will forget that thou art more than a common peasant, and will punish thee accordingly."

"Fetch the abbot's palfrey, Much," said Little John, "for it is not meet such proud guests should walk from Sherwood to Nottingham."

The palfrey was brought.

"I seek not any ransom for thee," Robin said to the Sheriff, "for thou hast been generous to us, and we will keep thy cups of silver, and think of the good Norman who for once has been so generous to the Saxon race. Go! I wish thee good speed."

The foresters obeying a signal from Little John, had slowly closed around the group, and when Robin uttered his parting words, some eight or ten stalwart outlaws laid hands upon the abbot and his kinsman, and before either could divine the motive for this sudden movement, they were lifted from the ground and placed astride the palfrey, their faces towards the animal's tail.

A thin cord secured their feet, then the mischief-loving Much cut the palfrey across the flanks with his bow, and caused the frightened brute to dart forward among the trees, as much alarmed by the double burden he bore, as by the roars of laughter from the foresters.

As for Friar Tuck, the tears streamed from his eyes, and he rolled about the greenwood, well-nigh killed by the comical sight.

---

## CHAPTER XXXII.

### THE COMBAT IN SHERWOOD FOREST.

There rides a warrior dark and glim,
Through Sherwood's sylvan glade,
And a battle-axe is held by him,
And keen is its polished blade.
And he is cased from top to toe
In panoply of steel;
From the nodding plume, I trow,
To the spur upon his heel.

THE next day the Outlaw Chief mounted his white steed, and armed with sword and buckler, pricked his way through the forest in the direction of the mill.

He went thus fearlessly in the open daylight and alone, for being of a generous nature, he had no suspicion respecting the Sheriff, who, he believed, having pledged his knightly word, would, as was the usage of the time, scrupulously adhere to the compact he had made, not to interfere with him or his men.

The vast forest was filled with the caroling, sweet-voiced birds, and ever and anon a deer would dart from the thicket, disturbed by the heavy hoof strokes of his horse.

It was a fair scene, such a one as is seldom or never met in England now, for bricks and mortar have taken the place of noble trees, and, where the red deer were wont to assemble, narrow streets have effaced the sylvan spots.

Robin Hood allowed the reins to fall upon his horse's neck, to give free play to the many matters of import that troubled his mind.

First, there was the state of England, which, in consequence of the fickleness of the King, and the absence of his son, then in the Holy Land, had become the prey of a nest of foreign favourites who thronged around the throne of Henry of Winchester.

There had been several meetings among the Saxon landowners—franklins, as they were termed, of the midland counties, to organise a rising, which should overthrow the power of the oppressors.

At these meetings the bold Outlaw had played a prominent part, for the conspirators were anxious to obtain the aid of one who could command such a warlike body of men.

He was pondering over these matters, and wondering when the oppressed people would take heart of grace and make common cause against the enemy, when he was startled by the heavy hoof-strokes of a war-horse, and the ring of the steel ornaments which depended from the animal's frontlet and housings.

The path he was pursuing was only of sufficient width to allow the passage of his horse, and, as it wound in a serpentine direction, he could not see the new comer, although, from the sounds just mentioned, he knew it could be none other than a knight or a free lance caparisoned for war.

The Outlaw gathered up his reins, and loosened his sword in its scabbard, for in those troublesome times no man's life was safe unless he was at all times ready to meet a foe.

Thus it was these precautions were more a matter of habit than any expectation of a coming conflict.

He had not long done this when there came towards him a figure, mounted upon a strong-limbed charger.

The rider was cased from head to foot in armour, and his visor was down, but from between the bars of his helmet Robin caught a glimpse of a pair of dark, restless eyes.

The forester and the knight rode forward until their horses' heads met, before they exchanged a word.

The mailed rider, no doubt confident in his superior arms, deemed the other ought to yield him place in that narrow path.

And Robin, from the long sovereignty he had held over the greenwood, thought it beneath him to yield, although to a man who was armed at all points.

As there was no possible chance of the horsemen passing each other, they were compelled to come to a standstill, the knight glaring upon the forester, and Robin no wise dismayed, scanning the noble proportions of the stranger's steed.

"How now, knave," the knight demanded, "is not the forest wide enough for thee that thou must come by the very path I have chosen?"

"By Saint Herman!" said Robin, laughingly, "I might ask the same question of thee, for thou hast come by a path I have chosen to follow."

The knight, as though disdaining further argument, put forth his hand to where his battle-axe hung by its leathern loop from the saddle.

"Rein thy steed back," he said, haughtily, "or by my valour I will cleave the brute's skull in twain with this axe."

"Far better," Robin said, "to cleave the rider's skull; go to, is it thus a knight makes war upon horses, not men?"

"Saint Christopher look down upon me," said the knight, angrily, "is it thus I am to be mocked by a mere churl?"

"Churl back to thy teeth," retorted Robin, "if my lineage is not better than thine, may the foul fiend claim me for his own! Rein thy steed back, Sir Knight, or by Saint Herman I will find a joint in thine armour for the point of my good sword to enter."

The knight made no reply to this, but, snatching his axe from the pommel of the saddle, he waved the heavy weapon above his head.

"Have at thee, then," Robin said, as he drew his sword, and slipped the loops of his steel buckler over his arm; "have at thee!"

There were a few blows exchanged in the narrow path, and the knight's war-horse, urged forward by his rider's spurs, slowly forced the fleeter animal Robin bestrode to fall back until they reached the open glade.

Here the combat was continued for some time, the well-trained horses wheeling about like falcons in the air under the impulse of their riders' hands.

The blows delivered by the knight were borne on Robin's steel buckler, and Robin's sword-strokes were bravely parried by the handle of the battle-axe.

Thus they fought for some time; the Outlaw, by the swift movements of his steed, making up for the other's superior arms.

A fierce blow, delivered by the knight at Robin's head, was caught upon the Outlaw's shield, but, so great was the power with which it fell, that the buckler was split in two.

The knight, exulting in his opponent's disaster, raised himself in the stirrups, and was about to repeat the stroke, when Robin, by a swift circular cut, severed the plaited handle of the trenchant battle-axe.

The knight felt for his sword, but, ere he could unsheath it, the Outlaw spurred forward, and, with the remains of the steel buckler, knocked the knight from his saddle.

The dismounted warrior was upon his feet in an instant, and his naked blade flashed in the sunlight as he rushed to meet the bold forester, who had dismounted when he heard the clatter of armour which announced the fall of the doughty knight.

Foot to foot they fought; but now the fight was in Robin Hood's favour, for his adversary, encumbered with heavy armour, could not move with the swiftness of his skilful foe.

The knight's long spurs, catching in the uncovered portion of the root of a gigantic tree, at the moment Robin Hood was pressing him very hard, caused him to stagger and partly unclose the grip of his sword.

In a second the weapon was wrenched from his hand, and went upward among the branches of the tree with such force that a perfect shower of leaves descended.

Following this advantage, the Outlaw, with a spring like an angry panther, seized his adversary by the throat, and, dropping his sword, drew his anlace, and, placing the point between the bars of the knight's helmet, he said :

"Yield! or look thy last upon the blessed sun!"

"I yield," answered the knight, and feel no shame at being vanquished by one so skilled in arms; who art thou, good fellow?"

"Unloose thy helmet," said Robin, "that I may see thy face ere I answer thy request."

The warrior did as he was requested, and Robin saw with much astonishment the fair handsome face of a young man, who could not have numbered more than twenty summers since he came into the world.

The youth smiled at the Outlaw's astonishment.

"So young!" Robin said, "yet so stout a man-at-arms! Well, Sir Knight, my name is Robin Hood. Hast thou one that can be as boldly spoken?"

It was now the knight's turn to be surprised, and he sprang forward and seizing the forester's hand, exclaimed :

"Robin Hood! Foul fall my hand for this day's work, and thanks to Our Lady of Saint Clothilde, my battle-axe has worked thee no harm ; it was thee I was seeking when we met in yon narrow path."

"Thou hast not told me thy name, Sir Knight," the forester said, releasing his hand from the other's grasp; "when I hear that I may fathom thy purpose in seeking me."

"My name, Sir Outlaw," the young knight said, "is Walter Henwulf. Hast thine ears ever heard it before ?"

"Full oft," said Robin; "has not the minstrel tuned his harp to thy praise, and the palmer returning from the Holy Land spoken of thy deeds ?"

Walter coloured to the eyes, for he was as modest as he was brave.

"I do not deserve this praise," he replied; "for my arm has done no more in defence of the Holy Sepulchre than many a man-at-arms."

"Thou wrongest thyself," said Robin; "for the deeds of the gallant Saxon knight are known far and wide, and those who sang them were always sure of a reward, for it has been so much the fashion of late to praise only Norman names and Norman arms, that it came pleasant to Saxon ears to hear some of their oppressed race had equalled the Normans in deeds of arms; but a truce to this, what was thy purpose in coming hither ?"

"To bring thee a message, good Robin ; a message from one who was once thy foe, but now thy friend."

"I have had many such. What is the name of him who has sent such a brave messenger ?"

"My cousin Roger, Earl of Mortimer."

"Ha! has harm befallen the noble earl ?"

"Alas! yes. In a council of state where there were none but Henry of Winchester's foreign favourites, Mortimer spoke up boldly for the people, who are every day becoming less, though human beings, by the crowd, who have come from Normandy, to portion and parcel out our fair realm."

"I am glad," Robin said, interrupting the knight, "to hear Earl Mortimer's stay under the greenwood trees has been of such good; sorry he has incurred the anger of the weak and vindictive King; but tell me what fruit bore the planting of this same tree in the midst of such a goodly assembly."

"Thou shalt hear," said the knight. "There was no mention made by the treacherous King of the offence he had given, but when Mortimer had gone to bed his room was filled with the King's myrmidons, who made him don his mail, and when this was done they left London, and took the road to Nottingham, and the leader of the party had a sealed letter for the Sheriff."

"By Saint Herman," said Robin, "this bodes no good for Mortimer; I know the Sheriff well; he would carry out any order of the King's. Have they lodged Mortimer in the castle yet?"

"About an hour since, for I followed them from London, and had I been in time, I should have tried a rescue."

"Thy single arm would have done but little, yet the motive that prompted thee was good."

"I wish to the saints," the young knight said, "I had had but the opportunity; I would have tried the weight of my battle-axe upon the knaves' skulls.

The Outlaw made no reply, he was thinking over the best plan to aid the Earl.

"It is a pity," he said at last, "that I knew not of thy coming; then a score of clothyard shafts would have relieved him. But it matters not; I would rescue him if we have to take Nottingham Castle down stone by stone."

"Generous, noble Outlaw," said the young knight, "sad it is to see one so good as thyself compelled to hide in a forest because of the cruelty of those who rule with iron hand over our hand."

"Nay, Sir Knight," laughed Robin, "be not sorry upon my account, for the life I lead is far easier and merrier than is led by those at court or camp. Come to horse, and I will show thee my band."

They mounted, and the knight sheathed his sword, which Robin handed to him.

Tracing the silent depths of the forest as amicable friends, as they had been but a few minutes before fierce enemies, the Outlaw asked more particulars of the Earl's arrest.

"How knowest thou," he asked, "the letter was given to the leader of the Norman myrmidons if thou wert so far behind the escort?"

"From my page," answered the knight. "I had sent him to the Earl's lodging, and he saw the whole of the affair."

"Is thy page handsome?"

"He is particularly so: fair of face, and with sunny locks such as many a lady has ...ried."

"So much the better; where is he now?"

"I left him near the castle, to glean what news he could from the loitering men-at-arms."

Robin smiled. He had thought of a plan by which he could communicate with the Earl, unless he was kept a close prisoner.

"By Saint Herman!" he said, "we shall yet outwit the Norman knaves. Ha, here, Sir Knight, is my band; what think ye of them?"

They had suddenly emerged from a thickly-wooded portion of the forest into a glade where the foresters had assembled.

"A lusty band, truly," said the knight, in undisguised admiration. "Report has not belied thy fame, Robin."

"It is a miracle, then," said the Outlaw, dismounting, and motioning for one of the foresters to take the knight's horse, "a wondrous miracle, for report is a common liar."

"It is so," said the knight, "but in this instance it has spoken truly."

"Come hither, Much." Robin said, "thou art fleet of foot; hie thee to thy fair cousin, and bid her for Our Lady's love, send by thee a kirtle and all garments befitting a maiden to wear."

"Body-o'-me!" said the grinning Little John, "heard ye that, friar? Our master is about to forsake the Lincoln green for maiden's garb. Ho! ho! ho!"

The fat friar and Little John were well matched; both were full of quiet humour, both were troubled with thirsty throats, and both could stand a bout at quarter-staff with any three of the band, Robin Hood and Allan-a-dale excepted.

"Thou'rt jealous, thou fat ox," said the friar, "because thy body would not go inside anything less than twenty yards of cloth."

"Thou barrel with arms and legs," retorted John, "thinkest thou thy paunch would go in less than a—a murrain on the knave, what's that?"

One of the foresters who was trying the strength of a new bow a few yards behind the friar, bent it until the ends met.

The wood was dry, and when thus doubled it split, and one half flew from the man's grasp and struck the fat friar on the shaven crown.

He jumped to his feet, and gathering up his gown started in pursuit of the forester who, as soon as he was aware of the mischief he had done, took to his heels.

"Ho, ho! Body-o'-me!" roared Little John, "Well done, Will; use thy legs, friar—ho, ho! trounce the knave, I saw him hit thee on purpose."

The latter portion of his speech, as may be supposed, was uttered when the Friar, in spite of his obesity, caught the luckless Will by the collar, and began to shake him.

The forester resented this attack by belabouring his priestly assailant with the broken half of the bow.

The young Knight, in spite of his trouble, could not help joining in the uproarious mirth.

"Come, Sir Priest," said Robin, "thou wilt be put down by our friend as but an ungodly son of the Church. I'm sure thy patron saint never used his fists as thou hast done."

"My patron saint," answered the friar,

rubbing the bruise upon his skull, " never had his saintly temper tried as that knave has tried mine. Relics of St. Anthony! but my pate feels as though I had been used for a battering-ram."

"Ho, ho, ho!" laughed Little John. "Friar, the bruise on thy skull does not match thy nose."

"How so, thou grinning thief?"

"Because, thy nose is red and the bruise on thy skull is blue."

"I'll give thee one to match."

The friar snatched a quarter-staff from a heap of these weapons and made a rush at John, who nimbly stepped back, and putting out his foot, upset the priest, and his nose coming in contact with the staff, caused a crimson stream to make its appearance.

"Paint thy skull with it," said Little John, as he took to his heels to escape his companion's threats. "Paint thy pate, fat priest, and it will match thy snout."

The friar gave chase, but Little John had obtained a good start, and after he had led the fighting priest thrice around the glade, he stopped.

"A truce," he said, as the friar, panting and out of breath, came towards him, " a truce, valiant friar, and we'll drain a cup of Rhenish to thy reverence."

Next to fighting Friar Tuck loved drinking, therefore, under the circumstances, as John had cried a truce, he set down the staff.

"A cup of Rhenish," he said, "after that race, to say nothing of the bodily injuries I have received, will not be amiss. Send for it good John, and mayhap our master here will send for another to pledge this comely knight and our sweet self."

"Hie thee to our stores," Robin said laughing; "hie thee, Will Scarlet, but have a care lest thou art tempted to touch the liquor."

"Not a drop, master," said Will; "unless, mayhap, the tankards may be filled too near the brim, then it would be unfair for me to spill such good liquor in the carrying."

"Now Much, haste to thy fair cousin," Robin said, "and give her the message thou knowest of, unless the bawling of these knaves has driven it from thy head."

"Not a word have I lost," said Much; "thy message shall be taken, and that part thou hast forgotten."

"Go to, knave, go to."

Will Scarlet came up at this moment, and by the appearance of the measures, the sewer had either not well filled them, or Will had prevented the loss in carrying.

"A malison on thy thirsty throat," said John, as he looked into the tankard. I believe thou wouldst swill at any hour of the day."

"Plague take thee," said the Friar, when he looked into the measure Will gave him; "were it not that my words would be useless with such an unbelieving knave, I would excommunicate thee with bell, book, and candle. As John says, thou wouldst indeed swill at any hour. A shame upon thee, I say."

"I drink to thy reverence," said Little John; also to thee, good Knight, and to my master here; I also drink to Little John, the best yeomen here present."

"I drink to thee in return," said the Friar; "I also drink to our master, bold Robin, and the comely Knight, and better than all, I drink to the saintly Friar Tuck, a true and good son of the Church, who may St. Anthony keep from harm."

The tankards went up to their mouths, and when they left there was not a drop in them.

There was a roar of laughter as the Friar and John looked comically into the measures, then at each other.

"Body-o'-me!" said the giant, "thou hast a swallow!"

"A swallow!" retorted the priest; "by the relics of my patron saint, that were but a draught for a fly! I scarcely felt it."

"By St. Hubert!" said John, "a drop of water on the dry sands of a desert would be as much good as that draught to my thirst! Out upon thee thou thief, or I will crack thy skull with this measure."

Will Scarlet retreated.

"Come hither, George-a-Green," said Robin; thou art fleet of foot, hie thee towards Nottingham Castle, and bring with thee a page thou wilt find there."

"Stay, good forester," said the Knight, "and I will give thee a description of the boy. He is slight of build and garbed in green velvet; thou wilt further know him by his long, fair locks, which hang far below his shoulders; haste thee, and a silver mark shall be thy reward."

The forester left, and Robin, with the handsome knight, seated themselves beneath the trysting tree and began to converse of matters which drew their attention from the somewhat rough practical joking of the merry foresters.

They were disturbed in their conversation by the sound of a bugle.

"From Nottingham side," Robin said; "ah! the abbot's ransom!"

Robin's surmise was correct, for a fat and jolly monk, whom he recognised as having been at the debauch in the refectory, made his appearance, between two of the foresters who had been out on sentry.

"Greet the all," said the monk; "which of this good company is bold Robin Hood?"

"I am he," said Friar Tuck gravely; "deny it not, Sir Priest, or I'll flay thy hide!"

THE COMBAT IN THE FOREST.

ALLAN-A-DALE IN THE COURT-YARD OF NOTTINGHAM CASTLE.

"Thou!" said the monk; "then Robin is a show for men to laugh at! I had always heard of him as being comely, and thou art far from being——"

"Reach me that staff, John," said Friar Tuck; "Relics of St Anthony! but I will teach this fellow a due respect for—— knowest thou who I am, Father Glib-of-Tongue?"

"Aye, right well, a lusty thief art thou, who——"

"Ashes of the d——, I mean St. Anthony, that staff, I say, John——"

"Peace!" said Robin, coming forward. I am he thou seekest."

"Ah!" muttered the priest; "the very knave who brought such scandal upon our order. So thou art bold Robin?"

"I am Robin Hood of Sherwood,"

"Right gladly do I greet thee," said the priest; and right glad am I to bear a loving message from my master."

"Unless I mistake much," thought Robin, "this fair speech is all this shaven rascal has brought! then he added, "the Lord Abbot's message, holy father, I listen."

"He greets thee well," said the priest; "and bids me say the money due from him to thee surpasses his power to pay; but he will, when the tithes are gathered, send thee it in full, with a fair and just interest for the time thou hast to wait."

"When are these tithes due, holy father?"

"To-morrow at noon," said the unsuspicious priest; "at that hour two of the brethren will go forth and collect them."

"And thy master will pay me then?"

"On the noon of the day following, good Robin, for it will take until nightfall for our brethren to collect them."

"Be it so. I will wait until the time thou namest, but mark me, not one hour later. Conduct this holy man to the confines of the forest."

"Friar," whispered John to Friar Tuck, "what think ye of waylayiug these priests, and taking the tithes?"

"A goodly notion," grinned the priest, "I am with thee, John, and we will baste their hides into the bargain, for I love to thrash a fat monk, John."

"It's a miracle, then," cried Little John, "thou dost not thrash thyself full often."

"I do, John, for do not the rules of my order enjoin scourging, fasting and severe mortification of spirit?"

"Aye," answered the forester; but dost thou keep to these rules?"

"Ask thyself; last Friday was a day of penitence——"

"Thou knave, I found thee drunk in the ash-grove that very night, and had to carry thee to thy bed!"

"Hear the heathen!" said the friar, lifting his eyes piously upwards; "thou thief, I was overcome with the severe scourging I had given my poor body when you found me."

"Body of St. Hubert!" exclaimed John; "did I not find three black bottles—each had held a quart, I'll warrant?"

"A quart of water, John, for I filled them myself from the well."

"Thou lying hypocrite! I put them to my nose, and they had the true aroma of the wine which they say comes from beyond the Rhine! Out upon thee for a hypocrite! out upon thee, I say?"

"Aye," retorted Friar Tuck, "out upon thee, I say; for hadst thou thought the bottles yet held water, thou wouldst not have stopped to have picked them up."

Little John laughed; the friar had spoken the truth, for John had fully expected to have found something worth drinking in one out of the three, and so great was his disappointment that he bumped the friar's head against the branches of the trees, as he bore the saintly man to his hut in the forest.

Next morning, when the friar awoke he had a splitting headache, which he attributed to the strength of the wine, instead of the raps his skull had received, when he lay like a log across Little John's shoulders.

"It would have required a very strong wine to have affected either Little John or Friar Tuck's brain, for they were the hardest drinkers in the band, and there were many who could boast of doughty deeds in this respect, for in those days a man who could drink well was esteemed much sober self-denying man.

## CHAPTER XXXIII.

### THE FAIR PAGE.

Robin set his horn to his mouth,
  And blew a blast full good,
That was heard by all his merry men,
  Far down within the wood.
I hear my master, said Little John
  And they ran as they were mad.

WHEN George-a-Green returned he was accompanied by the knight's page, a youth of such handsome features and small limbs that it was hard at first to believe that he was of the sterner sex.

"Well, boy," Robin said, "art thou disposed to serve thy master in all things?"

"To the death," the page answered, "If he needs it; for my life is Walter Hanwulf's."

"The saints forefend," Robin said, "that we should need such a proof of thy devotion. All we shall require will be a ready tongue, a bold heart, and watchful eye."

"For the first of these the boy said, "I can warrant I possess, or I would not have so often been termed malapert; for the second it behoves me not to speak; and for the last, I have eyes that fail not to notice all things that may pass before them."

"I will speak for the boldness of his heart," said the young knight; for he has followed me through the Paynim's ranks, and many a haughty Moslem crest has been brought to the dust by yon stripling's hand."

"It needeth not thy word, Sir Knight," Robin said, "to speak of this, for there is written in the boy's fearless eye that which tells he will make a name where doughty deeds and strong arms are needed.

The boy blushed at these words.

"Dost thou fear," Robin said, "to enter the castle outside of which thou hast been watching?"

"I fear not to do so, Sir Forester; but I wot there will be little good come of it, for I have been well marked by the crossbowmen on the towers—so well that every knave, I'll warrant, knows the escutcheon embroidered upon my breast as well as they know their greasy buff jerkins."

"This will matter but little," the Outlaw said, "if thou goest as I wish. What thinkest thou of wearing a hood and kirtle?"

"To dress as a maiden, Sir Outlaw?"

"Aye, boy," a skirt and thy fair face will be a passport to the inside of Nottingham Castle."

"I am willing, Sir Outlaw, but the saints preserve me, how am I to answer the Sheriff should he address me in the words of love?"

"Thy readiness of speech must carry thee out of that," Robin said; "thinkest thou it can?"

"It will go hard with me if it does not."

"Aye," laughed the young knight, "thy tongue will have altered strangely if it has forgotten to help thee from greater difficulties than this."

"It has not forgotten," said the boy. "So my master be not afraid of losing thy page because his tongue has lost its cunning. Now, Sir Forester, what plan am I to follow?"

"But a simple one, boy," Robin answered. "I will lend thee a palfrey, and one of my merry men shall attend thee as thy servant; and when the evening shadows come upon the earth, hie thee to the castle. Tell the warder thou hast lost thy way, he will admit thee; then thou must try and find out what are the contents of the sealed letter the man-at-arms brought from London with the earl. Whilst thou art doing this, the man will find out the chamber where the earl is confined."

"So far," the boy said, "thy plan is of promise; but concerning my leaving the castle, that has not been mentioned."

"Thou wilt leave to-morrow at matin song, and hie to the greenwood with all thou mayest have learnt."

"Aye," said the page, "if this Sheriff, who, I am told, likes well a comely face, will let me depart."

"If thou art not back by the noon-time, thy safety shall be my care."

"Sufficient," said the page. "I am ready to do thy bidding. Where shall I find the kirtle and hood of which thou just now spoke."

"It will be here anon," Robin said. "Until then, go with this holy friar; he will not only confess thee, but will find a choice nook of venison pasty and a goblet of wine to cheer thy heart."

"Of which dost thou stand most in need," Friar Tuck gravely asked, "the cup of wine and nook of pasty, or the ghostly comfort which mine office permits me to give to such as are weary of heart?"

"Of which of these things dost thou most practise thyself, holy father?"

"Meanest thou the ghostly comfort and the good things of this life?"

"I do, reverend father."

"The ghostly comfort, fasting penalties, and scourgings imposed upon mine order I pass my life in; yea, I do these things every hour."

"Thou mayest do so," the page said, "but I, being fonder of the good things of this life, prefer a cup of Rhenish and a nook of pasty before the rigours of thine order."

"Such is the thought of the giddy world," Friar Tuck said, lifting up his hand in pious zeal. "Oh! that it should be so."

They reached a secluded part of the forest, and seating themselves at the base of a large tree, awaited the coming of the man whom the friar had sent for the refreshments.

He soon returned, and, much to Friar Tuck's inward disgust, brought only a small goblet of wine with him.

"This fair youth," said the friar, "is sorely athirst, hie thee back, good forester, and bring another measure of this good liquor."

"Nay," said the page, "this will be more than sufficient for me."

"Thou art wrong, boy," said the fat friar, hurriedly; "thou wilt suffer the thirst of all who eat of venison pasty. It is for thy good I speak."

"Very well, bring the wine, good forester."

Friar Tuck's mouth watered when he saw the boy sipping the rich juice, and he was cudgelling his brain to invent an excuse to taste the contents of the goblet.

This did not take him long.

"Fair youth," he said, "is that wine of the best, for these foresters have a knack of bringing wine which is not fit for such lips as thine?"

"It is of good strength and sweet flavour, reverend father."

"Ah, sweet flavour, I could have sworn it. Reach me the goblet, I will soon tell thee whether it is the wine I spoke of."

The boy handed him the cup; and to his surprise the friar emptied it at a draught.

"As I thought," he said, "a plague upon the knaves, they would have poisoned thee. The saints be praised, I am doomed to suffer penalties; thus the drinking of this wine will do me no harm."

"Thanks, reverend father," the page said, laughing, for he began to suspect the true character of the friar; "I hope the flagon I see yon knave drinking from behind the tree is not of the vintage I——"

"Drinking! the knave tasting before he brings thee the cup!" exclaimed the friar. "Ashes of all the saints, but I will stop this scandal."

The priest ran towards the tree, his sandals making so little noise that he came upon the forester in the very act of tasting the contents of the cup.

"How now, thou knave," he said, "is thy thirst of more consequence than our good name for hospitality?"

The man was so astonished that he could not move until the friar snatched the tankard from his hand.

Then as though to avoid a thrashing, he took to his heels and bolted.

The friar looked into the tankard, which was nearly three-parts full.

"It is of the same vintage as the last," he muttered; "it will not do for this fair youth to drink too much; therefore I must, in spite of all pains of the colic, drink a little of it."

He did drink until there was but only sufficient to cover the bottom of the measure.

This he took to Sir Walter's page.

"This ungodly knave," he said, "has left thee but little of the good liquor; had I not been fleet of foot there would not have been even this left."

"Thanks, reverend father, it is enough."

When the page had refreshed himself he wandered about the forest, and conversed with many of the archers.

He found the sentence of outlawry which was out against them caused their minds but little trouble.

He saw but little of his master during the day, for Sir Walter and Robin Hood were busy in the forest hut laying out plans for a general rising throughout the midland counties to throw off the Norman yoke.

When the sun began to disappear beyond the trees the handsome page was apparelled in feminine garb, and, mounted upon a pillion, left the forest, attended by Allan-a-Dale, who was dressed as a serving man.

Robin Hood and the Knight followed them; but before they left the Outlaw Chief gave orders to Little John to bring twenty men and await his return in a wood near the town of Nottingham.

"John," said the fat friar, "my vows prevent me using weapons of steel; but as nothing has been said about a monk amusing himself by shooting arrows, I will go with thee, and should I feel in the mood to shoot, surely I am not responsible if my arrows are cleaving the air, aud a Norman knave's body runs against a clothyard shaft."

"Of a surety thou art not," said Little John, "for thy bow is not meant to kill; it is thy pleasure to send a few arrows through the air, and if, as thou sayest, a Norman carcase stops thy shaft, the blame is to the Norman, not to thee."

"My mind is at ease now, John, for thou knowest I would not do aught to bring disrepute upon my cloth."

"Out upon thee," said John, "for a lusty hypocrite!"

"The words of the scoffer," said Friar Tuck, meekly, "injure not the followers of so good a patron saint as mine."

Robin Hood and Walter Hanwulf had seen the page and Allan challenge the warder, and, after a brief parley, they were both admitted.

The Forester and the Knight had been so intensely watching the page that they saw not the approach of the Sheriff and about twenty men-at-arms.

They had been chasing the deer, for a noble buck was being carried to the castle across a strong horse's back.

The Outlaw and his companion were about to move forward and address the Sheriff, but the latter forestalled them by riding forward.

"A fair day, Robin," he said, and a look of intelligence passed between him and the leader of the men-at-arms; "I greet thee well, and would ask what has brought thee from thy forest?"

"But of little harm, Sir Sheriff," the Outlaw answered; "this knight, who has but lately returned from the Holy Land, took refuge with me yester-e'en, and to-day he could not leave without looking at the Castle of fair Nottingham."

The Sheriff sent a searching look upon the knight's features, but failed to glean any intelligence from the quiet, handsome face.

"Would thy guest," the Sheriff said, "deign to accompany me, he could then see the inside of the place which has so attracted his attention."

"I would gladly do so, Sir Sheriff," the Knight said, bowing; "but an oath I have taken prevents me from entering cottage or castle until I find a maiden who has been lost to me."

Robin Hood had noticed the look of intelligence which had passed between the Sheriff and his chief man-at-arms; and he saw that during the preceding conversation the men had gradually closed around the knight and his companions, and now seemed as though awaiting the signal to fall upon them.

The forester affected not to see this treacherous movement, but he was on his guard, and, as though by mere chance, his right hand toyed with the silver tassel of his bugle.

"Well, Sir Knight," the Sheriff said, "I will not press thee to break thy vow—perchance thou mayest pass fair Nottingham again; then shall I be right well pleased to offer thee such hospitality as befits my station and thy rank."

"Gramercy, Sir Sheriff, for thy kindness!" said the Knight; "I shall not forget."

The Sheriff turned to Robin, and a gleam of malice shone in his eyes.

"I would ask thee to share my hospitality," he said, "for I owe thee many thanks for the good cheer thou gavest me, and the high honour in which thou sawest fit to send me from thy domain; but it would not be meet for an officer so high in the King's favour to ask an outlaw to his castle; but for this, Robin, I would show my courtesy for thy kindness."

"Gramercy," laughed Robin; "how can I

xpress myself at such high honours being conferred upon me?"

"Although I cannot ask thee," the Sheriff said; "yet thou canst accompany us to the castle; my men here can take thee prisoner, and if thou makest thy escape after it will not be known that I had such friendly feelings towards thee."

"By St. Herman of the Wold," said Robin, "there is more in thy speech than its seeming fairness."

"Nay, Robin," said Geoffrey, "thou urgest me, and to prove this I will take thee to the castle, whether thou wilt or not."

He made a sign to his men as he spoke, and they attempted to close around the Outlaw.

Like a flash of lightning, Sir Walter Hanwulf's sword leapt from its sheath as he saw the treacherous Sheriff's intention, and with a ringing clash the blades of the pair met.

Sir Walter was an excellent swordsman but the Sheriff of Nottingham was a match for him.

By a dexterous movement the Sheriff wrenched the sword from the knight's hand, and with a quick blow stretched him on the sward beside his broken weapon.

"What hast thou done?" cried Robin Hood in anger, pointing at the same time to the apparently lifeless form.

"A favour I would fain have the honour of doing thee," answered the Sheriff sarcastically.

"Marry! and I am not dead yet," said the Knight, recovering from the stunning effect of the blow. "A malison on thee, thou knave of the blackest dye!"

The Sheriff gazed upon him in direst hate.

Seeing that the Knight was endeavouring, feebly, to rise from the ground, he raised his arm to strike him another blow. Quick as lightning Robin Hood turned aside the descending blade, and with a laugh of defiance he assisted the Knight to his feet.

"Upon them, knaves," said Geoffrey de Lois, throwing off all concealment; "ten marks for the man who takes the Outlaw, and five for him who takes his companion."

"Not so fast, my masters," said Robin. "Unless thou art tired of life, keep out of reach of this blade, or that held by my friend, this comely knight."

The reward was worth obtaining, and the men-at-arms closed upon the gallant pair, but before a blow could be struck the Outlaw placed his bugle to his lips and blew a loud blast.

## CHAPTER XXXIV.

### THE LADY ELFRIDA AND HER SERVING MAN.

The first loud blast that he did blow,
He blew both loud and shrill;
And Little John and Robin's men
Came running o'er the hill.

"BODY-O'-ME!" said Little John, stopping short in an argument with the curtal friar. "dost thou hear that?"

"Aye," answered the priest, tucking up his gown, "it's our master's horn, and tells he needs our help."

"Follow me," said John, "string your bows, ye knaves, as ye run, and hark'ee, the man who is last will I thwack with as good a staff as ever grew on tree."

The foresters rushed from their covert, headed by the fat friar and Little John, and when they came in sight of their chief, a most unsaintly oath came from the friar's lips.

He soon outstripped even Little John, and before they had reached the men-at-arms, who were by this time pressing hard upon the Knight and Robin, the friar's quarter-staff could be heard ringing upon the soldiers' morions.

"Bones of the blessed Clothilde!" cried the friar, "I will absolve thee—aye, even without confession."

The advent of the fighting friar and Little John's men had put quite a different complexion upon the affair, and the Sheriff, spurring his horse forward, made for the castle, followed by his men, and in such haste were they, that the horse with the fat buck across his back, fell into the foresters' hands.

Then they looked east, then they looked west,
For their eyes they were so keen;
But the Sheriff and his company,
Were no longer to be seen.

Foaming with rage at the failure of his plan, the Sheriff returned to Nottingham Castle.

He was met at the gate by Berthold, who, upon seeing his master's angry face, hung back.

"Well, sirrah," the Sheriff said, "what ails thee, that thou retreatest as though it was a sight to cause thee fear?"

"I crave thy pardon, good master," the man said. "I felt afraid lest I had done wrong during thine absence."

"What hast thou done?"

"Admitted strangers to the castle, good master."

"Ha, by my halidome! but thou shalt suffer——"

"I crave thy——"

"Silence, sirrah; did I not tell thee none were to cross the drawbridge since our prisoner came here?"

"Thou didst, master, but I thought there could be but little harm in giving shelter to a lady and her serving man."

"A lady! is she fair?"

"Of wondrous fairness, good master."

"Her serving man, where is he?"

"In the kitchen, for he is but a Saxon knave, whose breeding is not fit to permit him to sit with thy men-at-arms."

"Send for him hither."

One of the soldiers went for Allan-a-Dale, who approached the Sheriff in a shambling, loutish manner, and stared vacantly about him.

"Well knave, what brought the here?" the Sheriff said. "Answer me, and doff thy cap."

Allan looked more stupid than ever, and dragging his cap off revealed an unkempt mass of red hair.

"My horse brought me here, an' please your worship," he said; "how came you here?"

"That's not thy affair, fool," said the Sheriff, "so mind thy speech."

"Aye," Allan said, "that's the way; mind thy speech. What does your worship ask me?"

"Hold thy tongue."

"Aye, hold thy tongue, mind thy speech——"

"Fool!"

"Aye, fool. Well, my master, I wot I am a fool, or I would not, even for the love of my dear lady, have come here."

"Thy lady, who is she, knave?"

Allan grinned, fumbled with his cap, and put on such a loutish appearance, that the Sheriff could scarcely refrain from laughing.

"My lady?" he simpered; "that I must not tell thee, for she wants not to be known, and she gave me a silver mark not to tell."

"I will give thee two. So come, tell me."

"Not before all these men-at-arms?"

"Thou art right; to the ramparts, knaves, and keep good watch, lest the Earl of Mortimer's friends attempt a rescue."

The men-at-arms retired.

"Now, knave," the Sheriff said; "here are two marks."

Allan pouched the silver pieces, and the idiotic grin upon his face deepened.

"Good master," he said, "thou wilt not tell the lady what I tell thee, for she is quick of temper, and the whip she carries would soon be placed across my back."

"Not a word, by my knighthood."

"Thy word is given, and I know the Norman knights when they swear by this will be true."

"Come, sirrah; thou art wasting time."

"I had forgotten, good master, that thy race are so impatient; now the Saxon lords and franklins are not so quick of blood——"

"A murrain upon thee and the Saxon dogs! Speak only of thy lady, and tell why she has sought the shelter of Nottingham Castle?"

"For two reasons, worshipful sir, which, if thou wilt have patience, thou mayest hear."

"Patience! by my knighthood, thou wouldst try the patience of the blessed St. Ursula."

"Aye, like fire these Norman knights——"

"Wilt thou speak, fool?"

"I am speaking, good master, as fast as my tongue will wag."

"It will not wag much longer, if thou dost not mend thy speech. Come, of what quality is thy lady?"

"Of what quality, Sir Knight? she is of the purest Saxon blood; although she bid me, if I were asked, say she was but the daughter of a franklin."

"Ah! why this wish to conceal her real state? Dost thou know that?"

"But in part, good master; but in part."

"What is the part thou knowest?"

"I will tell thee; but mind thou must not repeat one word to my lady, for she is quick of temper; and once I can swear when a Knight Templar did utter words of love in her ears, she slit his face with her dagger."

"She must be a haughty dame."

"Thou mayest well say that——"

"To thy promise. Come, tell me all thou knowest."

"It is not much, but thou art welcome to it——"

"A malison upon the fool! am I to hear——"

"Good master, thou dost not give me time; for when the words come to my tongue thy fierce look frightens them away again."

"There, good fellow, I will be of more gentle speech."

"Gramercy for this, for thy looks and words have made me as hot as though I were basting the side of a bullock before the fire."

"I have told thee I will not do this more; now, here is another mark for thee, for thou art a good fellow."

"Eh, I will now tell thee all I know, Sir Knight; for thou art indeed a good and generous noble."

"I listen, good fellow."

"Well, Sir Knight, you must know my lady, the Lady Elfrida——"

"The Lady Elfrida! yes, good knave."

"The Lady Elfrida is betrothed to a young knight, who has but just come from the Holy Land."

"Ha! But proceed with thy story."

"But she likes him not; for, truth to tell, my lady has more favour for the Norman knights than the highest of the Saxon nobles."

"By the Saints," said the Sheriff, "she has good taste, this lady of thine."

"Of that I wot not; although, truth to tell, there is more of grace in these knights of Normandy than in the best of our Saxon nobles."

"Thou art right; to thy story, good fellow."

"Thou must know, Sir Knight, this

THE SHERIFF'S DISCOMFITURE.

Crusader, when he came from doing battle for the Sepulchre, wished to wed my lady, and he sent a messenger to speak of his coming."

"I listen."

"My lady," Allan continued, " heard the man's words; then last night, after all had gone to their chambers, she came to me and bid me saddle her palfrey and my own brown horse. I did this, Sir Knight, and, since the moon was in its full, have we been in the saddle, and stayed not to eat, drink, or rest until your warder courteously gave us admittance to thy castle."

"Return to the kitchen, good knave, and make merry, and if thy lady is as fair as I have heard, thou mayest stay here some weeks."

"Fair!" the serving man repeated, "by the soul of Alfred, she is fairer than a carle's lips like mine could find words to tell."

"It is not fit thy tongue should wag of this matter. Hie thee to the kitchen; I will see with mine own eyes this lady of such great loveliness."

Allan-a-Dale shambled towards the servants' portion of the castle. When his back was turned towards the Sheriff, he stuck his tongue in his cheek.

"By the mass," he thought, "I know not how to keep from laughing outright at the Norman knave. Well, so far all has gone well. Now to find the chamber where the earl is kept."

When the Sheriff left the courtyard, Allan,

in place of continuing his way towards the kitchen, turned suddenly and went towards the keep.

"If I am stopped by any knave," he thought, "I shall have but to say I have lost my way."

He shambled up a flight of stone stairs, and found himself in a corridor, from which there opened a number of doors.

"Vastly like prisons," thought Allan. "Ah! here comes a knave who will spoil my travels. I will hide."

One of the recesses enabled the forester to escape the notice of Berthold and two men-at-arms who entered the corridor from a stair-case at the other end."

One of the men bore a large platter of eatables, the other, a flagon of ale or wine—Allan could not see which.

They paused at one of the doors, and Berthold shot back the lock, and gave ingress to his men, who placed the food and flagon upon a rude table, then retired without exchanging a word with the occupant of the chamber. Although the glimpse the forester obtained of the interior of the chamber was but momentary, he was enabled to discover the form of the proud earl, who, with fettered hands, was striding gloomily to and fro.

Allan watched the men descend the stone stairs, then he stepped cautiously to the door of the earl's prison, and tapped as loud as he dared with the hilt of the hunting knife he had concealed beneath his servitor's jerkin.

The door was of solid oak, and plated with iron both inside and out; thus, if the earl answered his summons he heard it not.

"By the mass," grumbled Allan, "this door is thicker than the hides of the knaves who made it. Well, I cannot hold a parley with the good earl, so I must e'en do the best I can. By the rood! I should like to know what is the best to do?"

Looking about him in search of a cue to guide him in the laudable object he had in view, Allan saw a small loophole.

"The very thing," he said; let me see, there are four doors from this œillet; each room has a place for the admission of light Now if I can find a tree, a stone, or aught of like nature opposite this, my task will be easy."

Scrambling up to the loophole, he noticed an object directly in front of the aperture.

It was a blasted tree of gigantic size, and one Allan well knew.

"By the Rood!" he chuckled, "better and better; now let me quite understand, the earl's prison is four loops from the right of this; ah! but if I stand with my back to the tree it would be four from the left."

He cut a small cross on the back of his left hand.

"I shall not forget now," he said; "the fourth chamber from this cross, when my back is against the trunk of yon tree; now methinks I had better find my way to the kitchen and court the favour of the fat butler, who, if all Little John and Will Scarlet says is true, keeps a barrel of good October in the cellar for those he loves."

The forester's keen scent led him to the kitchen, for there welled upward from those regions a savoury smell of roast meats and tempting tantalising stews.

When the supposed lady was conducted by the major domo to the room where the Sheriff was in the habit of receiving his visitors, she watched the pompous servant strut from the chamber.

He no sooner had taken his effulgent person out of hearing, than the page took a most unmaidenlike stride across the room, and quietly shot a brass bolt into its socket.

"Secure from interruption," the page thought, "unless there are any secret doors behind the tapestry—I'll try."

He did so with the hilt of his dagger, and satisfied that he should be secure from interruption, the boy began to search among a pile of papers which were upon a table, and evidently left by the Sheriff not long before the arrival of the knight's page.

A cry of joy came from his lips when he caught sight of a packet, with the Royal seal hanging from it, and quickly folding the document, he concealed it beneath his flowing drapery.

He had only time to do this, when the major domo knocked at the door.

The page quickly slid the bolt back, and the pompous head-servant, followed by two serving men, entered the chamber.

The men brought a huge tray of choice viands and rich wines, and a silver dish of rose-water for the lady to cleanse her fingers after she had partaken of a meal a Sybarite would have envied.

"In the name of my master, the high and puissant Geoffrey-de-Lois, by command of the King sheriff of the shire of Nottingham, I bid thee welcome, fair lady."

He backed out of the chamber after this flourish, and the boy, laughing heartily, attacked the good things before him.

He had only time to finish his meal, when the door opened, and the Sheriff, bowing very low, entered the chamber.

---

## CHAPTER XXXV.

### A WINGED MESSENGER.

What wilt thou give me, said the Sheriff,
   In ready gold or fee,
To help thee to thy true love fair,
   And deliver her unto thee?

THE boy's graceful inclination of his body,

the look of modest confusion, and the partially turned aside head, was a consummate piece of acting, and would have done credit to a modern follower of Thespis.

The Sheriff bent very low in acknowledgment of the lady's presence, and with true Norman gallantry, said:—

"Welcome, fair lady to my poor castle, and if thou kneedest protection, the lance of Geoffrey de Lois is at thy service."

"Thanks, Sir Knight," the lady replied; "but I would not imperil thy life. I am but a humble maiden, and not of sufficient rank to have a warrior do battle for me."

"Lady," the Sheriff said, "thy beauty would give thee precedence above all the dames, and there are many fair ones at our court."

The lady blushed.

"I flatter thee not," the Sheriff continued, "I speak but as a knight whose vows hold him to aid the weak and oppressed. Speak, lady, wilt thou avail thyself of my good right arm?"

"Sir Knight," she said, "again I thank thee; but I dare not avail myself of thy kindness. I sought only the protection of thy castle for a few hours; grant me this, and I will go on my way to the Abbess of Kirkless Priory, who is a kinswoman of mine."

"To Kirkless, fair maiden—do I read thy intent aright—to seek the cloister?"

"It is even so. What else can aid me in this my hour of need?"

"Maiden, I am learned in the world's ways. Canst thou confide to me thy secret, that I may guide thee?"

"I have but little to tell, Sir Knight; but that little is sufficient to fill my heart with woe."

"So young," the Sheriff said; "yet so sad. I pray thee conceal nothing, fair maiden; and thou shalt have my advice as though thou wert my sister."

"Thou must know, then, Sir Knight," she said, "I was betrothed to a youthful warrior who went to the Holy Land to fight for the Blessed Sepulchre."

"A fair field, lady, for thy youth to earn his spurs."

"So I am told. But during his absence there came a palmer who reported the knight as slain. I mourned him, and my sire, when my grief had somewhat abated, brought to our dwelling an old noble, who made overtures for my hand."

'Ha! and thou?"

"I hated the man my sire had chosen for me; and upon the day we were to have been wedded there came a minstrel to my chamber, and from him I heard my true knight yet lived."

"It was sad he did not bring thee word himself."

"Alas, he could not, he was but crossing the seas; I feigned illness after this, and prayed for the return of my betrothed, but he came not; and my sire, no longer brooking the delay, bade me prepare for the hateful nuptials."

"Thy sire's heart," the Sheriff said, "must have been of stone."

"He is harsh, Sir Knight, yet I bethink me now, had I told him all he would have relented."

"Thou didst not tell him, then."

"Not one word."

"That was a pity; yet, peradventure, he had pledged his word to the noble, and could not save thee."

"I fear it was as thou sayest. Well, Sir Knight, the morn came that was to see me a bride, but ere any of the household were astir I roused my serving-man and we left my sire's roof."

"Thou hadst not seen thy true knight, then?"

"Alas, no."

"Dost thou think he has crossed the seas yet?"

"Of that I know not."

"Canst thou describe him to me, for I have seen many followers of the cross who have of late returned from doing battle with the infidels."

The lady drooped her head.

"I fear my poor description," she said, "will not be any great service; he is fair, Sir Knight, wondrously fair, and bears that look of the true Saxon descent which would single him out from an army of Normans."

"Ha!" thought the Sheriff; "the very knight I saw with that cut-purse Robin Hood. By the mass! I will soon have an opportunity to repay him for the ready aid he gave the forester."

"Hast thou," she said, "seen aught to resemble my true knight among those who have of late returned from the Holy Land?"

The Sheriff reflected before he answered.

He did not know for a moment which would be the best course to pursue, whether to answer in the affirmative, and endeavour to persuade her to stay in the castle, or whether to advise her to go on to Kirkless.

He decided upon the latter plan, for he justly argued she would be entirely out of sight when once past the Priory gates, and as he was a personal friend of the Lady Abbess, he could gain admittance, and work out a plot which had flashed to his brain during the preceding conversation.

"None, lady," he said, "have I met to answer thy description; but as every day beholds fresh arrivals from the Crusades, there is hope yet for thee."

"Oh, sayest thou so. My heart fills with joy at thy words."

"May thy heart be a true prophet of the joy in store for thee! Believe me, lady, I will do my devoirs as a true knight to find thy absent love."

"Thanks, Sir Sheriff, thanks; may the saints be good to thee and thine."

"Gramercy, fair lady, for thy wishes," he said. "Now that I have heard thy story, I will, if thou should'st wish, tell thee how I should advise thee to act."

"Whatever thou advisest I will faithfully follow."

"It is this, fair lady. When thou art tired of my poor castle, hie thee to Kirkless Priory, and await the coming of a messenger from me before thou takest those vows which will condemn thee to a life such as one of thy loveliness should'st shun."

"I will follow thy directions, Sir Knight; I will await thy messenger at Kirkless, and I shall watch the sun rise and set with my heart fluttering between hope and fear—hope that thou mayest find my true and brave knight—fear that he may have gone to the bottom of the sea."

"Let hope be thy guiding star, lady. I will soon send thee news of all ships that have brought their burden safely back to England."

"Again, thanks, Sir Knight. Now, as my palfrey has rested, I will leave the castle, for we have a long road to pass over before Kirkless towers are seen over the trees."

"It is not meet, lady, thou shouldst go alone? I will escort thee——"

"Nay, not for worlds, Sir Knight. I shall travel safely with my serving-man, who, though but of little wit, is a good and stout yeoman."

"I yield to thy wish, fair maiden; thy palfrey shall await thee by the time thou hast donned thy hood and cloak."

The Sheriff left the chamber in order that the maiden should resume her travelling garb; and when he was gone, the lady burst into a fit of laughter.

"Hoodwinked," she said; "ha, ha, ha! Most puissant knight, thou art overmatched by a Saxon page."

The Sheriff, as he descended to the courtyard, thus held converse with himself:

"So this fair beauty loves this knight I have so much reason to dislike. By the Rood! how well my speech suited the occasion; and she deems me the more thoughtful because I bid her seek the priory. Sister Agatha is a comely dame, and not proof against a bribe: this fair one, once in her hands, I can look upon her as mine; by the

mass, but she is fair, wondrously fair. A malison upon the knave—her serving-man; his speech was either to misdirect me, or the wittol's brains would not give him better knowledge."

He reached the courtyard, and despatched one of the grooms to fetch the horse; another to find the serving-man.

Allan-a-Dale appeared; his face flushed, and his gait unsteady, from the close acquaintance he had made with the Sheriff's ale.

"How now, knave," the Sheriff said; "is it thus thou appearest to ride forth with thy lady?"

"Appearest, Sir Knight! By my Saxon ancestors, I appear as a good yeoman should when he has been pledging the health of the lord of this castle. By the saints! it is not often a poor serving-man tastes such liquor as thou keepest."

"Go to for a drunken carle; canst thou sit thy horse?"

"Sit my horse! aye, Sir Knight, once on his back, the foul fiend himself would find it hard to drag me off."

He climbed into the saddle as he spoke, and made the animal curvet and prance about the courtyard, much to the danger of the toes of all who stood near.

The Sheriff saw the man was capable of managing his steed, and was about to give him a little advice about his duty to the lovely lady, when the page appeared.

His face was concealed in the silken hood, and the Sheriff went forward and assisted the Lady Elfrida to mount.

"Farewell," he said, kissing the gloved hand held out to him; "be of good cheer; my messenger will soon be at Kirkless Priory with the news thou art waiting for."

"Farewell, Sir Knight, may the saints keep thee from harm. Come, thou knave (this to Allan) the ale thou hast drunk has gone to thy face."

The lady and her lusty servant rode over the drawbridge, and when they were upon the green sward the horses quickened their pace, and soon bore them out of sight.

Plunging into the wood, which separated the forest from the castle grounds, mistress and man gave vent to peal after peal of laughter.

The echoes of their merriment brought an answer, in a high but cheery voice—

"Body-o'-me!" said the voice; "but thou art merry. Hast brought glad tidings?"

"Aye, John," said Allan; "great tidings. Where is our master?"

"Where every good master should be," the lieutenant said ruefully, "he's at dinner."

"And thou away; shame upon thee, John."

"Away! Bladebone of St. Hubert! our master sent me to look after thee, so hurry in, or not a scrap of meat or a drop of wine will be left."

Allan and the page trotted through the bridle path, and Little John, anticipating the loss of a dinner, struck through the brushwood and arrived at the glade, where the Chief and his followers were seated, some minutes before Allan and the page made their appearance.

"A place for hungry John," said the fighting friar; "a place, my merry men, or he will eat one of ye."

"A place!" grumbled the forester, looking savagely on an empty pasty dish which stood before the friar; "a place for what? bare bones and empty platters. A murrain upon thy gormandising, thou fat friar, not to hold me one little nook of as fine a pasty as ever was baked in Sherwood."

"Aye, thou art right," said Friar Tuck, folding his hands over his stomach; "aye, and for the matter of that, as fine a pasty as was ever ate beneath the greenwood tree."

"So it would seem, thou fat-paunched thief; but, by the Blade-bone of the——"

The appearance of Allan and the page stayed the forester's speech, and Robin and the knight, jumping to their feet, ran forward to meet the pair.

"What news?" the Outlaw asked; "come, tell unto me."

The boy drew from beneath his dress the royal parchment, and handed it to Robin, who read the clerkly handwriting aloud:

"*HENRY, BY THE GRACE OF GOD KING OF ENGLAND, &c.*

"*To our trusty cousin, Geoffrey de Lois, Sheriff of Nottingham, greeting. By these presents know ye that one Roger, Earl of Mortimer, is an attainted traitor, and, should there be a rising among the malcontents in the shire over which thy rule extendeth, at once bring Roger, Earl of Mortimer, to the block; should the malcontents remain at peace, keep him a close prisoner until thou hearest our Royal will.*

"*Given under our seal, at the Palace of London.*"

"*HENRY REX.*"

"So," Robin said, "this is the reward a king would bestow upon one whose good lance set him upon the throne!"

"Aye," said the knight; "such is the gratitude of princes."

"Come hither, Much," Robin said; "hie thee to my hut and fetch me a goose-quill and an ink-horn."

Much ran off upon his errand, and when he returned, Robin cut off a piece of the parchment with his dagger, then, placing it against a tree, wrote a few words.

"Where is Allan?" he asked, when he had done this; "I heard thy voice preaching that thou knowest the chamber where the earl is confined."

"I do, master."

"Is it beyond an arrow's flight to reach the window?"

"For a Norman cross-bowman it is, good master, but not for a Saxon archer."

"I am glad thou sayest so; take thy bow, and put this packet upon a grey-goose shaft, and send it inside the Earl's chamber; but harkee, knave, have a care lest thou sendest the arrow through the Earl."

"I will do my best, master; no man can do more."

Allan-a-Dale took the packet, and selecting a stout bow he left the forest.

"Thou hast chosen a good messenger," the knight said, "and a swift one."

"Thou art right," said Robin, "my winged messengers are sure and trusty, whether they are sent to friend or foe. Now, Sir Walter, let us leave these knaves to roar out their roistering songs, we have matter of more import in hand than to listen to them."

The knight followed the Outlaw Chief to a secluded part of the forest, and for upwards of an hour they walked to and fro in low and earnest conversation.

## CHAPTER XXXVI.

### THE TWO MENDICANTS.

Stand, holy friar; two mendicants
Crave thy gifts of charity.
'Tis nobler much to give than take,
Then listen as we supplicate,
For two beggars we be—
    Beggars poor be we.

"BODY-O'ME!" quoth Little John, as he leaned against a tree, "and gramercy, too, but they be long a-coming."

"Thy mouth waters, John, at thoughts of the fat pouches they carry. Is it not so?"

"Hunger and thirst sore press me. By my oath, they shall pay interest for this unseemly tarrying."

"Nay, friend John, thou lackest charity; peradventure they but tarry to rest their burdens."

"I warrant they'll be light enough when I lay my hand upon them."

"Hist!" exclaimed the friar; "dost hear they come to our calling with discreetness?"

The tinkle of bells announced the party as close at hand, on which Little John and his companion trolled out the following ditty:—

"Let thy pity loose, good sirs;
Help us earn our prayers.
    Thine alms we crave;
    The poor to save.
    Thy pity then vouchsafe,
    Good sirs, us to relieve;
    Help us! earn our prayers."

"Out upon thee! knaves; thy song is like thyselves—of poor account," said the foremost monk, as the pair of sturdy mendicants advanced.

"Hunger and thirst leave little room for song. We crave thy help, holy father," answered Friar Tuck.

" By the saints! yon fellow's countenance but ill accords with his condition. Didst ever see such a round paunch as he carries?" And both the monks laughed outright.

" 'Twill go ill with thee, an' thou keepest not a discreet tongue in thy head," growled Friar Tuck with bated breath, in allusion to the remark of the last speaker.

Little John smothered his laughter as best he could, for he was tickled at his companion's discomfiture.

" We have travelled far, holy fathers, and are sore pressed by want. Bestow on us of thy plenty but a groat," said the friar.

" Not a stiver. Hark thee, sirrah, trouble us no longer else 'twill go ill with thee," was haughtily answered.

Placing himself in their front, Little John said:

" We have fairly begged, holy fathers, for Charity's sake, and thou refusest to listen. We demand now thy money. Give, else thy plight will be a sorry one."

" The saints defend us! but list to the knave's assurance! Knowest thou our condition, sirrah?"

" But too well, holy father. 'Tis few who know thee better," naively answered Little John.

" Thy conduct is made worse thereby. Go aside, churl, else the Church's curse will smite thee sorely."

" A fig for all thy maledictions," answered Friar Tuck, placing himself beside his companion, and snapping his fat fingers as he bawled forth the following ditty:

" Let them curse, and they will; 'tis no harm, sirs;
Only cowards and knaves mind hard words, sirs;
For a well-filled purse will lighten any curse,
    Make us glad and none the worse.
'Tis no harm, sirs; let them curse, let them curse,
    That we came specially so meet thee."

" 'Tis well, too, that you should know, holy father——" spake Little John.

But before he could finish, Friar Tuck chimed in with:

" Aye, that it is. As we slept one appeared, telling us to take certain sums of money thou has in thy possession; which same we mean to do."

The monks' countenances now began to fall most awfully.

It was easy to see that their situation was none of the pleasantest.

Getting down from the mule that he bestrode, one of them said:

" Search and welcome. See I withstand thee not."

" Well said; thou art a jolly fellow after all," said Little John, as he and Friar Tuck proceeded to look closely at the saddle-bags.

To their utter dismay and astonishment, the clatter of hoofs struck upon their ears;

and on looking up, they perceived the other monk making off as fast as his beast could carry him.

" 'Tis a scurvy trick," exclaimed the friar, as his fat carcass shook with rage; and dealing one blow of his stout sinewy arm to the traitor monk, he jumped on the mule, and hied him off in hot pursuit.

Little John followed with swift strides; but his speed was greatly hampered by fits of laughter.

Friar Tuck sat his mule so unsteadily, and bumped from side to side so comically, that Little John was fain to halt and laugh immoderately, albeit much against his will.

" Oh, for my good bow and a trusty shaft; then would I bring thee to a stand," exclaimed Little John, as the fugitive gained upon him.

Luck favoured the pursuers in their extremity.

Stumbling over some obstruction in its path, the beast threw its rider heavily.

When Friar Tuck came up, he found the monk insensible, from which state he was in no hurry to arouse him.

When little John arrived, he was rejoiced to find the friar deeply engaged in counting out one of several bags of money which lay at his feet.

" 'Tis well worth the chase. By my halidome, but 'twill go hard but we pay ourselves for the holy fathers' discourtesies."

" Sawest thou ever such gold pieces? And see how bright the silver crowns are!" exclaimed Friar Tuck in raptures.

" 'Twill more than repay the debt due to bold Robin," answered Little John.

" But look you, John, here is something you love right well."

" What mean you?"

" Wine, my little man, that maketh glad the heart of man."

And taking hold of a large leathern bottle, Friar Tuck placed it to his lips, and drank heartily.

" Body-o'-me!" growled Little John, " 'twill be precious little my parched lips will suck, an' you proceed at that rate."

The portly friar thus admonished, ceased his suction, and handed the bottle over to his companion with a deep sigh, remarking:

" I am ever disappointed in the things I best love."

" Out upon you! for a swilling, round-paunched, hard-pated friar," said Little John with a merry twinkle in his eye; " my work will soon be done, thanks to your thirst."

" Ah, ah! I never heard better," replied the friar, laughing.

But when he saw that Little John was inclined to suck out the wine to the very dregs

ROBIN CLIMBING THE EARL'S WINDOW.

of the bottle, his aspect underwent a change. His fingers clutched the air nervously, his lips compressed themselves, and he made sundry gestures of disapprobation, all of which Little John totally disregarded.

"Body-o'-me!" quoth the giant, as he lowered the black jack, "'tis fine. Drank you ever better?"

"'Twas precious little you left for me to pass an opinion upon," growled the friar as he took up the bottle and applied his lips to it.

With an exclamation of disappointment, he threw it away from him.

"Look, you; you have overlooked this," exclaimed Little John, producing another bottle.

"I cry thee quarter, Master John," said the friar. "Bones of St. Hubert! but 'tis my first drink, I'd have thee to know."

"I would fain see that it is fit for thy digestion first," said Little John, with a merry twinkle in his eyes, and applying the bottle to his mouth.

Hold, John! Hold! by the mass, you'll burst outright. Think of thy condition, sirrah."

"Ah! that's fine," answered the giant, as he handed the bottle to the expectant friar.

While he drank, Little John sang :

"Rattle'm, rattle'm rig—
    A monk, as fat as a pig,
    Got drunk as a lord,
    Fell into a ford,
        With his rattle'm, rattle'm rig.

'Help, ferryman !' the monk cried ;
'Hie thee quickly to my side ;
    For the river is deep,
    And I fear its sweep,
        With my rattle'm, rattle'm rig.'

'Good monk, thou then may'st lie,
And in the river deep may tie ;
    For thou art of a sort
    That's not much worth,
        With a rattle'm, rattle'm rig.'

'My curse,' quoth the monk,
'Will thee always keep in a funk.
    No rest shalt be thine
    To the end of time,
        With my rattle'm, rattle'm rig.'

So the monk was drowned in the river;
And the ferryman walketh ever
    Along its shore;
    Wailing ever more,
        With his rattle'm, rattle'm rig."

"Well sung, little man," said the friar.

"Well, let me drink, thou guzzle, answered Little John, as he laid his hand on the bottle.

While he drank, the friar sang .

"Good wine I'll swill,
And drink my fill.
        Who cares?

Life is a vapour,
And goes out like a taper,
        With cares.

'Tis the merry twinkle
Takes out the wrinkle.
        Who cares?

Wine makes us glad ;
Grief makes us mad.
        With cares.

Let the grape grow ;
Its juice bothers woe.
        Who cares ?

It makes those who die
In peace to lie,
        Free from cares."

"We must be afoot, and that quickly," remarked Little John.   "The night draws on apace."

"I'm of opinion, friend John," exclaimed the friar with rather a thick utterance, "that the world's going round."

"'Tis the wine in thy pate, rather," was the humorous reply.

"Out upon thee!  By all the bones of the saints, thou blackenest my character past all bearing."

As he spake, the friar tumbled over the figure of the monk, who groaned heavily.

"A murrain seize thee, thou idle lout ! Rise up, thou sluggard, and depart."

And suiting the action to the word, the friar seized the monk by the legs and dragged him apace.

"Thou art too rough a nurse, friend," said Little John, laying his arm upon the friar's shoulder.

"Thou errest.   My leechcraft is not at fault.   A rough arousing best suits drowsy folks."

"Nay ; let's try something gentler.   Fetch hither the wine ?"

"If I do, may I be compressed into nothing. 'Twould be sheer waste, man."

"Robin would have speech of him, no doubt. 'Twere wise to bring him with us."

"A good thought, John ; a rare bit of philosophy.  Ha! ha! thou wag; thou wantest to find out the secrets of the cellar.   Thou can'st not forget the rich juice thy paunch has swilled."

Applying the bottle to the monk's lips, he drank and revived."

"Where am I, good people, and how came I hither?"

"By crooked ways and cross purposes, my son," replied the friar with half-drunken gravity.

"I remember. 'Tis plain. The rents. Ah! I'm undone."

"Nay, nay, good friend, thy plight is not such an evil one, an' thou rightly knowest it." said Little John.

"Come, drink, my son," exclaimed Friar Tuck, handing the bottle towards him.

The unsteadiness of his hand caused it to tip, and his poor victim was deluged with wine.

This caused some little merriment, in which, however, the monk did not join.

Saddling the mule, which had not strayed far, the money-bags were carefully slung, and the party commenced its march.

Their coming was joyously hailed by all the band, who quickly thronged about them.

The sight of the money-bags was exhilarating, and Robin specially commended Little John and the friar.

"But who is he?" the Outlaw asked, pointing to the monk.

"The gracious giver of this bounty," exclaimed Friar Tuck, mockingly pointing to the money-bags.

"Ah! I would have speech of him," exclaimed Robin ; "what ho, there, honest Will, lead hither yon poor woman."

Presently a forlorn-looking wench was led into the presence of the assembled company.

Anything more wretched than her appearance could not be conceived.

She was tattered and torn, dejectedly sad, and withal aged.

"Cast thine eyes upon this fellow of the cowl," said Robin to her, "and say if he is thy persecutor."

"My lord, 'tis he; this very morn I had a home and comforts; now I am the most desolate among women."

"Prithee explain, good father," said Robin with knitted brows; "'tis surely not thine office to despoil the helpless women of their homes and shelter."

"Her rent was overdue. A distraint upon her goods and chattels recovered it."

"To the crown piece, and no more? speak truly, I warn you."

"'Twas ever customary so to act," was the answer, insolently given.

"'Tis false. The Church has no such privilege. Extortionate dealings ill become its saintly character."

Then turning to the woman, Robin said, kindly and gently, "What was thy debt?"

"But five crowns when all was told, my lord."

"You sold her out for how much, fellow?" imperiously asked Robin of the monk.

"For what I got."

A sign from Robin brought a quarter-staff down on the saucy monk's shoulders, with a thwack which could be heard far and near.

The force of this strong argument was irresistible. It not only brought him to his knees, but also to his senses.

"Spare me, good sir!" he cried; "I received twenty crowns for this poor woman's house and chattels."

Turning to Little John, Robin said—

"Pay her,"—pointing to the woman—"twenty crowns, and five more for interest."

The money was given into her hand.

Falling on her bended knees, she said:—

"May Our Lady protect thee! may the God of the poor befriend thee—keep thine enemies under thee—prosper thy ways, and give thee sanctuary at last!"

"Amen, amen!" devoutly said several of the bystanders at the simple prayer.

"I thank thee, my good woman," replied Robin; "thy prayers are too good for such as me."

Turning to Will Scarlet, he said:—

"Give her safe conduct through the forest."

To the monk he said:—

"Harkee, good father. If by any chance you e'er again molest her, thou and thine shall suffer for it. An' she lacks her rent, I, Robin Hood, will pay for her."

Soon supper was spread on the greensward, and all hastened to do their devoirs by attacking the good things before them.

But despite their evil repute, they tasted not until Friar Tuck had said grace.

"Sit down, man," said Robin to the monk. "Partake of our homely fare, nor think that the king's deer will mar thy digestion. Thou wilt find it good, I warrant ye."

The invitation was readily accepted and soon the monk was doing his part of a hungry visitor right well.

The meal had nearly finished when a messenger arrived in haste, desiring audience of Robin.

"Tidings, sir, from Nottingham Castle. The Earl Mortimer dies by the gallows the morn after to-morrow."

"No such ill-fate will befall him. Hie thee away and say Robin will be there in time, mark you, in time."

## CHAPTER XXXVII.
### THE SHERIFF'S DISCOMFITURE.

I love thee dearly, maiden fair—
I cannot say how dear:
Georgeous apparel and costly array
Shall be thine. Then say me yea:
　For, oh! but I love thee dearly.

But I've a lover other than thee,
　And, oh! I love him dear—
His sweetest kisses are all for me,
And his presence is ever near:
　For, oh! but he loves me dearly.

"List to me, sweet Marian: thou knowest how dearly I love thee. Relent, and be mine."

"'Tis idle, Sir Knight, thus to persecute me. Thou hadst mine answer long ago."

"If thou knewest how madly I love thee! Night follows day, but to find me with thy sweet name on my lips, thy loved image in my heart!"

"A truce to such idle bantering, Sir Sheriff. Thou can'st ne'er be aught to me but distasteful."

"Methinks one of my degree should need not sue so humbly at thy feet."

"Then, why sue at all? Of a truth, thou art not wanted," replied Marian sharply.

"Ever thus haughtily repulsed," muttered the Sheriff between his clenched teeth, "it shall not be; but I must dissemble for yet a little time longer."

"Thou art expectant. 'Tis bold Robin, no doubt, whose coming is so greatly solicited," he said with a covert sneer.

"E'en so. 'Tis a name to thy liking, I wot," replied Marian with a malicious laugh.

"'Tis one derided and contemned by all good men. Thy fair fame receives a stain therefrom."

A rich, maidenly blush mantled her cheeks; her eyes glanced a furious hate, her fine form upraised itself, as she threw back his scorn in his teeth:

"None but a dastard knight would thus speak to an unprotected maiden. Bethink thee of thine ignoble manner, and begone ere that Robin, thou so much contemnest, arrives to smite thee for thy foul tongue."

"Bravely spoken," said the Sheriff, mockingly. "Thou lookest lovelier in thine anger than I before wotted of."

"And thou—— But 'tis idle to waste

words on such as thou. Thy chastisement but tarries."

"Nay, fair Marian, be not so coy. Bethink thee we are alone. Robin comes not."

"An' thou would'st lay so much as thy littlest finger upon me, thou would'st rue it. Back! I say, base fellow;" and Marian looked queenly in her wrath.

The Sheriff was abashed. Virtue conquered vice.

"By my halidome! sweet Marian, thou art a rare wench. I but tried thy temper from mere wantonness. Believe me, thou hast in me too true a lover to harm thee in any wise."

"I fear thee not. Our Good Lady protects those that in her trust."

"Now, hearken, Marian. Robin, whom thou lovest, must be mine some day, and that before long. For thy sweet sake I'll protect him; give me but encouragement to hope."

"Sooner would I see Robin a-dangling from yon tree than buy his ransom at so foul a price."

"God wot thou art hard to please, sweet maid," the Sheriff replied testily. "I brook thine insults with but little patience."

"'Tis thine own doing. Thou forcest thy company upon me, knowing full well the disfavour thou art held in."

"Dost know, proud wench, that Earl Mortimer is now my prisoner? How Robin's heart will ache when two morns more will see him die. Thinkest thou of these things when thou bravest my power and despisest my love."

"Earl Mortimer can die like a brave knight, an' it please Our Lady so to will it. Bold Robin knows full well how to avenge a friend's death; of that no speech of mine need remind thee."

"Be not so cruel, else will my passion o'er-master my reason."

"I've given thee too much license of speech already, Sir Sheriff. A good morn to thee."

Marian turned to go.

The Sheriff was quickly at her side.

"Unhand me, thou false-sworn knight," she indignantly said, as he placed his arm on her shoulder.

"Nay, sweet maid, I shall taste of the nectar of thy sweet lips, an' I be shot for it."

The next moment the Sheriff was rudely thrown backwards.

George-a-Green stood facing him.

"How now, thou varlet, knowest thou my condition?"

"Thou art Nottingham's Sheriff, and a bad man to boot."

"S'death, sirrah, thou shalt rue this. I will slit thy malapert tongue an' thou thus address me."

"Thou! thou king's minion," replied George-a-Green contemptuously. "I'll thrash thine hide till it is like unto a well-tanned one. This maiden requires thus much at my hands."

Furious with passion, the Sheriff rushed towards him with naked sword and hot vengeance in his eye."

George's quarter-staff flew nimbly about his head for a moment, then descended with force on the Sheriff's swordarm.

His weapon dropt.

The next moment he himself lay sprawling at the foot of a tree.

George placed his foot on his prostrate foe, and menaced him with his left hand.

"Robin, darling!"

"Marian, sweet love!"

The lovers were quickly locked in a close embrace.

The noise caused George to turn round unguardedly.

Quick as lightning, the Sheriff seized his leg and upset him. Like an arrow from a bow, he sped away, ere Marian had time to explain the matter to Robin, who had looked on in astonishment.

Regaining his feet, George-a-Green hied him after the Sheriff in good style. As he neared him he heard the Sheriff utter a peculiar cry. Whinnying with delight came a finely caparisoned, fleet horse.

Mounting its back, the Sheriff started off with the speed of the wind, and looking back defiantly at his pursuer, was soon out of sight.

When Robin heard from Marian's lips the story of the Sheriff's insults, he ground his teeth with rage, and swore an oath of fearful import that vengeance he would exact from him.

"'Tis for my poor sake thou sufferest these unseemly rudenesses at his hands; say, dearest, how can I ever repay thee for all this?"

And Robin looked tenderly and lovingly into her upturned eyes, in which floated a liquid flood of love-light.

"By ceasing to think of them, my sweet Robin. Believe me, thy Marian can endure as well as love."

"True, brave-hearted, noble Marian! Troublesome times are with us. Better days may come; my rightful patrimony may again be mine. Then, beloved, thou shalt shine as a star, resplendent in beauteous charms, in thy proper sphere!"

"I bemoan not my lot. Thou, Robin, dost ennoble any cause or station. More I crave not than thy love."

"It is thine, dearest; could'st thou but see into my heart, thy name, sweetest, would there be found deep engraved."

"Thy tell-tale eyes do this much disclose. 'Tis plain to thy Marian that she bears a place in her Robin's heart."

"But the Sheriff—said he aught of Mortimer, my dear friend?"

"Aye, that did he, and of evil import, too. Could aught of good pass such base lips as his?"

"His life is imperilled, I wot."

"Of a surety. The third morn from this is not his on earth. So discoursed Nottingham's Sheriff."

"'Tis the idle babble of a crazy pate. Fool! not one hair of brave Mortimer's head will be harmed. Robin's word on that."

"My mind is greatly eased. 'Twere sad were so brave a knight to perish. Ah, me! 'twould be sad—oh, so sad!"

"Even now things are in training to encompass his deliverance. With mine own hand will I strike off his accursed chains, and Mortimer will once again be free."

Robin's handsome face lit up with enthusiasm as he uttered this speech, and his finely-formed head poised itself more firmly on his graceful neck.

"But here comes George-a-Green. What news, my good fellow? Has he escaped?"

"I burn with shame to tell it. He has; and ere this is safely housed in his den. A murrain seize the villain!"

"His luck will not always stand him in such good stead. Mark me, Nottingham's Sheriff shall rue this day."

"Put his baseness out of thy memory, Robin dearest," said Marian; "else will it hamper thy free and generous nature."

"Have no fear, Marian. We crush the poisonous reptile under our heel, and scarce bestow a passing thought on its fate. Geoffrey de Lois is to me as such an one."

The pealing notes of a bugle horn were borne on the breeze.

"Hark! 'tis the signal. Fare thee well, Marian, love! God be with thee, sweetest!"

One ardent embrace, one impassioned kiss, and Robin hied him off.

George-a-Green waited to attend Maid Marian.

---

## CHAPTER XXXVIII.

### ROBIN GOES TO THE CASTLE WITH HASTE.

> For I doth thee scorn,
>     And all thy craven crew;
> Such silly imps unable are,
>     Bold Mortimer to subdue.

"'Twill but suit the moment for me to do as I have said," remarked Robin to the knight.

"It is a dangerous enterprise to thyself mostly. Consider the watch on the ramparts."

"Bethink thee, though, of the darkness of the night. By my halidome, I am eager for the risk, and deem the hours to go lazily by until it is attempted."

"Nobly said; I'll be with thee hand and glove."

"Thanks, Walter, thine arm is a trusty one, pledged to hew down Norman swine. By my soul, but it will be something to make all Nottingham ring again, and the Sheriff hide his diminished head for very shame."

"Of a verity this is well planned, and I doubt not of its proper execution."

"Doubt! I would as soon doubt myself. But harkee! hither strolls Little John. Beshrew me, but I like his voice; dost not thou? List!"

> "I have been in the forest, sir,
>     And a fair sight did I see:
> It was one of the fairest sights
>     That ever met my eye.
>
> Yonder I say a right fair hart—
>     His colour is of green;
> And a fine herd of seven score deer
>     Are with him to be seen.
>
> His antlers are so sharp, master,
>     I durst not shoot for dread.
> They've sixty points, or more—and I feared
>     I should be stricken dead.
>
> 'I make mine avow to God,' said the Sheriff,
>     'That sight I fain would see.'
> 'Haste you thitherward, my master, dear,
>     Anon, and go with me.'
>
> The Sheriff rode, and Little John,
>     Of foot he was so smart,
> And when they came before Robin—
>     'Lo, here is the master hart!'
>
> Still stood the proud Sheriff;
>     A sorrowful man was he.
> 'Woe be to thee, Reynold Greenleaf;
>     Thou hast now betrayèd me.'"

"Well carolled, by my knighthood—a likely ditty," said Robin's companion.

"John, this way; I would have speech of thee."

"I am ever at thy bidding, master," answered Little John.

"Not a trustier friend I wot of; as trusty as my own good sword—as true as my own good bow, John," and Robin laid his hand kindly on his shoulder.

"Thou honourest me too much, master mine, in thy speech. But this I know, for right loyal love to thee I trow I can challenge any man."

"Without a doubt, John, man. But list! To-morrow night sees Mortimer free or me a prisoner."

"Body-o'-me! master, the latter may not be."

"I but put it to thee at a venture. I climb the wall; you and a trusty band remain within bowshot to cover our retreat. Let two good steeds be in waiting."

"'Twill be so, master."

"And harkee, John, a file hard as a dungeon door, biting as the north wind, must be mine, and a stout rope to boot."

"Good! by the bones of St. Hubert, all will go merrily!"

"Let twenty trusty men be picked for service under this, my friend (pointing to the knight), to lie away to the right as an ambuscade, in case the Sheriff's men are drawn from their cover by your party. Hearest thou?"

"I do, master mine, and this will be the end of it:—

> "The Sheriff fled from Nottingham town—
>   He fled full fast away;
> And so did all the company—
>   Not one behind would stay."

"Ah, ah! friend John; thou art a soothsayer. 'Twill be even so, an' Our Lady will it not otherwise."

At this juncture a messenger came in haste seeking Robin.

"Good news I hope, lad," he asked; but say it quickly."

"'Tis black news, master. To-morrow at sunrise Earl Mortimer dies."

"How now? What sayest thou?" asked Robin hastily, "speak quickly."

"Brave Earl Mortimer at sunrise dies."

"Thou art certified of that?"

"Too surely."

"What unseemly haste! But explain to me an' you can how this has been brought about."

"Berthold doubting the page's appearance, caused him to be watched. His coming hither betrayed him. He hies to the Sheriff, and may I be excommunicated an' I ever saw man in such a rage as he."

"Haste, good lad, to the point, to the point."

"The steward suddenly bethought himself of the King's letter, but, lo, it was missing, With rage o'er mad, the Sheriff hied him to the earl, and with hard words assailed him, calling him traitor, false knight, and other such unseemly names."

"And the Earl?"

"Struck him to the earth with his iron-girt hands, and e'en forced the breath out of his body almost."

"Brave Mortimer! But what then?"

"But what I've shown. The earl dies at sunrise."

"Thanks for thy despatch, good lad. Thou shalt be rewarded."

Then turning to Little John he said:

"Sound an assembly. What I just now told you let be done with despatch."

To the knight he said:

"Thou heard'st the foul tidings? But Robin will make them fair ere the light of you star has dimmed its brightness, or the day dawn. To our purpose with despatch."

The clear, full notes of Little John's bugle sounded in the still night air.

Instantly all was astir.

Movement there was, but not confusion.

The foresters marshalled with order and regularity.

In a short space of time all were prepared.

With noiseless tread, the band moved forward to their respective stations.

On their way, two horsemen passed.

A repressed but audible cheer greeted the foremost of them.

It was Robin, the Outlaw, attended by a faithful lad.

Arrived near the castle, Robin dismounted.

"Stay you under yon tree. Come not, but for this signal," and Robin imitated the hoot of the owl three times in succession. "Dost rightly understand thine instructions?"

"Yes, master; thou shalt not find me tripping,"

"Good. But mark me, keep the beasts quiet. Hast provender sufficient?"

"And to spare, good master. They shall not e'en whinny. My word on't."

Facing the castle, and shaking his clenched hand in its direction; Robin said:

"Base Sheriff, thou little wottest of my presence here to-night. Thy perfidious designs will be frustrated, and thou, dear Mortimer, ere morning, shalt be free, or I perish."

With silent, but swift steps, Robin sought a dark object to the left.

It was the blasted oak.

"I will here pause till the castle is buried in deep silence," said Robin to himself.

Folding his arms, he leaned his back against the tree, and was soon buried in deep thought.

A hushed silence fell upon all around, unbroken save by the sentinel's tread on the ramparts.

"Now, for my ascent. Our Lady defend me, the risk is not so great."

Finding that everything he wanted was quite safe, he mounted the oak with the agility of a wild cat, and soon rested amid its scathed boughs.

"'Tis the loophole exactly opposite this tree. Good! now for a trusty messenger."

Taking a blunt arrow out of his sheaf, he strung it to his bow, and fixing to it a piece parchment, took aim and fired.

Earl Mortimer reclined on his hard couch. Sleep visited not his eyes.

His thoughts were busy with the past.

The future to him was to be but a short one.

Robin had promised his sure aid.

But the Sheriff had forestalled him by fixing the execution for the morning.

'Twas useless to hope now.

He would nobly meet his fate.

Ah! what was that?

ROBIN HOOD AWAITS THE COMING OF THE GUARD.

Something had struck the wall, and fallen at his feet.

It was an arrow, having affixed to it a parchment missive.

With eager hands he detached, and read it."

"I am in the old oak over against your cell. Be ready. Signal with your hand."

What joy unspeakable burst over Earl Mortimer's soul at this moment!

Escape was certain; for was not Robin near?

He waved his hand thrice,

A low whistle came in response.

Taking another arrow from his sheaf, Robin affixed thereto a string, to which hung a file.

With unerring aim it entered the loophole Mortimer filed, and Robin watched.

Slowly, but surely the bars were filed.

But it required assistance to remove them from the masonry.

Taking another arrow, Robin attached to it a thin cord.

Again it went with unerring aim through the loophole.

The cord was drawn carefully forward by Earl Mortimer.

To its end was attached a stout rope.

It was securely fixed.

Robin descended from the tree.

In a short time he was under the walls.

The rope was in his grasp.

He paused and listened.

## CHAPTER XXXIX.

### THE BLOODY SPECTRE.

At midnight's hour—so dark—
A figure, bloody and stark,
Haunted the ramparts high.
Its visage ghastly and wan,
Down its breast the red blood ran,
As the night-wind bore its sad sigh.

NOTTINGHAM'S Sheriff sat in his room quaffing the red wine.

"Ah, ah!" he said, "Earl Mortimer, thy hand, that struck me down like a dog, will be paralysed in death on the morrow's morn!'"

After a pause, he cried out:

"What ho! without there! send hither the captain of the guard with quick despatch."

He paced the room hurriedly as he waited.

"And Robin Hood! 'Twill go hard with me, but I so fix him soon— that the gallows will be no longer cheated of its just due. I but bide my time."

The captain of the guard entered and made a respectful salute.

"Is all in readiness for the morn? are thy men doubly watchful, sentinels alert, the prisoner secured beyond all possibility of escape?"

"Even so; guards within and without— drawbridge and portcullis closely guarded."

"Let a block be placed on the northern tower; let a spike be fixed on high there— the traitor's head shall be uplifted high."

"'Twill be done."

"And mark me, let the headsman bungle not—one sharp swift stroke. To thy charge I confide these arrangements; see that they are rightly executed. I would be alone."

The captain of the guard, bowing low, departed.

"I will keep the vigils of the night, that the morn find me no laggard."

Filling himself a bumper of wine, he quaffed it at a draught.

Pshaw!" he said, as if in answer to his own thoughts, "The King will hold me blameless. 'Tis a business once performed cannot be undone. The dead cannot be recalled to life!"

A low, sobbing wail struck upon his ear.

The hour-glass had just run its last grains. It was midnight.

With a start of horror the Sheriff looked out.

Again the strange noise was heard by m.

"Heavens! what do I see?" he said, as the perspiration stood in big drops upon his pallid brow, and his eyes well-nigh started in wild affright from their sockets.

A figure, ghastly and wan, with bloodstained vestments and eyeless sockets, from which blazed a dim, unearthly light, stood with uplifted arm and pointed finger.

The Sheriff was terror-stricken.

His parched lips refused to utter a sound.

His frame quivered like an aspen leaf.

His knees knocked together with an audible sound.

Step by step, slowly but surely, advanced the spectre like an inexorable fate.

With a loud cry of terror the Sheriff swooned.

Rushing in, his attendants found him thus.

The sentinels trod the ramparts watchfully and in pairs.

The two nearest Earl Mortimer's prison were extremely vigilant.

They conversed with bated breath of the gossip of the day.

"Is bold Robin expected that we take such precautions?" asked the first sentinel.

"Even so; the outlaw is daring and resolute."

"And kindly hearted, too."

"He is of the Evil One, I opine. 'Tis strangely true, his wonderful deeds. An' he had not some help not of this world he could not do them."

"Right. But hark! heard'st thou not that sound as of a voice calling in deep whisper."

"Nay; but I'll listen."

After a pause the last speaker said:—

"'Tis fancy, I wot. Heard'st thou it again?"

"Nay; it sounded like some ghostly whisper. I wot there are strange things to be seen at midnight's hour within these walls."

"Thou art right. I heard it from Ralph Pleydel but yesternight."

"What heard'st thou—aught ghostly?"

"Surely; and on this very spot."

"Nay, thou dost but jest."

"I jest not. Ralph discoursed so sensibly that I was fain to credit him.

"What saw he?"

"Listen, hark! heard'st thou not that voice again?" said the other without regarding the question put to him.

"Pshaw! thou dost but tamper with my credulity."

"Prythee spare thy pains."

"I could have sworn to it."

The last speaker leaned over and peeped into the black gulph underlying him.

"Nothing can I see," he remarked, " I heard the voice distinctly."

"Calm thy fears, man—but list to that, I heard it that time."

It was a low wail.

"Heavens! 'tis just as Ralph informed me."

"See, may I be hanged before morning if something comes not this way."

Gliding along came the same ghastly figure that had so scared the Sheriff.

Crouching low, the terrified sentinel quivered at every limb.

They too had swooned.

When the guard came to relieve them they had recovered.

But they spoke never a word of what they had seen until they reached the guard-room.

"Depend on't the Sheriff was scared by it. Heard'st not that he was found insensible in his room?"

"'Tis strange; I have oft heard of the phantom but ne'er seen it. Is it so frightful?"

But never a reply came from the sentinels, save a deep sigh of relief.

Their silence cast a gloom over the remainder.

The soldiers feared to keep watch, but said not so, except every man to his own heart.

---

## CHAPTER XL.

### HOW ROBIN ENCOMPASSED THE EARL'S ESCAPE.

Bold Robin he to the window hied—
Lusty of arm and strong of heart.
"Freedom to Mortimer, or death!" he cried;
"For 'tis nothing shall ever us part."

NAUGHT but the tramp of the sentinels overhead broke the stillness of the night.

"Now, Our Lady prosper me, and I vow to pay at her shrine one hundred golden crowns."

Placing his sword betwixt his teeth, he climbed quickly up the rope, resting himself at times by placing his feet against the castle wall.

His bugle-horn swung to and fro in the night wind, as his sturdy form mounted higher and yet higher.

It was a daring deed.

But bold Robin loved danger, and had braved death too often to fear it under any guise.

The stout rope strained and quivered under his weight, but not a strand started.

His ascent startled the birds that had nestled in the castle walls, and they whirled round the outlaw.

The bats flapped their black wings, and, in their stupid coursing flew butt against him oft.

He had reached three-fourths of the distance, when the glare of a torch shone o'er the ramparts, and a voice said:

"The outlaw has the daring of the Evil One. It behoves us to be vigilant. Look down. See you aught?"

Robin got as close to the wall as he could, and with bated breath, but a stout, fearless heart, awaited the issue.

"Naught but the deep blackness of the night, and the floating of birds, can I perceive."

"Ah! say you so. There must be cause for their nightly flittings. Hold the torch a little more to the right."

Robin gave an inward sigh of relief.

Had the torch been held to the left, he must have been discovered.

He listened for the voice of the last speaker.

"I see no cause for the disturbance of these birds. Yet, 'tis strange. Onwards! let our vigils be extended. The safe keeping of our prisoner depends on our watchfulness."

The voices died away in the distance, and soon all was hushed as before.

Robin worked his way upwards, every foot gained giving fresh strength to his energy.

At last he reached the window.

"Mortimer, 'tis Robin," he whispered low.

"Thine hand, brave friend; its pressure makes my heart's blood flow quicker, and sends it curling quick through my veins!"

"How has thy work progressed?"

"Bravely; it requires but thy help to complete it. But thou art in peril of falling."

"Nay, nay, have no fear; 'tis this requires wrenching out of the masonry. Stand aside —my strength is a match for it."

Twining his left hand with an iron grip round the rope, he pressed his knees against the wall, and with his right hand gave the iron bar a vigorous wrench.

It started from the masonry; but the impetus of his exertion sent Robin swinging a yard or more away. Fearing that evil had befallen him, Mortimer said:

"Speak, Robin, art safe? My God, he has fallen!"

"Have no fear, said Robin cheerily; "I'm safe, thanks to Our Lady. Do thou help me to loosen the bar."

With an united effort they wrenched it from its socket, and it was soon disposed of on the floor. Another was similarly treated, and room sufficient gained for Robin's entrance.

Once in, Earl Mortimer felt relieved of all care about Robin. They were soon locked fast in a friendly embrace.

"What! manacled! By my halidome! they must be removed, and that quickly, else those iron bracelets will retard thy escape."

"Aye, manacled. 'Tis not the greatest indignity I have suffered. But tell me, how hast thou and my friends fared since we last met?"

"Bravely, bravely. Thy condition alone caused us uneasiness. But how came the Sheriff to fix thy execution for to-morrow's morn?"

"Beshrew me, I wot not of this matter. He called but yestermorn, and discoursed such hard terms to me that I was fain, manacled though I was, to teach him manners."

"Noble Mortimer! In thee Saxon chivalry

finds its paragon. Would that all of Saxon blood were such as thou art."

"Patience, Robin; the day draws apace when the hated Normans shall hide their h ads for very shame, and England shall be freed from the hated foreign yoke."

"I agree with thee. Even now the peasantry are rife for a change. Let the King look to it, else will his throne be shaken to its overthrow."

"Hist, Robin, speak low. The night-guard approach. Crouch down under the truckle."

Flinging himself on his hard bed, Earl Mortimer feigned sleep, while Robin was hidden under it.

"Sentinel, is all well?" said the voice of the officer in charge.

"All's well."

"Onwards, march!"

When their retreating footsteps had died away in the distance, Robin came out and sat on the bed.

"I must to work, Mortimer," he said; "thy manacles must be removed."

"I will not say thee nay in this matter, good Robin. To thine office, an' thou wilt, with despatch."

As Robin filed, he and his friend conversed.

"Thou wert observing but just now, Robin, that the country was ripe for a change. Art thou certified of this?"

"My information is reliable. Thousands wait but the watchwords—Liberty!—death to the Norman dogs!—to rise."

"'Tis glorious news. Thou shalt hold thine own again."

"I would willingly relinquish all claim to my just inheritance to see beloved England free."

"Heard'st thou that noise, good Robin?" Mortimer asked, as a dull thud was distinguishable overheard.

"'Tis loud enough, in all conscience. What meaneth it?"

"The soldiers placing the block for my execution."

"A murrain seize the hard-hearted wretch! To treat one of thy degree so. S'death! a dog's death is too good for him."

"Say me. Is it not a refinement of cruelty thus to act? But Nottingham's sheriff little knows Earl Mortimer's heart. It is no craven, I warrant him."

"By Our Lady, no. But 'twill be fine fun to see his outrageous vapourings when the bird is known to have flown."

"Hearest thon not that wailing sound?" asked Mortimer.

"Nay, it struck me not. Thou art nervous, good Mortimer. Imprisonment has shattered thy nerves, and left thee a prey to strange fancies."

"Not so, Robin. Hark! list! heard'st thou it not that time?"

"Certes! I did; a most dismal wail it is. Hast thou a fellow-prisoner hither about?"

"I have no knowledge of such. But the saints defend us! Look, Robin!"

Standing near was the apparition that had terrified the Sheriff and the sentinels.

Mortimer was dumfounded, and sore dismayed at the sight.

Not so Robin.

He stood erect, gazing on the fearful thing.

"In the name of our Blessed Mary and the saints I adjure thee to speak. Whence comest thou?"

"*'Tis well thou hast spoken. My bones lie mouldering in the nethermost dungeon of this castle. Foully murdered was I!*"

"Thou seekest vengeance on thy murderer! Speak! 'tis whom?"

"*Geoffrey de Lois.*"

"Merciful heavens, the Sheriff!"

"Thou wilt avenge me?"

"I swear by high heaven!"

"*'Tis enough. For this thy safety is ensured. Follow me!*"

"Robin hesitated; the rope seemed the surest means of escape.

The spectre looked back and beckoned.

Robin and his companion seemed laid under an irresistible spell.

They followed.

The dungeon wall opened, disclosing a secret door to a corridor beyond.

In amazement they followed their ghostly guide.

It led them by an unfrequented way, and, after traversing many corridors, they arrived in a certain room.

The spectre vanished through a trap door.

Robin and Mortimer followed.

Down, down, it led them into the lowest dungeons of the castle."

The door of one of these flew open.

In a corner lay a mouldering skeleton.

Robin now understood why the spectre had brought them thither.

It was to give its remains burial.

Seizing an old rusty spade which lay on the dungeon floor, Robin set vigorously to work, and, with Mortimer's assistance, dug a deep grave.

In it they reverently laid the skeleton form.

The spectre had vanished.

"We are properly caged," observed Mortimer.

"Nay. My faith in the apparition is strong. We shall be at liberty ere long."

Issuing from the dungeon, Robin turned along a corridor to the left.

They had to use caution, and in places grope

their way almost, owing to the black darkness of the place.

"'Tis a mysterious matter, this spectre. What thinkest thou of it, Robin?"

"Rightly judged, 'tis no mystery. 'Tis some young girl entrapped, betrayed, and then foully murdered by the Sheriff, to quiet her importunities."

"These dank, dark places, make one shudder. Our Lady be thanked, I was not here confined."

"'Tis well remarked. In this matter, thou owest him a favour," said Robin, laughingly.

"But, hist! there are voices. Caution, as you value your safety."

Mortimer glanced down at his shirt of mail, and then scanned the apartment for some place of concealment.

Through the gloom he espied a large oaken chest. It was empty, and springing into it he closed the lid.

"Marry 'tis well," whispered Robin to himself, "hither comes the guard—they will pass through here, they are hailing the warder at the postern."

Robin was right in his conjecture. The captain of the guard having hailed the warder and received his reply, marched his men through the chamber into a long corridor at the farther end, and passed on unconscious of anything wrong.

Robin Hood remained in his concealment behind the door until the clank of the mail-clad feet died away in the distance, and the light of the torch faded in the gloom, then he released the Earl, who was glad enough to breathe the air of the place again, although it was dank and noisome.

"Now thou canst have freedom an' thou wilt," whispered Robin to his friend. "Hist! open well thine ears? We may learn something to our advantage."

It was as Robin said, for a voice gruffly and deep, remarked:

"'Tis nearing daylight. The keys thou'lt find to the right of the door on a nail. Mind, thou openest not the postern to any, save the Sheriff, an' he desires you?"

All was quiet again.

"Mark well the footstep, and discreetly follow," whispered Robin to his companion.

A silent pressure of Mortimer's hand, showed he was fully understood.

Cautiously picking their way, they followed the retreating footsteps, guided by the sound merely.

In a short time they emerged through an open door into the morning air, for the first streak of dawn had appeared in the eastern horizon.

Mortimer pointed to it with a significant gesture.

"'Twill all be well, trust me," said Robin

Tripping lightly across the ground was a young woman bearing a bunch of keys, which she rattled ever and anon.

"The lazy old curmudgeon," said Robin whisperingly, "is having his snooze out. 'Tis all the better for us."

Advancing with boldness, Robin accosted her with, "a good morn, fair dame."

The girl looked round affrighted, and would have screamed had not Robin gently placed his hand on her mouth, saying:

"Nay, my pretty fair one, cry not out, no harm is meant thee."

Seeing from the expression of the girl's face that she was somewhat more reassured, he withdrew his hand.

"Thou seekest exit hereby," she said, "but 'tis denied to all but the Sheriff. Who art thou?"

"An' the truth be told we are two roystering squires that were making merry last night in this castle, and losing our way found ourselves here this morning."

"Thou hast not the garb or speech of such," said the girl, shrewdly.

"We beg of you, sweet girl, to let us go before our masters wot of it," said Robin.

And placing his arm round her waist he gave her a hearty kiss.

"Out upon thee for a saucy knave," she replied, trying to catch Robin a smart box on the ear, but he adroitly avoided her.

"Squire, say you," she hurriedly said, catching sight of his bugle horn. "By the Mass, thou art bold Robin Hood himself. Thy garb is of green."

"Thou hast truly said, wench," he replied, "I am Robin Hood."

"And this is——"

"Earl Mortimer," replied Robin."

"Now the saints and Our Lady be praised," replied the girl, "thou shalt have immediate exit; why said you not your conditions before?"

Hurrying to the gate, she unlocked it in haste and held it open.

"Thy name, noble girl?" asked Robin.

"Madge Stukely."

"I shall not overlook this, thy great kindness, Madge. Thou hast made a friend of Robin."

"And of Earl Mortimer, too," said the earl

"Quick, quick," the girl replied, struggling from Robin's embrace, "my father comes this way."

"Madge," exclaimed a gruff voice, angrily, "to whom hast thou given exit?"

"To none, father. I but opened the gate to catch the fresh morning breeze."

Robin and Mortimer passed out of hearing They worked their way round to the spot where the horses were, and past the scene of the last night's adventure.

The rope dangled from the window, but half its length lay on the ground.

"We both escaped our destruction," remarked Robin, pointing to the rope.

"And such a death!" remarked the earl with a shudder.

"List!" said Robin; "the castle is alarmed! Thine escape has been perceived. Quick, as you value your life."

The castle was indeed in a commotion. At the dawn the captain of the guard had gone to rouse his prisoner, but lo! he was gone.

"Escaped! Quick, raise an alarm! to the ramparts! Hie thee to the Sheriff, and him acquaint of the matter!" exclaimed the captain in disjointed sentences. He feared for this misadventure the loss of his position, if not his head.

The window soon told the tale, for the rope was fastened there as it was left by Robin. The Earl's manacles lay upon the floor.

"Now a curse on Robin Hood! this is his work!" exclaimed the Sheriff, hastily entering the apartment. The storm of passion that he indulged in was indescribable.

The guards were to be executed forthwith, the captain first of all. He was surrounded by traitors and spies, and soforth.

"I would not have had this happen for ten thousand of the best gold pieces in this land!" the Sheriff exclaimed. "Now I shall be hooted at for a dolt—a fool—an incompetent! Oh! that I could crush my enemies under my foot! Thus and thus would I do it!" and the Sheriff stamped again and again in his impotent rage.

Going to the rampart, he heard a shout.

"There they go! 'Tis Robin, the outlaw, and Earl Mortimer!"

"Where, where?" said the Sheriff.

"'Tis them! 'tis them! a hundred crowns to the man that sends a bolt through their carcases!"

The cross-bowmen bent their bows.

## CHAPTER XLI.

### THE FRIAR AND THE STRANGERS.

I seek an outlaw, the stranger said:
  Men call him Robin Hood;
Rather I'd meet with that same outlaw
  Than forty pounds so good.

FRIAR TUCK accompanied the party under Little John, and looked gleefully forward to a brush with the Sheriff's soldiers.

"My conscience will not be sore troubled, an' I happen to smite one of the Norman dogs, what say'st thou, John?"

"'Twould take more than that to hurt thy sleep, friend. Thou are not of tender years, or conscience either."

"Thou art ever perverse in thy judgment respecting me, a man g' .en unto prayer and fasting."

"Out upon thee, for a hyprocrite! E'en now thou art troubled to digest thy last meal."

"Well, well; I must submit, I suppose, and bear thy slanders as best I can; but how long tarriest thou here, ere the potting commence?"

"Till morn, belike. 'Twill ill assort with thy slumbers, jolly Tuck, such vigils."

"I must bethink me of some plan to while away the time. I eschew idleness."

"Marry, and thou dost. But we are here."

Disposing of his men to the best advantage, and in accordance with the instructions given by Robin Hood, he threw out skirmishers on either hand, and in both front, and rear, to guard against surprises,

Those not on duty were to idle about without going too far.

This sort of business was not to the friar's liking, so he took the first opportunity to hie him off to the shade of some wide-spreading tree to sleep, if no better occupation presented itself.

When alone he drew forth from his satchel some venison, oat cakes, and wine.

"'Twas rare luck I fell into to get me this much. 'Tis scant fare enough for a hungry man, but it might be worse."

"I commend the cook for his art. 'Tis a rare art, too, Nature meant me for eating, not for praying. Egad, I unite the two profitably enough."

The wine, too, met with the friar's favour, and he was jolly enough.

"'Twere well to rouse these solitudes; 'tis lonely enough here for a churchyard. Think of friend Little John; but there was only just enough for one, not two. Besides that last steak was tough, and would have interfered with his digestion."

In a minute or two he carolled forth—

"The friar he is a saintly man;
He eats betimes and fasts when he can.
Of troubles he has not a few to meet,
But with scourging and fasting such foes he can greet."

"Bones of St. Hubert! I can remember penance in my younger days. 'Twas as nauseous to me as a dose of medicine Ugh!"

"To matins and prayers he gives his days—
Not to mend his own, but other men's ways;
For the fat things of earth he cares not a rush,
Though for all that he likes good wine at a push."

"Ah! things have mightily altered with me, and for the better. Robin is a good superior, not over troublesome. But, bones of St. Hubert! what is that?"

A rustling sound came from overhead.

"'Tis the wind, no doubt; I'll lay me down and rest—'twill refresh me."

Soon he snored loudly, and it was evident that he was fast locked in sleep's sweet embrace.

ESCAPE OF ROBIN HOOD AND EARL MORTIMER.

The noise caused by the approach of two horsemen failed to arouse him.

They were attracted by his snoring.

"Here is somebody," remarked one of them who can direct us in our course; I'm afraid we've lost our way."

"Thou canst be well certified of that. Marry! have we not been mouching about these last two hours or more? 'Tis a fact, God wot."

There was a touch of impatience in the last speaker's voice, which was of that soft tone, too, as to proclaim her a woman.

"I'll arouse the slumbering knave; perchance he can direct us."

Placing his mouth to the friar's ear, he shouted with all his might:

"Arouse thee, man! the house is on fire!"

This appeal, strong as it was, failed to make any impression on the sleeper.

"Certes, but be sleeps remarkably sound. What ho! thou knave. Dost hear?"

And the speaker gave the sleeping friar several rude shakes

"And he gave a thwack that broke his back,"

was the friar's dreamy response as he turned over, and snored louder still on the other side.

"Faith, thou deservest to have thy back broken, thou sluggard," said the speaker angrily.

"'Twere best to alight here for a time," said the lady. "'Twill not bring us nearer our goal an' we ride till morning's dawn."

"Fool that I was to trust ourselves in these places without a guide. But 'tis vain to chide myself now."

The lady dismounted, and tied her horse to a tree, an example which was followed by the gentleman.

"Throw thy cloak about thee, Maria, and sleep an' thou wilt, whilst I keep vigils till morning."

"Then Robin set his horn to his mouth,
And blew a blast or twain,"

mumbled the friar in his sleep, without, however, interfering with its peacefulness.

"By the Rood! the knave has named the very man we seek. Would that he were not so sleepily conditioned; then would I have speech with him."

"Patience will best serve us," remarked the lady. "I would I were not so faint with thirst."

"'Twere hard to relieve it here," said her companion, "unless this graceless lout has aught by him. I will see to it."

His search was rewarded by finding the remains of the wine and an oaten cake or two.

"I give thee joy, Maria; here have I to eat and drink for thee. Thou canst set to."

Hunger left no room for niceties about the condition of the provender, or the manner of obtaining it, so the lady did as she was bid, sharing with her companion

"He is not such an ill-conditioned knave, after all; but see, he stirs. I will accost him once more."

Before the speaker could do so, Friar Tuck awoke and groped about for the wine.

Finding it not, he grumbled lustily.

"Two travellers have lost their way, and beseech thine information."

"And I have lost my wine," replied the friar tartly.

"Thou shalt have enough money to buy a pipe of it, if thou dost but inform us of our road."

"Marry! the road is broad enough and straight enough to Nottingham good town. 'Tis only fools can miss it."

"Have a care, knave; thou answerest not a civility discreetly."

"I shall crack thy pate, an' thou usest knave to me again. Bones of St. Hubert! thy malapert tongue requires bridling with an oak-staff."

"Peace, sirrah, or I'll teach thee good manners."

"Thou! 'Twill be seen full quickly."

Grappling each other they wrestled for full ten minutes or more without an advantage on either side.

At last they were fain to stop for want of breath.

"By my halidome, thou art a sturdy wrestler. None I found could so stand as thou hast done."

"Thou knowest full well the tricks of wrestling, I perceive," answered the Friar, "and I fain would serve thee an' I could."

"'Tis easily done; I and my companion seek one Robin Hood."

"Robin Hood! Why man, the trees, the deer, every blade of grass hither about knows him full well:

"Come, listen to me, ye gentlemen
That be of freeborn blood;
I shall tell you of a good yeoman—
His name was Robin Hood.

Robin was a proud outlaw,
Whilst he did walk on ground;
So courteous an outlaw as Robin was,
Was never anywhere found."

"Thanks, friend, for thy ditty. Perchance, thou and bold Robin are acquainted?"

"Full well: full well. Friar Tuck and he are as thick as well-churned butter."

"Thou art one of his merry men, then?"

"Nay," replied the friar gravely, "thou mistakest; I am Robin's chaplain, and must, perforce, renounce merriment for penance."

"Thou knowest well the flavour of good wine," observed the stranger, "for that I drank just now was good beyond compare."

"'Tis to refresh my inner man, I take it," replied the friar. Thou knowest the old song, perchance:

"Good wine—'tis fine;
Give water to swine.
Never think to drink
Better stuff than wine."

"I would be going, an' it please you, good friar. My companion is tired, and craves repose."

"Robin Hood's merry men are near at hand, not two good bowshots off. Follow, an' thou wilt?"

"'Tis Robin I wish to see mightily."

"He is well employed on good business; but Little John, his lieutenant, can grant thee audience."

Friar Tuck drew Little John aside, and told him how that two persons of condition sought to see Robin.

"Their business? Disclosed they it?"

"Nay; but one is a hugeous fine wrestler. He came well-nigh tripping me. Thou canst now guess he is a man of some stuff."

Little John courteously welcomed the strangers, and, without directly soliciting their confidence, intimated that he was acting for Robin Hood, and would gladly assist them, if possible.

"Thanks for thy courtesy, good forester," replied the gentleman; "I would, an' it please you, discourse with you aside."

"I am at your service—say on," said Little

John, when he and the stranger had gone apart.

"My name is Richard Wykeham, or Sir Richard, as folks call me. My patrimony is wrested from me by the contrivances of Nottingham's Sheriff, because of the love that Maria Danvers bears me. 'Tis Norman against Saxon—the greedy dogs. My followers were taken at a disadvantage, and I and Maria are here to solicit bold Robin Hood's assistance."

"He ne'er refuses it to the oppressed. But he alone can decide in the matter."

"'Twas in my knowledge that he would do so, else had I not sought him. Can I not have audience with him soon?"

"Pressing matters engage his attention for a time. At Sherwood, thou shalt see him."

"Thy counsel is friendly; meanwhile I crave shelter for her who accompanies me. Thine hospitality will much benefit her."

Calling Friar Tuck to him, he desired him to go with the strangers to Sherwood and see after their comfort.

"'Twill be hard but I make them snug. Adieu, good John, my benison on thee and thine undertaking."

Sir Richard and his lady love departed, under escort of the friar, who beguiled the way with anecdotes of Robin's prowess, which were eagerly listened to by his auditors.

They were not destined to reach the end of the journey without adventure.

But this must form the subject of another chapter in due course.

## CHAPTER XLII.

### HOW THE ABBOT CURSED ROBIN AND LITTLE JOHN, BY BELL, BOOK, AND CANDLE.

He cursed him sitting, he cursed him lying;
He cursed him living, he cursed him dying.

WHEN the monks brought the tidings of the loss of the tithes to the abbot of St. Mary's his rage knew no bounds.

He raved and swore most unsaintly oaths that revenged he would be upon Robin.

He summoned his brethren in solemn conclave, and revealed to them the loss to the abbey.

"Curse him by book, bell, and candle!" suggested one of the monks.

"He cares not for such; he leagues with the Evil One," replied the abbot.

"It matters not; he cannot long defy our holy power. Let him be anathema maranatha!"

"But let us not lose sight of the power of the arm of flesh in chastising him. He is outlawed, and any man may lawfully slay or maim him without let or hindrance."

"Well said," replied the abbot. "A scheme must be devised against him specially, and next against that renegade Friar Tuck."

"'Twas he who assailed us. Would it were within these walls, that we might question him as to his backslidings."

"'Tis a thing hard of accomplishment, holy brethren," replied the abbot, " but nevertheless our rights must be protected."

"'Tis well said," "replied one of the monks. "To me are known two men or more, who, for a consideration, would lend their swords to our holy cause."

"Summon them to our presence; we would have speech with them," replied the abbot, significantly.

A messenger entered at this point to say that one was without, desiring speech of the lord abbot.

"Said he 'twere an important matter?" queried the abbot.

"Even so, my lord.

"Admit him to our presence, then."

The attendant bowed low and retired.

Presently there entered a yeoman from the castle.

"The Sheriff sends thee greeting, my lord," he said. "Earl Mortimer dies on the second morn from this."

"'Twill be one enemy to the Church and State the less," replied the abbot sententiously.

"He is not shriven, and would have some holy man to hear his confession."

"He is excommunicated, his death-agony must not be softened by the Church's holy comfort."

"But the Sheriff wots that important confession may be his to make."

"An' even were it so, 'twere not our pleasure to divulge such to any. The secrets of the confessional are inviolable."

"Am I answered in full, my lord?"

"Thou art. Earl Mortimer has consorted with the notorious outlaw Robin Hood. That damns him. My love and duty to your master, and say that the earl will not be shriven by holy monk or friar."

Earl Mortimer had not desired to be shriven.

'Twas the Sheriff's art to elicit the abbot's approval indirectly of his death.

When the Sheriff's messenger had gone, the abbot ordered a solemn assembly for the morn.

"Let notice be given thereof to all the country round. Let as many as will attend to hear our doom pronounced upon the enemies of our holy Church."

That very night three men of ruffianly exterior were closeted with the abbot.

"For twenty marks paid over to each of you, Robin Hood, Little John, or Friar Tuck will cease to further trouble us."

"We swear to execute thy behests," said

the leader; and each man laid his hand significantly on the hilt of his sword-dagger.

"Night would best subserve thy purpose. Watch vigilantly, and expose not thy precious lives to these men's taking."

"Thou need'st not admonish us of this. Our contract will be fulfilled, and to thy liking."

"Mark me. Reserve thy weapons for those I named to thee. Once rid of them, the band's dispersal would quickly follow."

"We would have guerdon of thee, for this is a desperate undertaking, of difficult accomplishment and dangerous involvings."

"Art thou distrustful? Thou hast no need."

"We must live. Five marks each would suffice. 'Tis not a large sum."

"Thou art importunate. But, as this is a holy service thou engagest in, take thy needs, and prosper in thy work."

Five crowns each were paid them.

They departed as they came—silently.

On the morrow, the abbot and monks walked in grand procession.

Such magnificence was never before witnessed by many of the simple country folk, who, prompted by curiosity, attended to witness the commination.

The large chapel was draped in black. The candles threw a dim, mysterious light over the place.

The funeral dirge was chanted in solemn tones, which sent the blood rushing back to the hearts of those who never before had heard it.

With stately, measured steps, the procession of monks defiled round the chapel. They knelt devoutly in silent prayer, then uprose, and, with folded hands and bended heads, listened to the abbot.

Robin Hood and Little John were publicly denounced as enemies to the Church.

Friar Tuck was not mentioned, the consent of the abbot's spiritual superior being required to such a proceeding being adopted in his case.

Then commenced the commination.

Anathema after anathema poured forth, in clear, uninterrupted tones, from the abbot's lips.

At the end of each curse the abbot laid his hand, with solemn gesture, on the Bible.

The lighted candle was extinguished.

The bell tolled its solemn toll, and the monks chanted a solemn amen.

It was a deeply awe-inspiring ceremony, and made a great impression upon the minds of the laity present.

Persons sheltering or assisting Robin Hood, or any of his band, would be excommunicated and cut off from all the rights of the church.

The commination was over.

The spectators dispersed.

The monks, with solemn steps, sought their cells.

The chapel was left deserted.

The abbot was alone, mourning over the loss of his money, for a very miser was he.

In thus trying to prejudice the minds of the common people against Robin the abbot committed a mistake.

True, there were some superstitious enough to be frightened at the anathemas pronounced by the abbot.

Nor was it to be wondered at.

To be excommunicated was in those days a serious matter.

It was to be afflicted with a moral leprosy.

Every person shunned the person under ban.

Food was not allowed to be sold him.

Nor house let to him.

Nor priest to confess or shrive him.

Nor surgeon to attend his ailments.

Nor Christian burial at his death.

The matter was much talked of when the meeting broke up.

There were two men in particular, who, apart from the crowd, walked and talked of Robin.

"Dost thou credit that these foreign words have aught of power to hurt bold Robin?"

"'Tis hard to say. But they sounded very dreadful to me."

"Bold Robin cares not for them, nor any of his merry men, either."

Looking cautiously round, he said:

"I join Robin's band to-night. 'Tis free living, and to my liking."

"Nay, Jack, lad, thou art joking, belike?"

"Not so. Bold Robin reckons me as one of his band; an' he likes to have me, that's certain sure."

"I should be lonely without thee, Jack. But think of the curse; think of the Sheriff's soldiers; think of the gallows, lad."

"Be a man, Dick. It takes not the joining of Robin's band to bring one into queer troubles. Hast not plenty of them now? Where be our bit o' land, our snug little cottage, our poor mother and sister. Thou well knowest. All gone, all! and in the churchyard drear."

"An' you love me, Jack, no more. It raises a sort of sensation like in my throat to talk of mother. I feel maddened, revengeful, and not the man I should be."

"What thinkest thou of the abbot's curses, now?" said Jack with a quiet sneer.

"I think more of our wrongs. Dick, my hand on't, I hie with thee to Robin the outlaw."

"Meet me under the large oak in Sherwood Forest."

"In Sherwood Forest, under the large oak,
I meet thee."
" 'Tis well."

## CHAPTER XLIII.

### HOW FRIAR TUCK AND HIS COMPANY DEFEATED THE ABBOT'S MINIONS.

To see how these together they fought,
  A full hour of a summer's night;
Yet neither of all would yield them aught,
  It was a most cruel sight.

"AND the Sheriff, say you, is in love with Maid Marian?" asked Maria Danvers of the friar.

"Aye, that is he, the ill-conditioned swine. Naught but so bonny a girl as she will suit him."

"And the maid loves Robin dearly, sayest thou?"

"Dearer than else in life. For him she lives alone. For his voice is sweet music to her ear. But thou should'st see her for thyself, lady, and thou wilt anon."

"Thou likest a free life, good friar," remarked Sir Richard.

"Truly, truly!

   " 'A life in the woods for me,
     With the fierce wind blowing free.' "

"Bones of St. Hubert! What's so pleasant as a home under the greenwood tree? Ha, ha! I laugh at the thought of it, and sing—

   " 'Ha, ha! 'tis well
    In the forest to dwell,
    With the green trees sighing o'er you.' "

"Thou art a jolly companion, good friar, and hast quite made us forget our fatigue. What sayest thou, Maria?"

"A very notably pleasant man, art thou, good friar, and rightly fitted for thine office with thy merry men."

"A shrewd remark, lady. Thou hast my liking for its point. Who would not sing and fight for bold Robin?"

"None but a churl, I wot," answered Sir Richard.

" 'Tis yet a good pace to your forest home?" queried the lady.

"It is naught, and will soon end. But I am wearying thee with my prating. Thou would'st fain have me silent, fair lady."

"Nay, say on, say on, I pray thee, friar. Thy speech is welcome, and cheereth exceedingly."

"Hast heard of Rob's adventure with Guy of Gisborne," asked the friar.

"But never the proper rights of it," answered Sir Richard.

"Would'st thou hear it? I wot I can give it thee in song right well. Thou must excuse my huskiness, though, for I am very dry:—

" 'Now tell me thy name, good fellow,' said he,
  'Under the leaves of tine.'
'Nay by my faith,' quoth bold Robin
  'Till thou hast told me thine.'

'I dwell by dale and down,' quoth he,
  'And Robin to take I've sworn;
'And when I'm called by my right name,
  I am Guy of good Gisborne.'

'My dwelling is in the woods,' says Robin,
  'By thee I set right naught;
I am Robin Hood of Barnesdale,
  Whom thou so long hast sought.'

He that had neither kith nor kin
  Might have seen a full fair sight,
To see how together those yeomen went,
  With blades both brown and bright,

Robin was reckless of a root,
  And stumbled up that tide;
And Guy was quick and nimble withal,
  And hit him upon the side.

'Ah! dear Lady!" said Robin Hood, 'though
  Thou art both mother and maid,
I think it was never man's destiny
  To die before his day.'

Robin thought on Our Lady dear,
  And soon leaped up again;
And straight he came with an awkward stroke—
  And he Sir Guy hath slain.' "

"Right well sung, good friar; an' thou pleasest thou shalt drain a stoup of good wine with me presently."

" 'Tis a thing I ne'er refuse. But I finished not all my song. I am hugeous dry, and were I to bawl further, 'twould crack my throttle, I wot."

"Seest thou aught beyond yonder tree?" asked the lady.

"Whither, lady fair? I strain, but see not," answered the friar.

" 'Tis but thy fancy, Maria, dear. This old forest hath queer, fantastic shapes for the mind's eye, I take, an' but the humour suits one."

"I could have certified to it. A man did appear from thence, and quickly lost himself again."

" 'Tis easy to see. Pause, thou, while I go forward."

Forward the friar went.

He had neared the tree, when, with a bound, he was beset by three men.

With a nimble quarter-staff, he warded well their blows, shouting out: "St. Hubert to the rescue!"

"Now stay thou here," said Sir Richard to the lady, "I haste to fight."

Dismounting from his horse he drew his sword, and was soon ranged by Friar Tuck's side.

Right well and lustily did the friar with quarter-staff lay about him.

Right well did Sir Richard parry and thrust, and guard and hew.

"An' take that for thy pains, thou knave," said the friar, as he brought his staff down with unerring aim on one of their crowns.

The man dropped as if shot.

"I cry thee quarter," cried he to whom the friar was now in turn opposed.

"Quarter thou shalt have after I have thee well thrashed. Out upon thee, thou cowardly knave. To thy guard and defend thyself."

The friar whirled his staff well and lustily. Never a blow did he get in return for the any he had given.

With a crack that could be plainly heard for a distance, he soon stretched the second fellow to keep company with the first.

But it fared not so well with Sir Richard.

His foot slipping, his adversary got him at a'vantage.

His sword point was at his throat when a stroke from an unexpected quarter, disarmed and badly wounded him.

"Well hit, lady fair, a good stroke. Rise, Sir Richard, thou art not hurt much."

"Not a scratch, good friar; and thou, Maria, hast earned anew my love by saving my life."

"I would that I had holpen sooner. But seeing that thou wast equally matched with thine adversary, I stayed my hand. It was thy mishap brought me to thy side."

Turning to the prisoner, who alone of the three could speak, the other two being in sorry plight, thanks to the friar's lusty arm and nimble staff, the friar said:

"Answer me, knave, thy name and condition, quickly as thou valuest sound bones in thy carcass."

"My name is mine own, my condition a soldier."

"Thou hast turned robber, I trow; was this errand of thine own seeking?"

"Nay, and thou trust me I will unfold to thee the name and condition of my employer."

"Thou art but a sorry knave, and deservest not a boon. But an' thou answerest truly, it shall be thine. Say on."

"The lord abbot of St. Mary's did us employ to thy destruction, and that of Robin Hood and Little John."

"Ah!" speakest thou in jest, or truly?"

"Of a truth; why else had I sought thee to thy hurt? Thou art no enemy of mine otherwise."

"By the Rood! this must be seen to. Thou must come with me. No hurt shall befall thee, I swear. Of Robin Hood thou must have audience in this matter.

"My liberty will be imperilled, life even. It will anger thy master, when he heareth of this thing."

"Not so. Thou hast fared the worst in the combat. I am free from scratch, as is my companion also—

"For a busy man he must be
To bring Friar Tuck to his knee."

Turning to Sir Richard, the friar asked his advice in the matter.

"Thou hast well advised in this thing, good friar. Let the knave accompany us, that Robin may have his own relating."

"Hearest thou that? So march, fellow, and mind thy conduct."

Leaving the two senseless bravoes to recover as best they could, Friar Tuck and his party proceeded onward.

"St. Mary's abbot! By the Rood! but he shall pay for this in gold pieces. He liked not our handling his tithes. Ah, ah! King Robin lets not money pass through his domain without crying snacks."

"Go now forth, said Robin Hood, .
And bring back unto me,
All that thou canst find in money fair,
All the marks that thou canst see."

"The abbot has furthermore excommunicated Robin Hood, and cursed him by bell, book, and candle."

The lady crossed herseld on hearing this. Seeing which, the friar said—

"'Tis naught when sin is not at the door. I wot bold Robin will sleep and eat, and laugh and sing, as if my lord abbot had not excommunicated him."

"'Tis a treacherous thing to thus appoint one's death at the hands of an assassin. It behoves not the Church's servants thus to act, and one of such high degree, too, as my lord abbot."

Thus spake Sir Richard in dudgeon, for he could ill brook such treachery.

"Let the hare sit," replied the friar; "an' he must be a bold man that would try conclusions with Robin Hood, King of Sherwood's forest.

"Bold Robin, he cares not a thing,
For abbot, or earl, or yeoman, or King;
With his merry men all, and the forest so free,
Bold Robin careth naught, not he, not he."

"'Twill go hard with him now he is excommunicate," suggested Maria Danvers.

"Thou hast a befitting reverence, fair lady, for our holy Church, an' which thing it pleaseth me to see. But thou wottest not of certain things, else wouldst thou think good Robin hardly dealt by."

"He little careth for such things, else hath report much deceived me," replied Sir Richard, laughingly.

"Who approaches, friend or foe?" was the challenge which rang out clearly upon the night.

"Friends, good archer, friends to Robin Hood and all good men."

"The word on your peril."

"Marian."

"Pass on, friends."

"What, Bill, knewest thou not thy friend?" asked the friar.

THE DUEL BETWEEN ROBIN HOOD AND THE SHERIFF.

"Right well. 'Twould be hard to forget thee. But what news from the front?"

Rare good tidings, rare. But, man, I am hugeous dry. Bones of St. Hubert! but my legs totter from thirst," and the friar seized a flask which hung by the sentinel's side.

"Thy throttle is so large, 'twould not so much as wet its sides such a drop as that, but thou art welcome to it."

The friar quickly drained the wine-flask, and gave a deep sigh of satisfaction.

"The news, man, what of it? Earl Mortimer is——"

"Still in prison, but Robin is with him by this. Our comrades stand prepared for action. All goes well."

"Who are those with thee?" asked the sentinel.

"Two friends of our master; one a foeman beaten, and now a prisoner. Thou need'st to keep sharp vigils. I would acquaint with the commander of the guard."

"Thine advice is welcome, and shall be well attended to."

The friar and his party passed on, and were soon resting.

Taking his prisoner with him, Friar Tuck sought the commander of the guard, and to him narrated what the reader already knows.

"Speak, sirrah,!" he said. "Hadst others with thee in this black affair?"

"None. Three only were of our number; myself, and two others now lying with cracked crowns where they were left."

"Thou must be secured past escape. An' thou art wise, no harm shall befall thee.

What ho, there! Guard well this fellow in safe custody.

"There tarry Sir Richard Wykeham and a fair lady under yonder tree. Little John commends them to thy keeping, until of Robin Hood they have audience."

"I will attend them. Perchance, they need refreshing. Thou, good father, canst well attend to that," said the commander with a laugh.

"Thou hast well spoken, for:

"'I love to make friends merry,
And treat them with good wine.'

But I waste but my time and they fasting."

Sir Richard and Maria Danvers were soon made comfortable.

Thanks to the friar's promptitude, a good repast was soon spread for them, at which he took good care to preside.

To see him eat and drink one would have thought that he had fasted for fully a week.

His jollity kept his companions in good humour, and the rich generous wine stirred up his wit and humour, until it bubbled up like a fountain.

The night passed without further adventure.

The garrison at Barnesdale waited news from the front; news of Bold Robin.

That news the morn brought with it.

### CHAPTER XLIV.

#### HOW THE SHERIFF AND HIS MEN PURSUED AFTER ROBIN AND EARL MORTIMER.

Bold Robin and Mortimer hied them away
From the castle at break of day;
The Sheriff's crossbowmen to slaughter them did vie,
But their bolts flew harmlessly by.

"SAID I not the Normans spied us out?" observed Robin, laughingly, as the bolts from the crossbows came whistling harmlessly by them.

"'Twill go hard but we escape them now," replied Mortimer, cheerily.

"Have no fear; but a little further, and there await us two steeds, once bestride them and the Sheriff may whistle for us, an' it please him."

Thickly the bolts flew past.

The fugitives seemed to bear a charmed existence, for never a bolt harmed them aught.

"Yonder come horsemen to cut off our retreat," remarked Robin, pointing to a score or more mounted men in the distance.

"'Twill be a close race," observed Earl Mortimer, "but Our Lady will befriend us."

"We are arrived. What ho! there, lad; the horses, quick," cried Robin.

Responsive to his call came the youth, but one horse only held he.

"The other beast, knave; speak quickly, 'tis where?" said Robin with impatience.

"Even dead. 'Tis but a moment since a bolt smote him and he died."

"A curse on the Norman swine for this misadventure. But we must e'en mount, Mortimer, and ride double."

The knight sprang nimbly up, and Robin vaulted behind him.

Turning to the youth Robin Hood said:

"Hie thee to Little John, and say, Robin is pursued by horsemen and flies northward."

By this time the horsemen, headed by the Sheriff in person, were near at hand—so near, in fact, that the latter could be heard as he shouted:

"Yield thee, Robin Hood and Earl Mortimer, 'tis useless to attempt to escape."

Onward dashed the gallant white charger with its double load.

The preciousness of its burden seemed to animate it to put forth its utmost speed.

Well, right well it breasted its course.

Like a pack of hounds in full cry came the pursuers.

Their foam-covered steeds urged and strained sinew and thew.

"What thinkest thou, Robin," said Mortimer; "gain they on us?"

"Nay, not a foot's pace, Mortimer. Our Lady send that the steed slack not its speed for a little space longer, and all will go well with us."

"Thy life shall not be imperilled by me, Robin," said Mortimer. "Better by far that Mortimer died than Sherwood's King should the Sheriff's captive be."

"Thou art too mindful of me, brave Mortimer. Hie onward, good steed, and soon shall we leave danger far behind."

Looking back, Robin perceived with sadness that their pursuers were gaining on them fast.

"Mortimer," he said.

And the tones of his voice were not so cheery as they had sounded but a few minutes before.

"Speak, Robin. What would'st thou say?"

"The Normans near us. Do thou obey my behests, I conjure thee?"

"An' it imperil not thy safety, thou hast my willing obeisance, Robin."

"Time presses us sore; yon thicket will shelter me. Ride on thou to Little John with tidings of my condition, that aid be quickly forthcoming."

"Never shall it be said that Mortimer thus acted to Robin. 'Tis I that will offer surrender to the Sheriff. Ride on thou!"

"'Tis folly, nay madness. Even now the hot breath of their steeds o'ershadow us. 'Twere not well both of us should fall. My woodcraft will stand me in good stead hither about."

With a bound Robin threw himself from the horse.

"Farewell, Mortimer!" cried he. "For my sake, speed onward."

Relieved from his double burden, the white steed bounded forward with redoubled speed, and soon distanced his pursuers

"Heed not the horseman," cried the Sheriff to his followers; "dismount, half a score of ye, and follow yon fellow. 'Tis Robin Hood; a purse of gold to the man who encompasses his capture."

With haste they dismounted, and dived into the thicket after the fugitive.

"Yonder he goes!" cried one.

"Circle out, circle out!" said another; "his capture will thereby be made more certain."

Acting on this advice, they spread so as to draw a sort of half-circle around the outlaw's wake, and so intercept him should he attempt to double upon them.

But Robin, bold woodsman was he!

Not a jot cared he for them pursuing.

He mockingly chevied them on, as, with swinging pace, he hied him through the thicket.

His heart bounded high and swelled with joyous emotions as the leaves o'erhead rustled to the swaying of the zephyr-like breezes.

He trod a spot he loved to tread, for was not he forest king?

Anon he had distanced all but three of his pursuers.

"They but tempt their fate," he muttered between his clenched teeth; "think they Robin to capture? 'Twill go hard with me but I teach them that one Saxon is more than equal match for three Normans!"

Actuated by a determination to halt and offer battle to his pursuers, he slackened his pace and rested against a fine old oak.

They saw him thus act with exultant glee.

"Now," they to each other cried, "Robin is ours! The purse will be ours to share. On to the capture?"

Disdaining to use his bow against them, Robin tarried their coming and breathed himself.

"Yield thee, Robin Hood!" cried the foremost; "thou can'st not cope with three."

Robin smiled a grim smile, and his trusty sword leaped from its sheath.

"'Tis what I have long wished for," said the Norman; "now will I test thy swordmanship; have at thee! Comrades, do thou stand by. This is a trial of swordsmanship."

"Thou art mad," exclaimed one of his companions; "let us all attack."

"Nay, thou know'st I am affirmed the best swordsman in these parts. I long to try my skill against yon fellow."

"Come on, prithee good fellow," exclaimed Robin. "Thou but wastest time in prating. The three an' thou wilt, 'tis not too great odds for Robin Hood."

"Have at thee, thou braggart."

Their swords crossed.

The bright blades clashed as point, guard, and stroke were dealt out skilfully.

"Thou a swordsman!" cried Robin, mockingly, as his antagonist's sword went flying through the air, and he himself received a wound in his sword-arm.

The other two were upon him

It required a quick eye to catch the movement's of Robin's sword.

Soon victory was his.

One of his opponents lay dead.

The other was badly wounded.

Wiping his bloodstained sword on the grass he returned it to its sheath.

With swift steps he swept onward as the remainder of his pursuers came up.

"Ah, ah!" he exultantly cried, "ye Norman swine, Robin bids ye take him an' ye can."

The forest echoed this taunt, and his pursuers gnashed their teeth with impotent rage as they saw him go bounding away.

"Not one of those churls but I could send to death," he muttered to himself. "My trusty bow could lay them low in turn. I seek not their hurt, but let them see to't they press me not too hard, else will my forbearance fail me."

Robin halted and debated with himself the best course to pursue.

"'Twill baffle them," he soliloquised, "an' I shape my course back towards the castle. I'll e'en try it. Come, to thy work, Robin, thy merry men await thy coming."

"Yield thee, my prisoner," a voice imperiously said.

Turning Robin confronted the Sheriff.

For a moment they stood eyeing each other.

Robin's look was calm and steady, and withal defiant.

The Sheriff's glance was full of malignant hatred and supreme satisfaction at the prospect of capturing the daring outlaw.

"Thou hast called on me to yield," said Robin haughtily; "to a Norman, and such as thou, that can never be!"

The Sheriff answered slowly and deliberately:

"Threescore men are within call. Thy capture is sure."

"Thou be'st a false sworn knight, insulter of weak and powerless women. Ere Robin yield to thee or thine, his heart's blood will be poured upon the greensward. Defend thyself!"

With a bound Robin Hood was upon him.

Right sore they fought.

"Thy men tarry apace," said Robin contemptuously, as he parried a downward stroke delivered by the Sheriff.

"Thou art ill informed on the matter," was the reply, as a straight lunge went at the outlaw's breast.

"Have a care, thou Norman robber," said Robin, coolly parrying it. "Thy carcass will soon dishonour the spot."

"St. Denis, help me!" replied the Sheriff as he dexterously guarded his head from a terrific blow aimed at it by his antagonist.

"That to teach thee manners," said Robin driving his sword through the fleshy part of the Sheriff's sword-arm.

But never a pause made he.

He fought him for his life right sturdily, and in his heart cursed the dalliance made by his minions.

Not a scratch got Robin.

His sword seemed a part of himself, so deftly did he wield it.

There was this advantage with Robin in all his encounters—he maintained his coolness, and let aught o'ermaster his passions.

The sun peeped through the trees at the combatants, and its beams settled now on one then on another with fanciful—nay, playful —effects.

Now they settled on Robin's sword's tip, making it bright with their golden rays. Anon they visited the Sheriff, stealing across his face with a slyness, and bringing out into bold relief the workings of his base, passionate nature thereon depicted.

But the swordsmen plied their calling merrily.

Neither had a decided advantage.

The Sheriff proved his swordsmanship to be of no mean order.

At length, a stroke from Robin disarmed him, but unluckily his sword broke off short in the middle.

"A malison on thy maker, thou traitor steel!" exclaimed Robin, eyeing the broken weapon with unfeigned disgust.

With a bound, the Sheriff had regained his weapon, and was upon him, thinking to take him at a disadvantage.

The combat was now a desperate one.

"Half a sword suffices for thy defeat!" exclaimed Robin, as he replied to the Sheriff's attack.

"Thou hadst better yield to my mercy. Bethink thee of thy sad condition else!"

"Thou hast the most cause for so considering," answered Robin, beating down the Sheriff's guard, and dealing him a blow that staggered him and dented deep his hauberk.

"Now shall the matter end," exclaimed the Sheriff, rushing forward with impetuous haste and uplifted weapon.

"Ah, ah!" answered Robin, "thou Norman braggart! what say'st thou to that?"

Springing forward, Robin, with wonderful dexterity, seized the Sheriff's sword arm, and held it aloft with an iron grip.

With a back stroke from the hilt of his broken weapon, Robin dealt him a chest blow that sent him reeling backward.

The Sheriff stumbled heavily, and Robin became entangled in his fall.

By a dexterous movement of the Sheriff, he got him uppermost.

With vicious grip he seized Robin's throat, and with his arm on his chest, exclaimed exultingly—

"Thou art my prisoner. Yield thee, thou outlaw."

But he little knew Robin's strength.

With a superhuman effort he flung him a yard or more from him.

They rested awhile by mutual consent.

The combat was resumed.

Wrapping his jerkin round his left arm, Robin once again assailed the Sheriff, who began to give evidence of weakness.

"Thou art undone, proud Sheriff!" exclaimed Robin, as the Sheriff defended himself with difficulty, and paced him backwards with uncertain steps.

"I yield not," he exclaimed. Ha! hither hie my men. What, ho! St. Denis to the rescue!"

The noise of approaching footsteps was heard.

Dealing the Sheriff a terrific blow that laid him low, as if bereft of life, Robin fled.

His exertions had so weakened him that he was unable to make much headway against his pursuers, who were close upon him.

Robin stood at bay.

With bow in hand, he sought his quiver.

But *three* arrows only there remained.

The remainder had fallen out.

*Twang!* and one of his advancing foes bit the dust.

The arrow had pierced his brain.

Robin's blood was awfully aroused.

He looked like a hunted lion at bay, so terrible his countenance, so noble his attitude.

The fate of their comrade warned them not to advance with temerity.

"'Tis useless to offer further resistance," exclaimed one of them.

"Speakest thou to a slave, thou Norman hind?" exclaimed Robin. "Have a care, else this Saxon arrow will best answer thine arrogance."

"Stand aside," a voice shouted. "This bolt will teach him to desist."

"Sayst thou so," exclaimed Robin.

With aimless aim almost Robin shot his second arrow.

The promised crossbolt came **not.**

The hand that had wielded it had become powerless in death.

"Ah, ah! thou Norman herd," shouted Robin, now thoroughly aroused and excited, "lettest thou one Saxon defy thee? By my halidome, thou art baser than I had e'en given thee credit for."

"S'death, an' thou thus tauntest us, devil or no devil, thou shalt suffer for thy contumaciousness."

A rush in a body, a cry of pain, a prostrate form with a Saxon arrow through his heart, and bold Robin was fearfully outnumbered.

His stout bow he unstrung and plied it like a quarter-staff.

Broken crowns there were, and aching arms, as Robin's blows descended fast and furious.

The very impetuosity of their onslaught defeated their object.

They huddled together so that their efforts to strike Robin down were impeded.

Right merrily fought the bold outlaw.

Not a thought of surrender.

With Marian's name on his lips, and his merry men in his thoughts, he fought desperately and well.

But such odds were overpowering.

With a desperate effort he shook off the grip of two stout fellows who had seized him, and placing his bugle horn to his lips blew thrice clear and loud notes, making the forest resound again.

He was now firmly secured.

His proud fearless heart was not subdued, though fetters held him.

Forward came the Sheriff, supported by two of his followers.

"Thou art mine now, Robin Hood, hated outlaw, and who is he that will deliver thee from mine hand?" and the Sheriff smiled triumphantly.

"Spare thy taunts and threats, base Norman. That thou would'st do my speech will not gainsay."

"Thy Marian, what will she say? The roses will fall from her cheeks, her eyes pale, and——"

"Silence! base Norman! pollute not her fair name by thine utterance."

"Ah, ah! by my knightly word 'tis a thing worth dwelling upon. But hearken, let the maid be mine, and liberty is thine this moment."

Robin's handsome face became purple with rage.

His whole form swelled with indignation.

With a desperate effort he snapped his cords asunder.

In a minute his hands were upon the Sheriff's throat.

Throwing themselves upon him they bore him off his half-strangled foe.

"By Our Lady! have a care, proud Sheriff,

how thou contemnest me again by such base offers, else will I force the breath out of thy dastardly carcase, though a thousand of thy minions guarded thee."

Robin looked kingly in his just wrath.

Gasping for breath, the Sheriff ordered him to be well secured and bound to a tree.

"Let him be quickly despatched," he said, with furious gestures.

"Fear I death? not I!" exclaimed Robin. "I have braved it too often to look on't as an enemy. Thy worst deed, caitiff, shall find Robin still unsubdued. St. George for merry England! Down with the Norman swine!"

A hushed silence fell on all around.

Robin waited calmly and fearlessly the advent of his merry men or death.

---

## CHAPTER XLV.

### HOW LITTLE JOHN AND HIS MERRY MEN BEGUILED THEIR VIGILS.

In the meery greenwood we hie away
From the sunshine so warm and gay;
When the moon's pale light shines o'er the night,
Then we skip it so merry and bright.

"I TELL thee, man, 'tis true. Did I not see them?" said George-a-Green, in an injured tone of voice.

"Thou didst but dream of this matter, good George," replied Little John.

"Nay, push him not too hard, John," remarked Will Scarlet; "'tis hard to gainsay such sights."

This conversation was the result of a disclosure by George-a-Green of what befel him in the forest the night after he had seen Marian safely home, as narrated in a previous chapter.

Robin's merry men were seated in groups, awaiting the signal for action, and whilst waiting gossipped about all sorts of things.

"Narrate unto us the whole matter, then, George, and let's judge of it in a lump. At present it ill suits my belief to pay credit thereto."

"Nay; I have no wish to tickle any man's ears with goblin stories," grumbled George-a-Green, in reference to Little John's previous disparaging remarks.

"The story—the story!" cried a dozen or more voices.

Reclining in various fashions on the greensward, under the wide-spreading oaks, the foresters listened, while George-a-Green narrated the following:—

"Thou all knowest the Hazel Dell?" he began.

"Right well," chimed in several.

"'Twas there I passed, as the moonbeams shone brightly on my path.

"My mind was not running on any matter in particular, and I tramped lightly along.

"There is a path—a short cut leads down

by a running stream—thither I hied me, with intent to reach home in half-an-hour, at least.

"Merry voices I heard carolling forth a sweetly strange ditty.

"The words were so pleasing that my mind has ne'er forgotten them since—

'The night we love, for 'tis then we roam,
　Gathering the dew from leaf and flower;
Hiding 'mid the branches of our forest home,
　Seeking mirth and frolic by the hour.

None to molest or intrude upon our mirth,
　With the moon's pale rays shining clear,
We frolic and gambol as we roam the earth
　Free from pain, or sadness, or fear.

Join our hands, and sing till the glade
　Re-echo with our blithesome laugh and song;
We'll enjoy what our Creator Great has made:
　Love ourselves, nor work our neighbours any wrong.

Then let the forest ring with joyful shouts,
　As we dance around the fairy rings so green;
Kiss the moonbeams as they chase us in and out,
　Bathing tree, and shrub, and flower in silv'ry sheen.'

"Thou art right, George," observed Little John; "'twas pleasant indeed for thee to listen to such a ditty."

"Ay' man, but proceed. Said they aught to thee?" said Will Scarlet, with a touch of impatience in his voice.

"Thou shalt hear. With curious intent I peered through an opening, and saw a sight not soon to be forgot.

"Hundreds of tiny figures roamed the glade, shouting, singing, dancing.

"Dreaming I surely thought I was, 'twas so uncommon a thing I beheld.

"Such merry imps I ne'er saw, and of such comely forms withal.

"Lads and lasses were fully bent upon fun.

"Cautiously I crept forward to more closely look upon so strange a sight.

"'Welcome, George-a-Green! Come forward,' said a score or more of voices.

"I trembled sore at thoughts of going among so strange a company, and held me purposely back.

"'Get thou from behind yon tree, and join our company, else thy case will be an evil one.'"

"Think of that; and what didst thou?" asked Little John.

"I e'en did as I was bid, and ïed me among them.

"'Thou shunnest better company than thyself,' said one saucily.

"'Welcome to Sherwood's merry forester,' said another; and blithely rang out their cheery voices on the night, in welcome to one so unworthy as myself.

"'Twas wondrous strange to look upon I saw.

"For the space of a good bow-shot these fairies held their merry revels, until thousands could not count their numbers.

"They were clad in green, and that of the best colour, like to ours."

"The lasses were decked in green kirtles, and their hair was fairly ablaze with jewels, like unto those worn at the King's court.

"Naught could I do but stare with main and might.

"'Drink, George-a-Green,' said one, offering me a tiny horn.

"Fearing to offend so brave and goodly a company, I e'en drank.

"It was but a drain of liquor, but had I drunken a dozen horns of wine, no such fancies would they have worked on me as did it.

"I laughed, sang, and danced, and was as blithesome as the best of them.

"'Ah, ah!' laughed one, 'the forester liketh our wine. Give it again to drink, while we sing:—

'Quaff, quaff the wine,
　Fill the horn up to the brim;
Drink it as the moonbeams shine,
　'Twill thee free from ache or whim.
'Twas distilled where violets grow,
　From the choicest flowery sweets;
If the secret thou would'st know,
　Search till the night the morning greets.'

"Suddenly the notes of a bugle horn sounded loud.

"Instantly the fairies hied them off affrightedly, hiding under thicket and brake.

"Rushing in mad career came a herd of deer, with riders to every one.

"The blood within me ran cold, for 'twas a most horrid sight.

"Circling round me came strange-looking fellows.

"Some had deers' heads, with branching antlers; others, heads of swine, dogs, birds, and such like things on a man's body."

"An' thou sawest them plainly?" asked Little John.

"Thou art not more plainly seen of me than were they.

"I stood in their centre, while with horrid glance they looked upon me.

"'George-a-Green! George-a-Green!' said one, that their leader appeared to be, 'long have we waited for thy coming. Thou wilt join our band.'

"My tongue clove to my mouth's roof, my limbs tottered, and helpless was I as a child of tender years.

"In accents harsh and unmelodious they carolled forth in chorus:

'Hunters merry and free are we,
　Sweeping onwards till break of day;
Nor daunted are we by aught that we see.
　'Tis nothing can bid us our course to stay

The owl gives out its dismal hoot
　As we ride swiftly and gallantly by,
With arrow keen the red deer to shoot,
　That under the greenwood so closely lie.

Blow a loud note on the bugle horn,
　Shout till the welkins do ring:
Night's shadows give chase to the morn,
　Onward, right forward, and merrily sing!'

LITTLE JOHN AND THE KNIGHT ARRIVE JUST IN TIME

" One blew a horn, and instantly the riders fell into rank by pairs, and dashed onwards.

„Last came a solitary rider, holding a deer by a leathern thong.

"An' I had been paid all the gold of the realm, I could not help going forward and mounting its back.

"With mad and terrible speed did we hie onward.

" Nor break nor thicket stopped our way, as the hunter's horn sounded loud in our ears.

" Our Lady and all the saints forfend me from all harm," I cried aloud.

" 'Twas hardly spoken ere the hunters vanished, and I lay on the greensward without life.

" The sun had well risen ere I roused, when I wended my way home, but never a word spake I of this until now."

" Right well told, George," exclaimed Little John. " I would thou would'st lead me thither some moonlight night to see such strange company."

" Thou would'st be fooled for thy pains an' thou did'st," exclaimed Will Scarlet.

" How so ?" queried Little John.

" Naught would'st thou see. Only at certain times are they visible to mortal sight."

" Body-o'-me ! they be strange folks outright," answered Little John. " They may revel and ride for me. But, Will, believest thou these mysteries ?"

12

"That I do.  Strange things have I myself seen ere now."

"The night is long," remarked one of the company, "and needs enlivening.  To thy story then, good Will."

The silence that ensued showed that his auditors were anxious for him to begin his story, which he did as follows:—

"'Twould be hard to find a sweeter spot than Leminton, on Devon's coast.

"I trow I could," exclaimed a forester, starting up.  "Where wilt thou find a finer place than St. Michael's, on Cornwall's coast?"

"Nay, I take thee a wager," exclaimed Will Scarlet.

Up started several of the foresters to arbitrate on the contending claims.

"Spare thy breath, merry men all," exclaimed Little John.  "Let the story proceed, else will the night run into the morning ere we hear one word of it."

This course was readily agreed to, and Will proceeded, taking care to preface his story with the above challenge again, which was not accepted, thanks to Little John's warning voice.

"Various caves are there to be found if sought after.  Fond was I of spending my hours wandering along the sea-shore, and dreamily stretching my length in the warm sun.

"Being thus engaged one day, methought a voice strangely sweet sounded in mine ears:

"'Beneath the wave in caverns fair,
    Safe from storms' harsh fury I dwell;
Decked is my couch with seaweed rare,
    Bordered by coral, costly gems, and sea shell.

Sport I merrily 'neath the bright-blue wave;
    Comb I mine hair by help of glass so clear;
Safe I recline when wild tempests do rave;
    Need not have I for anything to fear.

Come, then, with me to my bright sea home
    Mortal cannot find one so happy and free;
Bid adieu to sorrow, and never more roam;
    Come, love, come, 'neath the waves with me.'

"Rousing, I looked around, and espied a maiden, lovely and fair, reclining on the waves.

"With eager beck and smile so sweet she drew me near towards her.

"Spell-bound was I, and I could not find speech.

"Right into the sea went I so bravely.

"Her sweet smile so impelled me that I forgot home, parents, friends, all.

"Giving to me her hand, we sank 'neath the waves, nor feared I the going.

"In a spacious cave I soon reclined with the sea maiden near me.

"Attendants she had in plenty, hieing hither and thither at her beck and call.

"'Twas a sight to see her home 'neath the wave.

"I was e'en fain to close mine eyes, so dazed did its brightness make me.

"Lovelier maidens eyes ne'er rested on, and I was well content to dwell with her for ever.

"But it was not to be.

"My mother's hands had placed round my neck an amulet to charm away evil things.

"This could not the sea maiden resist.

"Furious with passion and hate, she bade her minions seize and bear me aloft.

"I came bereft of life; and on waking, found myself on the shore, with my father bending over me.

"The story I told to all, but was scarcely credited.

"Some said I dreamed, others that the warm sun had impressed my brain with fancies and imaginings.

"One thing none could gainsay.  The mark of the maiden's fingers remained on my right wrist, and may still be seen by the curious."

"What thinkest thou of that, Little John?" asked George-a-Green in triumph.

"Body-o'-me! 'tis hard to say.  Ne'er have I seen aught that had not flesh and blood like myself.  'Tis strange, so few folks see such."

Morning broke about this time, and the lieutenant marshalled his men in readiness for action.

"Our Lady send brave Robin is safe," he observed.  "His bugle hour summons is not yet."

"Hist! heard you not that signal, the owl's hoot.  'Tis tidings of Robin Hood, our master, depend on't?"

Will Scarlet was right.

With hot haste came the lad whom Robin had sent to Little John.

---

## CHAPTER XLVI.

### HOW THE ABBOT SERVED HIS FRIENDS.

The abbot he stormed at a furious rate,
    Ye slew not, he cried, my foes I wot.
"Slew!" cried the fellow, showing his cracked pate,
    "By my oath, a good beating from the friar we got."

"SPEAKEST thou truly," asked the lord abbot of an attendant who had just apprised him of the arrival of two out of the three bravoes he had hired to assassinate his enemies.

"They wait without, my lord; shall I bid them to thy presence?"

"Now does this matter assume strange import," the abbot soliquised.  "'Tis plain they are apprised of my hand in the matter.  Robin Hood's vengeance will follow."

"My lord, the two soldiers wait without."

"A malison on the knaves!" exclaimed the abbot, in a rage.  "Thrice five crowns have I paid them for failure."

"My message, my lord.  Shall I—"

" Peace, sirrah.  Desire the knaves to wait without till it be my good pleasure to have audience of them."

The abbot paced the room excitedly.

" All my plans of vengeance are frustrated, and by a rebel in arms against his King and country.  I'll to the King and secure his aid against Robin Hood.  But first I must have audience of these cowardly louts."

Summoning his attendant, the abbot desired him to show in the men.

They entered with sorrowfully dejected mien.

The friar's lusty arm and stout staff had knocked all sprightliness out of them.

" Answer me truly, knaves," said the abbot fiercely.  " Thine undertaking—what of it ?"

" Broken pates and bruised bodies, an' it please your worship," answered one acting as spokesman.

" Thou attacked whom ?"

" A lusty friar with oak staff; a malison upon him, he trounced us wofully."

" What, one man, and he a man of peace, to three soldiers !"

" Man of peace !" exclaimed the first speaker jeeringly.

" By my oath his hand is warlike enough, though he be a frocked and shaven priest."

" Aye, that it is.  Would that he had kept his stout thwacks for those of his own condition ;" and the speaker glanced slily at the abbot.

" Peace, knaves !  Thou givest thy tongues too great a license," exclaimed the abbot ; " discourse but of the matter on hand."

" Earned we not our money well, my lord ?  The balance is over due."

" Not a stiver—not a groat !  Thou hast had already too much.  But what of thy comrade ?  Speak !"

" We wot not of him.  Yon cursed friar's staff knocked our wits clean out of our pates."

" Was he alone," asked the abbot, " when ye fell upon him ?"

" Would it had been so ; then had we given good account of him."

" Thou did'st sadly bungle in this matter.  But thou hast not given answer to my question."

" There were with the friar two others.  'Twas our intention to strike him alone hastily, and in the confusion escape us hither."

" Thinkest thou your fellow is prisoned by the friar ?" asked the abbot.

" Thou hast rightly discerned our thoughts, my lord.  But we would thou would'st pay us that is our due, and let us depart."

" Said I not but just now, one groat more thou should'st not get from my purse ?" said the abbot sharply ; " have a care, lest thou fare worse than e'en the friar served thee "

" 'Tis better far to buy our silence with money than force our speech abroad by thy threats," said one of the soldiers boldly.

" Urgest thou such a thing upon my consideration ?" exclaimed the abbot angrily.

" Now, by Our Lady, it will be seen, and that soon, that I care little for thy outpourings."

At his summons an attendant entered.

" Call hither the lay brethren to convey these swine to the cell thou wottest of."

The attendant cast a commiserating glance upon the soldiers, and departed on his mission.

" We crave thy pardon, my Lord Abbot," said he of the bold speech.

" 'Tis too late.  Thy tongue will have little opportunity to wag abroad."

A significant look passed from one to the other of the soldiers.

With a rush they were upon the abbot.

Their daggers struck his side, but harmed him not.

Under his robe was concealed armour of the finest texture.

The next moment they were prisoners.

Despite their resistance they were borne away.

In a cell, dark and drear, they were thrust.

With refinement of cruelty, they were placed in a sort of stocks, chained hard and fast, and joining each other.

Their gaoler brought them food, bread and water, and placed it where their manacled hands could nearly reach it.

Struggle as they would, it was past taking.

The abbot had his revenge, ample and full it was, too.

He sat in his room in thought.

With knitted brow and clenched hands, he sought to shape his thoughts.

" Oh the morrow, I will e'en seek the King and him request to guard my rights from the power of the daring outlaw, Robin Hood."

Touching a secret spring in the wall, there was disclosed to his view a cavity of somewhat large dimensions.

It was filled with gold and silver.

The abbot's eyes glistened with a strange light as he gloated over his hoard.

He saw not another face peer cautiously over his shoulder at the glittering heap.

" All mine !" the lord abbot said.  Not a person within these walls wots of this hiding-place, but myself."

After a pause he continued :

" He whose cunning fashioned this concealment for me, lives not.  His work finished, with it ended his life.  'Twas a cruel necessity," he soloquised, " but much needed.  The dead tell no tales !"

Closing the aperture the abbot seated himself, and regarded himself with complacency in a steel mirror.

"Bold Robin Hood cannot find my treasure, cunning and daring as he is. Did he but know of it, not all the bars and bolts ever forged by man would keep him from it, I trow."

A low chuckle startled the abbot from his unanimity.

He looked fearfully around.

But nought saw he more than himself.

He saw not a figure crouched low under a large oaken table.

Nor dreamed he that Friar Tuck's presence was so near.

How he so mysteriously appeared must form the details of a separate chapter.

---

## CHAPTER XLVII.

### ARRIVAL OF THE MESSENGER AND RESCUE OF ROBIN HOOD.

"Thy tidings, speak quickly," said Little John to Robin's messenger.

"Robin thy master has hied him northward, whither thou and thy merry men follow with all despatch."

Little John placed his bugle horn to his lips, and blew an assembly.

While his men were forming he plied the messenger with questions.

"Went Earl Mortimer with him?"

"Aye, that did he. The twain sat one horse."

"One horse! Body-o'-me, had they not two?"

"One an unlucky bolt killed dead."

"Ah! pursues them any of the Sheriff's men."

"A score or more horsemen, with their master at their head."

"Said Robin aught else to thee? Bethink thee ere thou answerest."

"Naught but what I've unfolded."

Scouts came in to report a force of the sheriff's crossbowmen astir and proceeding northward.

"Hie thee to the knight, bid him follow cautiously after them with his party, to act as occasion requireth."

Having delivered this command, Little John turned to the messenger again.

"Seemed the beast at all o'erburdened with its riders twain?"

"'Tis a horse of mettle as thou knowest; and kept its own against those in rear while I looked."

"That's good. Bladebone of St. Hubert! my master, Robin, must not fall into the Sheriff's sharp claws."

Dismissing the messenger, he turned to his men, saying—

"Robin, our good master, has hied him northward with the earl, and bids us follow. Brace thyselves to use quick despatch in following. Forward, lads, to the rescue!"

"To the rescue!" was the shouted response by all the band.

With speed they moved onwards, keeping marked silence.

Each one listened to catch the call of Robin's bugle, but it came not.

"What's thy thought of this matter, John?" asked Will Scarlet.

"Robin has done his work bravely. Earl Mortimer is with him. Thou heard'st that?"

"I did with great joyfulness. Our Lady send they safe escape the Sheriff and his minions."

"Body-o-me!" growled Little John, "an' the base Norman hind but lay so much as his finger on him to his hurt, 'tis his to look to't. His days will be few, and I Little John promise for it."

"Heard'st thou that?" asked Will Scarlet.

Little John listened and replied:—

"'Tis but a bird's note. Robin's bugle hath a clearer sound."

"The friar was of our company a little while back; I saw him but now," said Will.

"He's at more congenial work, I reckon."

"How so? He was hot on flying his bow against our Norman foes."

"I sent him with a knight and lady—— But heard'st thou not that?" asked Little John interrupting himself in the thread of his remarks.

The sound of an approaching horseman became plainly audible.

"Our Lady send 'tis Robin," said Will.

"An' it be my master, I vow a pair of silver candlesticks to her shrine; that is, good Will, when I find some fat-pursed fellow to help me pay for them."

Nearer and nearer came the horseman.

Bounding forward, Little John cried:

"Halt, ye! whoever ye be, at thy peril!"

Earl Mortimer drew rein at Little John's side.

"Our master—what of him?" said Little John excitedly.

"He's in a thicket, a good few steps from here," replied the earl.

"And thou art here!" said Little John, half reproachfully.

"'Tis Robin's own doings, Little John; my word on't, I leave him not otherwise. But advance quickly. I can discourse to thee as we travel."

With quickened pace the foresters moved on.

"Thou must know of Robin's whereabouts," said Little John to the earl, "I pray thee move forward at our head."

"'Tis a grand doing," remarked Little John

as the earl finished his narration of Robin's daring adventure in the castle.

"Is his equal to be found in this our land?" asked the earl enthusiastically.

"None is before him. Would he were here with our company now. I begin to be fearful for him."

"His speech to me was cheery. He feareth no danger to himself," replied Mortimer.

"Body-o'-me! he never did—never will," answered Little John, as if half amazed at the earl's remark.

"I would have thee bethink thyself too that the Sheriff's men are accoutred and ill fitted for a chase through the forest after so good and crafty a woodsman as Robin Hood."

"There is comfort in thy speech," replied Little John, "but the Sheriff's crossbowmen are abroad too, knewest thou that?"

"'Twas a thing I lacked knowledge of. But forward, good John, each step advanced is Robin succoured."

"There go some of the Norman hinds," said Little John, pointing to some of the Sheriff's men in the distance.

"'Tis even so," replied Will Scarlet, who had by this time joined himself to the earl and Little John's company.

"A flight of arrows would deter their advance," remarked Earl Mortimer.

"Let them get entangled in the wood," replied Little John; "then will our fellows be more than a match for thrice their number."

"Well averred," said Will.

Turning round, Little John addressed the foresters as follows:

"Our master, good Robin, whom Our Good Lady have in her approved keeping, is in yon thicket. Between him and thee are Norman soldiers!"

A defiant shout greeted this harangue.

"Spread thyselves to the right hand and to the left, and teach these Norman clowns good woodcraft."

The cheer that greeted his speech told Little John that he was well understood.

Unaware of the near proximity of Robin's men in their rear, the Sheriff's men went forward.

"'Twill go hard, but Robin be captured this time," remarked their leader.

"Of that I am not well assured. His bugle horn hangs at his side. Its summons gets him instant help; of that thou art acquaint."

"Pish! He's but a mortal mould, and is found at disadvantage as are other men."

"I question not the soundness of thy speech, but it has ever been so, as I to thee have just said."

A flight of arrows in their midst made the Normans look round amazed.

"Advance quickly, one half," exclaimed the commander; "the remainder turn and let fly their crossbolts rearwards."

This was done, and a shower of bolts went whizzing through the trees.

But each forester had gained the shelter of a friendly tree.

Them the bolts assailed not.

With true aim and swift arrow, Little John's men harassed the foe.

In vain they returned their fire, not a mark to them was visible.

Several Normans had bitten the dust, more were grievously wounded, still they held their ground like hunted deer at bay.

Slowly, but surely, they were being surrounded to their destruction.

Clear and shrill upon the air came three notes of a bugle-horn.

"Forward, my merry men all," shouted Little John. "Robin is at hand, and in sore plight, I ween.

Regardless of the Norman crossbowmen, onwards they dashed with speed.

Each man struggled hard to be first in to the rescue.

Turn we now to the party under Walter the knight. Obedient to Little John's commands, he led them on cautiously in the footsteps of the party of crossbowmen.

By skirting a thicket his manœuvre was unseen by those on the castle ramparts.

With his good sword drawn, and Robin's merry men at his back, the knight kept on.

Little weened the Normans who were tracking Robin to his death, that behind came so many good men and true.

The sun shone out gloriously, and penetrated the forest's gloom, lighting on the helmed heads of the Norman crossbowmen.

'Twere easy for the knight to have annihilated a score or more of them, but prudence forbade one arrow being thrown away.

"They go to Robin," he said in reply to his men's importunities to attack the foe. "'Twill be perilous to stop their advance until we, too, see him whom we seek."

The determination proved a good one

In due time they arrived at a grove, and halting his men, the knight reconnoitered.

Three pealing notes from a bugle-horn wakened the forest echoes.

"'Tis Robin! 'tis Robin!" shouted he, and soon all were dashing forward.

"Little John's men here, too," said the knight joyfully, as they came in sight. "Now is Robin Hood safe; Our Lady be thanked!"

They formed quickly.

Peering cautiously in advance, Little John and the knight saw Robin bound to the tree.

The merry men bent their bows, and waited the signal.

## CHAPTER XLVIII.

Draw to the ear my merry men all;
 True to thine aim, sure thine eye;
The Norman hinds in scores make to fall,
 Till they and their master be forced to fly.
The merry men drew to the ear so true,
 Each arrow found place in a Norman breast;
There fell that day of men not a few,
 Brave Robin and his men to flight put the rest.

"MARK well, those three with bows bent at Robin our master's breast," said Little John, in a suppressed whisper.

The merry men let fly, and the first to fall were the three crossbowmen whom the Sheriff had appointed to slay Robin.

There fell also many others, so true did Robin's archers shoot.

With tremendous bounds Little John made for Robin's side.

His keen sword cut his bonds, and soon was his loved master free.

A warm pressure of the hand was all that passed between master and man.

They had other work to do.

"Take this sword, master mine," said Little John to Robin. "Body-o'-me! the Norman hinds must be vanquished quite."

With grim determination Robin rushed forward, dealing his blows right and left.

"Quarter to none!" he cried, as the bright blade he handled cleft in twain a stout Norman soldier's head.

Stoutly did the Normans resist.

Little John found himself hemmed in by a dozen of the Sheriff's men.

Right sore they pressed him.

But Robin was at hand, and Will Scarlet too.

The red blood ran from Little John's arm from a slight wound, but for no quarter cried he.

"That for thy pains," he cried, as with terrific stroke he felled the fellow that had wounded him.

Foot by foot he and Robin contested.

Around them the battle raged furiously.

"Ah! ah!" cried Robin. "Thou hast found thy masters, base hinds. True men and free are for slaves a match!"

"St. Denis to the rescue! Hew and slay! give quarter to none!" shouted the Sheriff, forcing his way towards where Robin stood.

Armed with a ponderous battle-axe, he struck down not a few of Robin's men.

"'Tis mine, the outlaw to slay!" he said, as with feverish haste he sought a place near his foe.

"Make way for the Sheriff," shouted Robin. "Way there, sirrahs, for Nottingham's Sheriff!" and a contemptuous laugh rang out clearly upon the air.

Face to face they stood.

The Sheriff's battle-axe was lifted high.

It descended not on Robin.

One terrific blow caused the Sheriff to reel.

It was dealt him by Little John, and he fell to the ground like a stunned ox.

Fiercer waged the battle o'er the Sheriff's prostrate form.

In the melée some of his men managed to draw the Sheriff away.

"Our Lady be thanked, they fly!" exclaimed Robin. "Pursue! pursue! my merry men all. Let vengeance still be taken upon our foes."

They chased them to the castle gates almost; and ne'er so bloody a fray was known in these parts for many a day.

The foresters lost not a few, but the Sheriff's company lost three to their one.

Right well did Earl Mortimer and Walter the knight ply their weapons.

Each man did his devoir in right gallant style for his master, good Robin.

Saxon bravery was that day well attested, and left its deep impress on Norman hearts.

"Welcome back, good master," exclaimed Little John, seizing Robin's hand. "Body-o'-me! but yon proud Sheriff will keep his dastardly knaves far from thee in future, I opine."

Little John's welcome was supplemented by a hearty cheer from the assembled foresters, until the forest re-echoed again with its ring.

"Thanks, a thousand times o'er, my men, good and true," said Robin, in response to the greeting. "This day thou hast more than proved thy devotion to me thy leader."

"Long live Robin! Hurrah! hurrah! hurrah!"

They were the same cheers as have been heard by Britain's enemies many a time since—terrible to such, but inspiriting to friends.

Robin waved his hand and said:

"For this day's work each man will receive ten crowns from the treasury. Those that have fallen their share will be doubled to their friends."

"Each man will share a stoup of the best wine at my expense," said Earl Mortimer; "I publicly thank ye all for thy help."

"Long live Robin! Long live brave Earl Mortimer! Confusion to England's enemies! Down with the Norman dogs!" and again went hearty cheers re-echoing through the forest.

"And thee, Robin, my friend and deliverer, what can I say to thee?" exclaimed Earl Mortimer, with emotion.

"Naught of praise deserve I for my friendly action in thy behalf. Thou knowest me as a friend, doubly endeared because of the cause we espouse."

"Thou hast bound thyself with strong cords to my heart, Robin. Perish Mortimer's memory if he should ever unbind them!"

THE TOURNAMENT AT NOTTINGHAM CASTLE.

"Ah, my friend," replied Robin, addressing himself in common, to all around, "adversity close binds where prosperity ottimes severs. What mine hand has done for Mortimer, I would do for any of my band: All are alike dear to me, alike true to each other."

Such a noble, disinterested expression of sentiment could receive none other than a warm response.

It was cheered to the full

Turning to Little John, Robin said:

"Good John, let the dead have sepulture, alike Norman and Saxon; six feet of earth is theirs in common. Let the wounded have tender care; prisoners, if any, strict guard."

"'Twill be so, master. God rest the souls of all alike!"

Many devout "Amens!" followed Little John's charitable wish: for the Saxon foresters carried not their resentment and antipathies beyond death.

A party was soon told off for these offices, and the remainder stood guard against surprises.

A list of the names of the dead and wounded was handed to Robin, and as his eye glanced down it, real sorrow marked his handsome features.

"Will Scarlet is missing, an' it please you," said little John.

"It cannot be," said Robin. "Will is too stout a Saxon yeoman to yield to Norman fetters. Inform thyself of this matter among the men; they may have knowledge of his whereabouts."

In a short time Little John returned with word that Will had been carried off prisoner by the Sheriff's men.

"By my halidome!" exclaimed Robin, "the Sheriff had well weigh the matter ere he lays a finger violently upon Will. I hold hostages on which to avenge him."

"Body-o'-me!" growled Little John, "Nottingham Castle will be imperilled, an' the Sheriff but hurt a hair of Will's head.

Every member of the band swore an oath to rescue their comrade, who had endeared himself to each one of them by his frank and open nature.

"Let us on now to Sherwood," said Robin. "Our rest this night shall have been earned right well. Onward! march!"

As they went, Earl Mortimer discoursed with Robin about the events of the past day.

"'Tis to me even as a dream," he observed. "Events have so rapidly fashioned themselves, that one's belief is put to the test thereby."

"'Tis nothing, Mortimer, replied Robin. "A life in the forest is as full of events as an egg is full of meat. 'Tis not any one's to say what a day will bring forth."

"'Twill impart such a lesson to the Sheriff, this of to-day's, that he will be fain to rest him e'er again he molests us."

"Intrigue and cunning will he next contrive, now that boldness has foiled his plans." said Robin, laughingly; "but he must play his game well to encompass aught of evil against me. Let him consider the reckoning.

"There fell full two score and a half Normans this blessed day," remarked Little John. It lacks not one of that number, for 'tis mine own counting."

"And of our merry men fell what number?" asked Mortimer.

"Three-fourths of a score to the man," replied Little John, sorrowfully. "Full too many for such an occasion."

"Fought they not well?" said Robin. "I trow I never saw Normans so well conditioned in bravery."

"Their's was a desperate case," replied Mortimer. "Like hunted stags at bay they stood, and in their wild despair they did the deeds of braver men."

"Well put, Mortimer," exclaimed Robin, who, of all men, liked a well-turned sentence. "But Saxon worth tried the baseness of their metal, and proved it beyond dispute."

"But what of the friar?" asked Robin suddenly. "His presence I wot is absent from us."

"Sir Richard Wykeham and his lady-love travelled hither seeking your protection," said Little John; to the friar's keeping I confided them."

"By report he is not to me unknown," replied Robin; "has aught of ill befallen him?"

"Ill! beshrew me! but worse than ill, master mine!" answered Little John.

"Discoursed he to thee of the matter?"

"That did he. 'Tis Nottingham's Sheriff is the despoiler of his property. Hast eve known the Norman different?"

"'Twill be mine to offer him means of r dress," remarked Robin; "Saxon ne'er crave it of me in vain, and that all men know full well."

"Stand; the password at thy peril!" challenged a sentinel.

"Robin Hood and his merry men!" replied Robin in quick response.

"Pass; God save ye all!"

Soon were the outlaws resting 'neath their old trysting places, holding converse of the past day's exploits.

A savoury odour from the foresters' kitchen betokened preparations for a substantial meal, wherewith to allay their hungry cravings.

Robin's first care was to see to the condition of the wounded, who had been borne thither on rude stretchers, formed by the boughs of trees.

Next he had the Norman prisoners brought into his presence.

Addressing himself to the chiefest of them, he said:

"The just doom of ye all would be a short shrift and a long rope; but our warfare is not of such sort."

"We are prisoners. Thy clemency is well received by us; our thanks are thine."

"'Tis not of this I would discourse," replied Robin; "the Sheriff, thy master holdest one right dear to me and all true men, named Will Scarlet.

"'Tis but one prisoner in return for us all," remarked the Norman.

"'Tis well said. I would out of thy number one be selected to bear my message to the Sheriff."

A hurried consultation was held among the prisoners, and one of their number selected for the service.

"Say to the Sheriff, I, Robin Hood, certify that, unless Will Scarlet be delivered up to me free of harm, within the first twain watch settings, two of those I hold prisoners will pay for it with their lives."

"'Twill be mine to deliver thy words as thou hast given them to me," the messenger replied.

"I further certify that each successive watch setting past the first twain that sees not Will Scarlet in our midst will prove the last of other prisoners, till the number be expended quite."

"I am certified of thy message."

"I, Robin Hood, have so said, and it shall

be done. Mine integrity is well known to the Sheriff. Advise him to instant compliance, an' thou lovest thy comrades' safety!"

"Trust me. 'Twill be mine office to so discourse, that my master will be fain to pleasure thee in the matter."

"Depart not yet till thou hast refreshed thy tired condition," said Robin. "Sound to dinner, and that with quick despatch?"

Little John blew an assembly, and soon the foresters were seated at the rude but plenteous board.

An unwonted silence reigned around.

Respect for the memory of those that had fallen in the strife that day, kept a still tongue in every head.

When the remains of the repast were cleared away, up rose Robin Hood, saying:

"Fill ye to the brim, one and all!"

'Twas done.

"Honour now my toast, I beseech you, my merry men all."

Holding his cup aloft, Robin said with deep feeling:

"To the memory of the brave dead. Full repose to both soul and body, and a resurrection joyful!"

The toast was fully responded to, and the foresters betook them to that rest which they so much needed.

The Norman messenger was conducted to the confines of the forest, and there bid to speed him on his errand with diligence and discretion.

Robin now held discourse with Sir Richard Wykeham and Maria Danvers, and they rested that night with light hearts.

The worth of such promise was too well known to be lightly esteemed.

## CHAPTER XLIX.

### HOW FRIAR TUCK GAINED UNLOOKED-FOR ENTRANCE TO THE ABBEY.

*The friar, he swore with a full round oath,*
*That to part from such a singer, he was loath.*

. . . . . . . .

WHEN Friar Tuck had finished playing host to the stranger knight and lady, he took himself aside to rest.

But so much had he eaten and drank that sleep visited not his eyes.

"A malison seize the thing! Here am I winking until mine eyes are right sore, and never a nap can I get."

With drunken gravity he staggered up and held a colloquy with himself.

"Friar Tuck, thou art weakening fast through necessity of drink and food. Thy limbs refuse their office. See thou to this matter, ere it be too late, and strengthen thine inner self, that thy limbs may behave themselves more seemly."

He paused, and surveyed his feet, apostrophising them thus:

"Out upon thee, for lazy fellows! Proceed. Good Robin will ne'er release Mortimer until thou leadest me to his side."

Whether it was that his feet disliked being rated, certain it is that they slipped from under him, and he rested firm on the broad of his back.

The first blush of dawn was in the eastern horizon, and the birds carolled their matins amid the branches of the forest, as the friar made another desperate attempt to rise, and succeeded.

"'Tis well for my character that that knave Little John is not here, else would he ascribe my present condition to somewhat other than weakness of limbs. Out upon him for a scandalising tongue!"

"A good man must needs be maligned;
   Fools prate, look wise, shake their heads;
Point as he walks, says he's lightly esteemed:
   Hang them—let them hie them to their beds.

If he drinks a horn or so of wine,
   Feeling dry, that increases by the score,
Why he's a good man still for all they talk so fine:
   Hang them for fools—let them roar, let them
      roar.

Jolly Friar I am called by foes and friends,
   'Tis a scandal cruel thus me to be-name
Let them prate, I will use the things that nature
      sends;
Did I not, folks would prate all the same."

After delivering himself of these verses in self-defence of his principle of non-abstinence the friar essayed to walk, and got along pretty well, though very slowly.

"My throat's parched," he said, with a thick utterance; "I will get me to the cellar and drink."

Mistaking the way in his drunken state, he steered an opposite course, and travelled in the direction of St. Mary's Abbey.

A donkey, ragged and hungered, saluted the morn, as the friar passed, in tones so lusty as to make himself heard far and near.

"Greet thee, friend," said the friar, with gravity, "a fine voice hast thou, I would thou would'st troll me a ditty."

As if responsive to the friar's kindly invitation, the donkey lifted up his voice and brayed e'en more lustily than before.

"Thy voice is not of ordinary sort, I wot," remarked the friar. "That quaver thou did'st so well execute tells that in Italy thine education was finished. I would I knew thy name and condition, friend, then would I take thee to my master, Robin Hood, to engage thine help in mass-singing, thy voice is so well fitted therefor."

"I would fain hear thy voice again," remarked the friar, after a pause, "and join mine own in sweet concert therewith an thou be so minded."

"Well, an' thou refusest I e'en must show thee the power and compass of my voice. Perchance it will or will not please thy liking."

Staggering over towards the animal, the friar placed his hand upon his back, and in that attitude commenced his ditty:

"Three jackdaws sat on a convent wall,
    In grave dispute, and sore perplexed,
When a shaven monk, so slim and so tall,
    To all three thus himself addressed:

'Give thee good morrow, sirs, one and all,
    Hast thou aught on thy minds, thou would'st lay bare,
'Tis mine office to hear when sinners do call,
    So confess thyself quickly, without shame or fear.'

The first jackdaw, with air so grave,
    Cleared his throat, wagged his tail, and loudly cawed,
Flapped his wings, hopped about, and looked so brave,
    That his companions did him warmly applaud.

With languishing eye, and look demure
    The jackdaw prepared himself to confess;
Quoth he, 'Holy monk, I'm not very sure
    That anything on my conscience doth press.'

The monk looked glum, the monk looked stern,
    Shook his head with grave gesture, and said;
'Unbosom thyself, lest haply thou mourn,
    When too late 'neath the sod thou liest dead.'

Said the second jackdaw, with sad mien;
    'Our thoughts we care not to disclose.'
Black must they be, then, I very well ween,'
    Quoth the monk, 'thou shalt not have repose.'

''Tis too bad thee to vex, holy friar,'
    Quoth jackdaw the third as he sat;
'The fact I'll disclose, and no longer thee tire—
    Our thoughts they dwell on yon cat.'

'He's a rogue, no greater doth live,
    'Cept us three and thou, holy friar;
To him due penance and stripes quickly give,
    As for us we go mounting up higher.'

In a rage the monk a stone he threw
    At the jackdaws that sat on the wall:
At which they but jeered with caws not a few,
    And mocked when the stone on the abbot did fall.

Poor monk, he got whipped, according to law,
    Stripes not a few on his back fell apace.
Three jackdaws came to his window to caw,
    And jeer him upon his most pitiful case."

"Excel that, and thou can'st," said the friar, on finishing his song.

Whether it was the friar's tones that stirred up the animal to bray, just as cocks do crow when challenged by their kind, does not appear; but a very ancient chronicler has it that the donkey did bray, and that most lustily.

"Well done! thou art well attuned and jolly. But canst thou do aught at quarter-staff or shoot?" said the friar with gravity.

No answer came to the friar's challenge.

Thou must e'en carry me, fellow, or receive three buffets for thy refusal. Dost hear? Bladebone of St. Hubert! but thou hast a rough hide, though thou art a well-favoured singer.

By dint of great exertions the friar mounted the animal's back; which, left to its own devices, hied it leisurely off towards the Abbey.

The friar slept as he rode, and was borne at last to the Abbey gates.

Looking out through the lattice, the warder espied Friar Tuck seeking admittance.

"Thine errand, father?" he said, on seeing the friar's priestly garb.

A loud snore from the friar was the only response.

"Our Good Lady save us! how he groans," exclaimed the warder; "some holy man doing penance, I wot."

Acting upon this assumption, he opened wide the gate and let the donkey in.

He shook the friar by the arm, but failed to rouse him.

"'Tis a miracle!" remarked the warder; "hither has this ass brought this holy man, and he fast asleep through grievous watchings and fastings!"

He had him carried in bodily, and placed in a dormitory, where the friar slept and snored his fill.

Waking betimes, and feeling a great thirst after his copious libations of the past night, he looked about him for means to quench it.

Seeing a room open of inviting appearance, Friar Tuck made bold to enter, and was fortunate enough to find what he was in quest of.

After satisfying his thirst, he looked about, and was not slow in recognising that he was not in his old haunts at Sherwood.

Though still greatly stupified by his inordinate drinking of the previous night, he was sensible enough to use wariness and discretion in his actions.

Selecting a quiet nook in the room, he coiled his fat person together, and settled himself to finish his slumbers.

When the abbot entered, he awoke, and peering cautiously forth, saw and heard what passed between him and the assassin he had hired, and whom the friar had so signally vanquished the previous night.

"'Twill ill betide me an' I show my face to the abbot. 'Tis quite clear he bears me no love," said the friar to himself as he listened.

Delighted was he to witness the closing scene of the interview as recorded elsewhere.

But more delighted still was he when, peering cautiously over the abbot's shoulder, he saw the glittering treasures of this miserly churchman spread out before him.

So engrossed was the abbot that he noticed not the friar's presence, although he was close at his elbow.

Taking due note of the position of the secret spring, the friar stepped back to his hiding-place.

Unfortunately he upset a stool, and the noise attracted the abbot's attention.

He turned round with great haste, but saw not the friar crawling under cover, else had it gone ill with him.

"'Tis strange how nervous I am of late.

'Tis the cares of mine office weigh heavily upon me," said the abbot on failing to see any cause for his fright.

"Mine hands will ease thee of some of thy cares," remarked the friar to himself, "or it will go hard with me."

His hand itched to handle the abbot's gold pieces, and he waited for a fitting opportunity to do so.

Soon this presented itself.

The abbot left.

Cautiously emerging from his hiding-place, the friar pressed the spring, and the abbot's treasure lay opened before him

His first care was to secure the door from within; that done he began to hide as many gold pieces about him as he could conveniently carry.

"Now St. Hubert be praised," he said, "but this is fine. Sawest thou ever such gold pieces, Friar Tuck?"

He was in raptures.

"Thou may'st stay here too long, my good fellow," he said, addressing himself, "so e'en get off with despatch."

Laden like a donkey almost, the friar left the abbot's room.

He was met on his way by some of the monks, and had to accept their kind invitation to a repast, although he tried hard to refuse.

He greatly feared detection at the hands of some of the confraternity; especially of those monks, whom he and Little John had eased of the tithes.

Being full of contrivances, however, he lacked not one for the present occasion.

He kept his cowl closely drawn round his face.

"Thy vow, good brother, debars thee from showing thy face to any," queried one of the monks.

"Thou hast rightly conjectured," Friar Tuck replied. "My vow is of such a sort. Nor is my speech to be too long.

"Thy voice hath a familiar sound to mine ears," observed one of the monks that had suffered from the friar's depredations.

"A good man's voice is always familiar to a brother. Goodness makes a bond of brotherhood between such."

After delivering himself of this well-turned compliment to his interlocutor, the friar modestly folded his hands across his fat paunch, and eyed the monks sharply from beneath his cowl.

"Thou art not that ungodly man, Friar Tuck?" asked one of the company, rather bluntly.

"But brother of his am I," replied the friar with imperturable coolness of speech and manner.

"Thou hast a strong likeness to nim," re

marked his querist. "Our Lady send thou resemble him not in rogues' ways."

Friar Tuck devoutly crossed himself as if the bare mention of such a possibility horrified him.

Inwardly he vowed a vow, mentally registered, to trounce his tormentor's hide the first favourable opportunity.

"Thou hast heard of his malpractices, doubtless," observed the monk.

"'Tis said his sanctity is not highly flavoured with scourgings and fastings," replied the friar; "I will teach him better things, and with mine own hands lay on the stripes thickly."

There was a general laugh at this.

The bare idea of anybody inflicting a scourging on Friar Tuck, strong-armed and lusty, was so preposterous that it quite tickled the monks.

"I wish thee well out of thine office," remarked the same monk, laughingly.

"Thou alludest, doubtless, to his strength of arm, and pugnacious condition," replied the friar. "But I, too, can strike a good blow."

Raising his arm he struck his tormentor, who stood near him, a blow which quickly felled him to the floor.

It would be difficult to say whether resentment or astonishment worked strongest in the minds of the monks assembled.

Certain it is that three of them seized the friar.

He was greatly disposed to give them similar treatment, but desisted for fear of consequences.

Assuming an air of innocence, he said—

"Nay, good brothers, be not angered. I but demonstrated my ability to deal with that n'er-do-well relation of mine. Besides, it was but a gentle blow."

"Gentle!" said the monk who had received it; "gentle, call you it? It was strong, and withal malicious. Hold him fast, while I hie to the lord abbott to acquaint him of the matter."

"Nay, nay, good brother, thou mistakes my motive in thus attributing maliciousness as its cause," friar Tuck said. "I pray thee think no more of it. Here's my hand."

"Let charity prevail," said the monk who had admitted the friar to the abbey; our good brother was in a sorry plight on his arrival. His weakness was so great as to unfit him to bestride his ass."

"What are those things I feel?" asked one of the monks who held the friar, in allusion to the gold pieces which he had stuffed away about his person in all directions.

"They be part of my penance," replied the friar, quite unconcerned; "stones and gravel have I placed next my person to mortify my body."

"Release him good brothers, I beseech you," said the friendly monk; "'twould be rank sacrilege to further molest such a holy man."

His intercession prevailed, and Friar Tuck was released.

His proffered hand was not refused by the monk he had so unceremoniously treated.

It was evident, however, that he little relished the warm grip of the friar's hand, which caused tears of pain to spring to his eyes.

He got him as far off as possible from his demonstrative brother, fearing that he would again illustrate some theory with practical force upon his person.

"I shall depart now," said the friar; "my benison I leave with you. Poor I came, poor I depart, to fulfil my vow."

The friar had only been enlightened a few minutes previously as to how he had come to the abbey, which circumstance up to that time was a complete mystery to him.

"Abide yet a little time longer," one of the monks replied; "I will acquaint the lord abbot of your presence."

"Concern not yourself, I pray you," Friar Tuck said. "I am unworthy of having speech of such a holy man."

He added mentally, "I am too well known to him to befool him as I have these."

Turning to the monk who had befriended him, the friar said:

"Let my beast be got ready, good brother. He is but a sorry creature, though well suited to one of my lowly, humble condition."

Friar Tuck stood at the gate bidding adieu to the monks.

He mounted his ass, and was just about to start when a loud outcry was heard.

"Secure him! Hold him fast! 'Tis Friar Tuck."

Before hands could be laid on him, he struck his heels viciously into the beast's sides, and went riding away at a good pace, pursued by the monks.

The friar laughed outright, and urged the ass on to greater speed.

"Bladebone of St. Hubert! won't Little John laugh when I narrate my adventurous stay in yon abbey? Robin Hood, too, will be mightily pleased. 'Twill be a standing joke for all our merry men."

On reaching the forest, the friar was met by a party who had been sent in search of him, headed by Little John in person.

"Body-o'-me!" growled the giant, thou art troublesome to find. Search have we made high and low for thee. I'm both tired, hungry, and thirsty."

"Ah! ah! ah!" laughingly shouted Friar Tuck. "Chide me not, good John, until thou art acquainted with all particulars of the matter."

"Particulars!" quoth Little John. "Where hast thou been, sirrah?"

"To visit the lord abbot of St. Mary's."

"Thou dost but jest; thy carcase would not be safe within St. Mary's walls."

"Ah! ah! list to this, John! list to this! Heard'st thou ever such a merry chink? Gold, too! all gold!" and the friar took out a handful of gold and chinked it up and down.

"Beshrew me! but it sounds of a good sort. Thy absence is ever welcome an' it bears such interest. Is that——"

"I am in search of our brother, our Friar Tuck, said the friar, laughing uproariously——

"Saw'st thou aught of brother of mine,
Sleek of person and strong of will;
Tell unto me, good reward shall be thine,
If not, I'll go seeking him still."

"Thou discoursest mysteriously. Beshrew me, I like plain speech best. Thy meaning to me disclose."

"Patience, good John; let's proceed. The lord abbot is mightily anxious to find me; I would rather be apart from him."

"Body-o'-me!" said Little John; "let but one of his shaven crowns be found by me within Sherwood's forest, an' 'twill go hard with me but that I make his pate ring for him!"

"Heed them not; but of my brother, John; sawest thou him?——

"Dark is his hair, sturdy his frame,
He rideth on beast of good breed;
Unto thee I cannot disclose his name,
Tell to me then, for great is my need."

"Ah! ah! hold me John, or I shall die outright! the matter does so tickle my fancy."

"I care not so long as thou art safe," replied Little John; laugh thy fill; 'tis a sorry time, though, for merriment."

"How so?" asked the friar, with seemly gravity; "hast aught befallen our master?"

"Our Lady be thanked! he is safe. But others rest them beneath the sod?"

"It grieves me to hear it. But how came it all about. Is the earl safe?"

I shall discourse thee on the matter at leisure. Meantime, tell me of thy adventures. St. Hubert! but we all gave thee up for lost."

Whereupon the friar told him all.

His arrival was greeted with acclamation by all the band, especially by Robin.

The sight of so many gold pieces was a welcome thing to all, for the treasury was beginning to get very low.

"I'm right glad," said Robin laughing, "that thou hast been so well employed. Sent my lord abbot his love or benison?"

"I stayed not to hear it," replied the friar merrily. "I was too preciously freighted to stay his pleasure."

THE NORMANS WAIT FOR ROBIN HOOD.

"Thou may'st seek thy brother, an' thou wilt," said Robin.

At this there was a general roar of laughter.

"With mine own hand will I scourge his hide," replied the friar; "but, St. Hubert! I am hugeous dry. Hast thou aught good in the cellar?"

"Not a drop," said Little John, with a merry twinkle in his eye. "Of water there is a plentiful supply."

"To the Evil One with thy water! 'Twill go hard with the cellarer an' he find me not something good."

"So, so, my lord abbot, thou art well re-paid for thy dastardly conduct," exclaimed Robin. "Assassins, too! Thou overreachest the Sheriff himself in evil intrigues."

After a pause, he said to Little John:

"Let the prisoner be brought before me. Thou knowest whom. 'Tis the lord abbot's minion I would see."

In a short time he was brought.

"Thou meritest nothing at my hands but death," said Robin sternly, "but I give thee thy life, because Friar Tuck hath promised thee it. See thou offendest not again."

The fellow was conducted to the confines of the forest, and then released.

13

"Should the Sheriff's messenger come during my absence, keep him until I return."

So saying, Robin turned and walked quietly towards St. Ann's Well.

## CHAPTER L.

Thou art ever welcome, Robin dear,
Thy Marian loves thee past compare.
That thou lovest me, thine eyes show clear.
In my heart thine image I always bear.

"Ah, thou truant," said a sweet musical voice, as Robin emerged into view.

"Marian sweet! thy chiding is undeserved, believe me!" exclaimed Robin as he pressed the blushing Marian to his heart.

"I did but jest, Robin dear. Thy Marian knewest what thou wert about, noble Robin."

She looked lovingly into his face, while her's reflected the happiness that in his shone.

"Stirring times have befallen me since I last pressed thee to my heart, dear Marian. The earl is free."

"The whole country rings with the account of thy noble exploit; my Robin is the theme of every tongue."

"Unworthy am I of such homage; I but helped a friend. Dastard is he that would not act as I did."

"The strife was sore I heard. But Robin, sweetest, tell me, art thou hurt, and thy Marian know it not?"

"Sweet girl, Our Lady protects those that in her trust. Thy prayers, too, are they not Robin's? And shelter they not him from danger?"

"Thine—all thine—are they. A present will I offer at Our Lady's shrine, for this her great blessing conferred on thee and me alike."

"Thanks, Marian, darling. But I desire to speak to thee of another matter."

"Say on; I listen.

"With me in Sherwood is a lady—one Maria Danvers."

"Nay, start not, Marian," said Robin, laughingly, nor be jealous."

"Thou merry gipsy; but say on."

"Her would I confide to thy tenderest care."

"Has she no protector?"

"One who values his life as naught in her service."

"She is welcome, dear Robin, for thy sake. Marian will be to her as a sister."

"Thanks; Robin knows not when he has asked aught of thee and been refused."

"I will wait her coming with impatience," said Marian.

"What of thine uncle, the miller, Marian? Of late I have seen but little of him."

"He is well, but sorely tried by the Sheriff's attentions to me."

"He likes not his wooing of thee then?" asked Robin with a roguish smile.

"He threatens to thrash his hide well an' he shows his Norman visage near the mill again."

"'Tis his meddling is my greatest concern. I would have both thine uncle and thee beware of Nottingham's Sheriff."

"Have no fear, Robin; he dreads thine anger too greatly to do aught unseemly."

"I cannot bear thee out in this. That he fears me is clear; but I opine he would anything brave to get possession of thee."

"Trust to Our Lady, and better times, Robin, dearest."

"Were I other than I am, Marian darling, thou would'st not lack my protection in a nearer, dearer form than now."

"I can wait, dearest. To know thou lovest me, Robin, is to me so sweet that aught else pales before the thought of my happiness."

"Dearest, thou little knowest how I crave for a quieter life. But it cannot be. The land groans under Norman tyranny; our liberties, our dearest, sacred rights are trampled upon; and shall I, Robin Hood, whilome Earl of Huntingdon, shrink from the dangerous task of avenging these wants and injustices?"

Robin Hood looked noble in his just anger.

"Never, Robin!" exclaimed Marian with enthusiasm, and hanging by her hand on his shoulder. "Never! Be thine the proud and glorious task to free our land. Then rest."

"Noble, devoted Marian, would that all were actuated by the same spirit, then would the hated Normans be driven from the land, and Saxons have their own again."

"Stay not thine hand, dearest, for thought of me," said Marian. "Bethink thee that beyond the grave is a happier life where we will ne'er be parted."

"Even so. Here I am hunted, outlawed, condemned by the rulers of the land. But my hand shall make itself felt among them Then welcome death if needs be."

"Spoken like mine own true-hearted love," said Marian. "But tell me, dearest, how fared my cousin in the fray?"

"He got him honour on his foes. Much's presence was where danger was most thickly strewn."

"I am glad. But see who comes this way. 'Tis the Sheriff and the abbot I wist."

"Truly; let us to cover—perchance they will discourse of things edifying to me."

Screening themselves effectually from observation, Robin and Marian listened.

"Sayest thou the friar thieved thy gold, and thou hadst no redress?" asked the Sheriff.

"'Tis true," answered the abbot, with an audible groan.

" Now by my halidome, this must be stopped."

" But how ?" asked the abbot.

" Hie thee to the King; of him ask help; show him thy losses, thine indignities, and the state of the country. I will endorse thy report."

" 'Tis well counselled. I myself had so determined, and my coming to thee was on this very matter."

" 'Tis a good omen of success I ween. But say, canst thou not counsel me by thine advice how to snare Robin Hood ?"

" Of this I have had thought too," said the abbot.

" Ah ! of what sort ?"

" Of this. Rememberest thou speaking of an archery meeting ?"

" Yes, yes ; but thou did'st not approve it."

" Now I do. Speak fair to Robin Hood, grant him thy protection in speech only. Arrange thy men to encompass his doom."

" Base churchman !" exclaimed Robin between his clenched teeth.

" Hist, Robin ; listen !" and Marian laid her hand warningly upon his arm.

" My perception of thy meaning is plain," said the Sheriff. " Beshrew me, but it promises well too."

" Be but discreet, and 'twill end well. Thou knowest full well that the King would favour any means for the outlaw's destruction."

" Full well. The outlaw's contumaciousness enrages him beyond endurance."

" Earl Mortimer, too," said the abbot.

" Have no fear. Let Robin Hood but fall, the earl is then undone."

" Thou owest neither any love," said the abbot with a low laugh.

" Nay, but rather dire hatred. But for Robin Hood's cursed interference Mortimer would now be past further mischief."

" 'Tis said the country is with him and Robin."

" 'This said, but requires confirmation. The people are ever for those who successfully rebel. Let but their leaders suffer defeat, and they scatter like frightened sheep."

" Of the fray of yesterday. Thou hast not yet spoken of it except sparsely."

" Name it not. 'Twas a bitter defeat. But it shall be avenged. I, Geoffrey de Lois, swear it."

" Believe me, nephew mine, cunning and stratagem oft encompass what force does not. Let my advice counsel thee, and thou wilt yet succeed."

" The archery match shall take place. I will e'en commence by granting him a concession."

" How so ?"

" I hold one Will Scarlet a prisoner. Him has Robin Hood demanded of my hand."

" Well."

" To hang him I had determined, despite the outlaw's threat to retaliate."

" And now ?"

" I will surrender him, and be soft of speech in the doing of it withal."

" I perceive thou art rightly proceeding in the matter."

" In a short while I will make advances, profess a friendship for Robin, and invite him to share my hospitalities."

" Have a care how thou proceedest. Robin Hood is shrewd, and is not caught like a foolish bird with chaff."

" Fear not," said the Sheriff. " To overthrow him I am bent."

" We will now return," said the abbot.

" When go you to the King ?"

" When you have arranged with Robin for the archery match," the abbot replied significantly.

They passed out of sight and hearing.

Emerging from their concealment, Robin Hood and Marian gazed at one another for a few moments in silence.

" Heard'st thou ever such shameless scheming ?" asked Robin at last.

" A churchman, too," remarked Marian. " The Sheriff I am not surprised at. He, I know full well, is capable of any wickedness."

" Fear not, Marian. This treachery will recoil on their own pates. Mark me in this."

Robin looked stern, and a flush of anger pass over his handsome features.

" Thou wilt not accept the Sheriff's treacherous invite to the archery match ?" queried Marian.

" Will I not rather ? 'Tis not fear of danger that will Robin deter."

A look of pain passed over Marian's beautiful features. Love made Robin susceptible of having pained her. She was hurt by his last remark.

He hastened to excuse himself.

" Forgive me, dearest," he said, " I spoke harsh, but not to thee, sweetest. Sooner be tongue of mine cut forth than that it utter one word to cause my Marian pain."

" Say no more, Robin, darling," Marian replied, as she imprinted a tender kiss on his cheek.

" Thus will I repay thee this loving kiss," exclaimed Robin, with tenderness in his voice.

Drawing her fondly to his bosom he kissed her pouting lips, and looked into the depths of her love-laden eyes.

" Thou wilt use every precaution, love ?" asked Marian.

" Of a surety. The Sheriff will not trap me like a wild beast. He will have cause to rue his malicious intriguing against my life."

"Thy trusty followers will attend thee?" asked Marian timidly, as if fearful of arousing her lover's ire.

"Fear not, sweet girl. Hast ever known Robin fail in aught he undertook?"

"Never; for which Our Lady be thanked. But see, hither comes my uncle. Shall we advance to greet him?"

"Even so. I must then leave thee, dearest. Duty claims my strict attention."

Running forward with light and graceful steps, Marian bestowed a caress on her uncle's cheek, saying,

"Greet thee, lovingly, uncle. How art thou to-day? Here is Robin."

The miller grasped Robin's hand with friendly warmth.

"I greet thee, noble Robin," said Much the Miller. "Thou hast well proved thy Saxon bearing."

"Indifferently, Much, but indifferently. Mortimer, as thou knowest, is safe."

"All the saints be praised for it," replied Much. "But, Robin, whom think'st thou I met but just now? Thou wilt never guess an' thou triest for a year."

"I wager thee twenty crowns against a sack of thy best flour that I tell thee truly," said Robin.

"Wager not, uncle mine," said Marian, laughing, "thou wilt lose."

"Thou seemest to know," said Much, half dubiously, as if debating with himself whether to accept or decline the proffered wager.

"The Sheriff and abbot," said Robin Hood, merrily.

"Thou would'st have won, man," the miller replied. "But what think'st thou they are concocting?"

"Ah! 'tis my turn now to challenge thee to disclose this, Much," exclaimed Robin.

"Nay, thou hast me there. Know'st thou?"

"That do I, and Marian also. We hid and listened to as base a plot as could be planned by man."

"Against thee, I can plainly perceive it was, by thy knitted brows."

"E'en so. But it boots not. The Sheriff will be overmatched."

"That will he," replied Much. "He must have a cool head, a brave heart, and steady hand that would plot against thee, Robin."

"Marian will disclose to thee what it is," said Robin; "but I would ask that not a word escape either of thy lips on the subject."

"Thou hast my promise," replied Marian.

"And mine," said the miller.

"Farewell, sweetest," said Robin, turning and pressing Marian to his heart, and imprinting an impassioned kiss on her ruby lips.

"Farewell, Robin, darling; Our Lady forfend thee from all harm."

"To-morrow Maria Danvers will be with you."

Much the Miller looked inquiringly.

"I will explain to thee, uncle," said Marian.

With a friendly parting Robin walked away and was soon lost in the forest.

Marian watched him with loving eyes until his manly form no longer met her admiring gaze.

---

## CHAPTER LI.

### ROBIN HOOD HOLDS A COUNCIL, AND RECEIVES AN INVITATION FROM THE SHERIFF.

So foul a thing I ne'er did hear.
　　Attend my words, my merry men all,
Bold Robin and thou hast naught to fear,
　　Though the Sheriff contriveth to make us fall.

"WILL SCARLET has not yet arrived," said Little John to Robin Hood, whom he had gone to meet.

"But shortly will," replied Robin with significant emphasis on his words."

"Body-o'-me!" said John. "Impatience grows apace on me. I would, good master, I had your permit to bring Will away bodily from Nottingham Castle."

"Which thou wilt not," answered Robin with a laugh. "But attend me, I would have speech with you on certain matters of import——"

"And the abbot, he turned him red with rage,
　　And vowed, with oaths, the friar to cage."

"Friar Tuck, comes this way," remarked Robin, as the lusty tones of the friar's voice reached him.

"What ho, there, chaplain mine," sang out Robin, "come hither, I much need thy wise counsels."

"Thou hast them at thy command at all times," replied the friar, emerging into view——

"'Tis ghostly counsel brings comfort and good,
　　'Tis better than drink, it's excellent food."

"Body-o'-me! but thou thrivest well on it," said Little John.

"Thou art ever malicious, John," replied the friar. "I vow I am grievously fallen away of late. Fastings and penances, stripes and discomforts——"

"A truce to this badinage, my lieges," said Robin jocularly. "Let's to council."

"I attend you," answered the friar.

Little John looked as grave as an owl, but said naught.

"What I now divulge," remarked Robin, by way of preface, "must remain in your secret keeping until I permit its disclosing."

"Thou art about to confess thyself, my son," said the friar with mock gravity.

"Even so, holy friar," replied Robin with a laugh. "Absolution I crave not; 'tis not my own sins but another's I would disclose."

"Proceed, my ears are itching to hear thy speech."

"And mine arm itches to give thee a buffet for thine interruption," said Little John to the friar.

"Peace; a truce to this bantering," replied Robin. "A short time since I was listener to a plot against our common safety."

"Now Our Lady be thanked!" ejaculated the irrepressible friar.

"Quiet thou prate-pate," said Little John.

"Treachery is engaged to cause our destruction. In friendly guise comes the Sheriff to invite us to his festivities."

"Has he a good cellar?" put in the friar.

"Thou never tastedst better than his providing could give thee," replied Little John, smacking his lips at the thoughts of his deep potations in the Sheriff's cellar, as related elsewhere.

"Thou wilt accept his graciousness?" said the friar interrogatively.

"Yes, jolly friar, and I would have my merrymen all at my back, but not perceivable," replied Robin.

"Ah, I perceive," remarked Little John; "yon Sheriff would hold a tournament."

"Even so, good John, and would us invite to an archery meeting, while the abbot hies him to the king to beseech his aid for our destruction."

"Thine informant, good master?" queried Little John.

"The Sheriff and my lord abbot," replied Robin with a bow of mock courtesy.

"Now this is mightily strange," put in the friar. "So tight-fished are the pair that such imprudent disclosures seemeth not to favour them."

"They recked not I listened, and spoke of their devices freely."

Footsteps were now heard approaching.

The new-comers proved to be none other than Earl Mortimer and Walter the knight.

"Welcome to our councils," said Robin, advancing, and shaking them by the hand warmly.

"I trust nothing of evil import threatens," replied the earl.

"Naught of great import, of a surety, brave Mortimer," answered Robin. "'Tis the Sheriff would fain encompass our destruction by stratagem and treachery, when all other means have so signally failed him."

"A base, false-sworn knight," remarked Walter.

"Thou dost truly describe him," replied Robin; "but thou shalt judge for thyself in this matter.

Whereupon Robin related in substance all that he had overheard the Sheriff and abbot discourse of.

"Being forewarned," remarked the earl, "thou wilt, of a surety, refuse to peril thy safety by acceptance?"

"Not so, Mortimer. He who would try conclusions with Robin Hood, must perforce be humoured to the full of his bent."

"'Tis as I have already avowed," put in the friar. "'Tis always better to humour one's longing, e'en if it be at the cost of a broken crown."

"So would I treat Nottingham's Sheriff," remarked Robin.

"I would that each of you consider well how to circumvent his designs, and inform me of your plans."

"Hist!" said Little John, holding up his finger, his practised ear having detected the noise of advancing footsteps.

The crackling of dried leaves evidenced the necessity of Little John's warning, and soon appeared a party of the Sheriff's men, having with them Will Scarlet.

"Thy business," said Robin, advancing.

Then perceiving Will Scarlet, he said, seizing his hand with a friendly grasp:

"What! Will, lad, amongst us once again? Now Our Lady be thanked. We owe her much for her goodness to theeward."

"Greet thee, master mine," replied Will, returning Robin's warm-hand pressure. "I am with thee, as thou seest."

"Speak I to Robin Hood?" deferentially asked the leader of the Sheriff's party.

"I am he; say on. What is thy master's good pleasure?"

"The good knight, Geoffrey de Lois, Sheriff of Nottingham, sendeth thee greeting on this wise, in answer to thy message, pertaining to the release of one Will Scarlet, whom I now hold in my keeping."

"Thou holdest," muttered Little John, in high dudgeon, and regarding the speaker menacingly.

"Grammercy," said the friar aloud and mockingly. "We are mightily beholden to thy master for his tender mercy. Beshrew me——"

"Peace," said Robin. "He but delivers his message to the best of his ability."

Turning to the messenger, he said—

"Say on, and take not offence at aught that has been said. My men are but rude of speech, and lack Norman polish."

It was doubtful whether Robin meant his concluding remark as a compliment or not; certainly his tones had a delicate vein of satire running through them.

"Norman roguery," exclaimed Little John aloud.

"Thou art but a Saxon churl," retorted one of the Sheriff's party.

"Have at thee, thou foreign knave," said Little John, springing forward.

"St. Hubert! but I am with thee," shouted the excitable friar.

But Robin was too quick for them both.

Hurling Little John back, he said, reprovingly—

"Is it thus thou would'st brawl with friendly messengers?"

"I crave pardon of thee, master mine," said Little John, apologetically, "but mine hand itched to trounce the fellow for his presumption. Body-o'-me! Saxon churl! An' I but meet thee, Our Lady be witness to the trouncing I'll give thy carcase."

The last part of his speech was delivered in an undertone, audible to none but the friar, who, by way of signifying his approval, gave him a hearty thwack on the back, for which he was well-nigh receiving a sharp return.

"Prithee proceed with thy speech," said Robin to the messenger, "and give heed to thy words, for my men are not wont to hear taunt or gibe, without giving fitting retort."

The messenger bowed, but could ill conceal his chagrin, which was evidently shared by his companions.

"My master bade me give over unto thee Will Scarlet, and receive, as thy own appointing hath put it, those whom thou holdest prisoners."

"I willingly, nay joyfully, receive thee back, Will," said Robin.

To the messenger he said—

"Tarry here; thy men will be forthcoming in a trice. Little John, do thou hie to quarters and bring with thee, free from restraint, mind thee, the Norman prisoners, to be forthwith freed."

When Little John had gone, the messenger said to Robin—

"I would, an't please you, have speech of thee aside."

"Say, say on; 'tis naught I would have concealed from these, I daresay," replied Robin, pointing to his companions.

"I crave thy patience," said the messenger, "but my master bid me deliver my message to thee alone."

"As thou wilt, then," replied Robin offhandedly, at the same time giving his companions a significant look.

When aside the Sheriff's man said, speaking low:

"My master sendeth thee excellent greeting and this missive, assuring thee of his great regard for thee personally."

"My indebtedness is great," replied Robin, bowing, but with an ill-concealed sneer on his handsome face.

"He further bade me tell thee that he wishes amity to exist between him and thee in so far as lieth within the scope of his office."

"'Tis a well-put request," replied Robin with a disdainful smile.

"I have finished mine office now, and await thine answer," said the messenger, who, to own the truth, felt ill at ease, and was wishful to be gone.

"Convey to the Sheriff my greeting, and acquaint him of my thanks for his proffered friendship. Answer to this he will have anon," said Robin, holding up the missive.

Cutting the silken thread which confined it, Robin read as follows:—

"FROM GEOFFREY DE LOIS,
Sheriff of Nottingham,

TO

ROBIN HOOD, whilom Earl of Huntingdon, with most excellent greeting.

WHEREAS, I, entertaining most friendly intent towards thee, notwithstanding and despite mine office of preserver of the peace of this part of his Majesty's realm, against thee, arrayed in rebellion, am wishful beyond degree to promote a better feeling between thee and me, do hereby specially invite thee, Robin Hood, and thy company, to a tournament of games and archery, to be holden contiguous to our Castle of Nottingham, holding thee and thine blameless for the time being for any acts committed against the King's Majesty, in virtue whereof I hereby affix my seal, in token of good faith and amity.

"At our Court     "GEOFFREY DE LOIS,
of   Shrievalty,              High Sheriff.
June 23rd, the
sixth year of        (Seal.)
His Most Ex-
cellent Majes-
ty's reign."

"Ha, ha!" laughed Robin, glibly; "by the mass! a well-laid scheme. So, so, sir Sheriff, thou essayest to play me false. Have a care, thou art but treading on slippery ground!"

After remaining buried in thought for a time he soliloquised:

"Out of this will I get me both honour and profit. 'Twill go hard with me, indeed, but that thou, proud Sheriff, rememberest till thy life's end the said tournament to be holden for my special delectation."

Robin smiled grimly, as he was wont when communing with himself on disagreeable topics.

Strolling leisurely back to the party, he remained in converse with the earl and knight until Little John returned with the Norman prisoners.

Friar Tuck had suddenly disappeared.

"The Normans are all before thee," said Little John, making the customary salutation to Robin.

"'Tis well."

Turning to them, Robin said:

"Thou art free to depart. Take not away embittered feelings to me or mine. We seek not thine hurt nor have ever."

"Our thanks are thine, bold Robin Hood," said one of their number, acting as spokesman for his comrades. "Treatment fair and honourable has been ours at thy hands. 'Twill be our duty to represent to our master thine honourable dealing towards us."

Robin bowed and dismissed them with a wave of his hand.

Accompanied by the earl, knight, and Little John, he walked leisurely towards the trysting place.

The party of Normans meanwhile pursued their way full of glee at their happy release, and full of what they had seen of Robin and his merry men.

Right in their path sat jolly Friar Tuck.

On sighting them he commenced to troll forth the following ditty, as unconcernedly as if such a thing as a Norman was a scarce article in the land:

"Findest thou aught foul or bad,
    Be assured 'tis Norman.
Rogues, liars, cheats, and knaves are they,
    To see such churls quite makes one sad.
Then to my toast, let none say nay—
    Confusion to the Norman."

"Hearest thou that?" remarked one of them angrily. "St. Denis! but he deserves chastisement."

"Heed him not, 'tis the mad-brained friar," remarked one in reply.

"Findest thou aught fair or just.
    Rest quite sure 'tis Saxon,
Good men, and true, and loyal too,
    Base Normans they can never trust.
In wine quite old and goblets new,
    Drink honour to the Saxon."

"By my halidome, 'tis too bad to hear yon shaven pate traduce us in this wise," remarked he who had retorted so fiercely to Little John.

"Thou art art at liberty to teach him better manners," answered the leader of the party, "but see that thou doest him no serious hurt."

Lagging behind his companions, the fellow watched them pretty well out of sight ere he approached the friar, who pretended to be unconscious of his presence.

"Thou wert exceedingly merry, just now," he remarked.

The friar looked at him, got up, and shaking himself together, gave a yawn.

The friar's silence nettled him exceedingly.

"Thou must e'en seek my pardon for thy rudeness in song, else will thy priestly office fail to keep thee from chastisement."

The friar began to count his beads, and continued to glance askance at him, but never a word said he.

"Hearest thou not, thou lazy, fat-paunched shaveling priest?" said the fellow furiously, as he advanced upon the friar to strike him.

"I pray thee excuse my mind's absence, my son," said the friar with imperturbable gravity. "Said'st thou aught to me of confessing thyself?"

The fellow aimed a well-intentioned blow with his fist at the friar's head.

But, marvellous to relate, he soon found himself sprawling on the broad of his back.

"I pray thee rise, my son," said the friar gravely, "'tis unseemly for a Norman to lie thus."

Foaming with rage, his assailant drew his sword and rushed upon him.

With quarter-staff so stout the friar did him quickly engage.

"My son, thou art but a sorry swordsman," remarked the friar, as he beat down the fellow's guard, and gave him a rap on his pate that sent the sparks flying in countless numbers from his eyes.

Rising, he essayed to fly, but the friar was upon him nimbly, and dealt him sundry thwacks on his back which made him roar lustily.

"Nay, my son," remarked the friar, as he plied his staff, "'tis for thy good I thus scourge thee for thy misdeeds. Thou wilt remember Friar Tuck, I ween, and his absolving, and come not again hurriedly to confess thyself to him."

Leaving him in pitiable plight, the friar turned and walked leisurely homeward, singing—

"With oaken staff
    And arm so stout,
At my foes I laugh
    And put them to rout.

For none care I,
    Naught troubles me long.
'Tis no use to try
    To do me a wrong."

Meeting Little John he appealed to him for a draught of wine to slake his inordinate thirst.

"Bones of St. Hubert! but I am hugeous dry," he said. "Ugh! trouncing Norman backs, though pleasant, is hard work."

"Thou hast never bestowed a good thwacking on that scapegrace, hast thou?" queried Little John, with a laugh.

"Be certified of it, little man, to thy great pleasurement. "Our Lady, how the fellow roared! Ah, ah!"

"Body-o'-me! thou must have a stoup of wine, in which I will join thee," said Little John.

"Grammercy, John, make it two stoups," exclaimed the friar, with lugubrious visage.

"By the mass, I could drink both myself at a single draught."

"Thou shalt have first drink, friend," answered Little John, "so attend me to the cellarer."

The wine was produced, and the friar was deep in the contents of the first stoup, when a messenger arrived summoning Little John in haste to Robin's presence.

He cast a wistful eye on the thirsty friar, but not a sign gave he of leaving the horn which seemed glued to his lips.

"Mind thou forgettest not that I have had naught as yet," said Little John, admonishingly. He then turned round with a huge sigh and grumblings not a few to attend his master.

"'Tis wine that will not keep," said the friar, casting longing eye on the other stoup which the cellarman had drawn. "And it will be a shame to let it spoil."

So saying, he seized and drank it at a draught; then hied him off to seek a secure place where to sleep free from Little John's anger.

Little John found Robin with Bayston.

"Hark thee," he said, "this abbot seeks the King; do thou go with him and contrive to learn his business and its ending."

Dismissing him he turned to Little John, saying—

"Let the Lady Maria Danvers be fitly escorted to-morrow to Much, the Miller's. He is acquainted with my intention respecting her."

"Body-o'-me!" growled Little John, as he turned from the spot, "this command would have kept; the wine will not, with that thirsty friar near at hand to it."

His prediction was verified; not a drop was left for him.

Giving vent to oaths and growls, and vengeful threats, the giant wrapped his mantle about him, and throwing himself down under the shade of a fine old oak, he was soon wrapped in slumber.

The stillness of the night was unbroken save by the hoot of the howl, and the "all's well" of the sentinels.

## CHAPTER LII.

### HOW ROBIN AND HIS MEN WENT TO THE TOURNAMENT, AND WHAT BEFEL THEM.

Such a brave sight could scarcely be seen,
  Gentle and simple, soldiers and yeomen,
Knight and fair ladies, on Nottingham Green,
  Did there meet with Robin, the Sheriff's brave
    foeman.

Two days after the events recorded in the last chapter, Robin despatched a messenger to the Sheriff, conveying his acceptance of the invitation to the archery meeting.

"Let the men be informed," he said to Little John, "to keep themselves ready for instant action, without any index to their suspicions of treachery."

"Body-o'-me!" growled the giant, "Let the Sheriff have a fair English fight for it, Saxon against Norman."

"True; but bethink thee, my friend, that hitherto he has been originally worsted in his contentions."

"'Tis any man's case to be beaten once or twice, or even thrice, but let him try on, and it seldom fails that in the end he is victorious."

"The Sheriff views it not thus. But fash not thyself about his treacherousness, 'twill receive its deserts, thou hast Robin's word for it."

"Hither comes the Sheriff's messenger," said Little John, pointing to him.

"Do thou bring him hither," said Robin. "Doubtless, he brings tidings I burn to know."

"Greet thee, gentle sir," said the messenger in courteous accents. "The Sheriff sends thee this," producing a missive.

Cutting the thread, Robin read:

"*The second day from this the tournament will be contested. Thy presence will be greatly welcome and looked for.*

"GEOFFREY DE LOIS."

Dismissing the messenger with courteous thanks, Robin read the missive to Little John.

"*My presence!* think of it, John. Hadst any thought of the Sheriff's subtlety being of such high order?"

"Thou knowest well, master mine, that for him I ne'er had aught of love. 'Tis Norman-like, thus to deport himself.

"Give it not a thought, my staunch friend," said Robin, placing his hand familiarly on the giant's shoulder. "But summon our men to target-practice, while I hie me to the butts."

Soon were the merry men engaged in shooting at the butts, when most marvellous shots were made. But none excelled Robin.

His arrow went true to its mark, with never a mischance intervening.

Next in point of excellence came Little John and Friar Tuck, between whom a friendly rivalry existed.

Things gave ample promise of a signal triumph for the foresters at the forthcoming tournament.

Assembling his men together, Robin, with brevity, explained to them his commands.

"Be not enticed or enthralled by Norman subtlety," he said, "and, before all, let not the wine-cup o'ermaster thee."

Hearty Saxon cheers rent the air as Robin concluded.

Could the Sheriff but have heard them, his sense of security in the success of his treacherous scheme would have been shaken to its base.

The auspicious morn arrived at last, and saw Robin and his men up betimes, as was their wont, for no sluggards were they.

In groups of twos and threes, each armed with a *short* bow, dagger, and some with staves, all of which were carefully hidden away, except the latter, the foresters hied them to the tournament, or to certain other positions assigned to them.

Robin, attended by Little John, the friar, the two knights, and Earl Mortimer, sought the abode of Much the Miller.

"Greet thee, Robin dear," said Maid Marian, throwing himself on his breast.

"Thou look'st thy best this morning, love," he said, tenderly, and affectionately saluting her blushing cheek.

"'Tis to do honour to my Robin that I tired with carefulness.

"Thou art welcome, brave earl," she said, turning to Mortimer," "and thou, Little John, and likewise thou, holy father (this to Friar Tuck).

"I salute thee, Queen of Beauty," said Earl Mortimer, gallantly dropping on bended knee, and reverently kissing the beautiful hand which Marian extended to him.

"Rise, good knight," said Marian laughingly, and with a deep blush o'erspreading her lovely features, "with knight so true I bid defiance to all competitors."

Robin introduced Sir Richard Wykeham in due course, and Marian hastened to summon Maria Danvers, who had not yet completed her tiring.

After the usual courtesies had taken place, the whole party adjourned to the tournament grounds beneath the castle walls.

The Sheriff hastened to welcome Robin, and smiled his blandest on Marian, who returned his courteous salutation with a hauteur bordering on disdain.

"Welcome gallant forester," said the Sheriff, " and thou sweet lady. Thy beauteous presence will add to the excellence of the meeting."

"Thanks," answered Robin, bowing low; " thy courtesy doth thee *honour*."

The tone in which these words were uttered, and the emphasis laid on the last word, caused the Sheriff to start and look fixedly in Robin's face.

But naught saw he there to fulfil his foreboding that his treachery was known.

Turning away to hide his confusion, he found himself face to face with Earl Mortimer.

They eyed each other defiantly for a moment.

Then bethinking of the part he had to play, the Sheriff proffered his hand to Mortimer, which he took, but did not press.

To Sir Richard Wykeham he gave a formal bow.

Robin's quick eye noted the presence of the Sheriff's men-at-arms disguised as peasants.

Their martial bearing betrayed their identity to one so quick of apprehension as Robin.

A significant glance passed between Little John and his master; both of them having detected the same thing at the same time.

With flourish of trumpets the Sheriff's herald proclaimed the conditions of the tournament, and then the lists were pronounced formally opened.

Robin, at the invitation of the Sheriff, opened the tournament, and gave a standard of test for the opening of the archery contest.

"Saw you ever so graceful a posture?" said a Norman dame who stood a little to the right of Robin as he prepared to shoot.

By his side stood Maid Marian and Little John, the Sheriff completing the group.

"St. Denis, a good shot!" exclaimed the Sheriff, as Robin's arrow hit a plug of wood in the target and drove it through, passing out at the other side with it transfixed to its point

"'Twill take no mean archer to better that," was the verdict of many of the bystanders.

Robin laughed within himself at these acclamations, for the shot to him was the easiest his skill could have been tested by.

The contest soon went on apace.

While it progresses, I pray your attention, good reader, to what was passing elsewhere on the ground.

Several burly-framed Norman men-at-arms were drinking freely at a small booth formed of uprights and covered with green boughs.

In their company were several loutish-looking peasants dressed in short cloaks of grey homespun stuff.

Near them loitered Friar Tuck, who pretended to be watching the antics of some merry-andrews who had collected a crowd around them, but who was really listening to the Normans' conversation.

"What think you of to-day's tournament?" asked one, of his companions.

"It has no attraction for me, save that of duty," was the reply.

"Here, wench," said one of the company, " fill this flagon with right good ale, and we'll drink confusion to the foresters."

"Have a care," remarked one of his fellows, " thy speech is indiscreet."

"Not so, by my halidome," was the reply,

"I scorn the whole lot of those thievish knaves of woodsmen."

"Thou hadst best be mindful of thy speech," remarked one, laughingly; "St. Quintin! saw you not the scowl yon fat-paunched monk gave thee?"

Friar Tuck had certainly lowered at the fellow who had spoken disparagingly of his merry companions.

"What, you shaven befrocked priestling, scowl at me! By the Rood! I'll e'en see to it."

Suiting the action to the word; he strode over to where the friar stood, and plucking him by his frock, said:

"Thou didst scowl at me?"

"My son, 'tis unseemly thus to accost one of my condition," said the friar, deprecatingly.

"Avow thyself, fellow; thou art of these foresters, knaves and rogues that they be."

Looking him straight in the face the friar placed his hand quietly on the fellow's arm and gripped it viciously.

"Unloose thy hold," said the fellow, with a lusty roar, "else will I stab thee with my dagger."

"I did but press thee with a friendly grip," replied the friar, in nowise disconcerted.

"Thou art in fault," said the Norman soldiers, gathering around their companion, "and must e'en beg his pardon or get thee buffets not a few."

The friar laughed contemptuously.

"My lineage is Saxon," he said. "Didst e'er know one of my sort yield to Norman?"

"Now, by St. Quintin, thou must pay for thine evil prating," said a great burly fellow, drawing back his arm and striking hard at the friar.

But the blow reached him not.

Raising his left arm the friar warded the blow, and dealt him such a crack with his staff o'er his pate as brought him to the ground.

Drawing their swords the fellow's companions were about to rush upon the friar, when the two peasants interfered and kept them off.

"I will fight the best of you at broadsword or staff," said the friar, raising his voice to a shout.

"A ring! a ring!" shouted several by-standers who had seen the whole of the matter.

Attracted by the voice, a dense crowd soon collected.

In the confusion, one of the peasants sidled up to the friar, and said in a low whisper.

"Good Friar Tuck, provoke not a quarrel. 'Tis Allan-a-Dale speaks to thee."

"St. Hubert!" answered the friar, "what thou! I knew thee not. But these braggart Normans must be chastised. Trust me, good Allan, naught ill will befall me."

"Now, thou fat-paunched friar," exclaimed one of the Norman soldiers, whose height overtopped the friar's by a span nearly, "defend thyself, for I vow by St. Denis, to trounce thy hide well, priest or no priest."

"Have at thee," replied the friar with a laugh.

The twain set to right merrily.

The Norman was no mean hand at use of staff.

"That for thy crown!" he exclaimed, aiming a terrific blow at the friar's head.

"'Tis naught, my son," said the friar, with ready guard. "That for thy Norman carcass."

A heavy blow on the shoulder caused the fellow to reel.

"Well dealt, father," said one in the crowd. "Our Lady be witness, thou art, for a man of peace, a heavy hitter."

The crowd cheered the friar lustily, who warmed to his work.

"Thou didst receive my compliment with an ill grace." he said, dealing the Norman another sound rap. "That to keep its fellow company."

Getting off his guard, the Norman dealt his blows wild and furiously.

"Ha! ha!" laughed the friar. "Bones of St. Hubert! thy staff is pliant, but how likest thou that?" dealing his antagonist a blow on his crown, which drew blood freely.

Seeing the discomfiture of their comrade, the other Norman soldiers essayed to attack the friar with their swords.

"Shame! shame!" shouted the crowd, many of whom threw themselves between the friar's assailants, and prevented his being hurt.

"St. Denis! but thou art a jovial friar," said one of the soldiers, getting the better of his temper. "Here is my hand, an' it please thee to press it in friendly mood."

"My refusal would be unseemly, my son," replied the friar, taking the proffered hand, "my ways are of peace."

"Thou must e'en drain a draught with us," exclaimed the friendly soldier.

"Aye, aye!" shouted his fellows, falling in with their comrade's mood. "Let's drink and be friends."

"A cup of good wine will not harm me," answered the friar, as he went in their company to the booth.

"Dost hear, wench? Let's have full horns of thy best wine, and that quickly," said the friendly fellow, as he motioned the friar to a seat beside him.

Nothing loth, the friar joined in the drinking bout; and managed to so ply them with wine and ale in keeping pace with his friendly toasts, that at length the soldiers lost all discretion, and began to prate about the Sheriff's designs upon Robin and his party.

These disclosures were listened to eagerly by the friar and the two peasants, to wit, Allan-a-Dale and Dick Withers, who were thus disguised.

"Fifty right good archers, the best in the north country has the Sheriff imprest," exclaimed one of the Normans, with drunken elatedness.

"For what purpose, my son?" asked the friar with an innocent mien.

"To slay him, Robin, and his principal men."

The friar exchanged significant glances with his two companions.

"Report has it, that the Sheriff has promised him safe conduct," said the friar.

"Believe it not. I vow to thee, that the Sheriff, my master, will this day slay Robin Hood."

"'Tis evil to shed blood, my son."

"But that is not all," said the fellow, unheedful of the friar's adverse opinion. "Maid Marian will fall to the Sheriff's lot."

"Ah! thy master is a rare contriver."

"A dozen horsemen will hover near, and will suddenly snatch her, and ride away like the wind."

The peasants' eyes were closed, as if they slept.

They listened keenly though withal.

As hoped, the soldiers now began to give evidence of dropping off into a drunken sleep, and the fellow seemed to have exhausted his stock of intelligence. The friar gave a sign to Allan-a-Dale and his comrades.

Rousing themselves as if from slumber, and yawning tremendously, they took leave, the friar alone remaining.

"Fill up again," said the friar, who wanted to see all the Norman soldiers rendered quite incapable of action through drink, being assured that they had been appointed to take a prominent part in the Sheriff's treacherous plans against Robin.

"Well put, my jolly cock," answered he who had acted as spokesman for the rest. What ho, there! fill up, fill up with right good liquor. I'll pay."

The friar chuckled to himself at the success of his manœuvre.

"Here, drink, good father," said the soldier, and favour us with a song. Thou art of the right sort to troll one."

"Ay, a song, a song," replied those of his companions who were not too drunk to give utterance to the request.

Willing to gratify their wishes for his own ends, the friar sang

## THE SOLDIER.

The soldier he's a notable man,
  Eager for fray and blunt of speech ;
He swaggers, struts, drinks, when he can,
  Always ready with sword, some foes to reach.
With smiles greets he each pretty wench,
  Vows that for her he's ready to die.
With wine such vows he's ready to drench,
  Swears by his saint she has a beautiful eye.
True as his good sword, sharp and keen,
  With oath and rush and ready blow,
Seeks he profit? not so I ween,
  The soldier's no knave, I'd have all men know.
Honour to him is dearer than gold,
  For fame and his country he perils his life.
If by foeman o'ercome, he never cries hold,
  But smiles, names her, and falls in the strife.
Charge to the brim, the merry wine cup,
  Shout ye this toast, each true-hearted holder,
Nor bate aught of breath as the red juice ye sup
  Honour, above all, to the warlike brave soldier.

"Honour to thee, thou jovial friar," said the soldiers, one and all.

"'Tis naught; I love the soldier; but false knights I detest," answered the friar, significantly; " an' thou would'st pleasure me," he added, " drink to my toast."

"That will we—the toast?" was the unanimous response.

" *Confusion and destruction to all false-sworn knights !"*

The toast was drunk by all but one with acclamation.

He was not so far gone in drink as to be unmindful of the drift of the friar's toast.

He tried hard to catch its full meaning, but his brains being muddled by the fumes of wine and ale, he failed.

Raising his glass, he drank the toast slowly and deliberately; then turning to the friar, he asked with thick utterance :

"Dost thou mean my master, the Sheriff?"

"Of a surety, a false-sworn knight is he," replied the friar in quick response.

"St. Quintin! thou shalt have thine ears slit," replied the fellow, essaying to draw his sword.

"Not by thee, thou Norman swine," replied the friar with a laugh and a push, which sent the fellow reeling to the ground, where he lay, in common with his companions in a thoroughly helpless condition.

Emerging from the booth, the friar wended his way to the archery butts.

He pushed his way stoutly through the crowd, and gave as good blows as he received while so employed.

"Here comes the friar, master," said Little John to Robin.

"Bring him here," answered Robin; "let him give evidence of his skill, that these archers may see it."

Plucking Robin lightly by the sleeve, Friar Tuck drew Robin aside.

"Saw'st thou Allan-a-Dale?" he asked in a low whisper.

"I did; my merry men are assembling e'en now. Fear nought; but be vigilant."

"Danger is abroad," replied the friar, "and to Marian."

"Have no fear, Robin will be scathless, Marian harmless; but to the butts, and show these braggart Normans thy priestly skill."

"Have at them," said the friar, walking forward with Robin.

## CHAPTER LIII.

### HOW ROBIN HOOD WON THE SILVER ARROW.

Such an archer as Robin, ne'er was seen,
None did him in shooting excel.
The silver arrow, with point so riven,
Was given by her he loved so well.

"A PLACE for our chaplain," cried Robin Hood.

"Cheerfully given," replied Little John.

"Welcome, friar," said Much, "your skill is greatly needed to teach these fellows good shooting."

"Ay, that it is," said Gilbert of the White Hand, "With so goodly an archer as thou, friar, 'twill go hard but our victory be rendered even more complete."

"Well shot, Reynold!" remarked Robin Hood, as one of his band slit the wand very cleverly.

"'Tis hardly fair shooting," remarked one of the Sheriff's archers.

"How so? Explain," said Robin, turning sharply upon him.

Soon an angry excited group collected, and the debate threatened to get from words to blows.

"What is it that causes this unseemly strife?" exclaimed the Sheriff in loud tones.

"'Tis not fair shooting!" exclaimed half a score of Norman voices in chorus.

"What sayest thou to that?" asked the Sheriff of Robin.

"'Tis a foul lie. I am ready to prove 'tis so on the body of any man uttering it."

"Thou art mighty boastful," replied a huge fellow, whose height towered far above Robin's.

"Thou mayest try me an' thou wilt," answered Robin. "Peradventure thou wilt find that our excellences are not confined to the bow's use."

"Nay, nay, master mine," said Little John, stepping forward, "demean not thyself in this quarrel. Let my hand deal chastisement to this fellow's presumption. Body-o-me! 'tis past brooking."

Turning to the Norman, who was surnamed by his fellows Grim Denis, Little John said:

"Thus I challenge thee to mortal combat an' thou wilt, with broadsword, bow, battle-axe, or aught else weapon thou can'st name."

Little John laid his bow with a light stroke on Grim Denis's shoulder.

An exultant smile passed o'er the Norman's countenance on hearing this open challenge.

"I accept thy challenge; but, as I am loth to shed blood on this festive day"—a malicious twinkle shone in Grim Denis's eye—"I as challenged, choose, in place of the weapons thou hast named, my fist. Blow for blow on each other's body, on chest or back."

His companions looked on Little John ominously.

Well they might.

Grim Denis had killed not a few by single blow of his ponderous fist.

"Accepted," said Little John readily. "Blow for blow, delivered in manly fashion. Let's about it at at once."

"What say'st thou, Robin Hood?" asked the Sheriff, who, knowing Grim Denis's prowess with his fist, sought to make Robin accessory to the duel by consenting to it.

"I would rather have met him myself in fair fight," said Robin, casting a contemptuous glance on the burly frame and giant proportions of Grim Denis.

"Thou afterwards, an' thou wilt," said the Norman sneeringly.

"'Tis not well to boast ere thy work is done," observed Little John, in high dudgeon. "Thou wilt not meet any other for a week or more an' I get but one blow at thy Norman carcass."

"Well, well," exclaimed the Sheriff, "loth though I be to spoil our merry-making in this wise, thou, Denis, and thou, Little John, hast my permit to do as thou hast agreed in this matter."

"Thou hast mine, John;" observed Robin. "Fear not, my trusty friend, Robin and thy faithful comrades guard thee."

"Thy meaning?" said the Sheriff, turning sharply round on Robin.

Drawing himself up to his full height, and with a countenance full of contemptuous anger, Robin answered—

"I hold myself responsible to none for words of mine uttered here or elsewhere. Thou hast mine answer."

The Sheriff bit his lip, and could hardly contain the anger that burned within him.

Curbing it with a great effort, he contented himself with saying—

"Thy speech is thine own. I sought not to challenge it to thy detriment. But let's to the ring, else will the day expend itself a full hour or two too soon for the right ending of our merry revels."

Robin made a gesture to Allan-a-Dale and Will Scarlet.

It needed nothing further.

They transmitted their chief's orders